Filthy Little Witch

ROYAL HARLOTS MOTORCYCLE CLUB
BOOK ONE

JENA DOYLE

DIRTY WORDS PUBLISHING LLC

Line Editing: Misha Robinson at Verity Ink Editorial

Sensitivity Read: Maria Gomez at Here For The Reads

Cover Art: Crimson Syn at Syn Ink LLC

*For the witches. For the deities. For the magic in this beautiful world.
Thank you for your many blessings.*

*And for Sam and Dean, and all the girlies who could never choose
between them.*

Royal Harlots Code

LOYALTY: Stand by your sisters through hell and fire. Blood in, blood out—once you're in, you're family for life. Any betrayal will be punished.

RESPECT: The patch is earned, never given. Honor it, wear it with pride and never let it be disrespected. **Respect** club law. **Respect** the patch. **Respect** your sisters. Disrespect a member and there will be hell to pay.

STRENGTH in UNITY: We stand as one. No sister rides alone, no sister fights alone.

RIDE FREE, RIDE PROUD: The road is our home, and freedom is our creed. Live boldly, ride hard, and never apologize for who you are.

TAKE NO SHIT: Stand tall and unshaken against anyone who threatens the club or your sisters. Sisters do not leave family behind.**CLUB** is **FAMILY**.

HONESTY: Never **LIE, CHEAT,** or **STEAL** from another member or the club.

EARN YOUR KEEP: Every sister has a role to play. No one rides for free. Contribute to the club with your skills, your strength, and your spirit.

SHOW NO FEAR: Fear has no place here. Face challenges head-on, whether on the road, in a fight, or in life.

RESPECT the ROAD: We respect the laws of the road and the freedom it brings. We respect our allies but bow to no one.

DEATH before DISHONOR: Being patched in is an honor, not a right. Your colors are sacred, not to be left alone, and **NEVER** let them touch the ground.

CHURCH is **MANDATORY.**

TERRITORY: You are to respect your sister's territory and follow their Chapter's club rules.

TRUST: Years to earn it...seconds to lose it.

Royal Harlots MC

1ST MISSION

Crimson Syn - The Duchess
J. Lynn Lombard - Calypso's Shield
Roux Cantrell - Heat
Barbara Nolan - Martina
Kathryn C Kelly - Dr. Feel Good
K.L. Ramsey - Ember
Elle Boon - Belle & Flame Royally Hacked
Via Mari - Pearl
Thetta James - Blaze of Retribution
JA Lafrance - Cuda
Quinn Slater - Femme Fatale
Jena Doyle - Filthy Little Witch
D Williams - Safe Haven
Kris Anne Dean - Katana
Elisabeth N. Harris - Sapphire's Gem
Chelle C. Craze - Lunatic's Asylum
Nevaeh Ryn - Melting Point

Follow the Royal Harlots MC:
https://linktr.ee/royalharlotsmc

I was used to existing in liminal spaces. Half witch, half biker. Both Catholic and pagan. Attracted to both men and women. A proverbial pie chart of ancestry that included Mexican, Scottish, and Indigenous roots. In many ways, this was what pushed me where I stood today. I existed everywhere, so I belonged nowhere. And in that desperate struggle, I forced myself to be better, to be smarter, and to work harder than everyone around me.

"Are you nervous?" my cousin, Bridge, asked from behind me. I glanced up at the mirror and looked at her, smiling as I shook my head. "Good. You're ready. You'll do great."

Tonight, I would be given my warrior, a partner supernaturally bonded to me whose sole mission was to keep me safe. I didn't take this privilege lightly. Looking at the leather vest on my shoulders proclaiming me a member of the Royal Harlots MC, I thought about how much it had taken me to get here.

Years of training. Years of learning from the elders. Decades of service dedicated to the coven. All of it would culminate tonight when the president, Lilith, finally announced the person who would stand at my side while I enacted my life's work. Getting patched in was one thing; getting bonded to a warrior sealed the deal.

"Was it painful?" I asked Bridge. She'd been inducted years ago, right around the same age as me, and had already completed several missions.

"Nah." She waved me off and winked, brushing her flaming red hair behind an ear, a blush on her alabaster cheeks. "It's over before you know it."

The Asheville chapter of the Royal Harlots wasn't like any other chapter in America. We were the most powerful witches this side of the Atlantic, and it took a lot even to be considered a prospect, much less welcomed into the club with a patch.

The Royal Harlots MC had only recently been recognized by Duchess, the president of the founding chapter, four years ago, but it was the local coven that had made it possible. Formalizing ourselves as Harlots gave us access to a nationwide network of empowered women, something that had been difficult to manage until recently. Since we all swore our blood and loyalty to the MC, we had their strength behind us, and it had made all the difference when we needed it. They looked out for us, and we looked out for them.

"C'mon," she said. "We're going to be late."

We left my bedroom, where my abuelita sat at her kitchen table with a steaming cup of tea in her hands.

"Oh, look at you!" She stood and held her arms out, gesturing me into her embrace.

I tried to hide the burning in my cheeks as I went to her and wrapped my arms around her midsection. When my parents died, Tita took me in without hesitation. I'd been a child, young and terrified of the world. But Tita had loved me through it all, through the nightmares and the rebellious teenage years, through the prospecting of my early twenties. She'd been a motorcycle-riding witch once upon a time, as had my mother. As much as she would rather see me off to college, doing anything other than what took her son and daughter-in-law from her, she also recognized that magic ran in my veins and I had always been destined for tonight.

"You look so beautiful," she said, pushing a piece of dark hair behind my ear. "How do you feel?"

"Okay." I smiled and tried not to shake. I'd heard the ritual could be taxing, sometimes deadly, but the club wouldn't have recommended me if they didn't think I could handle it.

"Remember," Tita said, "you are the strongest of us all. Your grandmothers are rooting for you." She touched the cross and the locket I always wore around my neck and grinned. For being well into her sixties, she didn't look a day over forty, which was a testament to the strength of the magic in our family. From her, I had inherited a long line of Mexican and Spanish ancestry, all powerful witches and healers. On my mother's side, I traced my roots back to the first settlers of Appalachia, equally strong and rooted in the natural energy of the world.

"I'll take good care of her," Bridge said as she grabbed my shoulders in a comforting squeeze.

"I know you will." Tita smiled at Bridge and kissed each side of my cheeks, cupping my jaw in a tender embrace before she touched her forehead to mine. She muttered a whisper to Saint Marta for strength and another to the Virgin Mary to look out for me. I closed my eyes and envisioned a shield of my abuelita's love coating my skin. Even if I had my disagreements with God, Mary, and most of the saints, I did believe in the force of my grandmother's love. It had gotten me this far.

When she was done, she let me go and hugged Bridge. Then she went back to her tea.

"Make sure you're back before supper," she said. "I'm making tamales and roasted chicken. The entire club better come, including your warrior."

"Okay, Tita." I waved goodbye to her and walked out of the front door, descending the stairs with knots in my stomach. I wiped my hands on my black jeans and adjusted my cut before kicking a leg over my bike and lifting it upright. Bridge got on her bike next to me and reached out to tug on my braid.

"It's gonna be fine, Marts," she said, using her nickname for me. "Trust me."

I wanted to. I really did. But Tita's mention of my warrior reminded me that this was real. This was happening. I'd been born into this family of witches, and despite what aspirations my parents might have had for me, there was never any other choice.

In my world, women were the most powerful practitioners. *All* women, even those who were misgendered at birth. We were the ones with the deepest connection to the earth, the ones chosen to wield magic to defend it. There were a lot of monsters out there—rabid shifters, chaotic vampires, ruthless demons. It was a Harlot's job to keep the rest of the world safe.

Normies didn't know we existed, not in any real sense. Even if some humans could tap into the unique reservoir of preternatural energy in their blood and the elements, they could not manipulate these forces the way we could. We worked our entire lives to perfect it, and once we came into our power, we spent most of the time fighting the real evil in the world.

But magic always came with a cost, and there was a downside to casting. It left the witch vulnerable to attack, especially if she used too much magic too quickly. She needed someone to defend her, to protect her, to channel energy into her if she got injured—hence the warrior.

A warrior bond wasn't inherently sexual, nor was it based on compatibility or mutual attraction. It was based on strength, on the ability to fight together with complementary skills. A witch could survive the death of her warrior, but a warrior would never survive the death of his witch.

I'd get mine tonight, and I tried not to think about who it would be on the long drive to the meeting grounds. There were dozens of unbonded warriors in the Harlot community. I prayed it was someone I got along with, someone I could put up with on long missions and even longer nights.

Instead, I focused on the weight of my bike between my legs, the wind in my hair, the brilliant blushes and pinks in the sky as the sun set over the horizon. God and I may have our differences, but I couldn't help but marvel at His creative splendor when the world came to life like this.

When we got to the mansion-turned-clubhouse way up in the mountains, we parked the bikes in the long row of motorcycles belonging to my sisters and walked to the treeline on the right. Rituals like this always happened outside during a full moon in our ancestral forest, one that had belonged to the witches in the Harlots for over a hundred years. Some could trace their lineage through Indigenous roots; their families had been practicing here for even longer.

I paused at the entrance to the woods and took a deep breath, wiping my sweaty palms on my jeans as I stared at the lit torches lining the trail deeper into the trees.

"It's too late to back out now," Bridge said, coming to stand on my right. She nudged me with her shoulder and smiled. "Your mom would be proud of you, ya know? So would your dad."

I thought of my parents and blinked back tears as I envisioned younger versions of them standing at this very spot, walking this path, making the same vow to pledge themselves to their coven. They had lived and died by that promise, and while some part of me resented that they'd been taken from me so young, I also understood that they'd died heroes. They'd gone down fighting, protecting the world, saving people, and I was proud to call myself their daughter.

"There you are," came a voice from in front of us. "We've been looking for you."

Our resident nomad, Valkyrie, walked forward, her dark hair pulled back in a braid, her leather cut firmly on her shoulders. She flashed a friendly smile and glanced between me and my cousin.

"All set?" Valkyrie asked.

"Just nerves," Bridge answered.

I scoffed and bumped my hip into hers. "I'm fine."

"Don't worry," Valkyrie said with a roll of her bright blue eyes. "We won't go easy on you. It'll be better that way."

I snorted and followed as Val led Bridge and me through the woods. The birds chirped in the distance, settling in for the night, and the cicadas buzzed through the pines and cedars. Lightning bugs had just started flashing around us, waking up for the night, and the frogs bellowed out their own version of a mating call, adding the perfect chorus to the September night. Our boots crunched on the dirt as we made the walk, and the closer we got, the more my heart pounded against my ribs.

No, wait.

That drumming sound wasn't coming from inside my body. It was up ahead, the riotous orchestra of voices chanting in time with each other, accompanied by the rhythmic *dum-dum-dum* of mallets on drums. We paused when we got to the clearing, and I forced myself to pull my shoulders back, to stand up straight, to not let the sight overwhelm me.

The entirety of the patched Harlots stood in a circle, singing to welcome the land spirits, to ask them for their grace as we performed our ceremony. Though the official members of the coven totaled thirty, another fifty stood around them on the outskirts of the clearing, near the trees. Some banged on drums, some clapped and danced to raise the energy of the spell, and others stood stoically in contemplation.

The warriors.

I recognized some of them as being bonded to Harlots, here to lend their energy should they need to. But a lot of them were unbonded. Any unbounded warrior was obliged to attend in case the magic selected them. I gulped and stepped closer to the circle, knowing I had to wait until Lilith called me forth to join.

I eyed the crowd, picking out a few people I'd known most of my life. Off to the left stood Leander, brother to the Harlots' secretary, Isobel. Next to him was his best friend, Lyr, twin brother to the treasurer, Lorelei. A few other family members milled around, but my attention caught on the Colt brothers in the far corner, standing in the darkness, shrouded by the trees and the impending twilight.

Atlas Colt stood on the end, dressed in a black jacket, matching jeans, and boots. He was the eldest at thirty-two, standing nearly six-three with broad shoulders and a strong jaw that gave way to lips permanently etched in a sneer. His dirty blond hair complemented his bright green eyes that sparkled in the firelight.

Wesson, his younger brother, stood next to him. He wasn't related to Atlas by blood, but he'd been the only child of Atlas's father's second wife, and when she died, he'd taken the boy on as his own. Wesson was taller than Atlas, nearly six-five, with dark, curly hair he kept cut short and skin almost as tawny as mine.

Neither of the Colts liked me, and truth be said, I didn't like them, either. Their father had been my mother's warrior, and three of them had been with my parents when they died. I didn't trust that they had nothing to do with it. They said my father died protecting my mother, and once he was gone, my mother went quickly after him. But if the brothers were close enough to see it, why hadn't they stopped it? Of course, they'd been new to missions at the time, but that mattered little when the result was the same.

Rage simmered in my blood for one heartbeat before I swallowed it back, remembering they had no other choice but to be here. Atlas and Wesson worked for the Harlots. Even if they weren't bonded warriors, they were family, whether I liked it or not.

The chanting stopped, and the sudden silence brought me back to the present, refocusing my attention on the witches around the fire. Circe, the vice president and second in command, walked to the center and held her arms above her head, her black hair tumbling down to her waist.

"On this night, we have gathered on sacred land to protect one of our sisters. She will complete her patching ceremony by bonding a warrior chosen for her." She turned in the direction opposite to me to call in the elements: North, East, South, and West, respectively.

Once the witches had finished their chant, the atmosphere changed. A chilling vibrancy now floated above us like an invisible mist, coating our skin and giving us an ethereal link to the world. Circe turned to Lilith, our president, and nodded, indicating she was done.

Lilith came to the center and took her place, looking toward the heavens, her deep umber skin shimmering in the firelight, her eyes completely white with the power of trance, the irises and pupils gone. "Great ancestors, grandmothers, grandfathers, all those who lived like us, loved like us, and thought like us, hear our call. Be with us tonight. Give us your wisdom and your strength as we seal an ancient rite. Hail and welcome."

The moon had fully risen now, shining in the sky like a heavenly beacon, illuminating us in a divine glow. A whoosh went through the air, lifting the hairs on my arms and the back of my neck as a loving warmth sank into my gut. I'd grown up with magic. My tita was powerful, and I'd learned to control my own energy from the very women in this circle. But this...This was the most potent and electrifying experience I'd ever felt. It was the ancestors letting me know they were here. It was the hundreds that came before me, whose blood still lived in my veins, and they would bear witness to my induction.

I thought again of my parents and chewed my lip, wondering if they'd made the journey. Were they here in the astral realm? Were they just beyond the veil, waiting with smiles and joyful expressions, hoping my bonding went according to plan?

Of course, I'd never heard of anyone *not* surviving the bond, but as with any magic, your mileage may vary.

"Elizabeta Marta Maria McDonnell-Ruiz, come forward." Lilith held her hand out to me, waving her fingers to gesture me toward her.

I took a deep breath and stepped closer, sensing the increased vibration from the circle as I did. It hummed against my skin and coated my tongue as I breathed, and when I reached the magical boundary, it rattled through my heart, twisting my stomach with excitement and anticipation. It wasn't evil, but it wasn't altogether good, either. It felt like the unknown, like a dark shape in the woods on a new moon.

"Marta, being patched in is an honor, not a right. You have earned that place, and so tonight, we pair you with a protector," Lilith said, bowing to kiss the back of my hand.

When she stood, I did the same to her, following the proper protocol of honoring the president of the Harlots and the high priestess of the coven. Lilith smiled and cupped my cheek, winking before breaking our connection and turning to the crowd.

"Our sister cannot stand alone," the high priestess said. "Every witch requires a warrior. Who is called to this position?"

Shouts of "I" and "Me" came from the onlookers, all the various men who had come to witness my induction and bond themselves to my sacred power.

"Brave Marta, you have heard those who are called," Lilith said as Circe came forward, holding the chalice. Lilith took her time pricking her finger with a ceremonial knife, holding it over the goblet so a drop fell inside. She handed the knife to me, and I held back a wince as I repeated the motion. Our combined blood sizzled as it handed inside, and I swallowed back my anticipation. The time had come, and now I would know.

"Place your hand over the cup and ask the ancestors for guidance," Lilith said.

I did, closing my eyes and whispering a prayer to the universe that it provide me with someone capable and strong, worthy and loyal. *Find me the right person. Mother, father, ancestors, help me.*

The cup grew hot, burning under my touch, and when I couldn't stand it anymore, I ripped my hand away and held it to my chest, grimacing through the pain.

A piece of paper flew out of the top, landing in Lilith's outstretched hand. She opened it, read it, and furrowed her brows.

"Colt," she murmured.

Colt?

No, that couldn't be. There were only two Colts in attendance. My heart sank, and my overheated blood suddenly froze like I'd mainlined ice water. A shiver raced down my spine.

"A.W. Colt," Lilith called, louder this time. She glanced around until her focus landed on the two men standing in the far corner. I couldn't bear to look at them, too terrified of what I'd see.

Wait...

A.W?

Which one was that? Was that Atlas's entire name? Were his initials A.W.?

"Atlas, Wesson, step forward," Circe said, waving her hand in their direction.

Boots echoed on the earth, breaking twigs and stomping through grass, and I felt their presence on either side of me.

"Which Colt?" Wesson asked, and the sound of his deep baritone ricocheted down my spine.

Circe looked at Lilith, who crumpled the paper in her palm before closing her eyes and leaning her head back toward the sky.

I sensed it before she said it. The weight of the energy in the atmosphere settled around me, and my intuition picked it up as if it were flashing a bright neon sign.

Both of them, it said. *Both of them.*

"Atlas...*and* Wesson," Lilith answered.

"Two warriors?" hissed someone close to me.

A chorus of murmurs repeated the surprise.

"I thought she was only supposed to get one?"

"Why two?"

"Both Colts?"

"That can't be right."

"Silence!" Lilith's voice rang out into the night, booming and deafening. "There has never been a Harlot with two warriors, but we do not question the ancestors. We do not question the magic."

I did. I had *loads* of questions, starting with, *"How fucking dare you!"*

The Colts were there when my parents died. I'd heard the rumors. Atlas and Wesson had stood by while some vicious demon tore my family apart. And now, I was supposed to bond with them? Rely on them for protection? I hadn't said more than two words to them in years.

"Lilith," I tried to say. "High Priestess, please. There must be—"

"Do you not accept this gift the ancestors have bestowed upon you?" Lilith asked, her tone suggesting I better not argue.

Once upon a time, she'd been bonded to her father's best friend, who eventually died protecting her. She hadn't been given another warrior since. And here I was, bestowed with two? Why two? Why *these* two?

In all the years I'd lived, I had more than enough reasons to be mad at God. Now, I had beef with the ancestors, too? Would the horrors never cease to persist?

I swallowed against my suddenly dry throat and licked my lips, hesitantly looking at Atlas on my right and his stepbrother on my left. Atlas glared at me, his emerald gaze and tight pursed lips radiating with the years of animosity between us. Wesson, on the other hand, looked destroyed, his jaw hanging open, his brows pinched together, his eyes nearly shimmering with hot, angry tears.

Even if I said I wouldn't accept the gift, nothing would happen. I'd never heard of them pulling another name from the chalice. In fact, I'd never heard of a Harlot rejecting their warrior at all. To be patched and blooded as a Harlot was an honor; to be given a warrior was the cherry on top.

"Yes, Lilith," I said, returning my focus to the ground in front of me. "I accept this gift."

"Good, all is well." She held out her hand, the same one she'd cut earlier, and waved her fingers for me to place mine in it. I did, and I shivered when Atlas put his on top of mine. Wesson moved to stand across from me, holding our fists under me. Lilith placed a red ceremonial ribbon on top of Atlas's knuckles before wrapping it over and around our combined embrace. Over and around. Over and around.

"I bind you together in the tradition of our beloved dead," she said. "Warrior to witch, witch to warrior. You will share your energy, your strength, and your magic. What the ancestors have bound, let no one tear asunder."

"What the ancestors have bound," the three of us repeated, "let no one tear asunder."

Lilith dragged her knife down the sides of our palms, scorching a hot cut along the outside of our hands, deep and fiery. It ached more than my blooding, and when Atlas's blood dripped down into my cut, I winced as a tether opened up between us. Circe brought the chalice over to us, catching the dripping liquid as it pooled under our bound fists. Normally, the warrior and witch drank of each other, and the ceremony concluded. But I didn't know how this would work with *two* warriors. Would they then be bound to each other? Would they have the same connection that a witch typically had with her warrior?

Circe handed the cup to Wesson, who took it with his free hand and held it up.

"Marta, witch of the Royal Harlots," he said, his voice trembling. He cleared his throat and stared up at me with dark mahogany eyes, holding my gaze as he said the next part of the oath. "I swear my allegiance and fealty to you as your blooded warrior." He drank, and my connection to him soared. His energy rushed into me like a warm campfire, like autumn bursting in my veins. He hadn't wanted to be selected because of how *I* might feel about it. He reeked of shame and guilt.

It wasn't like I could feel his emotions or read his thoughts; more like I got the energetic imprint of them. I understood them, even if they weren't my own.

"Marta," Atlas said when Wesson passed the cup to him. He sighed and shook his head, hanging it over his chest like the words took every bit of his energy to say. "Witch of the Royal Harlots. I swear my allegiance and fealty to you as your blooded warrior." When he drank, I gasped as his life force barreled into my chest, hot and fiery and reckless. It boiled with indignation and resentment. He *hated* me, almost as much as I hated him.

No, no, no.

This would not be a good match, not at all. How the hell was I supposed to run missions with them when we couldn't even stand to look at each other?

Atlas handed the cup to me with a squared jaw and hardened eyes; the green having almost disappeared around dilated pupils.

"Atlas Colt, Wesson Colt, warriors of a sacred line. I accept your allegiance and fealty as my blooded warriors. I swear to honor, respect, and protect you until the end may come."

"Until the end may come," the Colts repeated.

I drank from the cup, swallowing down the rich metallic taste, wincing as all three pathways snapped into place. Atlas groaned and Wesson winced, but undoubtedly, they now knew I hadn't wanted this, that I wished it had been anyone else. They knew I blamed them for every rotten thing in my life. They knew I hated them.

A small, vindictive voice spoke up from inside me.

Good.

"It seriously doesn't bother you that I've been bonded to the Colts?" I wrapped my arms around myself and followed Tita out her back door to the yard, where chickens clucked happily as they wandered the open space. My family had lived in this house for decades, and over the years, Tita had turned it into a mini homestead. She took great pride in growing her own herbs and flowers, and collecting eggs to do her own divination (and make omelettes). She insisted magic started where you created, and she loved taking care of it all. Goats and sheep bleated in the distance, and our donkey, Edward, hee-hawwed at our appearance.

Tita spread chicken feed on the ground and smiled as her avian pets gathered to eat.

"It's the will of the ancestors," she said. "You don't have much choice in the matter."

That didn't make me feel any better. After the ceremony last night, most of the Harlots had come here so Tita could feed them and celebrate. The Colts declined and instead slithered off to whatever dirty, dingy rathole they'd come from.

"I know, but...doesn't it make you mad? They were there when

Mom and Dad died." I didn't understand how she could be so calm about it. I'd been boiling from the inside out since it happened, fueled further by this ridiculous connection to them. I sensed their rage and indignation, and it stoked my internal inferno.

"Lots of things make me mad," she said. "Foxes getting into the coop. Weeks without rain. Granddaughters who don't always listen to their grandmothers."

I rolled my eyes and groaned. "Abuelita, please."

"It wasn't their fault, and they couldn't have stopped it. I've prayed about it, and the Virgin has guided me to forgive what can't be changed."

I sighed and rubbed the tension between my eyebrows. Praying had never gotten me anywhere. Why was it so easy for her?

"You're smart, Marta, and more than capable of handling those two." She turned to the coop and unlocked the hatch where the brooding hens kept their eggs, ignoring their squawks of protest. "You're looking for someone to be angry with. God, the Colts, fate. Where does your anger get you?"

I bit back my indignation at her arguably valid point, choosing instead to stick to my guns. They'd been there. They could have stopped it. They didn't.

"But isn't it weird?" I walked closer to her, holding up the first hen so she could reach under it to check. "No Harlot has ever had *two* warriors. Why me? Why now?"

"These are questions I can't answer." After gathering her spoils from the first hen, she went to the second, checking each egg to see if it was fertile or edible. "But I bet if you prayed on it—"

"No," I said. "God doesn't want to hear from me. Neither does Mary, I can assure you."

"Aww, my darling girl. The sweet Virgin still loves you, even if you are angry with Her." Tita moved on to the next hen. "She will welcome you back anytime."

That wasn't the problem. How could I worship an all-knowing being who took my family from me at the tender age of ten? How could I give my time and energy to someone who made my life so tragic? God, the Virgin, all of them could rot in hell for all I cared.

"That is the nature of faith," Tita said. "You still have to believe even when it's tough, even when it hurts."

I took a deep breath and let it out slowly, considering all that Tita had been through in her long life. She'd lost her husband, her only son, and most of her sisters, and still she remained steadfast in her devotion to predetermined destiny. Everything happened for a reason.

Bullshit.

"And you trust me to go out on the road with them? The Colts? You trust them to look after me, to protect me?"

She hummed and tucked another egg into her apron. "When I was your age, I went on my first mission with my bonded warrior, a man I barely knew. He was new to the coven, barely battle-tested." Tita turned to face me with a grin, her bright brown eyes hinting at something joyful and mischievous. "We hunted down chaos and took out the demon they'd summoned, almost didn't make it home. But I put my trust in my coven, in my ancestors. They'd picked the right match for me, and I'm sure the same can be said for you." She touched my cheek. "You're late for Church. You should go."

I checked my watch and swore under my breath. I had ten minutes to make the twenty-minute drive, or I'd miss my own freaking party.

"Damn," I said, giving her a quick kiss on the cheek. "Love you, Tita."

"Love you, too, mi hija."

I tried not to ruminate on her advice while I rode my bike into town. Why was it so easy for her to give her worries to God? How could she forgive Him for taking so many people from her? And why wasn't she more worried about the Colts? I was. I fretted about it all night and most of the day, and by the time I got to the clubhouse, my hands were shaking with nerves.

I parked my bike next to Bridge's and got off, ignoring the sinking dread in my stomach when I saw Atlas's 1964 Pontiac GTO sitting in the parking lot. They were already here. Of course they were.

The clubhouse had been in the coven for over a century. It was an old Victorian-style mansion gifted to us by one of the Vanderbilts in the late 1800s. She had been a witch, too, and died without any close heirs. Instead of it going to her estate, she'd left it to her witch sisters in her will, and it had been with us ever since. The outside was painted in bright whites and eggshell, but with the gothic archways and pointed turrets, it looked far too fancy to house a motorcycle club. It had forty-six bedrooms, fifty bathrooms, a bowling alley in the basement, and an Olympic-sized swimming pool. At its height, it housed a staff of over two hundred people, but those days were long gone. Now, the Harlots used their magic to clean and upkeep the place.

These grounds were sacred, warded by the blood of countless ancestors before it. As far as magical places went in the US, nowhere was more energetically potent or sanctified.

Hustling up the stairs, I opened the heavy wooden door to the foyer and glanced around at the warriors milling about. The clinking of pool balls echoed from the parlor off to the left, and the sounds of mingled conversation came from the gathering room to the right. I took a moment to admire the ornately painted ceiling depicting the founding members of our coven holding hands in a circle before I walked to the room next to the parlor, pushed the wooden entrance open, and stepped into the meeting room.

"Church is in session," Circe said, banging her thick metal rings on the circular table in the middle.

Whew. Just made it.

"Sisters," Lilith said, rising to her feet. "Thank you all for joining me tonight. We've got a lot to cover, so let's get started. Lorelei, how are we looking on finances?"

The Harlots' treasurer reported on our most recent trade deal with the Steel Roses MC in Madison County, Virginia. We'd started running guns for them in exchange for access to the DC ports. Next, she gave an overview of the most recent mission to help the Royal Bastards MC out in Helena, Montana. They'd returned the favor times ten.

"Their recent merger with Vanderbilt Holdings has been good for them," our road captain, Hekate, joked. Hekate had long black hair and deep olive skin. She'd gotten her road name because she was a devotee of the ancient Greek Goddess and claimed to trace her heritage back to that same source. Hekate knew these roads better than anyone else in the club.

The rest of the sisters laughed.

"Gullveig," Lilith said, glancing to our sergeant at arms. "What's up on the network?"

Gullveig had gotten her name from the Norse legend about a woman who burned three times on a fire and still lived. She had long blond hair and a bright, pale complexion, making her look like a Viking shield maiden come to life. In addition to being our sarge, she could manipulate fire with her bare hands, something that most witches spent years learning. She took a deep breath and rustled some papers in front of her. "The Bloody Femmes were seen riding out of our territory late last night."

Murmurs and gasps of surprise echoed around me. The Asheville Harlots controlled most of North Carolina, into South Carolina, and Southern Virginia. Even if we were stationed out of a small town in the Appalachian Mountains, we were responsible for keeping those bitches from sticking their noses anywhere near us.

The Bloody Femmes Motorcycle Club was the enemy of the

Harlots and had been responsible for more chaos and destruction than most first-world countries. They were magic practitioners, but calling them witches would do a disservice to all who lived in harmony with the earth and drew their power from the Great Mother. The Femmes wielded their power with reckless abandon, using it to summon demons and compel monsters. I doubted any of them were human anymore, and if they were, they'd long ago lost their souls to the dark magic in their veins.

Not that I believed in light or dark magic—there was only chaos and order, action and consequence. All magic could be light or dark, depending on how you used it. The earth, after all, needed both day and night to survive. But the more a witch dealt out harm, the more tainted their soul became, twisting and perverting until the thing that made them human no longer existed. The Bloody Femmes had been running rampant up and down the East Coast for decades, well before the Harlots were incorporated.

"Any strange reports coming out of that area?" Circe asked.

"I've got a few things from the local news," our tech guru, Aradia, said. She was tall and statuesque with reddish-tanned skin and dark features. She had a photographic memory and knew more about computers than anyone I'd ever met. "There have been a few mysterious deaths, but nothing that would jump out. I'll check the tabloids and the socials."

"While she's doing that, where do we think the Femmes are headed?" Lilith asked, raising an eyebrow. Though she was our leader and arguably the most powerful of us, Lilith had become the president for a reason. She was strong and independent, and after losing her warrior some years ago, she went on missions by herself, surrounded only by her sisters. None of us liked it, but she said after watching her best friend die right in front of her, she couldn't do it again. I didn't blame her for that.

"They crossed into the Georgia chapter's territory late last night," Hekate said.

"Fuck." Lilith pinched the bridge of her nose and sighed. "I'll call Blaze and let her know."

Blaze was the president of the Atlanta chapter, but their territory stretched up to meet ours.

"Okay, I got it," Aradia cut in. "People on the socials report strange behavior in Biltmore Forest and Hope Springs."

"What kind of strange behavior?" Circe asked, inhaling on a cigarette.

"Wait, that can't be right," Aradia said as she typed faster on her keyboard.

"What?" Circe asked. "What are you seeing?"

"They're saying people are devouring each other." Aradia furrowed her eyebrows.

"What? Like cannibalism?" Isobel asked.

Aradia shrugged and pulled up a video, turning the volume so everyone could hear it.

"I know this sounds crazy," said the girl on the app. "But what's happening in Biltmore is a nightmare, and no one's talking about it. My best friend went to see her boyfriend last night, and now they're both in the ICU. They wouldn't stop, and now she's got an infection and his skin is peeling off."

"What the fuck?" Bridge asked. "Is this for real?"

Aradia showed another video. "This won't be reported on the news because no one believes it, but I swear to you, America, Hope Springs is literally boiling from the inside out. I walked in on my grannie having an orgy last night."

"Fucking hell." I rubbed a hand over my face, trying not to laugh. It sounded ridiculous, borderline hilarious.

"This is a prank," Morrigan, our tail gunner, said. She had flaming red hair, almost as bright as Bridge's, and dark eyes that contrasted with her alabaster skin. She'd gotten her nickname from her association with animals, particularly crows. She said she could speak to them, and after observing her interactions with them only a handful of times, I believed her. "If something like this were actually happening, it would be all over the internet."

"We've heard weirder," Lilith said, looking at me. "Marta, Bridge, Isobel, go check it out. Report back on whatever you find."

I nodded, pleased to have my first mission. Hopefully, it would turn out to be nothing but a joke, but the chance to flex my skills as a Harlot twisted hope and excitement in my belly. The meeting carried on for another hour as the prez assigned missions to the other witches. By the time it was over, I couldn't contain my anticipation.

Bridge and Isobel met me in the front room, crossing their arms with serious looks on their faces.

"We handle this like any other mission. It's not that far away, so we can call in backup if we need it," Isobel said in her Scottish brogue. She was the most senior of the three of us, having been inducted into the Harlots almost a decade ago. She was from a small town in Scotland, and her family traced their lineage back to Isobel Gowdie, the so-called Queen of Witches. "We'll ask the locals and the PD. Go round up your warriors. We head out in an hour."

"Got it," Bridge said with a nod before walking over to Leander, Isobel's older brother. They were a good team, and as far as I could tell, always kept things professional. Isobel headed off to find Caspian, Circe's twin brother, and I turned to the back of the room, where Atlas and Wesson sat on the couch, huddled together in quiet conversation.

They went silent when I stood next to them and cleared my throat. Wesson's dark eyes flicked up to me.

"Yes?" he asked, raising his eyebrows.

I took a deep breath and steeled myself against the hesitation burning through our connection. I couldn't tell if it was mine or his...or both.

"We have a mission," I said. "There are reports of people

screwing each other to death in Biltmore Forest. We're heading out in an hour."

Atlas snorted and sipped his beer, raising an eyebrow at Wesson in silent communication with his brother.

"Screwing each other to death?" Wesson smiled and shook his head. "Didn't know the Harlots put so much stock in tabloids. What's next? Aliens?"

"We don't," I said, crossing my arms. "But it's worth investigating. It could be a demon or a vampire playing tricks."

At least, those were the first two things that came to my mind.

"And you need both of us for that?" Atlas asked, his sardonic tone hinting at the years of animosity between our families.

"No," I sniped. "I don't *need* either of you. But you are my warriors, and the ancestors thought otherwise."

"Ya know, I'm curious about that little ritual." Atlas pushed to his feet, towering over me from his height of six-three. "Who says Lilith didn't make it up? I didn't see that slip of paper. It could have had anyone's name on it."

"Atlas," Wesson warned.

"Did you *want* us to be your little gopher bitches?" Atlas sneered. "Did you think it would be funny to have us cater to your every—"

"I would rather trudge through steaming hot shit than be tied to you," I said and squared my jaw, glaring at the eldest Colt brother with hatred burning in my blood. "Either of you."

"That can be arranged." Atlas stepped closer, bringing his face inches from mine.

"Alright, enough." Wesson stood and grabbed his brother's arm, yanking him back from me. "You've made your point."

"You signed up for this, remember?" I glanced between them, suddenly realizing how much smaller I was, how much easier it would be for them to manhandle me. Luckily, I was the one with the magic in my veins. "You knew what being a warrior would require, what it would demand. You dug your grave; now we all have to lay in it."

Atlas rolled his eyes, and Wesson's cheeks turned a bright shade of blush. Was he ashamed of his brother? Or did he feel guilty that he'd known they shouldn't have come but had anyway? I didn't care.

"Get your shit," I said. "We leave in an hour."

Then I turned and headed out of the estate to pack my bags for the trip.

"Witches are bullshit," I said from the driver's seat of my GTO. We'd been on the road for thirty minutes, following behind the Harlots as they led us on what would most likely be a wild goose chase. "This whole thing is bullshit."

"She's right, though," Wes added from the passenger. "We knew what we were signing up for."

"And what were we gonna do, huh?" I shook my head. "Not attend a bonding ceremony just because it's her? Dad would kill us if he were still alive."

"It's surprising both of us were chosen. I'll give you that," Wes said, flipping a page of his book. Such a fucking nerd, my brother. Sometimes, it was difficult to tell that we'd been raised by the same dude, even if we had different biological parents. Wes had been with me since he was four, so he might as well be my brother in every way except blood. When Dad came home all pissed off and angry, he yelled at *both* of us, not just me. Yep, connected by trauma didn't even begin to describe how fucked up our little so-called family was.

"What? The ancestors couldn't figure out which of us would

be the *worst* match for her, so they picked both?" I laughed and let the disappointment roll through me. At least twenty other prospective warriors were waiting in the wings; any of them would have been a better choice. But nooo, fate was a fickle bitch and wouldn't let us have any breathing room.

"The ancestors don't do anything by chance," Wes said, glancing at me with a disapproving side eye. "If they wanted it this way, it's for a reason."

"Yeah, let's live our lives following a bunch of dead idiots that were stupid enough to get killed in the first place," I said. "There's a bright idea."

"You didn't have to come," Wes said. "I could have taken this one."

"And let you have all the fun?" I reached over to hit his book on the spine, sending it flying toward his face. "Not a chance."

"Hey, knock it off," he said, shoving my shoulder. I responded by knocking his book out of his hands again, which only made him punch me in the bicep. "Asshole."

"Cunt."

Wes pursed his lips and grabbed his phone to scroll through the socials for anything relevant. Marta said people were screwing each other to death, whatever the fuck that meant. Maybe it was a demon or a poltergeist, possessing all those poor fucks and forcing them to wear down their meat-suits. It could be an easy fix, and if it were, we'd be back in Asheville by the weekend.

Good. The less time we spend with her, the better.

It wasn't that I was pissed about the warrior bond, though that was a whole other bag of cats entirely. It was just *her*. Why *her*?

Twelve years ago, Dad had taken us on our first mission, which was a mistake. I was twenty at the time, Wes only eighteen. It was supposed to be an easy job, in and out, a quick fix, and we'd be on our way. At the time, I'd been thrilled about becoming a warrior. I thought it was my destiny.

Killing monsters. Saving humanity. All that stupid, idiotic shit.

We got to the haunted house, quickly realized it was infested with demons, and tried to make a swift retreat. Marta's parents got caught in the crossfire. Dad told me to take Wes and get the hell out of there, but I couldn't stand the thought of leaving him, leaving all of them. But always a good little soldier, I did what he told me to do. I took my brother back to the motel and waited for Dad, his witch, and her husband to return. They never did. We later learned all three of them had gotten chewed up and spit out, hardly a body part left to bury.

Marta blamed me for what happened, blamed Wes and me both.

Maybe that was why I hated her so much. She'd never heard our side of the story, and she didn't want to. No, she'd rather simmer with her own wrath while Wes and I bore the brunt of the fallout.

"It could be a Cupid," Wes said, drawing me back to reality. "Or maybe a siren."

"Cupids don't make people go rabid," I said.

"Are we sure that's what's happening?" Wes asked, scrolling through the evidence Aradia sent to us. "A few videos don't mean anything." He clicked on his screen before leaning over to show me. "Check out the local PD reports. Ten victims so far, and six more they're not sure about. Four of them were still...chewing...by the time EMS arrived."

"Chewing?" I grimaced and skimmed the intel as best as I could while driving. Sure enough, the impacted people had escalated from fucking to cannibalizing each other alive. "Fuck. That's gnarly."

"Granny from the orgy was rib deep in human pit beef when they carted her off to the ICU. They had to sedate her to keep her from breaking out to finish him off." Wes scrolled through a graphic, gory mess.

"So if it's not a Cupid, are we going with a siren?" I looked at Wes, waiting to see his reaction.

He rubbed his hand over his mouth and sighed. "Maybe, but sirens usually only go after men."

"C'mon," I teased, grabbing his shoulder to give him a shake. "It's 2025. Sex-obsessed monsters don't care about stupid things like gender anymore."

"You would know," Wes added with a chuckle.

I shot him a glare. "Prude."

Yeah, I'd been known to fuck around with anything that moved. I, too, didn't care about stupid things like gender. Chances were, if I liked you, I'd probably want to play with whatever was in your pants. I guessed that made me pansexual or some shit, but I always thought of myself as an equal opportunity sex-enthusiast. In my short thirty-two years, I'd been around the block more than I'd ever admit. Practically run through, at this point. But that didn't mean I'd stand for being shamed by it.

"No, this is worse than that," he said as he ran his hand back through his dark curly hair. "If people are consuming each other, that's heavy-hitting magic. My money's on demon."

I took a deep breath and ran through my mental monster encyclopedia. Demons in this world weren't like the impotent villains in comic books or the snarky antiheroes from some long-running television melodrama for tweens. These fuckers were cruel and ruthless. They came from the darkest pits of the afterlife, here to wreak destruction and chaos. At least fifteen of the last twenty serial killers in modern history were possessed by demons, and it wasn't as easy as exorcising them back to hell. The witches we ran with didn't banish; they said it cost a witch part of her soul. Most of the time, demons crawled out of whatever shit-stained veil they could find and walked among us like average people. The only way to get rid of them was to trap them in a liminal or destroy every piece of them in this plane of existence.

Liminals were pocket realities created by magic, sort of like a bubble in the space-time continuum of the human realm. It was the easiest and safest way to ditch a demon. Gather a group of witches, create the porthole, and shove the fucker in it. Piece of cake. But the magic required to do the spell took even the best witches out for days afterward.

Destroying every piece of a demon was harder. Unfortunately, demons knew their own kryptonite, so they typically left chunks of themselves hidden throughout the human realm. A lock of hair here. A graph of skin there. A molar in a suit jacket sold at a thrift store. These bitches were relentless, and they could re-manifest using any piece of their body.

Because of their connection to the afterlife, they packed a mean punch. They had the entire weight of hell and the undead behind them, so they could influence humans in truly despicable ways.

"If it's a demon," I said, "there'd be other signs. Cattle mutilations. Desecrated ground. Dark rituals and—"

"Low blood supply at the Red Cross," he added. "A week ago, the local blood bank reported a break-in. Nearly sixty pints of O-Neg were stolen. They blamed it on local teenagers pulling a prank."

"And there it is," I said. "Did you replenish the salt stores and the holy water?"

"Of course," Wes said, a sharp sting of defensiveness in his tone. "I'm not an idiot."

"Just checking," I said, holding up a hand to show I meant no offense.

My own mother died when I was five, and Dad married Wesson's mother shortly after that. Then, she'd died a year later, leaving my old man with two little boys to raise on his own. I'd like to say he did his best, but he was never the same after that. He rode both of us hard, forcing us to train and shoot and learn how to fight. Our home was more like boot camp than a safe space for children, and Dad had been our drill sergeant until he died.

I had to be perfect. Always the best. Which was why I probably pushed myself the hardest in these missions. Be better, faster, stronger. Softness was a weakness. Love was a vulnerability. So I never let myself open up to anyone. Sex was one thing. Relationships carried too much baggage, especially in this life. People died all the time, and I didn't have the patience for it.

Wes and I had a fucked-up relationship. We fought like brothers, probably because we spent far too much time together, but we were more than that. We always had been. We were two sides of the same coin, attached at the soul. If we were to end up on some therapist's couch, they'd probably say we had something unhealthy and codependent about us, but fuck all that. Wes was the only person in my life I truly cared about.

He didn't want this life. He wanted to go off to college and get married, maybe end up with two-point-five kids and a golden retriever. He even tried it once or twice. And as much as I loved him, I hated him for that. I saw this life as my duty, my birthright. He saw it as an obligation.

"When we get to the motel, let's regroup with Marta and let her know what we think," Wes said. "She might have better ideas on how to handle it from the magical side of things."

"It's a good thing Lilith sent three witches," I said. "If we need to make a liminal, three will do it."

"It would be better with four," he muttered. A few minutes of quiet went by before he ran his hands over his face and sighed. "You think Marta knows what she's doing?"

I snorted. "I think Marta's in over her head. Yeah, she helped with those shifters out in Montana, but does that mean she's ready for missions?"

Wes shook his head. "I feel bad for her, ya know."

"Feel bad *for her*? Why?" I narrowed my gaze on him and tsked through my teeth. "We didn't have anything to do with her parents' death? We lost our dad that day, too."

"Yeah, but that doesn't mean she deserves *this.*" He gestured between us, as if to say she didn't deserve the burden of being bonded to us.

"Deserves what? Two highly capable warriors with a lifetime of experience?" I scoffed. "Yeah, poor her."

"C'mon, Atlas," Wes said. "She hates us. And we haven't been exactly kind to her, either."

"Whatever. I just hope there's cheesecake at the diner." I reached forward and turned up the radio, blasting classic rock to shut him up.

I'd always admired Atlas. Once he'd made up his mind about something, almost nothing could deter him. Marta hated him? Fine, he hated her, too. Both men and women wanted to fuck him? Fine, he'd fuck them both, and screw anyone who dared look down on him for it. I'd always lived in his enormous shadow, and no one wanted to fuck a god's little brother.

I, on the other hand, never knew what I wanted until it was too late to do anything about it. Decision paralysis plagued me, a result of the anxiety I felt about making the wrong choice. One incorrect decision, one reaction a second too late, and everybody died. My parents, my stepfather. It didn't matter much in the grand scheme of things. Everybody left, no matter what. The only one who hadn't was Atlas.

I did feel for Marta, though I'd never say I pitied her. She was too strong for my pity, but if I were in her shoes, I'd curse the ancestors and damn us all to hell. The night our parents died was a blur, and if I was honest, I'd mostly blocked it out. I didn't want to remember my stepfather's screams as Atlas hauled me from the burning wreckage of that cursed house. I didn't want to return to that night every time I smelled roasting barbecue. I wanted to get out of this life, before and after the incident.

But I wouldn't leave Atlas. We were bonded by more than a legal relationship. He was...well, the conventions of modern society didn't have words for what he was to me, what he meant. I never let myself wander down those twisted roads. In my darkest moments, when the weight of my desire for freedom pressed in on me from all sides, he was the reason I stayed. The thought of him out here, doing this alone, kept me firmly rooted to him. Our story was a tragedy that would undoubtedly end with one of us burying the other, and knowing that still did not push me away.

Now, poor Marta had been pulled into our disaster, and she didn't even know the destruction she'd walked into. She didn't deserve the weight of this. I wasn't good enough for her, and I never would be. If it had to be one of us, it should have been Atlas. Just Atlas. He was more capable, more exacting, and I was just a fucking mess.

By the time we got to the motel, Isobel had already doled out the rooms. I'd be with Atlas (shocker) and Marta would stay with Bridge in the one next to us. It wasn't much more than two full-sized beds and a grungy bathroom, but I'd slept in worse places, so I dropped my bag on the mattress and sat on the edge to check my gun.

"Cozy," Atlas said, taking the one closest to the door. "Reminds me of that shit-hole in Dayton." He cracked his lips into an eager grin. "You remember the one."

I snorted and shook my head. "Sure. When you met that stripper at that sleazy club and she brought her boyfriend back to the room with her?"

He hummed appreciatively and dug his pistol out of his duffel, checking the clip before loading the chamber. "Fuck yeah."

I rolled my eyes. "I didn't see too much of the room. I slept in the GTO that night."

"You were invited," he said with a teasing wink.

I sighed and shook my head. Between us and sex, things had always toed a line. Which was understandable given how much else we shared in this life. I'd be an idiot not to admit that Atlas was objectively attractive. I wasn't blind. We'd hooked up with people in the same room, hard not to when we always split a motel. On one disastrous occasion, we'd ended up with a poly throuple where the guy wanted to watch his girlfriends fuck us both. That night had been sweaty and complicated, and I woke up wondering if there was an edge Atlas wouldn't hesitate to throw himself over.

Nothing had ever happened between the two of us, but if it ever came to it, I wasn't sure if Atlas would balk or encourage it. After all we'd been through, I didn't know if I would, either. We were brothers, yes, but the conventions of societal taboos had long since been thrown out the window. In his mind, who cared what the world thought when we were constantly putting our lives on the line to save it?

I'd catch myself watching him with someone and wonder what it would be like to be the object of his affection. I'd watch his hands as he cleaned his guns and marveled at their strength and dexterity. Then I'd shake myself back to earth and remember he wasn't into me like that, and I wasn't either. Perhaps it would have been better for him if I had left for college all those years ago. Maybe it would have been for everyone.

"Right," I said and pushed to my feet. "We should check in with—"

The door to the room opened, and the Harlots walked in, followed by their warriors. Isobel put her hands on her hips and glanced around while Bridge wrapped an arm over Marta's shoulders. Leander and Caspian hung toward the back. The rush of Marta's spirit raked over me, tickling my insides with unfamiliar anxiety. Almost like she was just as nervous to be around us as I was to be around her.

I was still adjusting to the warrior bond, though I wasn't sure I'd ever get used to it. Sensing her energy, her pain and joy, it squirmed like a phantom limb, like an itch I couldn't scratch. How did the others deal with it? I'd have to ask Leander one night, maybe after a beer or two.

"Aradia sent us some more intel," Isobel explained. She'd always been the type to jump right in, never wasting a moment. "There's evidence of rituals in Biltmore Forest and a farmer who claims he lost his entire flock of sheep in one night."

"Demon signs, sure as shit," Leander said.

"I agree," Bridge echoed.

"So we split up," Isobel continued. "Marta, Atlas, and Wes, you'll take the morgue. Check out the victims. Look for any signs of foul play."

"You mean besides the partially digested body parts in their stomachs?" Atlas added with a smirk.

Isobel ignored him. "Caspian and I will go to the hospital to see the survivors, maybe get some clues about what actually happened. Leander and Bridge hit the forest and talk to the farmer. We'll meet back here at 18:00."

"Got it," I said as more words of understanding echoed around me.

I met Marta's gaze and tried a smile, but her cheeks flushed and she looked away, the burn of hesitation and uneasiness zigging through my chest. No, I couldn't imagine anything about this being comfortable for her. But, like us, she was a soldier, a trained Harlot, capable of fierce magic and immovable stubbornness. She'd see this through to the end.

My focus lingered on her silky dark hair, currently braided at the back of her head with little whisps decorating the area around her face. Mahogany eyes gave way to delicate cheekbones and full, pouty lips that begged to be licked. Objectively, Marta was all beautiful curves and soft, supple muscle. And if I weren't me, and she weren't her, she was exactly the type of girl I'd go for.

But she'd never want me, and I understood that.

Her gaze connected with mine, and she furrowed her

eyebrows, perhaps confused by my leer. I quickly looked away. Knowing what we would have to do once we got there, Atlas and I took turns changing in the bathroom. Our everyday jeans and T-shirts wouldn't pass for business casual, so once I had the button-down and tie number on, I emerged and slipped on the suit jacket.

Marta let her gaze drift over me, and the weight of her appreciation zapped through my midsection. When I glanced up at her, she quickly looked away.

Atlas clapped me on the shoulder. "You ready, brother?"

"Sure," I said, clearing my throat as I loaded up my weapons and followed them out of the room.

"We should take my car," Atlas said, nodding toward the GTO. "It'll be less conspicuous that way."

Marta scoffed. "That rust bucket is about as inconspicuous as a sledgehammer in a china shop."

I winced internally, knowing Atlas's reaction before it happened.

"Rust bucket?" He balked, jaw gaping. "How dare you?"

She put her aviators on and crossed her arms, raising an eyebrow. "What's that thing get? Like two miles to the gallon?"

Atlas looked at me. "You hear this shit? She's insulting Josephine right in front of her."

"Josephine?" Marta shook her head. "It has a name?"

"Of course it has a name." Atlas opened the driver's side door and flipped the seat up, gesturing Marta to squeeze in the back. "Are you done making your comments? Any more and you'll be taking that grandpa bike instead."

"Grandpa bike?" Marta grimaced and stepped closer. "It would make this POS eat dust in two seconds."

"Oh, you're on, little witch." To anyone else, the exchange might have sounded flirtatious, but I knew my brother, and insulting his car was the quickest way to get on his shit list. Marta ducked into the back as I squeezed into the passenger side, curling my long legs under the dash so I could move the seat up to give her more room. She wasn't tall, but I was nothing if not a gentleman.

Once Atlas was in, he started the beast and revved the engine, shooting her a shit-eating grin in the rearview.

"Show off," she muttered, but Atlas reversed out of the parking lot and peeled off onto the main road like something was chasing us, rock music blasting on the radio.

Five minutes into the ride, I turned it down so we could plan our story once we got to the ME's office.

"We have our fake IDs," I said. "We play this like we normally do."

"What's that entail?" Marta asked.

"We say we're Feds," I explained. "We flash the badges and give them a nice smile. They usually don't question it."

She raised her eyebrows. "Does that work?"

"It hasn't failed us so far," I said. "Though now that you've mentioned it, we'll probably get held up."

"It's just..." She pursed her lips, crossing her arms.

"What?" I looked back at her.

"You don't look like Feds," she said. "Neither of you. Not even in the cheap suits."

"And how do you propose we get past the red tape, huh?" Atlas said in a biting tone. "Just wave your magic fingers and do a Jedi mind-trick on them?"

She shrugged. "There's an idea."

"Can you do that?" It surprised and intrigued me. What must it be like to wander through life, knowing you could manipulate anyone you wanted?

"I could," she said. "But I won't. The memory charm rarely lasts for very long, and I don't want to waste my energy if I don't have to."

"So, we're back to square one," Atlas said. "Wes and I play the Feds, you play the nosy, uptight assistant. That shouldn't be too hard for you."

She glared and gave him the finger, but I only snorted and shook my head, facing the front for the rest of the ride.

As it turned out, we barely needed the disguise. The ME was all too eager to have a second set of eyes on her work.

"I've honestly been waiting for someone to show up," she said as she led us to the morgue. "I've never seen anything like it."

These rooms always gave me the creeps, but I swallowed it down as the chill washed over me, raising the hair on the back of my neck. Marta and Atlas went first as Dr. Ballard gestured to the six bodies on separate gurneys, each with a white blanket draped over it.

"We read that the cause of death was blood loss," Atlas said. "Is that your opinion?"

Marta walked to the first body and peeled the sheet back, revealing an older woman with deep gashes up and down her torso. Big chunks had been taken out of her arms and neck, the unmistakable curve of teeth marks indicating how it had been done.

"Technically, yes," Dr. Ballard said, nodding toward the bodies at the far wall. "Blood loss for some of them, missing vital organs for others." She pulled open the sheet on a tall male with worse lacerations than the first person. "As you can see, they took bites out of each other while they were engaged in intercourse. They didn't stop until they were dead, and even then..."

I raised my eyebrows, anticipating her answer even as I suspected what it might be.

"The ones left alive kept eating." Ballard pointed at the wall of cadaver freezers to my right. "I've got four more skeletons in there, nearly picked clean."

Nausea rolled through my gut, but it wasn't mine. Marta had gone pale, and, try as she might to hide it, her throat convulsed and she swallowed hard to keep down her breakfast. Of all the missions Atlas and I had ever run, this was by far the most gruesome. Normally, we investigated demon rituals gone awry or some reckless vampire who'd invaded the wrong territory. But this? These were humans with an insatiable appetite for each other. Admittedly, I'd never seen anything so violent.

"I'm still waiting on the tox screen," Ballard said. "But my guess is some kind of ecstasy laced with a neurotoxin."

"Do you know of any kind of neurotoxin that could do this?" Marta asked.

Ballard shook her head. "But new stuff shows up on the drug market all the time."

"Fair," I said, stepping closer to the older cadaver. "What about strange markings? Notice anything during the autopsy? Any kind of tattoo or brand?"

"Brand?" Ballard raised her eyebrows. "Are you thinking a cult ritual?"

I shrugged. "Weirder things have happened."

She shook her head. "The only thing I'll add is that they were all missing their hearts."

"Hearts?" That got Marta's attention. "All of them? Even the ones at the end?"

Ballard nodded.

"Did you find evidence of their hearts in their stomachs?" I asked, watching as Atlas ran his gaze over a young woman, the last in the row. He inspected her arms and eventually her legs, looking for signs of a demon mark.

"It's difficult to tell," Ballard said. "By the time they dropped dead, they'd been at it for hours. Some of it was partially digested."

Marta nodded.

"The PD didn't find anything at the crime scenes," Ballard continued. "But you can't live without your heart, so my guess is once everyone else was dead, the last one standing ripped their own out to eat that, too."

"What about the survivors?" I asked. "Do you notice any commonalities?"

"Well, they're certainly not missing any vital organs," Ballard said. "But other than that, I wouldn't know. I'd have to see their medical reports to be sure."

"But based on what you've heard?" Marta pressed.

Ballard shrugged. "Could be related. If they got the same bad dose or maybe ran into the same rotten dealer? I heard they went at it until they were raw, until they bled and peeled the skin away."

It sounded horrific, and I wondered again what type of monster we were working with. Certainly a demon. Maybe an incubus?

"But I have no clue why they didn't progress this far or what would have stopped them from feasting." Ballard raised an eyebrow. "If you want to see the full workup, I can send it over as soon as I have the toxicology results."

"Thank you, doctor," I said.

A bell rang from the front desk, and Ballard sighed. "Feel free to examine the rest of the bodies, if you'd like. I'll be right back."

She walked out of the examination room, leaving us alone to speak freely.

"I don't know of any demon that is capable of this," Marta said as she walked to the body next to the older woman.

"What about an incubus?" Atlas asked, damn near reading my mind.

"Incubi want to impregnate. *They're* the ones doing the fucking," Marta explained, glancing over her shoulder. When she confirmed we really were alone, she rubbed her hands together and placed them over the chest of another young woman, right above the Y-incision. Marta closed her eyes and mumbled to herself as a white light emanated from her palms and fingertips. I held my breath, half expecting the corpse to sit up and start talking, but when Marta gasped and the energy dissipated, she only shook her head and sighed.

"There's something there, but it's..." She rubbed the space between her eyebrows and went to another body, eventually performing the same spell on all of them. "It's like...I'm being blocked."

"Is it because they're dead?" I asked. "Maybe Isobel will get something from the survivors?"

She hummed and hugged her midsection, a sudden wave of deep dread sinking into my gut as it flew across our newly formed bond.

"What is it?" I asked, taking a step closer.

"Whatever did this is more powerful than anything I've come across," she said. "The magical residue left behind is sickening. Vile."

"Well, they're all vile," Atlas said. "I've never met a demon I liked."

I understood what she meant, maybe even better than Atlas, based on his nonchalant response to her explanation. It rankled under my veins. Whatever darkness had permeated into our reality coasted down the space between Marta and me in a truly despicable way.

"We should get back," she said. "There's nothing else we can do here."

Atlas glanced at me, raising his eyebrow as if to suggest her input wasn't remarkable. I disagreed. Marta might not be the most powerful witch in the Harlots, but I'd been bonded to her for a reason. So had my brother. The sooner he accepted that, the stronger we would be.

I'd always believed in an afterlife. Despite my issues with God and whatever collective divinity watched over us, I'd never wavered in the idea that places like Heaven, Hell, and Purgatory existed. The power I had came from my long line of ancestors, and evidence of their reassuring presence made itself known in my everyday life. The sound of birds chirping in the morning, the peaceful energy radiating from the earth, the calming hum of trance and meditation. This was where I felt them most.

But those bodies...there was *nothing* in them anymore. When I placed my hands on them, the magic pulsing back made me ill. Their souls had not been passed onto the fade. It was almost like they had been devoured. Gone. Poof. Right into nonexistence.

Monsters like incubi or succubi could feed from souls for years and never fully extinguish them. Demons thrived on the chaos they created, reveling in the violent energy of humans under their thrall. But this? I had no idea what we were dealing with. It could be a demon, but maybe one I'd never heard of before.

On the drive back to the motel, Atlas and Wes talked in the front seat while I breathed through the rotten agony boiling in my veins. My skin prickled like I'd touched a live wire or stuck my tongue in an electrical socket.

The more we drove, the worse it got.

The sun had started to set over the horizon, painting the sky in brilliant violets and hushed roses. It should have been a beautiful sight, but my paranoia had only escalated. The hair on the back of my neck rose, and the churning in my stomach had me checking the back window every five seconds, one hand on my pistol, the other on my cross necklace. There was nothing behind us, but that didn't mean we weren't being followed.

Atlas slowed the car to a stop at a crossroads as that prickling awareness scratched over my scalp and down my spine.

"I don't know, Wes," Atlas said. "I've snorted and swallowed almost every drug out there. Nothing's ever made me feel like I needed to fuck my way to an early grave."

"Well, you're hardly a reliable source," Wes countered with a smirk. "You'd fuck anyone with a pulse and a warm hole."

"Hey!" Atlas smacked Wes's shoulder with the back of his hand. "Don't slut shame me."

Wes laughed, but movement in the woods off to my left got my attention.

"I don't think you have the emotional capacity for shame," Wes replied.

"Shhh," I cut in, narrowing my focus to the thrashing grass and swaying leaves.

"What? You side with him?" Atlas said. "Typical."

"Shut up," I said again, harsher this time. "Do you see that?"

Thick, heavy energy coated my insides, the air seizing in my lungs. We *were* being followed, and the thing was massive, whatever it was.

"What?" Wes said, following my line of sight to the tree line.

"What the fuck?" Atlas leaned closer, squinting to try to see better.

The ground thumped like a giant had taken a step toward us,

and the windows of the car rattled, vibrating with each heavy footstep. Anticipation had me yanking my gun out of the holster and reaching for the bottle of holy water in my satchel. If it was a demon, it was big and likely all hopped up on soul energy.

Which meant we were fucked.

"Go," I said, pounding on the back of the driver's seat. "Go. Go. Go!"

Atlas stepped on the gas pedal, but before we could move, something massive slammed into the car from the left side. My head smashed against the window, and the world darkened around me, stars blinding my vision. The white noise of tinnitus rang through my ears, and I clenched my eyes closed as the car flipped on its side. Metal crushed against asphalt as sparks flew into the back seat.

I struggled to focus, to come back to reality, my heart pounding and my hands shaking, my entire reality now upside down.

Just when the car would have toppled, I murmured a spell and blasted energy to the right, forcing us back onto four wheels. A black cloud spiraled outside, coalescing into the shape of an enormous human with glowing red eyes.

Demon.

Not just any demon. This was more colossal than anything I'd ever encountered.

It rammed into us again, growling and spewing venomous words in a language I didn't understand. Like Aramaic, but a much older version than the one I'd been taught. I caught bits and pieces through the high-pitched whine in my eardrums, but it was enough for me to realize it meant to kill us.

Consume, it snarled. *Consume. Take.*

Atlas raised his gun and fired off rounds right into the beast's midsection, but that only pissed it off more. The beast stumbled back, growled, and hit the car again.

Dizzy and disoriented, I scrambled to get out, shoving my

weight against the door until it finally gave way and I tumbled onto the asphalt.

"Marta!" Wes shouted, scrambling after me. But I had a plan. Holy water and a few enchantments should force it away long enough for us to figure out what to do. Wes joined me outside, sprinting behind me to the back of the car.

Mustering all the magic I could, I held my hand up and forced the energy through my palm, shouting in Latin.

"I expel you," I screamed. "Be gone, demon. I command you. Leave this land! Leave this place, immediately."

It turned to face me, crimson eyes gleaming, and curled its lips into a deadly, toothy grin.

"Ancestors, hear me!" I grounded myself in my mental safe space and reached out to the land, the heavens, and the other side of the veil. "Saint Marta, help me. Grandmothers, give me your strength."

White light beamed from my palm, energy surging through my fingertips, hitting the monster in the chest. I tossed the bottle of holy water at the demon, reveling in its groan as it stumbled back.

"I call upon the powers of this great mother: earth, wind, fire, water, spirit. Erase this monster from our sight. Erase this being from harming your children."

Atlas joined Wes at my side, and something tugged inside of me, that immature bond blaring to life. One Colt grabbed my right hand, the other grabbed my left, and magic surged between us, uncontrollable and untamed. Wes's calm stability clashed with Atlas's wild energy, burning through my earthy groundedness like wildfire. I couldn't contain it, and it poured out of my chest in a bright white beam, decimating the space between us and the demon, blinding me. Something warm trickled down my lips, over my chin. Ignoring it, I continued my assault, and the demon leaned into the force field, like a peon trying to withstand a hurricane.

A strangled growl tore from my chest, and just when I thought I would pass out, the demon dissipated into a cloud of obsidian.

Exhausted and panting, the connection to my warriors sizzled out, and I let go of their hands, leaning forward to put my weight on my knees. I'd never channeled that much energy before, and doing so made me lightheaded. Wes heaved deep breaths while Atlas stared at what remained of his precious POS.

"Fuck!" he shouted, clutching at his chest. But I didn't know if that was because of the car or the energy he'd just exerted.

I grabbed my phone and called Bridge, who answered on the second ring. I told her what had happened and asked her to get us, seeing as Atlas's vehicle wasn't going anywhere anytime soon. But that wasn't the major issue.

No.

When I searched deep down inside me, they were still there, lingering like electrical currents under my skin. This was *more* than the bond. This was chaos in my blood. This was their souls mingling with mine. It was too much. Too much indeed. It kept zinging back and forth between us, caught in a feedback loop. It passed through Atlas, into Wes, back into me. Over and over, gaining momentum as it went. I didn't think I could withstand it.

I ignored that for the time being, and eventually Bridge showed up, taking us back to the motel.

"Here," Bridge said, holding out a bar of chocolate after I collapsed on the bed. "It'll help."

"Thanks." I took it from her and sheepishly bit into a piece.

Atlas sat on the other bed, cleaning a wound on his head, and Wes stood next to Leander at the edge of the room, his arms crossed over his chest.

"Well?" Isobel said, raising her eyebrows. "What happened?"

"It was a demon," I replied.

"No shit, it was a demon," Isobel said. "Did you get an idea of what kind?"

"A big one," I answered.

Isobel's silent glare was enough to have me wilting into the mattress. I did my best to explain as I chewed. *Damn, this chocolate was good.* I got to the part where the warrior bond burned through me, *was still* burning through me, and I stopped. No one had ever had two warriors before. What if this was normal for that kind of thing? Was there even a reason for concern? Could Wes and Atlas still feel me this intensely? Still feel each other?

"I just...couldn't control it." I avoided the stare from both Atlas and Wes as it drilled holes through me, almost like they could see all the way down to my soul. Atlas didn't trust me, but his adrenaline was still high, so he was riding the waves of antici-pating another fight. Wes seemed more level-headed, like a tiger hiding in the bushes, patiently waiting for the right time to pounce. The bond's whirlwind energy didn't seem to frighten them as much as it did me, and maybe that was because they didn't know any better. "I don't think it's supposed to be like this. It...it scared me."

Isobel looked at Caspian while Bridge glanced at Leander.
Yeah, definitely not.

"You're okay now. Rest up," Isobel said. "We can't have you frying out in the middle of the ritual."

I swallowed and drank water from the glass on the table next to me, avoiding her scrutinizing gaze.

"It kept saying consume and take," Atlas continued, bringing their attention back to the demon. "My money's on some kind of deadly sin. Maybe gluttony or lust."

"What did you find out at the hospital?" I looked from Isobel to Caspian, praying they learned more than we did.

"One survivor is still in a coma," she explained. "The other was too traumatized to talk about it. He did say that it came on quickly. One second, they were normal. Then he was overwhelmed with desire...like if he didn't have sex, he would die. Literally die."

"So a lust demon then," Leander said. "Wonderful."

"The farmer was pissed about his sheep," Bridge continued. "It was a massacre. He'd already cleaned most of it up, but from what I could tell, it had all the signs of a ritualistic sacrifice."

"What about the woods?" Caspian asked.

"We didn't find much more than candle wax and leftover salt," Leander added.

"The magic residue was overwhelming." Bridge ran a hand over her face and back through her hair. "I brought a few books with me, anything I thought would be important, but there's nothing like this in there."

The Harlots had the most extensive collection of metaphysical and esoteric texts in the country. Our grandmothers had been gathering texts for decades, and now we maintained all of that knowledge to pass on to future generations. Bridge had the best catalogue of every book in there, even if I'd spent a large portion of my childhood roaming its shelves myself.

"Someone conjured something they shouldn't," Bridge continued.

"The Bloody Femmes?" Isobel raised her eyebrows in expectation.

Bridge nodded. "I think so. The energy was dark. Desperate. Almost...evil."

"What if it's THE Deadly Sin demon, the one who created the others?" Wes suggested. "Or maybe Babalon."

"He's super old," Isobel said. "Esoteric. Why would the Femmes haul him outta hell?"

"It doesn't matter why," Bridge said.

"Would a liminal even work on him?" I asked. "To create one, we need to know what we're working with."

"We'll do a summoning spell," Bridge replied, "quickly followed by an exorcism to the pocket world. Once we know what we're working with, we can adjust the spell accordingly."

"What about the salt ward?" I shook my head. "I've never seen anything that powerful. He might be able to walk right through it."

"There are three of us," Isobel replied. "And four warriors. That should be enough."

Should be.

That didn't make me feel better.

"Great." Isobel shook her head, sighed, and glanced at the rest of the warriors in the room. "The moon is conjunct Mars tonight at exactly 9:03 p.m. We'll go to the same spot where the Femmes conjured the son of a bitch and pull on that power to build the liminal."

That, too, made sense. We could pull on any residual energy left there to trap this specific monster.

"We leave in twenty minutes."

Twenty minutes? I doubted I'd be ready for a walk, much less a ritual, in that time. Especially with all this warrior energy buzzing around my molecules.

That decided, Isobel and Caspian left, quickly followed by Bridge and Leander, leaving me alone with my warriors. I licked the rest of the chocolate off my lips and swung my legs around to stand, wanting to head to the room I shared with my cousin. But when I sat up fully, my vision swam, and another wave of unease rocked through me.

"Hey, take it easy," Wes said, grabbing my arm to help me up.

I shrugged him off. "I said I'm fine."

"Clearly, you're not," he snapped.

I glared at him, suddenly irritated with his fussing over me. I didn't *need* his help. Either of them. I sensed his frustration and disappointment as I walked outside to ground myself in the earth's energy before we left.

Sitting cross-legged near the tree line out behind the motel, I wrapped a red ribbon around one hand and sank the fingers on my other into the dirt, diving my consciousness into my body. This particular ribbon had been given to me by my tita when my magic first manifested.

"It will protect you if you treat it with respect," she'd told me. In her tradition, red was a symbol of power, and ribbons, in particular, represented a barrier against harmful spirits. Once I had it wrapped around my wrist, I went to my safe space in my mind—the forest near my abuelita's house. The trees rustled in the wind, the birds chirped overhead, and the steady stream of trickling water echoed nearby.

Focusing on my breathing, I pulled energy up from the ground, channeling it into my heart, absorbing it into my soul. I reciprocated by sending my own back down, starting an ebb and flow between us.

I walked through my internal woods, touching the bark on the trees, my fingers sparking with strength and renewed determination. Just when I got to an area where the creek water crashed into rocks, a strange sensation cascaded over my arms and up the back of my neck. I glanced around but found nothing unusual. This was, after all, my sacred space.

"Mi hija," came a soft voice from behind me.

I whipped around, gasping, preparing to defend myself, but my focus landed on a tall, beautiful woman with blue flowing robes. Her dark hair fell in ringlets around her shoulders, and she held her hands out to me, beckoning me forward, almost like she wanted me to embrace her.

"Who are you?" I asked. Of all the times I'd come to this place, of all the times I'd centered and grounded myself in seclusion, no one had ever randomly intruded.

"Listen closely," she said in Spanish, completely ignoring my question. "The time has come when you must fight. You must forsake your rage at what isn't and focus on what is. You must channel your anger into faith, and faith into action."

"What?" I didn't understand what I was hearing. Who *was* she? Why had she chosen now to contact me?

In all my years as a practicing witch, I considered myself faithful to the things I could see and touch. The elements. The moon. My own spirit. But this? Was I imagining this?

When I finally got close enough to her, she put her hands on my jaw and tilted her glowing face down, meeting my eyes with resplendent ones of her own. They glittered with ferocity, with force and command. Whoever she was, she demanded my complete attention, my utter rapture. And I didn't have the willpower to resist.

"You will want to give up," she continued. "You must not do this. You were given many gifts, mi hija. Do not let them go to waste."

"I—I don't understand." The words fell from my lips in a stutter. I wasn't scared of her, no. She emanated a fierce but compassionate vitality that infected me with pure bliss. I could have stayed there with her forever. I could have basked in her radiance until the end of days.

Then she straightened and let go of my face, her expression morphing from stern benevolence to that of a parent chastising a child throwing a temper tantrum. I got the sense she had said all she would on this matter, and between one blink and the next, she was gone.

I glanced around, sure I had misunderstood or perhaps imagined the whole thing. This was, after all, my sacred mental space. It wouldn't have been impossible to have conjured the entire conversation from my subconscious. But I had never done anything like that before.

Why now? Why here?

"Who are you?" I shouted to no one. "Come back!"

I whirled around again, and when I returned to the spot where she'd once stood, a great giant cloud of black smoke filled my vision. Glowing red eyes raced toward me, gleaming sharp teeth encased by an evil grin. The demon reached out toward me, wrapping its arms around my throat, and just when I thought it would suffocate me in my own head, I opened my eyes back in the living realm.

I gasped, sucking in air, as I glanced around.

It isn't real. It isn't real.

I repeated the mantra as I blinked and focused on what I could see, what I could hear, what I could touch. The birds in the trees. The cool ground under me. The woods and the undergrowth and the faint sound of water running somewhere up ahead.

It isn't real.

Certain it was just a dream, just a trauma that hadn't quite been processed, I pushed myself to my feet and went to find the others.

We parked our bikes and walked into the forest, the relentless tension in my chest increasing exponentially. The trees hummed with ominous energy, seeming to emanate a warning that we were not welcome here. They'd already been scorched with chaos magic and would tolerate no more of it.

That should have been our first clue to tuck tail and run.

Wes and Atlas walked on either side of me, and the fiery bond between us vibrated intensely at the proximity. Despite not trusting it or knowing how to use it, I couldn't deny its captivating hold. Their emotions rattled deep down inside, nearly indistinguishable from my own. Wes was nervous, his heart pounding and his chest tight. Atlas was more resolute. His white-hot fury at having been attacked was compounded by how the demon had wrecked his car. He wanted revenge.

When we finally stepped into a clearing, I knew immediately it was the place where the Femmes had brought this entity into our realm. The aura of the trees changed to a sickening threat, one that coated my skin in raw evil, making the hairs on my arms stand on end. This was a *bad* place.

"Here," Bridge said, pointing to a spot on the ground where the undergrowth had been charred in the shape of a perfect circle.

Isobel reached into her bag and retrieved a tall glass bottle full of Holy Water. She popped open the top and poured the liquid on the decimated area, chanting a spell to cleanse the space. It smoked when it touched the ground, gray wisps rising as it reacted to the malicious energy. I read them as they appeared in zigzag crosses and interweaving tendrils.

Tread carefully, it warned, and my thoughts returned to the woman in my safe space.

The time has come when you must fight. You must forsake your rage at what isn't, and focus on what is. You must channel your anger into faith, and faith into action.

Was this what she meant? Would I need to start fighting now?

I cleared that from my mind and returned to the ritual. It would require all of my focus and mental shields.

Isobel set up the white candles, placing them at the four corners of the circle, while Bridge sprinkled a concoction of herbs in the center. I interspersed my own candles around Isobel's, calling on my ancestors to help us, calling on the woman from my meditation.

When it was done, I poured a salt circle around us, including our warriors, still unsure about whether it would be able to hold back a demon of this magnitude.

"Don't step outside it," I said. "No matter what happens."

Leander and Caspian had been through this sort of practice before, but Atlas and Wes had only ever gone on their own missions. I didn't know if they'd ever witnessed the creation of a liminal or understood the severity of the consequences should they take matters into their own hands. We'd need everyone to get through this.

Once the space was cleansed and set up, I stood on one side of the circle and held out my hands for Isobel and Bridge. Our palms connected, and the power of the coven rushed through me, tremendous and overwhelming. I nearly buckled at the knees. Holding firm, I closed my eyes and took deep, steadying breaths, sinking into the weight of my feet on the ground, the magic of the Earth cradling me through this.

"Ancestors, hear us," Isobel began. "Powers of light, wielders of magic, healers of the bloodline. We call to you now."

We took turns welcoming the elements and seeking any deities that would assist us with this work. Then we began the summoning chant.

"Demon that was resurrected here, we call to you. Show yourself. Bring yourself forward to us. We summon you. We summon you."

We repeated the command over and over, and the weight of our combined words rested heavily on my shoulders. The energy shifted around us, darkening, rolling a sick, threatening aura under my skin.

It's coming.

"We summon you! We summon you!" Our cries grew louder, the magic whipping around us like a hurricane as it raised the hair around my face. The wind picked up, and tendrils of vibrating power twisted around my legs from the earth below.

"Uh...guys," Atlas said, drawing my eyes open.

The dark sky had turned violent with rolling storm clouds, illuminated in the moon's soft light. My stomach bottomed out as the trees rustled, the ground rumbling, the air turning electric.

Isobel's hand tightened around mine, and I took a long, slow breath to steel myself against my nerves. A part of me wanted to run away and let this small town consume itself. To hell with the consequences. But I was better than that, stronger. I'd taken a vow to protect this world against whatever was coming for it.

A smoky pitch cloud broke through the tree line, coalescing into a tall monster at the center of the circle. Its bright red eyes met mine, and it smiled. I bit back my shiver.

"Cursed filthy witch," it snarled. "*Consume.*"

I forced my feet to stay still and my hands to hold on to my sisters so I didn't break the circle. Together, we'd created a bind that the demon couldn't break, but if we let go of each other, it could attack us...or worse.

"Demon," Isabel said. "Identify yourself. What is your name?"

It bucked against her command, twisting one way and then the other like her words burned.

"I compel you," she continued. "What is your name?"

The demon rolled its wispy head along its shoulders and clenched its eyes shut. "I do not answer to you."

"You are in my realm. You WILL answer to me." Isobel's voice grew stern and overbearing. "What are you, demon? What do you want?"

"Chaos," it said before muttering in an ancient language I

couldn't understand. At first, it rambled in soft whimpers, the words barely audible. Then, as we continued chanting, it grew irate, its voice booming over the rush of wind around us.

"Your name, demon!" Isobel yelled over its rambling.

"Harlots," Atlas cut in as he held up his pistol and cocked the chamber. "We've got trouble."

More smoke rolled in around us, surrounding us, pushing up against the salt border. They became monstrous human forms as their crimson eyes stared past the warriors, dead set on us.

"Don't break the circle," I said. My heart pounded and sweat beaded down my temples, my legs shaking, my stomach clenching. I'd never seen this many demons in one spot before, and if anyone broke the boundary, they would ambush us. We were suddenly outnumbered.

"You think this little show scares me?" Isobel laughed while Bridge continued saying the words that would hold the monster in place. "Tell me who you are!"

Despite Isobel's insistence, we were only tormenting the beast, pissing it off. We needed to force it to tell us specifically what it was so we could set up the right liminal.

The demon's voice grew louder, and I focused on trying to decipher what it said. I caught bits and pieces of words I knew, things like *god of lust* and *Asmodeus,* which he'd muttered in Latin. But I'd been forced to learn the dead language when I was a child, so I understood.

Asmodeus was the demon of lust, king of wanton desires and chaos, but he was too ancient to have been unleashed here. This was likely one of his offspring, one of his firstborn. We weren't dealing with a Deadly Sin demon, but this one was just as powerful, if not more so. The Sin demons took their inspiration from this one's father. How in the hell did the Femmes summon him here? How had he broken loose from the confines of the nether realms?

"It's an Asmodeian," I shouted, but that angered it more. It thrashed against the protective force field, throwing its misty body as hard as it could against our magic. The weight of its force rocked against me, throwing me back so hard I nearly lost hold of my sisters.

Gunshots echoed from behind me, the blast so loud, it rang in my ears. I ignored it. I had to believe that the warriors would handle whatever was coming our way. I focused inward, slowing my inhales and exhales, the words from the liminal spell surfacing in my mind.

"Bridge! Marta! Start the spell," Isobel shouted and squeezed my hand so tight, my knuckles twisted together. The strength of the coven flowed out of her, into me, into Bridge, and back again. I sensed Atlas's wrath as he fired bullets at the demons trying to protect their leader. I pulled on it, sucking it into my soul. Wes's panic and stoic focus came next, just as overwhelming. I yanked it into me, unwilling to trust it but knowing I needed it to help Bridge create the liminal.

A dark swirling vortex started to form in the middle of the circle, right in front of the Asmodeian as it struggled, twisting and warping in an attempt to break free.

More deafening blasts sounded from behind me, but I kept my focus on the words, tasting the syllables as they poured from my lips, imbibing them with as much magic as I could. Bitter and sweet, tingling and rapturous, I sang the ancient words, watching as the black hole grew around the beast.

Just when the magic reached an apex, something hard slammed into me from behind. I tumbled forward, my vision darkening, the ground steadily rising to meet me.

My hands slid from my sisters, and the world fell away.

CHAPTER 7

Atlas

here were two things in this world that I cared about more than my own life: my car and my brother.

Watching that Asmodeian motherfucker destroy the first one had enraged me. I wouldn't watch it kill the second.

Everything happened so fast, and before I knew it, something had knocked my Goddamned lights out. My insides punched and pulled. My soul got ripped out of my body and shoved back in the wrong way. I screamed, but no words came out.

I landed hard on my back and all the air rushed out of my lungs on a loud cough. For a moment, I lay there, staring up at a midnight sky, blinking into the moonlight.

Late summer heat clung to my skin, the humidity of North Carolina in September sticking to my throat as I sucked in an inhale.

Reality came into focus, and I remembered what happened.

A dark arm wrapping around Wes's throat.

Sharp, pointed claws digging into his chest.

Hot sticky blood pouring out of his torso.

My desperate shout for my brother...my best friend...my only friend.

"Wes." I tried to scream, but it came out on a wheeze as I turned on my side and pushed up on my hands. "Wes!"

"Over here," Marta said, kneeling in front of a prone body. He lay face up on the forest floor, his shirt ripped open, with deep gouge marks down the front of his torso. The Harlot's hands were covered in his blood as she waved them over him, muttering an incantation I couldn't make out. I struggled to my knees, crawling over to him as my heart thudded. "Heal, Goddamn it. Heal!"

"Is he breathing?" I croaked as I touched his chest and prayed for movement. "Is he alive?"

"I don't know," she snapped. "Be quiet. I need to focus."

Be quiet?

I shot her a glare before I checked for Wes's pulse. A faint, dull thud hit my fingers, and I scrambled for my brother's shirt, peeling back the layers so I could assess the damage.

The wounds wept with black pus, ruby red mixed with agonizing pitch. Marta's white light emanated into them in sputtering pulses, but she must have been weak from the spell it took to push the demon into the liminal.

"Here," I said, holding my hand out to her. "Use me."

She ignored it, clenching her eyes shut and continuing to chant.

"Fuck you, Marta. Now's not the time for your bullshit." I shoved my hand in her face. "Pull from me!"

When she opened her eyes, they glowed bright white, the pupils and irises completely disappeared. With her squared jaw and lips pulled back in a grimace, she looked damn near as formidable as the monster we'd just defeated.

But she didn't argue. She grabbed my hand, interlaced our fingers, and started the spell again. Nothing happened. She didn't pull on me. When I spotted her wide eyes and open mouth, I realized she was trying.

"I can't—" She shook her head. "The bond isn't working. It isn't—"

"What do you mean it's not working?" I cut in. "Fix him!"

"Shut up," she said, breaking the contact between us to return to her work. Pale wisps trickled from her palms in sputters, hardly the power she'd had during our first fight with the demon. My heart nearly pounded out of my chest as I waited for her to kick her magic into high gear.

More obsidian ooze leaked from my brother's chest until it finally ran red, and once it was gone, the wounds stitched back together. She kept chanting until a translucent patch of purple skin knitted over the claw marks, and Wes's eyes opened.

"Fuck," he murmured as he arched off the ground, clearly in turmoil.

"Wes!" I grabbed his cheeks and stared down into his dark brown eyes, the gnawing ache of relief flowing through my nerves as I brushed the hair out of his face.

Wes tried to sit up but groaned and fell back, thumping his head on the ground. I moved around him to wrap an arm under his shoulders, helping him into a reclined position on my knees.

"What happened?" His strangled voice nearly brought me to tears, and it wasn't until I heard it that I realized how close I'd come to losing him.

No. That wasn't a possibility. I wouldn't let that happen. There was no world in which Wes didn't exist, and if there was, I didn't want to be a part of it.

"That's a good question," Marta said, looking at me.

"You nearly became demon bait," I explained, shaking my head in disbelief. "Good thing I was there to pry him off you."

"Pry him off?" Marta raised her eyebrows, opening her mouth. "You touched the demon?"

"I touched *a* demon, not the one you were shoving into a liminal."

"We were trying to shove *all* of them into the liminal." The accusation in her tone raised my hackles. "What did you do?"

I looked around. We were still in the woods, probably the same forest where we'd done the ritual. But the other Harlots were gone. The circle, the candles, the demons, all vanished. Save for the wind in the trees and the birds chirping overhead, we were the only sounds in the place.

"I don't know." I tried to remember, but it all happened so quickly. Had I stepped over the salt line? Had Wes? How had the demon been able to grab him in the first place?

"Are we dead?" Wes wheezed.

"If we are, we're certainly in hell." Marta let out a sad laugh and bent her knees so she could rest her arms over them. "I doubt any heaven would put the three of us together for all eternity."

I tried to act like the insult didn't sting. After all, I hated her as much as she hated me, but worse things were waiting for us in hell, me especially.

"You should be so lucky, witch," I snapped, grabbing my cellphone out of my jeans pocket to check for a signal. When I had none, I held it up higher and hoped it was just the trees fucking it up.

She shifted that angry gaze to me, her eyes narrowed into tiny slits.

"What the fuck did you do, Atlas?" she snapped. "We were chanting. The liminal was opening. And then..." She closed her eyes, seemingly remembering the last moments before we went ass over teakettle into whatever this was. "You knocked into me."

"No," I snarled. "Your shitty wards fell. One of those fuckers got Wes. I had to protect him."

"You were supposed to be protecting *me.*" She tried to push to her feet, only to slam back on her ass with a resounding thud, almost like she'd lost her balance or stood up too quickly. "And if it weren't for those wards, we all would be dead. No thanks to you."

"No thanks to me?" I scoffed. "I'm the only reason you're still in one piece, Witch."

Marta opened her mouth to give me some nasty retort, but Wes cut in.

"Stop," he said, wheezing as he tried to suck in a deep breath. "Stop fighting. We have to get somewhere safe. We need food and rest."

Leave it to the one who almost died to bring us back to reality.

"Fine," I said, garnering my strength so I could push upright. Stars twinkled in my vision, and my head spun, but I put my hand out to a tree to steady myself. When my blood pressure caught up to the rest of me, I straightened my shoulders and looked at my wayward companions. "Can either of you stand?"

Marta struggled to her feet, and once she had them under her, she took a deep breath and looked at Wes. I reached out a hand for him, and he grabbed it so I could haul him upright. He groaned and winced against the ache in his chest, especially when I ducked myself under one of his arms to hold his weight on my shoulders.

"Which way?" I asked, glancing at Marta. She looked around and shrugged, holding up her cellphone to move it right and left. I guessed she didn't have a signal either.

"That way, I think," she answered.

"You think?" I took a deep breath and swallowed the irritation bubbling in my chest. What good was the witch if she didn't know where the hell we were?

"Do *you* know which way to go?" She crossed her arms and raised an indignant eyebrow, jutting a hip out.

I rolled my eyes. "No, of course not. But I'm not the one with magic. Can't you do some location spell—"

"It doesn't work like that," she said. "After the ritual and then healing Wes, I'm tapped out."

"Use me," I said. "Use us."

"I can't. Something happened when we got knocked...wherever we are. The bond is gone."

"What do you mean *gone?*" I'd had just about enough of her bullshit. We didn't have to like each other, but we were supernaturally connected regardless. She might as well use that to our benefit.

"The road between us is closed," she said.

"Well, open it," I growled.

"I can't!" Marta closed her eyes and sighed before pinching the bridge of her nose. "Let's just...go this way and see if we hit the road. Maybe Isobel and Bridge went back to the car to get something to help us."

I didn't argue, but in my gut, I doubted Isobel and Bridge were here. I had a sickening suspicion we'd fallen victim to our own spell, that instead of creating a liminal for the Asmodeian demon, we'd done something far worse.

We stumbled through the woods, Marta leading the way while I struggled to carry most of Wes's weight. He could barely hold himself upright, and it took us nearly double the time to get to the road. But at least he was alive.

At least we're both alive.

"What do you think happened?" Wes asked. He gasped through the syllables like each word hurt him to say, and based on the horrifying bruises starting to form on his chest, I bet it did. Marta had only put a magical bandage on him. He'd still need time to recover fully.

"Those fucking witches screwed up the magic. Now we're trapped." In all my years of hunting monsters, I'd seen some fucked-up shit. I'd seen ghosts and poltergeists that fling people around entire houses. I'd seen undead creatures that burst into disgusting blood bubbles if stabbed with iron. Fairies, vampires, shifters, all of it. But when I woke up in the woods with only the two of them, my internal what-the-fuck-meter blared loud and clear.

"Trapped where?" Wes asked.

I had an idea, but I didn't want to go wandering down that road until I had more reason to.

Marta cleared the tree line to the street, Wes and I stumbling out after her. Her bike sat in the same spot next to Bridge's and Isobel's with Leander's car behind it. But there was no sign of the other Harlots or warriors.

"Bridge!" Marta called out. "Isobel?"

She held her phone up and squinted at the screen, waving it around as she tried to find reception. I checked mine again but came up short. No WiFi. No connection.

"Fuck." I slid my phone into my back pocket and hitched my brother higher on my shoulder, glancing up and down the road. "This is ominous, huh?"

"Where do you think they went?" Marta asked.

"I don't know," I said as Wes's head lulled down in front of him. "But if we don't get him to an ER—"

"No doctors," Wes muttered. "They'll ask questions."

"Shut up, man." I wasn't prepared to watch him waste away from an infection when his pride was the only thing standing between him and a shot of penicillin. "Witch, open the door."

Marta helped me load Wes into the back seat, where he promptly slumped over, before she started for her bike.

"Come with us," I insisted. "Leave the bike."

"Hell will freeze over before I do that." She scrunched her features, scowling at the thought of leaving her precious behind.

"I get it," I added. "But we shouldn't split up, not until we know what's going on."

She remained hesitant, heels dug into her spot.

"We'll come back for it later. Get. In. The. Truck."

The disgruntled look on her face made me think she would ignore me, but when she only nodded and climbed into the passenger seat, I went around to the driver's side and set about dismantling the panel under the steering wheel. Most modern-day vehicles couldn't be hot-wired because of push-button start and anti-theft nonsense. But Leander drove an early '90s pickup, so getting it started took almost no time.

"Should I even ask why you know how to do that?" Marta asked with raised eyebrows.

"This ain't my first rodeo." I winked, put the truck in drive, and set off toward the hospital.

CHAPTER 8

Atlas

It didn't take us long to realize that something was really fucked up about where we were. The streets were empty. We didn't pass any other vehicles on the roads. The shops were open, and the lights were on, just as they had been when we'd driven past them to go to the ritual, but there weren't any people inside, almost like everyone had blinked out of existence.

"You thinking *Avengers: Infinity War* or *Zombieland*?" I asked, raising an eyebrow at the witch in the passenger seat.

She didn't answer; she just glowered out the window as we passed a popular department store that should have been bustling with people. Instead, the parking lot looked like a junkyard where cars went to die.

"The hospital on Route 9 is closer, but the one in Asheville is better," I said.

"No hospitals." Wes groaned from the backseat.

"Shut up," I said, glancing at my brother in the rearview. He looked like shit, his skin pale white, his features twisted in excruciating pain.

"I can heal him," she said. "I just need some rest, and then I'll be able to do the spellwork."

"Forgive me if I don't trust your secret special magic powers, not after what just happened." I rolled my eyes and shook my head. "You're not a miracle worker."

"I've healed demon wounds before." She clenched her fists in her lap. "I need to recoup my strength. Maybe the others went back to the motel. We should check there."

"The others?" I scoffed. "Look around you, witch. There *are* no others."

"We need sacred ground," she continued, like my protests meant nothing. "We need to head back to the estate. I have herbs and candles there, not to mention the eons of ancestral magic in the earth."

"Herbs and candles?" I scoffed. "Look at him! We need stitches and antibiotics and—"

"Listen to her, Atlas," Wes said. "She can heal me. She knows what she's doing."

Yeah, I fucking bet.

I took a deep breath and debated what to do. Even if we went to the hospital, I didn't know what to look for. Yes, we needed penicillin, but would that even work against demon magic? How much was I supposed to give him?

On the other hand, witches had been known to do a better job of treating and patching up wounds than the best doctors. Maybe with a little rest and some witchy-woo-woo shit, she could get Wes back on his feet.

"Fine," I snarled. "Where to?"

"The motel first," she said. "If this isn't our own personal hell, maybe my sisters went back there. If it is, we'll head to Asheville."

I didn't like it, not one fucking bit. But if Wes was on board and Marta thought she could fix him, I'd hesitantly go along with it. Like she said, the hospitals in Asheville were better than the ones out here in the sticks, so I figured I could always hit it up if it came to that.

But the closer we got to the motel, the more that ominous pit in my stomach grew. The roads were abandoned, and cars literally stopped in the middle of the highway like their drivers had disintegrated behind the wheel. When we finally got there, I grimaced at the desolate building straight out of every one of my favorite horror movies. The lights flickered on the sign, and the rooms were dark inside, no doubt containing flesh-eating monsters ready to peel our skins from our bones.

"Well, this is cheery," I said, grabbing my pistol to check that it was loaded. I'd emptied my clip during the ritual, but I had another in the bed.

Marta didn't respond, just opened the passenger door and rushed out.

"Wait!" I shouted, but she didn't listen to me. "Fucking hell."

I glanced in the back seat and checked that Wes was still breathing. He leaned back with his head on the rest, his inhales labored and his exhales pained. But at least he hadn't faded yet.

"I'm gonna go in there after her," I said. "You stay alive, understand?"

Wes gave me a half-hearted thumbs-up and grimaced.

I got out and went to the back of the truck to retrieve my extra clip before loading it up. Then I followed Marta into the room she'd been sharing with Bridge. Holding my gun out in front of me, I cautiously pushed the door open, preparing for a zombie or a demon or I didn't know what, something gruesome. Instead, I lowered my weapon when I found the witch coming out of the bathroom.

"They're not here," she whispered.

"Don't fucking run off like that again," I said.

"They're not here," she repeated, louder this time, curling her hands into fists at her side.

"Yeah, I heard you the first time," I said. "Did you check the other room?"

She shook her head as I headed outside and down the corridor leading to Isobel's room. But it looked the same as it had when we left. That sneaking suspicion became a full-blown conspiracy theory when I went to the room after that, and the room after that, and found no one.

The motel office was empty. The rooms were empty.

This entire world...empty.

When I got back to Bridge's room, Marta stood next to Bridge's bed, gathering books into a suitcase.

"Witch," I said, "there's no one here."

She glanced over her shoulder before returning to her task.

"I need you to take me back to my bike," she said. "And then we'll head to the clubhouse."

"Are you sure we should leave the area?" I walked closer to her, watching as she packed her things. "What if the other Harlots can fix this? Maybe we should stay close to the woods."

Marta took a deep breath and sighed. "I think we're in the liminal."

There it was, the thing I'd been dreading to say out loud, and she'd just flopped it into the atmosphere between us like a dead fish. Even if I suspected it, all the air rushed out of my lungs, and my stomach lurched.

"Have you ever heard of anything coming back from a liminal?" She raised an eyebrow and looked at me.

"Well...no," I admitted. "But that doesn't mean there isn't a way."

The witch clenched her eyes shut, a blush creeping up her neck and into her cheeks, almost like she was holding back tears.

"We're fucked, Atlas," she said. "This is so much worse than I thought."

I didn't know what enraged me more: that she'd so easily sunk into this useless despair or that it was her stupid coven that had gotten us into the mess in the first place. Blinding white fury snaked up my spine, pooling in my mouth, and I couldn't stop what came out next.

"Yeah? And what did you think? That a demon clawing

through the wards to slice and dice my brother meant we'd end up in fucking Eden?" It was cruel, but I had nowhere else to direct my anger, and I couldn't contain it. "That you could wave your magic fingers, and it would all be over? Wake up in Aruba, perhaps? No, you fucked this up, witch. Now, fix it."

She snapped her gaze to me and squared her jaw, her pouty lips pulling into a thin line.

"This wouldn't have happened if you hadn't touched the demon in the first place," she snarled. "The spell should have worked."

"Well, it didn't," I roared, taking a step toward her.

She countered with a step toward me, staring up my body with those bright mahogany eyes, burning with indignation. "I can see that. I'm not fucking stupid."

"You're also not a fucking quitter." I towered over her, heat pluming off me, mingling with the reckless inferno burning in her stare. "So stop feeling sorry for yourself and get your shit together because, if we *are* in a liminal, we have bigger things to worry about now than who fucked up what part of the ritual. And..."

I trailed off as I realized how close we were. Our torsos were millimeters apart, our pants combining in the electric space between. For half a heartbeat, I thought about leaning down to kiss her, to collide the decade's worth of tension brewing between us and let out a little steam. I dropped my focus to her mouth, where her delicate pink tongue swiped against her perfect lips.

"Did you find anything?" came the pained voice from the doorway, punching me back to reality. I blinked and jumped back from Marta, turning to see Wes slumped against the door.

"What the fuck are you doing?" I rushed toward him and wrapped an arm around his waist to hold him up. "I told you to wait in the truck."

"You were taking a long time. I thought about dying but figured you'd kick my ass if I did. So I came to check on you."

"You're Goddamned right." I couldn't even *think* about losing him.

"To answer your question, no," Marta said, returning to her books. "No one's here. We're alone."

"Are we..." Wes winced and tried to straighten himself. "Are we in the liminal?"

"I think so." She zipped up her bag, slung it over her shoulder, and turned to face us. "Maybe the demon was too powerful for the salt circle. Maybe *someone* fucked it up. Either way, it doesn't matter now. We should head back to the Harlot estate. I can pull on the strength of the magic there."

Wes swayed in my arms, his knees almost buckling under me.

"You should go wait in the truck," the witch said. "You're practically a ghost."

He snorted a soft laugh. "That sounds about right. How many times have we almost died, Atlas?"

"That's not funny, brother," I said, helping him out of the room and back toward the vehicle.

"I mean, at least ten," he said. "Fate was bound to catch up to us someday."

"I don't want to leave my bike," Marta said, drawing my attention. "But I also don't think we should split up. If this is the liminal, then that demon might be around here somewhere. I don't know if we managed to pull him in with us."

I shuddered at the thought. Trapped all alone in a pocket reality with a witch that hated me and a lust demon certainly sounded like my own personal hell. Maybe Wes was right. Perhaps fate or the ancestors or some twisted, fucked-up karma had led us here just to punish me for all the shit I'd done. How could we possibly hope to defeat a demon in the prison we'd created for it? It wasn't like we had the power of other witches to help us create another liminal, if that was even possible. But first things first.

"I don't wanna leave Josephine, either," I said, my heart yanking at the thought of my baby all alone at that repair shop, busted into pieces, no one to put her back together again. "But we don't have another choice. Besides, we're in the liminal. None of this is real. Your bike, my car, they're waiting for us in the human realm, so we should spend our time figuring out how to get back."

Marta nodded and walked toward the passenger seat. "Go get your things. Let's head home."

Ididn't remember much of the drive back to the clubhouse, only the part where Atlas and Marta carried me into the mansion-turned-hangout and through the foyer into one of the bedrooms downstairs. They laid me down on the bed, where I promptly passed out from the exhaustion and agony of what had been done to me.

Most of it was a haze, all except one recurring nightmare that plagued my sleep. I was back in the woods where we did the ritual, alone, standing in the salt circle the witches had drawn. The forest was disturbingly quiet—no birds chirping, no wind in the trees— just me and my heartbeat. I turned around, looking for someone, anyone, only to find myself completely desolate.

"Hello?" I called. "Atlas? Marta?"

No answer came. A small part of me knew I shouldn't step outside the salt line, but I couldn't stay here. Just as I started to cross the boundary, the clouds turned a dark, angry gray, rumbling with the threat of thunder and lightning.

"I wouldn't do that," whispered a soft, feminine voice.

I jumped and twisted around, reaching for my gun, which

wasn't in my belt holster, where it should be. Neither were my knives. I was precariously unarmed.

"Who's there?" Panicked, I turned back the other direction, finding no one.

"Wesson Colt," came the voice again. "Child of Nathaniel Smith, adopted son of Xavier Colt."

I straightened my shoulders and prepared for a fight. Just because I didn't have my weapons didn't mean I was hopeless. I'd been training since I was a child, and I could hit nearly as hard as Atlas.

"You should not have come here," the voice said. "But I am pleased to see you."

"Yeah, I fucking bet," I snarled. "Why hide? Come out. Show yourself so I know who I'm dealing with."

"This is my domain, my realm. Your witch made it for me," whispered the voice. It echoed from all around, seeming to come from the air itself.

"Asmodeian demon," I said. "I summon you. Show yourself."

"Tsk, tsk, tsk," it said. "Such arrogance. You cannot compel me, boy. Not here. Not anymore."

I didn't like the sound of that, but there was nothing I could do until I put eyes on the beast itself. "Where are you? Come forward. If you're so almighty and powerful, why are you acting like a coward?"

Yeah, I was baiting it, but some clawing need inside urged me to make sure it was the demon so I knew how to handle it.

"Are you sure?" Its sinister laughter made the hairs on my arms stand up, sending shivers down my spine. "You might not like what you see."

"I'm not afraid of you," I said. Though the demon that had torn open my chest nearly killed me. Maybe I should have been more scared than I was.

Silence fell again before a burning sensation tunneled through my stomach into my lungs, ripping apart my veins, boiling my muscles. I gasped and dropped to my knees, scrambling for my shirt to rip it over my head. My blood had turned a sickly shade of black, my skin suddenly translucent enough to see the vile stuff pumping through my molecules. I scratched at my skin, trying to get it out of me, but it only grew worse. Agony raced through my sternum, up my throat, over my tongue. I spat out brimstone and sulphur, my eyes scalding, my skin sliding from muscle and bone. My ribs popped, and a thick, dark hand exploded from my chest like something out of an '80s movie.

Screaming, I lurched up, and the nightmare fell away. I was back in the bedroom, the soft glow of little flames flickering from all around me. Marta sat on the mattress at my right, a washcloth in one hand, a burning white candle in the other.

"Hey there," she said, leaning down to pat my forehead with the cool cloth. "You're alright. You're safe."

I grimaced against the headache between my eyes as I remembered why I was laid up in this bed in the first place. I glanced down my body, gaze narrowing on the deep purple claw marks across my chest. They looked as bad as they felt.

"How long have I been out?" My voice sounded like someone had taken a sandblaster to it, and my throat ached from the raw force of talking.

"A week," she said. "We're back at the Harlot estate, but I just regained enough magic to heal you properly."

I stared at her, taking her in fully. She looked rough—heavy bags under her eyes, dark shadows in her cheeks, her hair in a frizzy ponytail around her head. None of that distracted from her beauty, though. She still looked like she could kick my ass in stilettos.

"Where's Atlas?" I asked, pushing myself up into a seated position against the headboard.

"Whoa, take it easy." She leaned forward to help me, but I pushed her away. I needed to move, to do this for myself. "You're still in rough shape."

"I'm okay," I said. "Where's my brother?"

She sighed and rubbed a hand over her forehead. "Raiding the bar, I'm sure."

"Sounds about right." I snorted and shook my head. Atlas was hedonistic at the best of times. Where I relied on logic and a clear head, he lived to fuck and fight and drink. Sometimes, I couldn't believe we were raised by the same man.

"He wouldn't leave your side for the first few days," she continued. "I had to force him to take a break today."

I ignored the heat in my cheeks at the embarrassment of Atlas being worried about me. "Any sign of the demon?"

I fought the shiver that went through me at the mention of the reason we were in the first place, and I touched my chest, where the burn of my nightmare still lingered, almost like the monster was still trying to claw its way out.

"No," she said, sitting down on the mattress next to me. "But we haven't left the house since we got here. He wants to ride around, see what we see, but I don't think we should leave the protection of the wards."

I could see both sides. While it would be a good idea to understand precisely where we were and what we were dealing with, until she had her magic back and until I was back on my feet, doing that could be dangerous. Atlas couldn't defend himself alone, and we needed to regain our strength.

"Smart," I said. "The wards here are strong. Nothing's getting past that front door."

"Exactly," she said. "But he does have a point. We should know if we're the only ones here."

I nodded and glanced at the candle, still flickering and dribbling wax down to her fingertips. "What are you doing with that?"

She smirked and put it on the bedside table. "Fire scrying. I was trying to get the spirits to tell me what's going on, but they're being unusually quiet."

"Those bastards," I teased.

Marta furrowed her brows and glanced back at me. "What were you dreaming about?"

A sharp slice hit me in the sternum, and I glanced at my lap as the memory of anguish crept through my veins.

"Nothing," I said, my cheeks burning. "Just a bad dream is all."

She nodded and stood to grab a tea from the table, handing it to me. "Drink this. It'll help."

I took it and brought it to my nose, wincing at the earthy compost smell wafting off the steam. "What is it?"

"Herbs," she said. "Rue, chamomile, garlic, pepper. They have natural antibodies and healing derivatives."

"It smells like grass," I said.

She raised an eyebrow. "If you don't want it, give it here."

"No," I said immediately, bringing it to my lips. I chugged it down, ignoring the weedy taste and the mild burn in my throat. It settled in my stomach like warm soup, comforting if not entirely palatable.

"Good boy," Marta said and took the mug from me.

Heat snaked down my chest, into my abdomen, and not just from the tea. A low simmering tension gripped my lower stomach, yanking until my cheeks burned hotter.

Fuck my praise kink.

"The bond is still blocked," she said, "and I don't know why. I've been in the library for the last few days, and I haven't found anything worthwhile. You should try to get some more rest."

"No, fuck that," I said, shifting around so my legs hung off the side of the bed. My torso stung and my muscles twinged, but I wanted to help. "It's been a week. If you're researching, I'm researching."

"Wes." She groaned. "A week ago, you were demon mincemeat."

"And I'm feeling much better now, especially after your grass stew."

She laughed, and the sound rattled something deeper inside me, more profound than her calling me a good boy.

"I can rest just as easily in the library as I can here," I said. "Besides, it's shocking you and Atlas haven't already killed each other."

"Well, that's easy to do in a place this size. We just avoid being in the same room."

"See?" I pushed to standing, wobbling as my core nearly gave out under the stress. She lurched to help me, but I held a hand up, stabilizing myself on the table. "I'm okay."

She heaved a deep sigh.

"What do we know about the liminal?" I asked. "Any quirks or weird stuff happening?"

She shrugged. "Every day resets like Groundhog Day. Any food we eat gets replenished at midnight. Any chances we make reset. It's like we're living the same day over and over again."

"Wonderful. At least it's a starting point."

She smiled and nodded, stepping toward the door. Just before she left, I stopped her.

"Thank you," I said, meeting her timid gaze. "For healing me. For your...amicable bedside manner."

Marta grinned and gestured toward the dresser. "There are some clean clothes in there. You know where the shower is. Other than being alone, it seems like everything else is exactly as we left it."

She left, and after I ambled to the shower, I stripped and got under the heated spray. The water stung the wounds on my chest, but washing away the sweat and grime from the last week of bedrest made me feel better. Of course, there was the problem of the ache in my cock, which hadn't let up since Marta had called me a good boy in that silky tone of hers. I palmed the thick length, telling myself it would be okay just this once...just to let it out... to deal with the problem so it didn't escalate.

No.

No, it wasn't right. She deserved better than some fucking creep like me lusting over her.

The sight of a demon bursting from my chest had the problem deflating as I hung my head under the spray and supported my weight on the wall. *It was just a dream. Just a bad dream. That's all.*

After I got my shit together, I dressed and limped down the hallway to the parlor, where Atlas sat on a loveseat, hovering over the coffee table in front of him. Parts of his guns were spread out across the wood grain next to a glass of amber liquid, rags and brushes at varying degrees of dirty. He'd obviously been cleaning them for a while.

"Hey." I grimaced, plopping down into the seat across from him.

"Jesus, man," he said. "You look like shit."

"Have you seen yourself?" Like Marta, he had dark circles under his eyes and his hair stood on end, like he'd been running his hands through it for hours.

"You should be in bed," he said.

"I'm fine," I said, leaning forward to grab his glass and bring it to my nose.

Whiskey.

I took a deep swig and set it back down, letting the burn soothe away any lingering effects from the nightmare. Atlas went back to stuffing a brush down the barrel of his pistol and raised an eyebrow at me.

"What do we know?" I asked. "Any luck getting in touch with the Harlots?"

He shook his head. "Without her magic and without the bond, we're hanging on by a thread."

"This is my domain, my realm. Your witch made it for me." The sound of the demon's voice rattled around in my brain, making me wince. I pushed it away.

"I want to go back to Biltmore Forest," he said. "There's got to be a clue there somewhere. Maybe in the woods. Maybe—"

"You think that's safe?" I raised an eyebrow as he ran his hands over his face and reached for the whiskey.

"I don't know, man," he said. "It beats sitting around here, waiting for something to happen. That fucking witch has been holed up in the library since we got here, and the longer we wait, the more likely it is that we might never get back."

"I've never heard of anyone bringing a demon back from a liminal," I said.

"But we're not demons," Atlas countered, and I conceded that fact. The implications of it were mind-numbing. Was it just our souls trapped here? Or had our physical bodies fallen into the trap? That Asmodiean fucker had been nothing more than black smoke and metaphysical energy. How then did we live through the spell? Was this all in our heads? And if so, how would the Harlots get us back in our bodies?

"If we're trapped in a liminal, then none of this is real. It's a made-up reality, a ripple between realms," he continued. "If she can summon demons from hell, I have to believe she can figure out how to get us out of this."

I glanced down at the gun parts again. "You planning on helping her or—"

"I *am* helping her," Atlas growled. "By staying out of her way. That witch is a pain in my ass, and—"

"I'm sure the feeling is mutual," I added with a small laugh.

"You're taking her side?" He scoffed. "Typical."

"What?" I blinked at him.

"One pretty girl bats her eyelashes at you, and you fall ass over teakettle."

"Fuck off." I grabbed a pillow and threw it at him, but he caught it before it could hit his face.

Atlas rolled his big green eyes and licked a drop of liquor off his lips, and I pretended like the sudden urge to swipe my tongue over his mouth was just a lingering side effect of Marta's appreciation.

I quickly averted my gaze and squashed down the heat in my cheeks.

"There are no sides, Atlas," I continued, bringing myself back to reality. "We're stuck in this together, and we're gonna need to work together to get out of it."

"Whatever." He downed the rest of his whiskey and poured himself another glass. What was it? Noon? One? What did it matter? Like he said, nothing was real. In the liminal, societal norms didn't matter. Nothing mattered.

"I'm going to help her research." I pushed to my feet.

"Alright, nerd," he said. "Can't wait to get your greedy paws on those books, huh?"

"This can't be the first time this has happened," I continued, ignoring his jape. "And if we can get the bond working again, maybe there's a way out of this." I headed toward the door, but turned back at the sound of his disgruntled sigh. "But I agree with you. Give it a few days, and we'll circle back to Biltmore. There's got to be something we missed."

"Hey," he called out just when I got to the hallway. "Keep your head on straight, right? I still don't trust that witch."

I nodded and left him to play with his toys, and as I slowly strolled through the house toward the kitchen, I debated the best way to heal the rift between them. It wasn't just the history with our family, though that was a big part of the problem. They were very similar, almost mirrors of each other. Headstrong, arrogant, and confident in their own righteousness. Like magnets with the same polarity, they would continue to push each other away until someone forced them to make amends.

Since I was the only other person here, I figured that person had to be me.

I sat at a table in the massive library, surrounded by three stories of bookshelves lined with ancient tomes. It was something out of a Disney movie, and I pitied my rotten luck that I'd been stuck here with the worst beast of them all. But like I told Wes, as long as Atlas and I stayed out of each other's way, we could keep the peace.

At least until he saw the book in front of me. I found it in my room at the estate on the first day we came here. I'd never seen it before, and I certainly hadn't pulled it before we left Asheville. So that pegged the question—how did it get there? And why did it reset to that same spot every day?

The uncertainty was enough to make me leave it alone, but when I read the title, my curiosity got the better of me.

Signa sanguinis et animae.

Signs of Blood and Soul.

It looked like any other book in the library: black leather cover, dusty faded pages, ornate-swirling script. But when I picked it off my bed, a wave of magic coasted through my veins so powerfully, I nearly wilted. That should have been my second clue to leave it alone.

It was written by a witch named Constance in the late sixteenth century, which was legendary, seeing as most women couldn't read or write at the time. She'd been bonded to two warriors. Immediately intrigued, I'd spent the last week devouring it, only to pick it back up and read it again.

Most of it was her diary, detailing the days of someone spent trying to survive in the throes of a witch-craze. Challenging enough in itself, but being bonded to two warriors had presented its own struggles. They struggled to find a homeostasis between them, each person connected in their own ways with their own bond, to the point where magic ricocheted through them with reckless abandon, creating "chaos and unmanageable emotions." Finally, the tether snapped, cutting her off from the two people meant to protect her.

Rather than go to her coven, she started experimenting. The first half of the book seemed like her journal, detailing the daily tribulations of working with two warriors. When the bond was severed, she concocted three rituals meant to create something similar, but more powerful. They were dark spells that scared me to contemplate — things like bloodletting and magical coitus and sensation pairing.

The three rituals built on one another, creating greater magical resonance with each step. First, a blood sacrifice to connect their energy. Then, a flesh-bind to demonstrate their commitment to each other. All three had to participate in the sexual exchange, even her warriors. Finally, a soul-bond to seal their emotions and share their combined essence amongst all three. After the instructions for the third ritual, the rest of the pages were blank.

"Must not have gone that well if there's nothing else," I muttered to myself.

Because she didn't want her sisters to know the bond had dissipated, she'd done it all by herself. I didn't know if that spoke to how powerful she was or to how deeply she'd fallen into a mental health crisis.

Still, her words intrigued me, and the similarities between Constance and me couldn't be ignored. Like her, I'd been bonded to two warriors, and the bond had seemingly disappeared once we got trapped in the liminal.

I'd been at the Harlot estate for a week, and I already felt my magic starting to return, which boded well if we wanted to attempt any sort of reconciliation to the bond between us. I didn't know if Constance's spells would work, but we wouldn't be able to get out of the liminal without our combined power.

I shifted to the notepad at my left and began a list.

1. Get my magic back

-R&R at Harlot estate

-Attempt grounding in Sacred Forest

-Contact the woman in mental space?

2. Repair the bond

-Research Constance - Delusional or mastermind? (Is there a difference?)

-Figure out how the warrior bonds were created

-Research her rituals - any validity to them? Anything to back them up?

3. Get out of liminal

-Mirror scrying - attempt to contact the coven - Estate or Tita's house?

-Smoke divination - Ancestors, please help.

-Find evidence of someone getting out

"Hey," came a gruff voice as Wes sat down in the seat opposite me. I shut the book, glanced up, and smiled at the sight of him biting into a sandwich.

"I'm glad your appetite is back," I said. "You probably should have started with applesauce and soup."

"At least it's not grass tea," he teased with a wink.

"And look at you now." I gestured to his massive body and healthy pallor. "It worked, didn't it?"

"Hmm." He took another bite of the sandwich and nodded to the book. "Find anything good?"

I shifted *Signs of Blood and Soul* closer and shrugged. "Maybe."

I wasn't quite ready to share with the rest of the class, not if I didn't even know whether it was credible myself.

"The way I see it, we have three places to start." I ran down the list with him, skipping over the part about Constance and her warriors. Once I had a firmer grasp of who she was and what may have happened to her, I would let him in on the book.

"I don't think there's much I can do about getting your magic back or contacting your sisters, but I can dive into the warrior bond." He glanced at the stack of books on the end of the table, pulling one closer to him. "Any running theories on why it stopped working?"

"Having two warrior bonds is strange," I said. "Most witches only get one. I know it's divine in nature. It manifests from the ancestors, and Lilith has to drop into trance to receive revelation. But I don't understand the mechanics behind it." I ran my hands over my face, trying to recall anything I might have learned growing up. "It would be easy to say it's magical and leave it at that. We don't understand magic, and we likely never will. But in order to know what went wrong, we need to know how the bond works."

"Do you think the liminal is blocking it somehow?" he asked as he flipped open the pages of *Soul Bonds: Theory and Practice,* his deep brown eyes scanning the pages.

I shrugged. "Could be. Or maybe it was something in the ritual. I was connected to you both when things went wrong."

"Do you feel us at all now?"

I grabbed another book on demons and religious theology, placing it on top of Constance's ramblings before flipping open to browse the pages. "No. Which should be a blessing, seeing as none of us wanted this in the first place. But now..."

He glanced up at me and frowned, and I focused on the way his full pink lips thinned into a tiny line. I thought about asking what was going on behind those pretty chestnut eyes, but decided against it. We all had our secrets. I didn't need to pry.

We worked like that for several hours until the sunlight faded into darkness, and my back creaked from leaning over the desk for so long. I found him to be a companionable research partner, his energy soothing rather than distracting. At least he didn't live to get on my nerves like his brother. Occasionally, he'd stop to write down a note or place a piece of paper in the pages, marking something to come back to. I appreciated his quiet presence after spending a week wondering if I was about to lose him and find myself trapped here alone with Atlas.

The demon book didn't yield many exciting details, only things I already knew about Asmodeus or demons related to him. He was a demon of lust and, in some mythologies, had given birth to the seven deadly sins. A slice of Hell had been specifically carved out just for him because of how powerful and overwhelming his energy could be. It made me wonder if the Bloody Femmes had summoned a child of Asmodeus or the being himself.

And if it was the Granddaddy of things that go bump in the night, was our ritual even powerful enough to have trapped him? Could we have been doomed from the start?

After that, I moved on to some theoretical texts about liminal spaces and magical interference. It was so dry and scientific, I could hardly keep up. I didn't have a background in physics or energetic abundance, and I feared I'd need ten PhDs to understand half of it. But if three Harlots from North Carolina had managed to create a liminal without this in-depth knowledge, I figured it probably wouldn't help us get out of it, either.

Hours passed, and eventually, Atlas came to find us to announce he'd made dinner if we were hungry. Deciding to take a break, Wes and I joined him in the kitchen, where he gave us a plate of sliced ham steaks and roasted vegetables. My stomach grumbled on cue, the delicious scents reminding me that I hadn't eaten since breakfast that morning.

"Thanks, Atlas," Wes said, sitting down at the breakfast table off to the side. "This smells amazing."

I sniffed it again and sat down opposite Wes, debating whether I should actually consume it. Over the last week, we'd eaten separately, and everything I ate had been made by my own hands. Atlas and I weren't friends, barely acquaintances. The last conversation we'd had ended with us snarling in each other's faces. With my magic still damaged and the bond absent, now would be the perfect opportunity to—

"It's not poisoned," Atlas said, plucking a broccoli off my plate and shoving it into his mouth with a despicable wink.

I raised an eyebrow but didn't answer as I picked up my fork and knife to dive in.

"I didn't think so," I said. "I was just wondering where a warrior learned to cook."

"Ugh, you wound me," he said, clutching his chest in fake offense.

"It doesn't take much to find food in the fridge and put it in the microwave," Wes teased, causing Atlas to reach over and slug him in the shoulder.

"Cunt," Atlas said with a grimace.

"Asshole," Wes replied, rubbing at his chest.

"Hey, knock that off," I cut in. "He's still healing up."

"He deserved it," Atlas grumbled, diving into his dinner.

"Good thing everything resets at midnight." Wes stuck a piece of ham into his mouth and chewed. "At least we won't run out of food."

"If everything is as it was when we created the liminal, then the grocery stores should still be stocked," I said. "We can make a run later this week, if there's anything you want that we don't already have."

Atlas raised his eyebrows. "You think it's going to take that long to get out of here?"

"We didn't find anything helpful today," Wes said. "Lots of theory and conjecture, but nothing solid."

"I'd like to go out to the sacred forest tomorrow," I said. "I can feel my magic returning, and a trip to hallowed earth will help."

"If your magic is returning, shouldn't the bond come back with it?" Wes asked.

I thought about Constance's book, about how the feedback loop exhausted itself between three people until it shut off. I didn't know if that was happening to us or if it was something about the liminal itself.

"I don't know," I finally said. "But it's a start."

"Atlas, you'll need to go with her," Wes said. "I'm still too injured to be any help if the demon shows up."

Atlas sighed and reluctantly nodded.

"I can go by myself," I said. "This is ancient ground, even in the liminal. The demon can't get me here."

"Yeah, and we thought that about the salt ward, too. Didn't we?" Atlas smirked, and I hated that he had a point. "Until we know more about where we are and why, no one goes outside alone."

As much as I didn't like it, I had to admit it was reasonable. We ate the rest of our dinner in silence, and when it got late, we went back to our separate rooms to sleep.

Atlas took me to the forest the next morning, the same place where I'd been inducted into the coven and bonded to the two of them. Despite how much he lived to goad me, he didn't say anything on the walk there.

Once I had my hands in the earth, I retreated to my safe space in my mind. I pulled on the energy of the woods and the power of my ancestors, sucking it into me as I reciprocated with my gratitude and relief that the connection still existed, even in this terrible place. I tried calling out to the woman who'd assisted me before, that ethereal being with light pouring out of her.

But she didn't answer, and she didn't show herself. Nor did the demon, neither in the physical realm or the mental.

Once I was more grounded and the remnants of my magic pulsed through my veins, I opened my eyes to find Atlas sitting on a log, twirling a knife between his long, capable fingers. He hadn't noticed that I'd returned, so I took a moment to look him over. Even if he acted like a terrible little shit, he was a beautiful man, his face perfectly imperfect, his jaw square, and his bright green eyes twinkling in the sunlight. Both of the Colt brothers were attractive, and if it weren't for the years of animosity between us, this whole stuck-together thing might not have been so bad. At least they were pretty to look at.

He glanced up and caught me staring at him, and I quickly darted my focus away, forcing myself to my feet.

"Good meditation?" he asked.

I nodded. "My magic is returning. We can head back now."

"Uh-huh." He lifted one side of his perfect mouth into a smile, and I ignored the rush of heat to the center of my gut.

When we got back to the mansion, Wes was already in the library, deep into *Darkest Magic and Darkest Souls*. I didn't disturb him, just sat down in my spot and grabbed another book from the pile.

We read for hours, researching and debating new ideas until our eyes burned. And that night, I tried mirror scrying for the first time since we'd been there. I lit divination candles and watched the smoke for signs of disaster. When the flames stilled, I dropped into a meditative trance, chanting my intentions to see into the human realm.

"Let my sisters see me, let me see them. Open a line to my coven. Let me be heard." I repeated it nine times before opening my eyes to stare in the mirror, letting my gaze go unfocused, willing my consciousness to connect with my blooded witches. I'd been inducted into the Harlots. I was part of them. They were a part of me.

Let them see me. Let them see me.

Bridge. Isobel. Lilith.

Anyone. Please.

An hour passed with nothing to show for it, and when my knees ached, I broke the spell and stood, blinking back the tears in my eyes.

I need to get stronger. Then it will work.

Three weeks went by like this, and we got no closer to a solution. In the mornings, I went to the sacred woods to meditate, and each time, I returned stronger and more resolute. I worked out in the training room, sparring and boxing, determined not to lose my physical prowess, just in case the demon ever did show up. In the afternoons, Wes and I read every book we could get our hands on, deep diving into any subject remotely adjacent to our predicament. Occasionally, Atlas joined us, but mostly he minded his own business, fucking around in other parts of the mansion.

Wes got better, and after several days of rest and my magical "grass tea," his wounds had faded to pink scars. The muscles underneath were gradually getting stronger, too.

"These are fading nicely," I said, wiggling my hands a few inches from Wes's shirtless torso. God, these warriors were built like statues. Yes, I was focused on sending healing energy into his wounds, disinfecting any lingering darkness, but I couldn't help the girlish tingle that went through me at the sight of his massive shoulders and sculpted abs.

Never mind how long it had been since I'd had a lover, the close quarters had taken its toll, and it was becoming more difficult to remember why I wasn't supposed to like either of them in the first place. Atlas was gruff and mean, but Wes and I complemented each other, especially when it came to our research abilities.

"All thanks to your magic," Wes said. "I'm glad it's coming back. You must have just wiped yourself out during the ritual."

I nodded, having come to the same conclusion. Unfortunately, the same couldn't be said for the bond. But I remained determined to continue my research on Constance and her experiments. I hadn't come any closer to figuring out who she was, but that was only a matter of time. And in the liminal, all we had was time.

Still, a shiver of unease passed down my spine and into my marrow. My meditation this morning had been shoddy because I couldn't stop focusing on the trees. They whispered in hushed tones, telling me to beware, to remember what my guide had said.

"The time has come when you must fight. You must forsake your rage at what isn't and focus on what is. You must channel your anger into faith, and faith into action. You will want to give up. You must

not do this. You were given many gifts, mi hija. Do not let them go to waste."

A flock of crows had squawked in the distance, and the wind had picked up when I recalled the determination in her face. The earth was trying to tell me something, trying to get me to pay attention. I just didn't know to what.

Was the demon lurking out there somewhere, waiting to strike? And if it was, what was it waiting for? Why hadn't it shown itself by now?

When I finished the spell on Wes's wounds, I stepped back and gestured to his shirt next to him. "You're all set."

"Thank you, Marta," he said, meeting my eyes. "Truly."

"Yeah, no problem," I replied, leaving him alone to get dressed before heading to the library to start my research for the day.

The Colts and I gradually grew closer. We ate lunch and dinner together. We bickered over stupid things like laundry and leaving dishes in the sink, but it was obvious they had spent their lives side by side. We lived around each other, our worlds intermingling as we made the best of an impossible situation.

In the evenings, they'd hole up in the parlor to drink until their eyes were heavy. I never joined them. They exuded a fraternal atmosphere, laughing and teasing with countless inside jokes. I didn't want to intrude. It had always been them against the world, against me, and I didn't like being the third wheel. I let them have their alone time to decompress.

But as the days went on, my body revolted against me. I'd find Wes shirtless after a run and clench my thighs together to keep from ogling more than necessary. Atlas would return from lifting in the gym, muscles tense, cheeks red, and I would force myself to ignore the heat building in my lower belly.

It was like being surrounded by temptation and knowing I couldn't touch. It wasn't just me, either. One day, I heard a loud boom while I was in the middle of a shower, so I wrapped a towel around me and went to investigate. Wes and Atlas were wrestling in the parlor, and when I interrupted, both sets of eyes focused on me with heat and something distinctly masculine dancing behind him.

I made dinner one night, and when I couldn't reach a bowl on the top shelf, Wes saddled up behind me, extending a long arm to grab it for me. He rested his other hand on my hip, the entire front side of his body pressing against my back, and I could have sworn he moaned as he brought the glass down to the counter. I caught his eyes on me in the library, his soft focus raking over my body before he quickly looked away with his cheeks flushed.

Yes, he wanted me. They both did. And I struggled to keep a lid on my own nascent attraction. I had certainly gone weeks without sex before, but living in such close proximity to these two gorgeous men tested my patience in ways I was quickly losing control over. Evidently, they were feeling the same.

That was where it ended. Looks filled with desire. Gentle caresses. Flirtatious remarks and late-night laughs. I couldn't let it be more, despite how much my body ached to give in. To have one left out the other, and I couldn't reconcile what it might look like to let myself have both of them.

That could only last so long.

One morning, I woke up early, determined to put in a few hours in the gym's training room before spending the day with Wes combing through ancient texts. I started with a few laps around the track before moving on to the boxing bags. Just as I was five minutes into my fifteen-minute routine, a loud snort echoed from behind me, and I rolled my eyes, gritting my teeth at the interruption.

Of course.

"You keep lowering your guard hand like that, and we'll never survive a demon fight," Atlas said, stalking around to my right side.

"Yeah?" I kept going, suddenly fueled by animosity to hit harder, pretending it was his beautiful, smug face. "Who asked you?"

"Seeing as I'm your bonded-unbonded warrior, I think I have a say in how well you fight." His ridiculing grin set me off, and I huffed out my annoyance, turning to face him.

"I bet I could still take you down," I said and raised an eyebrow in challenge.

He laughed. Actually laughed. Right in my face.

"I'm serious." I didn't appreciate his input or his presence, so showing him up to knock him down sent a sick pleasure straight to my filthy little witch heart.

"Oh, I'm sure you are." He shifted his shoulders and stepped toward me, and I ignored how delightfully sweaty he was, wearing nothing but a pair of gray gym shorts. His broad torso was lined with muscle and scars, and I ached to know where he'd gotten them. I wanted to trace the story of his body with my tongue. Frustrated by that asinine thought, I forced my gaze back to his eyes, swallowing the burn in my cheeks when he caught me staring at him. Again.

"What? Are you scared?" I teased, tilting my head to the side in mock pedantry.

"Of you?" He shook his head and came closer. "Not a chance. But what will your ancestors do to me if I put their precious cargo on her back with two moves?"

"You should be more afraid of what *I'll* do to you once I get you on your back."

The sexual innuendo hung between us, and his glittering gaze traveled the length of me before he licked his lips and grinned again.

Ugh, I hated him.

"Okay, little witch," he said. "Here are the rules. No magic. Nothing lethal. And nothing you can't heal with a spell or two, got it?"

Ohhh, he'd left open a whole wide world of hurt.

"Fine," I said. "First to tap out makes dinner tonight."

"Fine," he said. "I hope you remember your abuela's tamale

recipe because I've been dreaming about that braised pork since she had everybody over last New Year's."

I winced at the mention of my grandmother, and I reminded myself not to be upset that I hadn't ventured to her house. Yet. I still didn't know if it was safe to venture off the estate, but I'd concluded I couldn't reach my sisters from here.

But Atlas's flippant comment added gas to the inferno in my gut, and when he held his hands up to indicate he was ready, I launched at him.

He blocked my first few swings, and I ducked under one of his right hooks, side-stepping out of the way as he tried to swipe my feet out from under me. The sounds of AC/DC's "If You Want Blood" echoed through the space, adding the perfect symphony to the decade's worth of tension finally exploding. He jabbed again, and I blocked. I countered with a hit to his ribs, and he almost wilted, jumping back at the last second with a wicked grin and illuminated eyes.

"Thought you said two moves, Colt?" I teased. "What? Is the liminal making you rusty?"

He laughed and kicked at my stomach, but I shoved his foot down, parried, and kneed him in the chest. I jolted when he grabbed my leg and swung me around, pushing me onto my back. I landed with an *oomph* that I quickly transformed into a roll back to my feet.

Our fight quickly became a dance. He moved; I countered. I moved; he countered. He went for the face, I went for the jugular. Panting and sweating, we took out our frustration on each other. He landed a few good blows to my stomach and one (admittedly light) jab to my cheek, and then he chuckled and tsked through his teeth.

"I told you to keep your guard hand up."

That only pissed me off. Without thinking about it, I grabbed a knife from my thigh holster and threw it at him. To my immense surprise, he caught it by the handle just as it whizzed by his cheek, leaving a tiny scratch and a faint trail of blood down his jaw.

"Hey!" he snapped. "Nothing permanent."

"I can fix that," I snarled.

He growled and threw it back at me, where it nearly lodged in my shoulder. If I hadn't ducked out of the way in time, I'd have met the business end of my own weapon. Minutes turned into centuries as we practiced, and as much as I was loath to admit, it was the most fun I'd had since we'd gotten stuck here.

Just as I was starting to wear down, I found a weakness. When he swung with his left hand, he shifted his weight to his left foot, which left his right foot open to attack. Ever the opportunist, I took advantage. I goaded him into another punch, and just when it would have landed, I kicked and hooked my foot around his right knee, sending him toppling to the ground.

Heaving for air, I grabbed another knife, climbed on top of him, and held it to his throat, pinning his right wrist above his head as I leaned over him.

"Give," I said, pressing the blade deeper under his jaw.

I expected him to be pissed, to toss me off and demand a rematch. But the look in his eyes wasn't rage. No, it was darker and incredibly wanton. He curled his pouty lips into a smile and leaned into the blade, bringing his face closer to mine.

"Go on, little witch," he whispered. "You've got me on my back. Now what?"

God help me, but the energy in the room shifted immediately. My lower stomach tightened, and my thighs clenched around his hips. When I shifted my weight to hide it, he grabbed my waist with his free hand and lowered me down his body. I gasped when my clit lined up with the thick swell of his cock, so perfectly hard and poised for depravity. He smelled like sweat and man and honey, and my heart pounded at the heat radiating off him...off us both. The new position stretched me along his body, my chest on his, our breaths mingling in the minuscule space between us.

Stop this. Get off him.

I didn't. I didn't move. Just stared down at those green eyes and wondered how far he would let this go. He hated me as much as I hated him...right?

Maybe it was the weeks stuck with him in the liminal, maybe it was the sudden release of all these years of pent-up aggression, or perhaps it was finding someone who could match me blow for blow. But I couldn't stop myself. I rolled my hips, dragging my cunt along the bulge between us.

He hissed in a breath and moaned, leaning his head back to expose the column of his throat, where my knife still rested under his jaw. That sound reached inside me and plucked a guitar string I never thought would sing for him. When I did it again, his fingers tightened into my flesh, guiding me over him, pushing me down on him harder.

"Fuck, witch," he said, dragging his tongue over his lips. Suddenly, I wanted to know what they tasted like. I wanted to know how sweet his mouth could be when all it had ever thrown my way were nasty words and insults.

Against every instinct telling me not to, I leaned down and licked across his lips, swallowing his groan and the salty taste of his overheated skin.

When I met his gaze again, his emerald irises were gone, now replaced with wide, dilated pupils, hungry for more. A thick heady lust clenched in my abdomen, and I couldn't fight it any longer. I rocked against him, searching for that primal release, compelled by the sound of his moans and fueled by the euphoria skating through my veins.

I dropped the knife and put my hands on his chest for better leverage, and he grabbed my hips, digging his fingers into my skin to pull me tighter against him. My nerves burned, shooting antici-pation and sparks of energy through my limbs, amping up my strokes.

"God, yes." Atlas moaned. "Right there, right there."

"Shut up." I put my hand over his mouth, but that only egged him on, and he sank his teeth into my palm, latching on like it was the only thing keeping him grounded.

The sharp pain collided with the pressure between my legs, and I exploded, muscles tensing, my climax yanking me under its tremendous force. I gasped, wiggling against Atlas as the aftershocks of pleasure rippled through my body, overwhelming and powerful, making me crumple under its weight. I floated lifeless in that room for two mind-numbing moments before the weight of reality sucked me back down to earth.

I stared down at Atlas under me, his big eyes blown wide, his breath coming in pants through his nose.

Oh. Oh, no.

No, no, no.

I started to climb off him, but he tightened his hold on me, keeping me still, continuing to rock his pelvis against mine. Too sensitive, I squirmed and let out a small noise of protest, but he didn't stop. Two more thrusts later, he curled in on himself and groaned behind my hand. I watched him fall apart, the gorgeous lines of his face tightening, intoxicating me, reeling me in. I memorized it, despite how embarrassed I was. Then he relaxed against the training mat and heaved a deep sigh.

Heart pounding and disgust warring with relief in my chest, I pushed upright, grabbed my knife, and stalked out of the training room. Wes came out of his room as I passed by in the foyer, but I didn't stop to talk to him or take in his adorable rumpled appearance.

"Hey, what's—" he tried.

I marched up the stairs to the room I'd claimed for myself, shut the door, and slammed the back of my head against the firm wood.

"Fuck!"

I was nothing but a man of my word. I happily made dinner for all of us that night, even giving Marta a wink and a smile as I placed her plate in front of her.

"Thank you," she mumbled softly.

"Yeah, a deal's a deal," I said, taking my usual seat next to Wes.

"What deal?" he mumbled around his steak.

"Nothing," Marta said at the same time I said, "She beat me in training this morning."

"She beat you?" Wes raised his eyebrows and laughed, glancing back at the witch. "You don't look too happy about it. I figured you'd be gloating."

No, I realized she wasn't thrilled when she promptly got off me, rushed out of there, and avoided me for the rest of the day. Even when I came into the library to help them research, she didn't say more than two words before disappearing into the Christian occult section and not returning for a few hours.

It wasn't the first time a woman had hit it and quit it, but admittedly, it was the most action I'd gotten in over a month and would likely be the *only* action I got until we figured out how to get out of here. Watching her walk away stung, and the ache in my chest pissed me off.

I shouldn't care what she thought about me. I didn't even like her. But watching her get herself off on top of me, her knife to my throat, her hand over my mouth...*Goddamn,* I got hard just thinking about it. I might have even gone back to my room and fucked my fist thinking about it a few hours later.

"She cheated," I teased, pointing to the wound on my cheek that she'd yet to heal.

That got her attention. She gasped and dropped her jaw, staring at me. "No, I didn't! The rules were nothing permanent."

"This is gonna scar," I said. "I probably need stitches."

Wes chuckled harder, but Marta only growled and stood, raising her hand toward me as she muttered something I couldn't hear. Her white light started to beam out of her fingertips, but I ducked out of the way before it could reach me.

"No, none of that," I said. "I want you to see it every day and know the error of your ways." I let the double meaning hang between us, raising an eyebrow at her cute indignation. "Besides, chicks dig scars."

She ran her tongue over her teeth before glancing at Wes and finally returning her attention to her dinner. Our conversation turned to figuring out how to get out of the liminal. Then Wes and I went to the parlor to drown our sorrows. Marta didn't join us. She never did.

"What'd you do to her?" Wes asked when she stalked up the stairs.

"Nothing she wasn't asking for, brother," I teased.

He raised an eyebrow and let it slide.

But when I went to sleep that night, I dreamt of the things I wanted to do to her, the way I wanted to roll her over, tear open her leggings, and stuff myself inside of her. I'd hold her down and fuck her until neither of us could talk, until we were wrung out and gasping for air. It got so intense that I didn't realize I was dreaming. I could almost feel her heart beating next to mine, could sense the heat rolling off her, could squeeze my hand around her throat until she pulsed around my cock.

One final shove into her, and I detonated with a resounding fury that ricocheted down my spine and into my legs before surging back up again. I opened my mouth to groan with my release, but the only thing that came out was black smoke, wisps uncoiling from my mouth in thick, devastating waves. Shocked, I sat back as it poured from my nose and lips, smothering the space between us. It replaced my hand around Marta's throat and tightened until it pulled her up. The smoke coalesced between us like a sickening tether, scalding the connection between us. She opened her mouth to suck it in, and it poured down her windpipe, revitalizing our bond with an evil depravity that I'd never known before.

It should have terrified me. It should have made me wonder if we were possessed or worse...becoming demons ourselves. Instead, I relished it. I held her down while the mist pummeled out of me and into her, shoving myself in between her legs again, filling every part of her with *me*.

I shot out of bed, sweaty and gasping, clutching at my mouth like I could get it out of me, like the smoke was real and would suffocate me if I didn't eradicate it. But when my brain caught up with my body, I realized I was alone in the dark with nothing but the streams of moonlight filtering in through the curtains.

Marta wasn't in the training room that morning. Nor was she in the kitchen when I finished my routine and made myself breakfast. I found her in the library, hunched over a pile of books with my brother sitting across from her in his usual spot. Over the last few weeks, they'd gotten close, partly because of their shared love for nerding out on history.

I didn't think we'd find a way out of here by looking through books. The Harlot library housed thousands of texts, some in languages no one spoke anymore. We could probably spend the rest of our lives stuck here, poring over them, and still have nothing to show for it.

We needed to get outside. We needed to go back to where the ritual was, hold another one, and cut through time and space to get home. Of course, mentioning it only caused a fight.

"We don't have our bond, Atlas," Marta would say.

"We don't know what we're doing," Wes would agree.

I had no arguments for that, so I shut the fuck up, drank my beer, and let them take their time. But anxiety clenched my chest when I thought about staying here, and the longer we went, the harder it might be to break out again.

"Alright, it's been weeks," I said, plopping down in the seat next to Wes. "How's the research going? Find anything good?"

Marta raised an eyebrow and kept reading, continuing the whole ignoring-me gig. It still hurt, even if I was used to it by now.

"It might go a lot faster if you helped," Wes said, turning a page.

Fine.

I sighed and grabbed a book from the top of Marta's stack, and that got her attention. She whipped her gaze up and tried to grab for it, but I clutched it tighter to my chest.

"Ohhh, what do we have here?" I said, running my hand down the smooth black leather. "Signa sanguinis et animae." I pursed my lips as I translated. "Signs of Blood and Soul."

"I didn't know you read Latin," she said.

"I know ten different languages," I replied with a smirk. "Give me a break."

It was true. Dad had been a strict drill sergeant, forcing Wes and me to learn as much as we could about magic, including all the ways it had been created. Then, I flipped through the pages, shivering against a sudden gust of energy that surged up my arm. Ignoring that, I glanced over some of the words, focusing on a ritual or two.

Blood magic. Flesh bonding. Sex magic. Soul tethers. Knives and carving and consuming.

"This is a dark book," I said, looking back up at Marta with a raised eyebrow.

"Yeah, it's...uh...a bit out of touch," she said.

Then my attention caught on something about a witch with "two warriors." I squinted and leaned in to make sure I'd read it correctly.

"Wait." I leaned forward on the table. "She was bonded to *two* warriors?"

Marta visibly swallowed and glanced at Wes, whose eyes widened and back straightened. He looked over my shoulder and then gazed back at Marta.

"I don't know how much to buy into her ramblings," Marta said. "It seems like she was trying to experiment with her warriors to make something more powerful than the bond."

"Hold on," Wes said, grabbing the book from my hands. "She had two warriors and lost their bond?"

Marta licked her lips and stayed silent, clearly caught red-handed.

"And you didn't think to mention this?" Wes scoffed as he quickly ran his gaze down the words.

"I didn't want to give us false hope," Marta said. "The last entry is her attempts to knit their souls together. Since she didn't come back to say whether it worked or not, I have to assume it didn't, and they all died trying."

"Yeah, but this is a start," Wes said.

"Listen, that book is full of chaos magic," she said. "I felt it as soon as I touched it."

Yeah, I'd felt it too, and I wasn't even a witch.

"Where'd you find it?" I asked.

"It was in my room when we got to the estate," Marta answered, clutching the pendant around her neck. "I've never seen it before, and I certainly didn't put it there."

I heard what she didn't say. If she didn't put it there and she'd never seen it before, then maybe it had always been in the liminal. Perhaps it was the demon playing games with us. But that only pissed me off more.

"You've had this book the entire time and didn't say anything?" I shook my head and took another sip of beer. "Typical."

"What was I supposed to do?" Marta pushed to her feet, spreading her hands on the table, and I countered, towering over her, making sure she understood that I didn't appreciate being kept in the dark. "Say here's a book full of strange magic. Let's do some and see what happens?"

"This bond affects all of us," I said. "We're trapped here, the same as you."

That gorgeous blush filled her cheeks, her eyes glittering with the start of a fight. It took everything in me not to grab her neck, bend her over the table, and fuck her into submission right here in front of Wes.

On second thought...could be kind of hot.

"The least you could do is be honest with us," I growled.

"I wanted to make sure I understood what it was before I brought it to you," she snapped. "This could hurt us. This could *kill* us."

"Or it could fix this whole fucking mess," I shouted.

"Alright, enough," Wes said, holding out a hand to my shoulder, forcing me back into my seat. "Arguing with each other solves nothing. We need to work together."

Marta hugged herself and sat down. "I'm sorry I kept it from you. I was trying to protect us."

"What else do you know?" Wes said. "Have you found anything else about Constance and her warriors?"

She shook her head. "I've read through it a few times. Some of the rituals are terrifying. Some are just bullshit, but it's obvious she was desperate to fix the bond...or create something like it."

Marta explained what she'd read, highlighting how the bond had torn through the three of them violently before dissipating altogether. It sounded like what happened to us when the demon attacked us at the crossroads.

"I think something about three people affects it," she continued. "I have my magic back. I can try to contact the human realm. And once we have our bond, maybe we can..." She stopped and shook her head. "Open another portal back to our side."

"It took three witches and four warriors to create the liminal," Wes said. "You're going to try it alone with the two of us?"

"If I can get in contact with Bridge or Isobel, maybe they can pull from that side while we push from our side and...I don't know, squeeze through. Constance talks about using her rituals to gift her magic to her warriors, making it stronger than it was before." She glanced between me and my brother, but when we didn't respond, she rubbed her hands over her face. "It's ridiculous, but it's the only idea I've got. We've been researching for weeks, and we barely have anything to show for it."

Wes drummed his fingers on the table and glanced at the book again, flipping a page over before looking at me.

"I suppose trying one of them won't hurt," he said with a shrug.

I widened my eyes and scoffed. "Oh yeah? Which one do you wanna do first? The one where we fuck each other under the full moon or the one where we carve sigils onto each other's hearts and lick the blood off?"

Wes frowned. "No harm in trying both of them."

"What?" I couldn't believe what I was hearing.

"Do you wanna get out of here?" He raised his eyebrows. "To do that, we have to get our bond back."

"Why don't we try the original spell? The one Lilith did at the choosing."

"That took a full coven," Marta said. "Lilith entered a trance to speak to the ancestors while Circe guided her, and Val acted as a tether to the real world. Doing that without assistance can leave the witch lost. I could get stuck in the Under Realm. I could lose a piece of myself there."

I had no desire to have any of them carve anything into my body, much less watch my brother fuck the woman I'd made come on top of me yesterday. And yet...the moment the thought was in my head, my cock twitched and something stirred in my gut, forcing me to shift my hips to keep my cool.

Living in close quarters with Wes for most of our lives had naturally blurred the line between us. I'd woken up, drunk and spinning, in motel rooms, only to look over at the spare bed to see my brother railing some chick we'd met on the road. There had been times when I'd hooked up with men and women, sometimes both at the same time, and caught a glimpse of Wes sneaking out or trying his best to pretend to be asleep with a tent under the bedsheets. There was even that night with the cuck and his girl-friends, and I'd be lying if I said Wes wasn't hot when he was plowing into some chick.

Perfectly submissive. Bendable and willing. A gorgeous mouth to match his fascinating mind. In my darkest moments, I let myself regard Wes, especially when he was inhibited and letting his guard down. His strong forearms gave way to broad shoulders, and his perfect mouth had been made to be bitten. Hell, it was no surprise the guys I went for were usually taller and bigger than me, even if I dominated them.

But...for as much as we'd fucked around and developed a rela-tionship that would fund a therapist's salary for years, we'd never pushed that boundary between the two of us. And this ritual required active, *willing* participation from all parties. An exchange of sweat and seed. The thought both scared and excited me for reasons I didn't want to pick at.

"You're on board with this?" I asked the witch, grabbing the book from Wes's hand. "You're okay with 'connecting flesh under the power of the full moon until the sun rises?'"

She pushed her fingers back through her dark hair. "I'm not okay with any of this, but I don't know what other choice we have."

I licked my lips and sighed, downing the rest of my beer in one desperate gulp. "Fine."

"Fine," she repeated.

"We don't have to do that one first," Wes said.

"It's best if we work from the outside in," Marta added. "Blood's the sacrifice, flesh is the bond. Soul is the seal. They have to be done in order."

"Cool," I said, adding as much sarcasm as I could. "Drinking blood in the woods at midnight. Wonderful."

"One problem," Wes said. "The moon is the same every night. It never grows full. What are we supposed to do about that?"

Marta sighed. "The moon is conjunct Mars, the same as it was the night we created the liminal. We'll have to work with that. We can do it tomorrow."

"Tomorrow?" I blinked and swallowed the clench in my chest. "You don't think that's jumping the gun?"

"You wanna get out of here, right?" Marta shrugged. "Why wait?"

"What about ingredients?" Wes continued, bringing us back to the rituals. "Some of this stuff is obscure."

"We have most of it in the stores," Marta said. "I'll gather them, and then we need to cleanse the space and ourselves."

"I'll help," Wes said, pushing to his feet.

"Great. Perfect." I kept my gaze on the book, purposely ignoring them. "I'll just...keep reading to make sure we don't miss anything."

Wes and Marta nodded before leaving the library, but I sat there for too long afterward, wondering what the hell I'd just agreed to.

"You don't have to do this, you know," Marta said, glancing over the shelves in the closet where the Harlots kept their herbs and candles. It was practically an occult store by itself.

I grabbed the bottle of vervain and placed it in the basket, moving on to the next item on her list.

"I don't want to be in the liminal any more than you do," I said. "If this will help us get out, I'll do anything."

"It's just..." Marta placed a bottle of cemetery dirt in the basket and leaned on the table, tilting her head as she looked at me. I ignored her scrutiny and kept going.

Five-finger grass. Five-finger grass.

Why the hell weren't these bottles alphabetized?

"The blood bind is one thing. The flesh..." she said. "You and Atlas—"

"I'm aware." I cut her off, unwilling to think too much about it. Though now that she'd brought it up, I couldn't *stop* thinking about it. I'd always loved my brother, and even if we weren't related by blood, we were raised together. It should have been weird. I should have refused the idea and insisted we find another way. Instead, I went along with it because...

Well, I didn't have a good excuse. Saying I wanted to get out of the liminal seemed like too much pressure to put on the uncertain outcomes of Constance's rituals, and saying I didn't mind...er... joining flesh with my brother seemed too fucked up to put into words.

But one thing at a time. Blood came first. We had a little while before we had to worry about the rest.

"Have you and Atlas ever—" She raised an eyebrow, a mischievous glint dancing behind her gaze.

"No," I answered. "Not together. Not like that."

"But other things?"

I cleared my throat as memories pummeled me. "We've shared a room since we were kids. It's...complicated."

"Complicated. Right." She crossed the room to stand in front of me, interrupting my search. "So then why did you agree?"

I took a deep breath, trying not to let my uneasiness show.

"It wasn't just *you* we bonded that night in the woods," I said. "We bonded each other, too. I could sense him. He could sense me. And for the first time in our whole lives, I felt..." I almost said *peace* but stopped myself before the words tripped over my lips. That was too small a vocabulary for it.

Whole. Complete. Soul-shattering wonderment.

She seemed to understand without my having to say it out loud.

"You know," she continued. "Tita says the ancestors never do anything without cause. If they put us together, the three of us, there's probably a good reason."

I rolled my eyes and laughed. "Don't tell me you're okay with this?" I gestured between us.

She shrugged. "Atlas isn't as bad as I thought, and you..."

Marta smiled, shook her head, and turned to move away. But I caught a whiff of her cherry-scented perfume and the floral essence that was just *her,* and I grabbed her wrist to pull her back.

"Go on," I said, moving to trap her between me and the table behind her. "What about me?"

"You're tolerable," she said with a laugh, avoiding my gaze.

I put my finger under her chin and lifted her face so she had to look me in the eyes. I hadn't forgotten the way she'd stared at me while she was patching me up, the heat in her cheeks, and the soft flick of her tongue over her lips. I watched those lips now, so full and pouty, so perfect and pink. I wondered what they tasted like.

"Only tolerable?" I feigned offense. "And here I thought we were connecting over our shared love of old, dusty books."

She laughed again and shoved at my chest, at first pushing me away, but then she wrapped her fingers in my shirt and tugged me closer, her hips connecting with mine, my cock suddenly very interested in where this conversation was going.

"You're smart, Wes," she said. "And you know you're easy on the eyes."

I chuckled and brushed a piece of dark hair behind her ear. In the weeks we'd been trapped here, I'd come to know her as incredibly intelligent herself. She saw connections where no one else did. She could smack my brother into place like I'd never seen before. And me, she complemented my dark, solemn parts with her grounded luminescence.

I didn't deserve her attention. I was scum on her shoes. She should laugh in my face and tell me I was ridiculous. But fuck if her rapt attention didn't call to the part of me that ached to be adored and accepted.

"You're beautiful, Marta," I murmured. "I'm sorry you got stuck with me...with us. You're so much better than this, but I don't regret it."

"I'm starting not to regret it myself," she said, focusing on my mouth.

The thought of doing this while Atlas moped in the library

passed through my mind. Certainly, we didn't need any more tension in the house. But if he were here, he wouldn't waste a fucking opportunity like this. I'd wanted her since I'd woken up with her standing over me, and I'd fucked her in my dreams every night since. I couldn't help staring at her, and I touched her every chance I could, almost unable to contain myself. If she wanted this too, who was I to deny her?

"I want to do this before the ritual," I said, leaning down to rub my nose against hers. "Before our minds get clouded and we don't know what we want anymore."

I didn't wait for her to respond, and when I pressed my lips against hers, she moaned and wilted against my body. I ran my hands up her shoulders, holding her neck while my tongue swept inside her decadent mouth, and she scratched her nails up the back of my neck to my hair, gripping it to hold me tighter against her.

Fuck, it was hot. Sharp ricochets of arousal raced down my spine to my balls, pulsing my dick to life between us, where I rocked against her, desperate for more touch, more action, just *more.*

I sucked her tongue when it wrestled with mine and grabbed the back of her legs to hoist her onto the table, jostling glass bottles and dried herbs. When she hooked her ankles around the small of my back, I rutted against her, possessed by hunger and wanton desire. Had I ever *needed* somebody the way I needed her? Had I ever felt so starved for touch, for affection, for sickening sweet kisses?

We broke apart, only for me to trail my mouth down her jaw to her neck, where I ravaged the skin over her pulse with famished bites and trembling licks. She moaned and leaned back, arching her chest toward me, and my greedy hands took advantage, rubbing over her perfect tits. When I found her nipples, she sighed and reached between us, cupping my aching dick to massage it. My abdomen twisted, and an alarm in the back of my mind told me to stop, that this wasn't right.

But fuck that. We were an inferno, blazing out of control, and there was no putting it out. Marta and I had danced around each other for weeks now, and this tenuous passion inside me needed a release.

"Wes, touch me," she said, grabbing one wrist to bring it to the wet spot between her legs, and I rubbed a thumb over the seam of her denim, finding the spot that made her cry out with disturbing ease.

Nothing in the world could have slammed the brakes on this runaway train. We were careening toward a cliff, knowing it would end in travesty, but fuck, the ride was so good. Too good. I wanted all of her. I wanted to consume her and decimate her and leave nothing left but bones.

I needed and I yearned, and when she clenched her eyes shut, her climax imminent, I bit the side of her throat on instinct, shoving her off the edge. Marta bucked against my hand, riding the waves of her euphoria, and watching her come undone flipped a switch in my brain. I wanted to yank her off the table, bend her over it, and shove myself inside her. I wanted to hold her down while she soaked my cock again and again.

"Did you like that?" I hissed, tugging on her ear with my teeth. "Do you want more? Are you so fucking wet for me, Marta?"

"Yes," she whimpered, reaching for my cock again. But I pushed her hand away. If she so much as ghosted a finger over me, I'd explode and embarrass myself more than I already had. Instead, I went for the button on her jeans, unzipped her pants, and shifted her back so I could shuck them down to her ankles. Then, I lifted her legs, stuck my head under the denim, and rested her knees on my shoulders so I could lay her down and feast on her the way I wanted.

She didn't stop me, and when she moaned while tunneling her fingers through my hair, I took that as consent to keep going. One lick was all it took for me to get addicted to her. She tasted like sin and sacrament, like the most delicious poison and the most decadent venom. I sucked her into my mouth and drank everything she gave to me, digging my fingers into her thighs to hold her still. I fucked her with my face and lapped at her with my tongue, relishing her breathy moans and soft cries for "more, more, harder, harder."

Yes, some twisted voice said. *More. Take more. Give it harder. Ravish her. Devour her.*

My cock ached behind my jeans, thundering my arousal into my legs and up my torso. She dug her nails into my scalp, and that only urged me on. I pulled back to spit on her cunt, delighting in the way she squirmed at the sight.

So my girl has a spit kink. Fuck yeah.

"Come for me, Marta," I said, rubbing her clit with my palm. "Come on my face and show me how much you like when your warrior takes care of you."

When I ducked my head back down to her, Atlas's bright green eyes and enduring sneer passed through my mind's eye like a yellow light telling me to slow down, to take caution. But this driving need inside me propelled me forward like I couldn't control it, even if I wanted to.

I pushed a finger inside her, rubbing at that soft, spongy spot that had her bucking against my face, riding me like she was as caught up in the chaos as I was. And when I pushed the second inside, she clamped down on me and forced my head where she wanted, her second climax claiming her. Her thighs squeezed my ears. Her cum painted my mouth and tongue. Her praise echoed off the closet walls.

It sent me over the edge. My orgasm rocketed through my cock like a teenager, and I spilled in my pants, completely rung out and spent.

Despite this, I kept licking her. I swallowed her cum and her sweat, and when she could handle no more, she pushed my head away and opened her legs so I could lower her trapped legs to my back. The most depraved part of me wanted to yank my jeans down, pull out my rapidly deflating cock, and spear her with it to see how narrow she could make my refractory period.

But a quick movement by the door caught my attention, and when I glanced up, I saw Atlas standing in the hallway, his cheeks flushed, his eyes focused on us, his lips wet and parted. He had a beer in one hand and the other firmly wrapped around the bulge in his jeans, grabbing the tip seemingly to alleviate the pressure.

The sight smacked me back to reality, one where we shared this house with him, one where we were preparing for a "blood-joining" ritual tomorrow, one where the tension between Marta and him was almost as tangible as it was between him and me. He had every right to storm in here and deck me, or maybe explode in a rage of jealousy fury.

Instead, he canted his hips, adjusted his cock, turned, and walked away.

"Fuck," I murmured, disentangling myself from the trap of Marta's legs and jeans. I ran my hands through my hair and started to go after him, but Marta grabbed my arm to stop me.

"Hey," she said.

I paused to look at her while she pulled her pants up, fixed her hair, and smiled. Then she pressed up onto her toes and kissed me, melting the panicked part of my soul that had thought to react first and respond second. I leaned into the touch, and when she broke away, she nodded back toward the supplies.

"Let's finish this, okay? Then we'll explain."

Explain what, I didn't know. It had all happened so fast, too fast for me to understand where it went wrong or why it happened in the first place. Yes, Marta was attractive, and yes, I had feelings for her that were complicated and difficult to put into words. I felt the same way about the bond with her as I did with Atlas. I didn't like it when it happened, but now, its absence ached like a void in my chest.

Together, we were unique and complete. And now...now I

didn't know what the fuck was wrong with me, but I needed to fix it.

At dinner that night, Atlas didn't say anything about what he saw, just carried on like nothing had happened. I made food, and we sat at the breakfast table to eat the same way we'd done in the weeks prior.

"So everything's ready?" Atlas asked, digging into his chicken parmesan.

Marta nodded. "I plan on cleansing the space tonight and praying to the ancestors for their blessing. We'll need to bathe tomorrow before the ritual." She went through the steps, including the specific oils we would need to use and the amount of time we would have to spend in the water for it to take effect. Cleansing the body would ensure we didn't accidentally invite something wicked to come this way. "The wards around the estate should protect us, but I'll cast protection spells and anoint us all in protective ointments before we go."

"And what do we expect to happen?" Atlas asked, raising an eyebrow at her. "Once the ritual starts?"

She shrugged. "I honestly don't know. Some of the texts describe a trancelike, almost euphoric state of consciousness. Blood magic is powerful, but almost always overwhelming. I don't expect it to be more cumbersome than our original binding, but... again, that was a full coven. This is just us."

"Have you done blood magic before?" I asked, trying to keep my voice as clinical as possible. "On your own?"

"Not like this," she said. "But blood creates sacrifice, and sacrifice is always an energy exchange."

Atlas shifted his weight, and I straightened my shoulders,

meeting my brother's gaze for half a second before he quickly looked away.

"I don't think it will alter our consciousness to the point where we don't know what's going on," Marta said. "But there could be some after effects. Euphoria. Giddiness. A magical rush. I'll act as the connection point between the three of us."

"And you're used to that, huh?" Atlas murmured under his breath, barely audible, but both Marta and I picked up on it.

I sighed, anticipating the argument between them, and she grabbed Atlas's wrist to stop him from biting into another piece of food.

"If you've got something to say, out with it." She tightened her features, perhaps preparing for the attack.

I readied myself for the fight. He'd seen what we'd done. He'd watched us from the doorway and said nothing. He didn't stop it. He didn't even condemn us after it happened.

Atlas glared at Marta and ran his tongue over his teeth before glancing at me.

"Did she tell you about the training room?" he asked.

I raised my eyebrows, a sinking realization hitting me in the gut.

I wasn't first.

Of course, I wasn't first. Why would she pick me over him? Why would I think I'd ever come before Atlas? I was nothing compared to him.

"What?"

"Yeah. Me. Her. A sweaty session on the mats," Atlas said. "She makes this cute little groan when she—"

"Okay," Marta cut in, glancing at me. "Enough."

I wanted to be angry. In the real world, I probably would have been. Atlas and I had never shared a woman between us, even if there were some hazy nights where it came close. I sat there, willing the wicked, fiery slice of jealousy to come, but it never did. Instead, the thought of the two of them fighting and fucking sent a different kind of heat to my stomach, one that clenched my balls and made my cock twitch.

I would have liked to have seen that.

I bet it was hilarious. I bet it was hot. I bet—

"If we're going to perform some fucked-up ritual in the woods, we might as well put all the cards on the table," Atlas said. "You can't fuck both of us and expect us not to say something about it."

"Yeah? And what about you, huh? Standing outside the storage room, watching us like some kind of creeper—"

"Alright, stop it, both of you," I cut in with a chuckle, surprising myself. "Look, we're not exactly in ideal circumstances. Trapped here in this big empty mansion, a fucking lust demon on the loose somewhere. Let's just...make the best of it."

"What?" Atlas balked. "So you're not jealous?"

I laughed and shook my head. "If we plan to do all three rituals, this was going to come up eventually. Jealousy won't get us home."

The words rang true in my heart. I wouldn't begrudge either of them for taking their frustrations out on each other. We *were* in a frustrating circumstance, made even more irritating by the limited prospects of getting home. What if we were stuck here indefinitely? Would I expect them not to act on what they felt between them? And what happened once we got the bond back and those emotions were amplified? What if we couldn't control it like before?

"Are you?" I asked Atlas.

"Pfft." He balked and sipped his beer, clearly searching for the right words to say. When he sputtered something that sounded like "I don't know," I took pity on him and said my thoughts out loud.

"What if we never get out?" I asked. "What if it's just the three of us until we grow old and die?"

"There's something about this place," Marta said. "I feel...out of control. With both of you. Like I can't stop it."

"Me too," I said.

"Ditto," Atlas agreed.

"That's got to be the demon," I said. "It was making people consume each other in the real world. What would it do with the three of us in a reality made specifically for it?"

Atlas sighed, and Marta shook her head.

"It's only going to get worse," she said. "We might be somewhat shielded behind the wards, but when we leave this place...if we ever venture out there...it'll fuck with us."

"So here's what we do," I said, my rational mind quickly searching for a way to organize the chaos, a way to keep us going. "Anything that happens in the liminal, stays in the liminal. If doing this ritual gets us a step closer to getting home, we'll do it. Whatever happens in the meantime is...nuance."

"Nuance?" Atlas barked a laugh. "Jesus Christ, I can't believe this is my life."

"Look, you and I have never had many boundaries between us," I said. "We were raised in motel rooms and the back seat of Dad's pickup. I'm honestly surprised this is the first time something like this has happened."

Atlas met my gaze then, his emerald eyes shimmering with a tumultuous mix of fear and anticipation. Something else danced behind them, too. Something depraved and licentious, like maybe the thought didn't bother him as much as it should. Like maybe this wasn't the first time it had crossed his mind. Like perhaps some part of him was even looking forward to it.

Am I?

I couldn't think about it.

"When we get out there," Marta said. "Let the magic guide you. Open yourself up to it. Whatever happens stays here. It's just us."

Atlas nodded, and I agreed. Later, after she'd gone to bed, my brother and I stayed in the parlor, lounging on the antique couches with a bottle of whiskey between us.

"C'mon, man," I said. "It's just you and me now. How you doing?"

Atlas ran his index finger over his eyes and sighed. "I've been better."

"Are you stressed about the ritual tomorrow?" I wouldn't blame him if he were.

"No," he said. "Oddly, I'm okay with whatever happens."

"Then, Marta?" I was ready to talk him off the ledge again. We didn't need to have alpha-male animosity between us. There didn't need to be mine or his. There could just be ours, just like our entire life had been ours.

Atlas took a deep breath and drank the rest of his whiskey in one gulp before pouring himself another, topping off my glass as well. "I should be pissed, but I'm not. And then I'm worried about why I'm not, but that's not it, either."

I waited for him to continue and picked up my glass to sip the amber liquid, relishing the mild burn as I swallowed it down.

"You ever wonder what our lives would have been like if we weren't raised in *this?*" He gestured around the ornate room and decorative crown molding, indicating generations of wealth before the Harlots inherited it.

"I imagine you would have been a mechanic, and I would have gone off to college," I said. "But it doesn't do any good to wonder what could have been. We're here. This is our life."

"Right," he said. "*Our* life."

"Don't tell me you regret it," I said. "You're the one who convinced me to stay when I got accepted to Yale."

"I know." Atlas frowned and drank another swig of liquor. "But what if I was wrong? What if you should've left years ago?"

I narrowed my eyes at him. "What? What's that supposed to mean?"

"You wouldn't be here if it weren't for me. You wouldn't have gotten sliced up by demons or been trapped in the liminal—"

"Yeah, it would have been you instead. You, here, alone with a witch you can't stand." I snorted a laugh. "Couldn't stand."

"Hey," he said. "Hate-fucking is a thing, alright. Just because we let off some steam doesn't mean we're besties."

I reached across the space between us to grab his shoulder and give it a squeeze in solidarity. "I stayed because I wanted to, Atlas. It's you and me, no matter what. Always."

He looked at me again with that same mix of trepidation and yearning, the same one that had nearly stopped my heart at dinner. It seemed like he wanted to say more, that he had a lifetime's worth of things he wanted to say. Instead, he let out a sad laugh, gulped the rest of his whiskey, and stood.

"I think that's enough for one night." He patted my shoulder as he passed me, leaving me alone in that room with a million thoughts rumbling around my pathetic brain.

Maybe I should have felt some regret for grinding on Atlas one day and letting Wes go down on me the next. But I refused to be slut-shamed by any of it. Like I'd told them, I couldn't control it, and the longer we were stuck here, the more I worried I wouldn't want to.

I spent the day of the ritual preparing myself and debating what to do about Wes and Atlas. Tonight would change a lot of things, even if it was just a blood binding. We weren't *joining flesh*, not yet anyway, but it could create something chaotic and untenable between us.

Constance hadn't been specific about the details.

I tried to block that out. Who the hell knew whether Constance was in her right mind or not? The ritual was sound, as far as blood rituals went. I didn't have a coven to do another summoning, and I didn't have a high priestess to bind us with limited fallout. We'd have to improvise and pray for the best.

I created the protection oil and made sure the Colts understood how to use it in their baths. I mixed up a concoction of road-opening oil, containing vervain, five-finger grass, and lemon balm. While it was brewing, I dropped an old key into the oil and stirred it while chanting my intentions.

"A bond is blocked; let it be opened. Our magic is closed; let it be cleared. Our way home is unclear; let it be known." I repeated my mantra nine times while stirring, channeling my magic down my arms, into my hands and fingers, visualizing the power of my ancestors as I did.

Then, I prepped the candles. I bathed them in the road-opening oil and rolled them in herbs to hasten the spell, things like camphor and cinnamon for luck, roses for extra protection, and lavender for peace. I added a little extra coffee to speed up the process. The sooner we got out of here, the better.

In the human realm, it was the middle of October, and a thought occurred to me while I tracked the dates. November 1st was Día de Muertos. The day of the dead. The time when the veil between the realms would be the thinnest. Tita and I would spend the day making sweet bread and decorating our ancestor altar, preparing ofrendas as we remembered our beloved deceased. The thought of her made my vision blur, sending tears down my cheeks. Would she carve out a spot for me on that altar this year? Would she think I was as lost to her as my father?

Or maybe...maybe we could use that to our advantage. If we could complete the rituals, restore the bond, and gather enough energy, perhaps we could push from this side while my sisters pulled from the human realm, and we'd scoot through.

That would require contacting them to let them know. I'd been scrying every night since we arrived but hadn't had any luck. Maybe I was that much of a masochist that I tried again with similar results. Either they couldn't hear me on the other side, or I still wasn't strong enough to break through. I glanced down at my hands, tingling with the fury of my magic.

It's there. I know it's there.

I'd been performing mirror scrying since I was a little girl. I'd perfected it eons ago.

Why isn't it working?

It must have had something to do with the centuries-old blood wards in the estate walls. Nothing in. Nothing out. If I were going to get a hold of *anyone* from the other side, maybe I would have to go someplace sacred *to me*. Perhaps I had to go to Tita's house. It might still be too risky to go outside, but if it worked, it would be worth it. Refusing to give up hope, I let it go for the night and told myself I'd pick that thread tomorrow.

At nine o'clock, I ran myself a bath with three drops of cleansing oil, rue, rose petals, and salt. As I sat in the water, I enchanted it with my intention — ward away bad energies, cleanse my body for optimal ritual magic, and protect me (and my warriors) from ill harm. Closing my eyes, I grounded myself in my sacred space. I went back to my spiritual woods and listened to the birds chirping in the trees. I called to my ancestors and asked them for their blessing, and when the wind picked up, blowing my hair around my face, I smiled as the sensation of gratitude washed over me.

"The time has come when you must fight. You must channel your anger into faith, and faith into action."

The words echoed in my mind, the sound of the woman's gentle voice calming what little hesitation I had left.

I'd just been about to thank her again for her guidance when dark clouds blocked the sun, obsidian wisps wrapping around me.

"Filthy mortal," came the deep growl. "You cannot escape me. You cannot escape this place."

Panic seized my chest, gripping my heart in a vise, and I spun around, searching for the source of the voice. Bright crimson eyes glowed in front of me, razor-sharp teeth extending from behind a bloody grin.

Gasping, I opened my eyes and sat up, splashing water over the side of the tub.

There was nothing here. No one in my bathroom except for me.

"Fucking hell." I ran my hands over my face and back through my hair, taking deep, calming breaths to slow my racing heart.

It's not real. It's a bad memory. Just a bad memory. That's all.

Once the water had gone cold, I stepped out of the bath and let the droplets run down my body. Air drying allowed the magic to sink into the skin. I dressed in my white floor-length dress, braided my hair, and anointed my amulet with protection oil.

After gathering all of the supplies, I went downstairs to join the guys. They were dressed in white linen pants, their chests bare and hair brushed back as I requested. Wes wore a pentagram around his neck, attached with a long rope. Atlas wore his around his wrist on a brown leather bracelet.

"Here, let me," I said, walking toward them so I could rub protection oil over their charms, just in case. "Ancestors of the order, I pray to you now. Please protect us in our work. Saint Marta, slayer of dragons, ancestor of my own namesake. Watch over us. Guide us."

A shiver ran down my spine in answer, and I took that to mean she had our back, at least for this.

"Well?" Atlas asked, nodding toward the bag in my hand. "Are we ready?"

I nodded and glanced at Wes, who smiled in that gentle, reaffirming way of his, filling my chest with a confidence I only slightly felt.

"Let's go." I turned and led the way out of the house, around the gardens, and toward the tree line where I'd initially been bonded to them. I'd come out here every morning since we'd been stuck in the liminal, but it never felt quite as powerful as it did then. The crescent moon shone overhead, illuminating the trail with an ethereal radiance that made the world more effervescent. Frogs and crickets sounded in the distance, providing a chorus for our meditative walk, and when we got to the clearing, I sighed at the pulse of energy surrounding me.

This place was old, even older than my coven, and the wind

bustling through the trees whispered ancient secrets that only a select few would ever be privy to.

Atlas set the wireless speaker down on a log while I grabbed the holy water to bless the space. Wes lined the candles up in a wide circle around the edge, in almost the same spots they'd been when we were bonded. I chanted prayers and offerings of peace to the land spirits, expelling any negative energy from the space so we could do our work in peace and harmony with nature.

Even if this was a questionable spell. Even if this was chaos magic in its rawest form.

"You're sure this is the right playlist?" Atlas said, glancing down at my phone.

"The one that's called Ritual One," I answered, completing the cleanse before going back to my bag for the dried herb bundle.

"This has AC/DC and Led Zeppelin on it," he said.

"Music is important," I said. "It heightens the energy and welcomes the spirits to join us."

He raised his eyebrows and shook his head. "Whatever you say, little witch."

"Here," I said, pointing to the fire pit as a primal instrumental song played in the background. "Stack the logs up. I'll start the fire."

Atlas did as I asked, and I picked up a candle, lighting it while I walked the circle to cast a ward around our magic. "Candle and flame, light the way. Keep our magic safe, we pray."

The moment I completed the circle, the world around us went quieter. The night faded into the background, leaving only my warriors and me and the anticipation of what was to come. Atlas had set up the fire pit, so I used my magic to light it, casting a spell that would keep it from burning out while our energy still permeated. Firelight flickered across Atlas's features, making him seem more fearsome and demanding. Wes walked to join us on the other side, his body powerful in the nighttime glow.

"Remember what I said," I told them as I set up our altar on a log between us. "We're safe inside the circle. Just...open yourself up to the magic. Let it flow through you. No matter what happens."

Atlas nodded as I placed our offerings on the wooden stump. I'd brought dried roses and a card depicting Saint Marta. I set up red and white candles in the center of a circle made of cinnamon and carnelian. Finally, in the middle, I put the ceremonial knife.

Even though this ritual would entail us exchanging blood, we would also be carving a symbol into each other's chests, right over the heart. The wounds would be deep, but I'd brought satchels full of healing herbs. I just prayed I had enough magic left over at the end to close them up so they didn't get infected.

Wes glanced at both of us before handing me the book, which I placed next to the chalice, open to the correct page. I licked my lips and swallowed the little bit of anxiety creeping up my throat.

It'll be okay.

Have faith.

Anger into faith, faith into action.

I can do this.

We can do this.

I grabbed the goblet, having already been cleansed earlier, and held it above my head, calling the four elements to assist us as I walked around the fire. I called to the ancestors and the ancient spirits of this land.

"Hail, and welcome," I said.

"Hail, and welcome," Atlas and Wes repeated.

I came back to the altar and held my hands out to either side to grab onto my warriors, and they clasped palms opposite me, completing the triangle. The wind picked up, the trees rustled louder, and the cicadas buzzed fiercely in the background, echoing over the drums and deep vocals of the music.

"Gentle spirits, we call thee here to witness the binding of our blood. A sacrifice made so our magic may flow. We ask for your blessing, or let your disagreement be known."

I focused on the candles and listened to the earth, reading the signs in the flames. They danced and flickered in the wind for only a moment, indicating initial hesitation. But then the fire glowed brighter, bursting with energy and willingness. Our sacrifice had been accepted.

"Here we go," I murmured, picking up the knife and turning to Wes on my right. I turned my corresponding hand up and carved a triangle into the fleshy part of my palm opposite my thumb.

"By thorn and chain, by ash and rod, by serpent's breath, by raven shod. I bind thee fast, I bind thee near, to walk with me through flame and fear." I handed the knife to Wes, who gently cupped my left hand and carved a triangle into the same spot on my palm. I winced as the blade pierced my skin, but held firm through the spell, knowing it was a test of my strength.

Then I walked to the altar and squeezed my palms over the herbs, letting my blood drip onto our sacrifice as the candle flames glowed brighter, welcoming my magical essence.

Wes repeated the incantation as he carved the design into his right hand before turning to Atlas, holding the knife out, and gesturing for him to repeat the carving on his left. He added his life's essence to the altar, and I watched as the crimson swirled together, sizzling and rippling with preternatural energy.

Atlas went next, saying the words as he sliced open his right before holding the knife out to me to do his left. His fingers shook as I held them, but I stared into his eyes, hoping to reassure him that it would be okay. We had the ancestors' blessing.

We're doing the right thing. This is the only way.

Atlas added his blood to ours, and once he stepped back, we took hands again, our wounds sealing together with warm, sticky liquid. A surge of power went through me, dense, potent electricity cascading from me and around me and into me.

It's working.

"Blood to blood and bone to bone, what is ours shall be ours alone. Breath to breath and soul to soul. Thy will be yoked. Thy spirit be whole."

The guys repeated after me, echoing the spell as the world faded away, leaving the three of us holding hands around the altar. We said the next part together, reading from Constance's book, reciting the old words as magic danced from the ground, ricocheting up my legs and into my torso, spreading out to Wes and Atlas on either side.

"By fire that burns black and red, by the realms that hold all the dead, by water deep, by air that flies, I claim thee now with eternal ties."

Wind swirled around us, but the flames held steady. The clouds brushed over the moon, casting an ominous shadow on our work, but we kept going. I steeled myself against the ecstatic vibrance burning through my veins, remembering what I'd told them earlier.

Let it flow. Open yourself to it. That's the only way this works.

"Come shadow, come serpent, come raven, come crow. Witness the vow and the binding we sew. Let no man break it or spirit undo. This chain we weave is permanent and true."

As we said the last word, a visible blast went through us, blinding white and nearly scalding. I gasped, sucking in the essence of both of them. Atlas's raging fury mixed with Wes's calm demeanor and forced itself into my lungs. It was almost as strong as the original ceremony, almost as potent. We were nearly there.

The energy died away, leaving us all wide-eyed and panting. I looked at Wes, who raised his eyebrows and grinned, and then at Atlas, who seemed as shocked as I felt. I broke our hands and grabbed the knife again, knowing what would come next. It would be the most challenging and most tender part of this ritual, but it would seal our words and our vow. It was the third mark. Right over the heart.

Stepping toward Atlas, I held the blade toward him, gulping as I met his hesitant stare.

"Now's your chance, witch," he whispered, raising an eyebrow. "Push too deep and this is all over."

I scoffed and shook my head. "Quiet, warrior. I promise not to make it hurt too much."

He chuckled as Wes came to stand next to me.

"By moon that shines, by sun that dies. I bind thy heart. I seal these ties." I pressed the blade into his chest, right over his heart, and sliced half of the triangle, trying not to let his trembling muscles ruin the design. This was, after all, meant to scar. Wes took the knife from me and completed the sigil as he repeated the spell. Then, together, we leaned down and licked the marks, taking Atlas's blood into our bodies, making it our own. I closed my eyes against the sweet, delicious taste. I expected it to be metallic, but oh, it flowed down my throat like ambrosia, and I had to physically force myself to stop.

Atlas balked when I opened my eyes again, and Wes stepped closer, running a finger over my cheek.

"Your eyes," he murmured.

"Here." I held the knife out to him so we could do the same to Wes. "Do it quick."

He seemed surer of the outcome, his torso sturdy and upright. When Atlas and I licked over his skin, the hum of magic grew steadier, settling in my torso, wrapping my heart in comfort and ease like a fluffy blanket on a cold winter day.

Finally, it was my turn. I lowered the straps of my dress and covered my breasts, holding them so Wes could slice the first half of the sigil. It burned with euphoric fury, pain and pleasure combined, and I grimaced, maintaining my composure as Atlas completed the mark. And when they lowered their heads to lick the blood from my body, I gasped as pure, unfiltered rapture raced through my nerves. My head fell back on my shoulders. Bliss erupted over my skin. The blood tie was almost complete, almost at its height. And if this was the result of a sigil marking, I trembled with anticipation of what would come once the last word was said.

They stood, lips red with blood, the same blood dripping down my chest, and I tried to hide the shaking in my muscles at the amplification of power connecting us. They looked magnificent in the glowing firelight. Fierce and powerful and covered in our life force. I wished I had a camera to capture this moment forever. I had never been more attracted to two people with equal ferocity.

And they're both mine.

When they opened their eyes, I understood what had happened. The iris and pupil were gone. In their place was a sparkling ruby color that filled the entire space.

I barely had time to register that before a blast of magic shot through us like a shockwave, nearly debilitating in how forceful it hit us. I stumbled back, clenching against it, but when it subsided, warmth and contentment vibrated through my gut, leaving me with the unfettered knowledge of being supported by them.

Them.

Atlas.

Wes.

Mine.

The ritual was complete, but we were far from done.

Things got blurry after we carved the sigil into Marta's chest. Magic ripped through us, almost knocking me off my feet, and then I wanted...I didn't know what. Both of them. All of them. All of us.

It was fucking confusing and absolutely fantastic. It was the best high I'd ever had, more potent than the best whiskey, more exhilarating than the purest cocaine. I could have gorged myself on this ecstasy for the rest of my life.

Marta glanced between us, our blood fresh on her mouth, crimson dripping down her naked chest, a similar look of desire and energy twinkling behind her sensuous gaze.

For half a heartbeat, we stood there, staring at each other. Then Wes acted. He grabbed Marta behind her neck and pulled her to his mouth, devouring the remnants of our spell. He licked and kissed, wrestling his tongue with hers while she moaned into the touch.

Fuck me.

The sight made my cock twitch, sending that delicious heat coasting down to my balls and the back of my legs. It was like watching them in the supply closet, except this time, I *felt* the kiss on my own lips. Their combined passion rattled through my torso, echoing through my heart and stomach. I should have been jealous. Maybe some small part of me was.

But Wes had hit the nail on the head. We'd spent our entire lives together. What was mine was his. Forever. Marta was gorgeous; I couldn't deny that. But Wes was...powerful. Strong. Beautiful. I'd always thought it, but I could never admit it, at least not out loud. Not until now.

It could have been the aftereffects of the spell. Or maybe it was the combination of the fire and moon lighting him up like a Greek God. Whatever it was, I'd never been more attracted to both of them.

When they broke apart, Marta turned to me, her stare hungry and greedy. I didn't think, couldn't think, just reacted. I grabbed her throat, yanked her toward me, and consumed her mouth. Her lips tasted like sugar and Wes and *her,* decadent magnificent her.

Us.

She tasted like *us.*

She ghosted her hands up my bare chest to my neck, where she tangled her fingers in my hair, raking her nails over my scalp. I groaned and wrapped my arms around her lower back to bring her closer, and *fuck,* when her belly rubbed up against my cock, a shiver wrenched through my nerves.

I wanted her.

I want both of them.

When she finally stepped back, she licked her lips and glanced at Wes, who stared at me with the same desperate affection that had been in Marta's eyes moments ago.

Everything in me wanted to taste him. My entire body wanted to press against his in a way I'd never experienced before. I knew everything about him. I was familiar with every part of his personality and his habits and the way he sighed and relaxed just before he drifted off to sleep. But this...

The way I wanted him now didn't just toe the admittedly

blurry boundary between us; it set the fucking thing on fire and danced around the ashes.

He stepped closer, and my heart pounded. He curled his hands into fists, and my breath caught. He tilted his chin up to stare down his nose at me, and I nearly sobbed with ache.

When he reached up to grab the back of my head, that imaginary boundary exploded. I launched at him, wrapping my hands around his neck and bringing his face to mine.

The ground went out from under me. My knees shook, and his massive chest pressed against mine, the fresh triangles on our ribs lining up. Something in that tiny intimacy made me more feral for him. We didn't kiss. No. We battled for power, for strength, for lust. He wanted me as much as I wanted him, and the haze of the magic lingering in our bodies fueled the frenzy.

He lapped at my lips with his tongue, seeming to devour the forbidden essence of what had been building between us for decades. And I let him. I opened my mouth and sucked him in as deeply as I could, curling my arm around his neck to bring him closer. Always closer.

I could have stood there for eons, drowning in the despicable craving between us, but Wes stepped back entirely too soon, breaking the connection. He exhaled on a sigh, pressing the palm of his hand to my heart, right over my new triangle mark. Our eyes met, and his sparkled in the moonlight, making the ruby-red seem even more entrancing.

Marta stood next to us and rubbed her hands over our shoulders.

"Let it flow through you," she murmured as she pushed up on her toes to lick a path across my neck, and fuck, I was done for.

Everything after that was a blur of hands and mouths and murmured sighs of content. Marta dropped to her knees in front of us and tucked her fingers under the waistbands of our pants, shoving them down to our ankles in tandem. Wes was just as hard as I was, and when she took my cock, I jolted from the shock of pleasure that went through me.

I'd had threesomes before. I'd even been involved in foursomes that had escalated to full-blown orgies by the end. But nothing had ever turned me on more than watching her swipe her tongue under Wes's cock while she stroked mine. Even though she was doing it to him, I sensed the thrill of her mouth on my skin, the wet warmth, the magnetic pull of flying high with endorphins.

A deep, guttural groan escaped my throat, and I rolled my head back on my shoulders to let the sensations have me. And when she wrapped her perfect mouth around my dick, I nearly lost it and came on the spot. My hips jerked forward, seeking more of her, longing for her throat.

She teased me. She flicked her tongue over my slit and let me go with a loud pop before going back to Wes and doing the same thing. She was face-fucking him, but I felt it like she was doing it to me, too.

She was doing it to *us*.

Us.

Ours.

"I'm losing my fucking mind," I said, running my hands over my face and back into my hair.

"Aww, you're making him blush, sweet girl." Wes laughed and sank his fingers into her hair to guide her head as she worked him. "I think he likes it."

"Hmm," she said, letting him go to return to me. "I think he wants more."

She stared up my body with those blood-soaked eyes gone to magic and lust, and a wave of yearning hit me so hard in the gut, I almost wilted. I reached down to tangle my fingers in her hair, and I touched Wes's hand as he nudged her toward me. The contact rattled me, and even in my drunken haze, I knew we were doing something irreversible.

The tether in our blood magic amplified the experience.

"Want me to drain you dry, warrior?" she asked, raising an eyebrow. "Want me to suck your soul out through your—"

"Don't fucking talk to me like that," I whimpered. "I'm barely hanging on as it is."

Wes laughed harder and stepped closer to me, kissing a trail up my neck to my jaw before latching onto my earlobe.

"Such a strong man turned to mush by a sweet little sinner," he whispered. "Tsk, tsk, tsk. What happened to the guy who could go all night, huh? Or don't tell me you're so turned on by seeing my cock that you've lost your stamina?"

Wes's words, combined with the way Marta massaged my dick, had me panting and gripping her hair just to ground myself in reality. But I couldn't hold on. It was too much—the sinful thirst for both of them, the sounds of the night mixing with classic rock on the radio, the way she pumped me and sucked me.

I lost my composure and exploded in her mouth like a teenager on prom night. It was embarrassing. It was amazing. My soul soared into the sky, rounded the universe, and collapsed back into me with an earth-shattering eruption. I jerked and shivered and moaned while she swallowed me down, smiling up at me with a victorious grin.

Dizzy and enthralled, I dug my aching palms into my eyes to come back to myself. My legs wobbled, for Christ's sake. But when I came to, Marta had moved onto Wes, sucking him off with as much vigor and enthusiasm as she'd done to me. Except he was much more in control of himself. He had both hands wrapped in her hair, rutting his hips toward her face like he was chasing his first orgasm ever.

My cock twitched to life again, and it was only then that I wondered exactly what we'd unleashed in these woods. But payback was fair game.

I took advantage of his distraction to lean in and lick a trail of sweat beading down his throat, causing him to moan and tilt his head back to grant me more access, which I greedily took. He tasted like salt and man, and I wanted more of it.

"Do you know how hot you look like this?" I whispered, reaching up to grab a fistful of his dark hair and yank his head back farther.

He let out a low chuckle and flashed a devil's grin, something wicked and dark that only spurred me on.

"Watching her suck you off turns me on more than you can possibly imagine. Watching you eat her pretty little cunt nearly made me bust in my pants." I tightened my grip on his hair, and he hissed. "I bet you wanted me to see, didn't you? I bet you were even thinking about me when it happened."

"Fuck." He clenched his eyes shut, his features twisting into a grimace laced with euphoria.

"That's right," I said. "I know you, Wes. Just like I know you're going to fuck her throat and come on her tongue and replay this memory for months to come. And when you do, you're going to think about me." I yanked his hair harder and kissed his jaw, relishing in the delicious little sounds he made. "Now be a good boy and give her what she wants."

I sank my teeth into the side of his neck, and that was what did it. He shuddered and froze, his muscles tensing, the veins in his arms bulging, and Marta gulped him down like she was starving for him. His pleasure became my pleasure. His explosion echoed deep inside my chest, down to my bone marrow, and when his cum settled in her stomach, I knew her contentment like it was my own.

When she finally let him go, she smiled up at both of us, a little drip of his cum sliding down her chin. And fuck, I couldn't resist. I took the back of her neck, guided her up, and licked the rest of him up, swallowing down the salty leftovers. I'd given head thousands of times. I'd tasted cum from countless men. But Wes mixed with Marta's essence was the sweetest ambrosia I'd ever had the privilege of tasting.

Pulling back from her mouth, I weaved my hands into the hair at the base of her neck and tilted her head up so she had to stare at me, her eyes still unfocused and blissed out.

"You," I growled and pressed a tender kiss to her mouth, "are such a naughty girl."

"The ritual didn't require any of this," she said with a sly grin. "You wanted it. Because you've always wanted it."

"And you wanted it too, huh?" I shook my head and licked my lips. "Did you enjoy yourself?"

"Immensely." She didn't even have the decency to be embarrassed.

Good.

I like my partners unashamed.

Wes regained his composure and stepped next to me, eyeing our witch with mischief behind his gaze.

"Take off your dress," he snarled. "Get on the ground. Knees up. Legs spread."

Fuck. Yes.

"What?" She widened her eyes. "No, we don't have to—"

"If you think we're letting you get away without seeing that adorable come face you make, you're sorely mistaken." Wes raised an eyebrow.

"Are you going to play nice?" I asked. "Or do I have to make Wes spank you to get you to listen?"

She bit her bottom lip. "Don't threaten me with a good time."

I let her go with a little shove and glanced at my brother, who tilted one side of his mouth into a grin. He wanted it. She wanted it. And even if I was certain I'd feel every single one, I'd had a red ass before. It might even make my dick harder (if that were possible).

Wes moved toward her to grab her, but she held up her hands and laughed.

"Okay, okay," she said and slipped out of her pale dress, shoving the fabric to the ground and stepping out of it. God, she was perfect, like every part of her had been designed to tempt me. She lowered herself to the grass and bent her legs, spreading them wide enough for me to see the glisten on her cunt.

She was just as turned on as we were, and sucking us off had gotten her there.

"Look at that, brother," I said, slinging an arm over Wes's shoulders. "The little witch likes having our cocks in her mouth."

"Did you like drinking our cum, too?" Wes laughed at her shiver. Clearly, she did.

"Answer him," I said.

She took a deep breath and let it out on a shaky, "Yes."

"There's a good girl," Wes said, patting me on the stomach. "Wait until you taste her cunt. You haven't devoured anything sweet until you've tried her."

"Hmm, don't mind if I do." I knelt between her legs and trailed kisses down her inner thigh, laughing when she trembled harder. I did it to the other side as Wes circled to lower himself by her shoulders. Just as I leaned into kiss her clit, he licked her nipple, and she arched off the ground. One of her hands tunneled through my hair while the other grabbed his, holding us to her.

I took that as a sign to keep going. I shifted myself around so I was lying on the ground with my legs out behind me, settling in to feast on her. And when I licked through her wet heat, she moaned and mumbled something that sounded like, "Fuck, that feels good."

Wes whispered to her while he alternated sucking and lapping at her tits, but I went to work between her legs. I found the spot that made her hiss and lavished attention on it until she shook, nearly on the verge of climax. But no, she wouldn't get off that easy. I sucked her entire cunt into my mouth, swirling her before going back to that sensitive spot again.

She grew wetter, the taste of her arousal making me rock my hips on the ground, seeking friction. But it wasn't enough. I ached to touch myself, but I *had* to make her come on my face. Like Wes,

I sensed everything I was doing to her. When I flicked my tongue over her clit, the tip of my cock throbbed. When Wes ran his hand down her stomach and up to her throat, it was like he circled mine. And when I stuck a finger inside her, it was like someone had rubbed up against my prostate, massaging me from the inside.

The whole experience set my skin on fire, and as I continued to devour her, Wes traced her lean curves with his lips. He ravished her while I took from her, murmuring sweet nothings against her pussy. I stuck a second finger inside her, coaxing her from the inside while I lapped at her outside, relishing her delicious taste, covering myself in her distinctive cherry scent.

Wes amped up his attention to her nipples while I escalated on her cunt, and then she tensed, reaching her own orgasm. She tightened her grip on my hair, her thighs clamping around my head, her pelvis pushing off the ground as she moaned, and the waves of her ecstasy rolled through me.

Fuck, it was fantastic, and I shot another load on the grass under me, surprising myself. I had never done that before.

Wes looked up with a huge smile, nodding toward me. "Did you just paint the grass?"

I hung my head and laughed. "Don't bring the attention to me. This is about her."

"Right," Wes said, rising on his knees to scoot down next to me. "My turn. Move."

"What?" Marta lifted her head and gasped. "No, I'm too sensitive. I can't."

"Yes, you can, sweet girl," he said, putting a hand on her stomach to lay her back down. "I know you can."

She whimpered but did as he asked, and I crawled up her body, peppering kisses on her torso as I went, licking off blood and sweat. When I got to her mouth, she moaned into the touch, licking at my lips like she was trying to get her taste off me. I let her. I kissed her and touched her with free abandon, memorizing the image of Wes's head between her legs and the feel of her breathy sighs on my skin.

We worked her through it. Wes ate her out like he was starved, and I sucked her neck, her tits, her mouth like they were my only lifeline to reality. When she came again, she rocked into Wes's face, and I swallowed down her cries, consuming them and praying it would always be like this.

Now that I'd lived it, I never wanted it to stop. I'd just come twice in a row, and still I wanted more. My cock ached painfully, and I squeezed the tip with my free hand, trying to stave off another embarrassing combustion.

"Atlas," Wes said, drawing my attention back to him. "Get down here."

I didn't question it. I just went, my body compelled by his command.

"Wes," Marta murmured. "Atlas. It's not supposed to be like this... It's not..."

Wes spread her knees wider, exposing her to both of us. The sight of her dripping in front of us, slick with want and need, made me groan.

"Together?" I asked.

He nodded. "Together."

"You think she can handle it?" I raised an eyebrow at him while I lifted one of her knees over my shoulder.

"She can handle anything," Wes said. "She's our good girl, our sweet little sin. You want it, don't you?"

Marta sobbed and nodded. "Yes. Yes, I want it."

"There ya go." Wes trailed kisses down her thigh while I settled myself on the ground again, anticipation twisting in my gut. When our tongues met at her cunt, she rolled against the touch, and my mouth touched Wes's, and the combination of the three of us turned the boil in my blood to an inferno. We alternated sucking and licking, battling for control of her pussy. Our tongues ricocheted across my cock, like the affection was focused on me instead of her, but fuck, that made it even hotter.

Eating her out with my brother was the most erotic thing I'd ever done. He stuck a finger inside her first, his fist bumping my chin. Not to be outdone, I put my hand under his and fucked her with my fingers, too. We worked in sync, sliding in and out and in and out together, massaging her, working her into a delirium.

"Fuck, I'm close," she said. "I'm so close. Just like that."

Wes and I sucked her together, smashing our faces to get more of her. Always more. I spread her open wider, pushing her knee out to the side so there would be room. But that didn't help. We worshipped her, our witch, the tension growing inside her. It pulsed out of her, into me, and out of me into Wes before going back into her. It rebounded between the three of us, going on and on until she finally broke.

She came with such a force that it coated our faces and hands, drenching us in her orgasm. I came again, my cock shuddering through the third climax with an exhausted sigh, spilling myself into the grass while I finished her off, lapping and swallowing everything she gave us.

"No more," she said with a hoarse throat, pushing our heads away. "No more. Please."

I rolled off to my side and stared at the starlit sky, panting down the excitement of the ritual, knowing I could go again. This indestructible need inside me hadn't been satisfied by what we'd done, and I wondered what it would take to make it go away.

Would it ever go away?

Or had we just kicked open a bees' nest that would drag us down into its stinging hell?

CHAPTER 16

Wesson

Words couldn't describe what happened to us out there in the woods. Once the blood bond had been sealed, I couldn't stop myself from taking them. Over and over and over again. Atlas wasn't the only one who came while going down on Marta. I was nearly spitting dust by the end of it.

When we could finally breathe, we cleaned ourselves up as best as we could. Marta reopened the circle while we gathered our supplies. And then we went back to the estate.

It was tempting to return to my room alone, but after what we'd done together, it didn't seem right. I was still riding the high of magic and endorphins, soaring through bliss like I had a first-class ticket. Thankfully, both Atlas and Marta were thinking the same thing. She grabbed our hands and guided us to her room, taking us to the bathroom with no argument from either my brother or me. When I glanced in the mirror, I wasn't even startled to find gleaming crimson eyes staring back at me. Atlas and Marta were still sporting the same thing, too. We shared a shower, laughing as we took turns scrubbing the dirt, blood, and sex from each other's skin.

"I still feel high," Atlas said while he dried himself off. "I'm fucking giddy."

Marta hummed her agreement. "That's the magic. It'll wear off eventually."

"What if I don't want it to?" Atlas raised his eyebrows as she giggled and pushed up onto her toes to kiss him.

"It'll still be there in the morning," Marta said, walking her cute little ass into her bedroom to leave my brother and me in the bathroom alone.

"That was the best fucking sex I've ever had," he admitted. "And we didn't even fuck her."

"It looked like you were fucking her pretty good with your face," I said, shivering as the image of his head between her thighs floated to the top of my mind.

Atlas was certainly more experienced in this department than I was, but even with my limited encounters, nothing had ever topped the energy we created together tonight. Was it because of the magic? Was it because of Marta and Atlas? Or was it something else, something more sinister than we could have anticipated?

I didn't know, and with the lingering effects of the ritual tingling through my veins, I didn't care. I kissed Atlas and followed Marta out to the room, swatting her ass playfully as she crawled into bed naked. I walked around to the other side and scooted in next to her, sighing in contentment as the smell of her sweet aroma plumed around me. I grabbed her waist and dragged her closer, tucking her ass against my pelvis, which got my cock's attention. It reluctantly jerked at the contact as if asking to go again, both exhilarated and annoyed that the answer might be yes.

Marta giggled and teased me by rubbing the soft swell over my dick again, which made me bite her shoulder in response.

"Careful, sweet girl," I said. "Brats who tease get spanked."

"Hmm." She settled in against my chest and hummed. "Any other time, I'd be on board with that. But I'm too tired. You both wrung me out."

I glanced over her shoulder to see Atlas standing at the edge of the bed, his hands on his hips, seemingly unsure about whether he should climb in on the other side of her.

"What's wrong?" I asked.

"Nothing, I just..." He rubbed a hand over the back of his head.

Marta pushed up on an arm and pulled the blankets back, nodding into the space next to her. "C'mon, then."

He furrowed his brows like he was trying to solve a complicated math problem, and a sense of unease shimmied down my sternum. It wasn't mine. He wondered if he was intruding, like maybe he should leave Marta and me alone.

"Atlas Colt," Marta demanded. "Get in this bed right now."

He laughed, and I focused on the way he squinted when he smiled. Had he always done that? Fuck, he was gorgeous when he was happy. He scooted into the spot next to Marta and wrapped an arm over her waist, his heavy hand landing on my hip. Together, we drifted off to the best sleep I'd had in years.

The nightmare didn't come that night. I wasn't alone in the woods with demonic smoke trying to claw its way out of my chest. Instead, I dreamt of crescent moons and dark hair glittering in the firelight and crimson eyes sparkling from the feel of my kiss.

A sharp slice of pain between my eyes woke me the next morning, and I squinted against the trickle of sunlight creeping in through the crack in the blinds. But I wasn't in my bed. I wasn't in my room.

I glanced around and quickly realized I was in Marta's bed. Alone. The lingering scent of her shampoo and soap assaulted my nose, and I licked my lips. The bitter aftertaste of blood mixed with sex and a long night coated my tongue, but an ache in my chest had me looking down.

The sharp red lines of a triangle marked my skin right over my heart. I rubbed a hand over the cuts and winced when my palm twinged. I had matching lines on the fleshy part near my thumbs.

The ritual.

Suddenly, memories from the night before raced through my mind.

Marta cutting a triangle into my hand
Me slicing the same into Atlas.
All of us marking each other's chests.
And then...
Oh God.

A fiery brand of shame squeezed my lungs and twisted around my heart, made even more intense by how I'd woken up alone.

They left me.
Of course they left me.
I'm no good for them. I don't deserve them.

I closed my eyes and sensed something else inside me...something that *wasn't* me. Two somethings. Almost like a homing beacon pointing me downstairs. My instincts said whatever it was would lead me to the kitchen.

Them.
Us.
Ours.

I remembered that, too. Last night, we'd nudged open a door between our sensations. When one of them came, I felt it. When Marta sucked Atlas off, it was almost like she was doing it to me.

Christ, what did we do?

I slowly sat up, grimacing as my headache protested the movement. My muscles twinged like I'd run four marathons yesterday, and I swung my legs to the side of the bed, preparing myself before I stood. Even taking it as lightly as I did, I still got lightheaded and had to hold on to the banister of her four-poster bed to stabilize myself.

I wrapped a damp towel around my hips and limped down the hallway to the stairs, taking them one at a time until I got to the first-floor landing, gingerly making my way to my room at the far end of the house. I went to the bathroom, and when I glanced at myself in the mirror, I had to blink at the person staring out at me. Despite feeling like shit, I looked amazing. My skin glowed with a healthy radiance like I'd been on a week-long juice cleanse, and my torso had gotten bigger. Stronger. I figured it must have been the magic and went to get dressed. At least the red eyes were back to my normal mahogany.

When I walked into the kitchen, Marta and Atlas sat at the breakfast table, whispering to each other over two cups of coffee. They stopped when I came in.

I would have been worried about that except they, too, had experienced changes overnight. Marta's hair was shinier and fuller, her complexion just as magnificent as mine. And Atlas had gotten bigger as well. His shirt was tight around his biceps, his chest broad and more defined.

"Morning," I grumbled as I took the seat between them.

"Good morning," Marta said, pouring me a cup of coffee before handing it to me black, the way I liked it. "How are you feeling?"

"Like I drank an entire liquor store last night," I said, taking a sip.

Ahhh, caffeine.

"Same," Atlas said in his gravely, just-woke-up tenor. It sent chills down my spine, and I tried to ignore the images of him biting into my neck as I came. Or the way our tongues had tangled while we dined on Marta's delicious cunt. Their combined tastes had done something irrevocable to me, and I feared I would never be able to go on without it. When this was over, when we got out and they realized I was not worth their energy, how would I ever get over it?

But last night was part of a ritual, right? Surely, we wouldn't repeat it outside of that magical space. We couldn't. We shouldn't. If this much damage had already been done, what would it be like once we completed the other two?

"It's the magic hangover," Marta explained, rubbing her temples. "It'll pass."

We fell silent as we drank our coffee, the awkward tension of this new pull between us tightening my chest.

"What were you two talking about?" I glanced between them as they avoided my gaze, distinctly avoiding each other as well.

"It's just..." Atlas cleared his throat. "Last night was a lot."

"Understatement," I said. "But we agreed. What happens in the liminal stays in the liminal."

My brother shifted his hips as Marta pulled her lips between her teeth.

"And I was reminding Atlas that we still have two more rituals to do," she explained. "I can sense you two inside. It's almost as strong as the bond was before, but...I think we should continue. The next ritual has to be done soon, within a week if we can manage it. We're running out of time."

"As much as I want to get out of here, and I do... I think we need some space to think about things," Atlas said. "To reassess where we stand now."

"And where do we stand?" I raised an eyebrow at him, taking a big swig of coffee. It burned on the way down, and Atlas coughed while Marta cleared her throat. That, too, came roaring back. I *felt* them. I knew Atlas was uncomfortable with how far we'd pushed ourselves. Anxiety raged through his chest like a sledgehammer, beating away at his lungs. For him, this was dabbling in something we didn't understand. One wrong move, one wrong decision, could push someone into something we liked to hunt.

Marta, on the other hand, was exhausted. She'd drained more of herself last night than she'd intended, and the soreness between her legs matched the rest of her muscles. It was like she'd done a triathlon and then fucked ten people afterward.

"Look, we all knew what would happen when we went into the woods last night," I said. "We all agreed to it."

"I didn't think it would be that intense," Atlas confessed. "And the next one..." He grabbed the book and flipped it open to the flesh-binding spell. "If blood binding felt like that, flesh binding is going to kill me."

"Or make us stronger," Marta argued.

"You don't know that," he said. "You don't know how any of this is going to turn out. Constance stopped writing after the last soul ritual. This is..." He shook his head. "This is *dark* magic."

"There's no such thing as dark magic," Marta said, the ire in her tone forcing Atlas to grind his teeth.

No love lost between these two.

Despite what we'd done, they were still at each other's throats. Maybe it would always be this way.

"There's only chaos and order," she said. "Everyone walks the line between both."

"Then what are demons, huh?" Atlas said. "Vampires? Rabid shifters?"

"Forces of chaos," she said. "They thrive on it."

"And last night was your definition of order?" Atlas sighed.

"The spell worked as intended, even if it was a little...unorthodox," Marta rebutted. "We are one step closer to being able to share magic."

"But without a full coven, we don't know if what we'll end up with will be the same thing we had before we got stuck here," he growled. "What if it's worse? What if we unleash something we never should have fucked with in the first place?"

"As long as it gets us home," Marta snarled. The frustration ricocheted between them like a ping-pong ball, bouncing back and forth, feeding off each one's anger and pent-up aggression. "The end will justify the means."

"I'm not sure about that," he said, pushing to his feet.

"So you want to stay here for the rest of eternity?" She shoved upright, getting in his face.

"Alright, knock it off." I slammed my hands on the table to get their attention and break the cycle. "You said we had a week, right?

We'll keep researching. We'll keep scouring the library and trying to connect to the other side."

Atlas pinched the bridge of his nose. "I don't know, man. Something's wrong."

I narrowed my eyes at him. "Wrong, how?"

He glanced between us as a thick wave of trepidation coursed through the bond.

"I feel...*different,*" he said. "I've been having these dreams."

That got my attention. "What dreams?"

He looked like he was about to say something life-altering, but instead he shook his head. "It doesn't matter. I don't want us to forget what brought us here. We created this liminal for a lust demon. Asmodeius. People were consuming each other, fucking each other to death."

"Your point?" Marta asked, drumming her nails on her coffee mug.

"What if the demon's here?" Atlas cleared his throat. "What if it's inside us? What if it's fucking with us? We already feel like we can't control our impulses. This is just making it worse."

"Even more reason to keep going with the rituals," she said.

Atlas had a good argument. I almost hadn't been able to stop last night, and even now, sitting next to them and not touching them took an incredible amount of restraint. I wanted to lick the sweat off Atlas's abs. I wanted to bury myself between Marta's legs. I wanted to fuck them both, consequences be damned, society's ideas of taboo be damned.

"Look, creating that amount of magic at one time..." Atlas rubbed his hands over his eyes, pushing them back into his hair. "Demons feed off that shit. They live for it. It may not have shown itself yet, but that doesn't mean it's not here."

Marta squared her jaw and nodded once, reluctant resolution settling in her gut.

"You're right," I said, glancing up at her. "Do we have to be outside for the flesh binding? Can we do it indoors, behind the wards?"

She nodded. "I think so. Outdoors is better, but as long as we protect ourselves and we start at the right time of day, it shouldn't matter *where* we do it."

Atlas sighed, his anxiety momentarily quelled. But my mind went back to something else Marta had said.

"What do you mean we're running out of time?" I asked.

"In the human realm, it's the middle of October. In two weeks, it'll be November 1."

"And?" Atlas raised his eyebrows.

"Día de Muertos." She blinked as a wave of regret and anguish flickered down the bond. She explained it was the time of year when the connection between realms was at its most potent. "Usually we think about it in terms of the living and the dead, but—"

"It could mean this realm, too," Atlas finished.

"Exactly," she said as a burst of exhilaration exploded from her chest. "If we could get my coven to pull from the other side while we push, maybe we could overwhelm the veil and slip through."

"How do we get them to pull?" I asked. "You haven't been able to contact them."

"I think it's time we leave the estate," she said. "If I go to Tita's house, I might be able to reach her from there."

"How?" Atlas asked. "Do you and Tita have some kind of telepathic connection?"

"No, but we have a direct bloodline." She took another sip of coffee and sighed. "It's not like the coven, not like our blood binding. We share DNA. I'm hoping I can reach her through the mirror."

He raised his eyebrow as a wicked heat of disbelief twisted through his chest. "A mirror?"

"Mirrors have long been believed to be the doorway to other realms," I said. "You think that will work?"

"I've been trying to reach the coven from here, but I think the heavy protective wards around the space are keeping me out. Tita's house is warded, too, but not by hundreds of years of witch blood. This is her blood, *my* blood. It could work."

"I thought you said it was too risky to leave the grounds," Atlas said.

"It is," she admitted. "But I don't think we have another choice."

My brother looked at me and raised an eyebrow, a silent question of whether I agreed.

"It's worth a shot," I said. "If it gets us home. But I don't think you should go alone."

"I'll go with you," Atlas added. "I'm dying to get out of this place, and I could use the drive."

Marta nodded and licked her lips.

"Okay." I agreed, but I didn't like the thought of the two of them out there while I was stuck here with no way to help them if something went wrong. But someone needed to keep researching. "I'll go to the library to hunt down Constance. Maybe there's something in the lore that will help us with the liminal."

"I'm wiped from the ritual, so we'll wait a few days before we go. In the meantime, we can test the bond. See what we're working with," Marta said. "Even if I can't reach her, as long as the rituals work, we *might* have enough juice to do it without the coven."

CHAPTER 17

Marta

Ten days went by with no luck, and we were staring down the barrel of almost two months trapped in the liminal.

We trained in the mornings, the three of us. Atlas and Wes were skilled at fighting together, having done so their entire lives. But now that we shared sensations, it became more challenging to get a leg up on either of them. I anticipated their moves before they acted, and they knew which way I planned to dodge before I'd even thought of it myself.

I tried to keep my worst impulses contained, but after the ritual, I couldn't help but stare. Atlas's muscles had been carved out of stone, all lean ripples and strong curves. Wes's hands were capable of immense strength, made even more attractive by how gentle I knew they could be. Whenever one of them caught me staring, I quickly looked away and ignored the burn in my cheeks.

After breakfast, we huddled together in the library, poring over dusty old books until our eyes hurt. My magic returned a little more each day, bringing with it more sensations of them. Atlas's reckless hedonism and Wes's strong, stoic countenance.

I grounded in the woods as often as I could, and they took turns escorting me. The demon didn't show, and I began to wonder if it *was* only us that had gotten stuck here. Once I was feeling up to it, we tested the strength of this new connection between us.

We sensed each other's physical and emotional states, clear as day. When I pricked my finger with the tip of my knife, both Atlas and Wes felt it. But when I grabbed their hands to try to pull on their strength the way I'd done before, nothing happened. It felt like a gaping chasm, a void in space, a rope leading nowhere.

"We'll keep going," Wes said, giving his brother a nod.

Atlas didn't seem happy about it, but he didn't argue, either.

We researched together. We ate dinner together, and at the end of the night, we drank together. They told me hilarious stories about their life on the road with their father, living out of cheap motel rooms and getting into as much trouble as they could. And once we were well past the point of inebriation, we stumbled our way upstairs to my bedroom and passed out in my bed.

It wasn't even a question or a conversation. After the ritual, it seemed right. After a few days of that routine, I didn't think I could sleep without them on either side of me. I felt safe in their combined embrace.

Nothing happened...nothing sexual, anyway. Sometimes, we giggled until our sides hurt. Sometimes, Atlas and I fought over the covers. And other times, we simply drifted into unconsciousness to the sounds of each other's breathing.

Día de Muertos was only two days out now, and with nothing more to show for it, we had officially run out of time. As much as I feared the risk, I couldn't hold off going to Tita's any longer.

I stood on the sidewalk in front of the white rancher and swallowed the lump in my throat. It looked the same as it had when I left it, when I'd argued with her about faith and the Virgin Mary and the wisdom of our ancestors. It had only been two months, but it felt like years ago. I had aged decades since then.

The wind chimes on the porch sang in the wind, and the birds chirped from around me. But there were no goats in the backyard and no chickens clucking around their hutches. Where had they gone? Were they not a part of the liminal? Or were they considered only part of the human realm? If that was the case, why were wild animals separate from that?

My mind raced with questions I didn't have the answers to.

"You okay?" Atlas asked, stepping up next to me.

I tried to smile and nodded, walking up the steps to her front porch and through the front door.

God, it even smelled the same—like tea and incense and the comforting scent of *her.* I almost expected her to walk around the kitchen corner and chastise me for waiting so long to come home.

"Can I do anything to help?" Atlas stood in the center of the living room with a reluctant look, like he didn't really believe me and hoped I would tell him to be quiet and stay out of it.

His hesitance to complete the rituals still hung heavy between us, making me painfully aware of how much he didn't trust me. Not that I expected him to follow me mindlessly, but I was the witch in this situation. I'd been trained in spells and folk magic since I was a child. He was a warrior, a glorified hunter, even if I could admit that proceeding with Constance's books scared the daylights out of me.

"Just keep an eye out," I said. "Let me know if you see anything strange."

"You mean like a big smoky demon?" he muttered under his breath.

I ignored him and went to the household altar in the kitchen. In the drawer to the right, she kept a handheld mirror that she used to communicate with our ancestors. I put that on top of the altar and grabbed the matches. As I took one out, I whispered my intention.

"Child of fire, connect me to my abuelita. I need to talk to her. I need to see her. Will you help me?" I struck it on the side of the box and lit the tall white candle on my left, watching as the flame danced and flickered. The smoke twisted at first but eventually settled into a thick stream, indicating the candle would assist if it could. I used the same match to light the matching candle on the other side with the same result. I grabbed Tita's rosary and placed it in the center of the altar, sprinkling rue for protection, marigolds for communication, and cinnamon for luck. After pouring holy water in the offering bowl, I said a prayer to any ancestors listening that they would accept this sacrifice and help me in this work.

Then I closed my eyes to ground myself, to pull from the earth and summon the spirit of this house, of any benevolent energies that would assist in this work. It spun through my nerves, sparking in my blood, tingling as it coursed through me.

When I opened my eyes, I gazed into the mirror, letting my focus soften. Staring at myself, I willed my mind to go blank, trying to force myself into a trance. Behind me, Atlas shifted and sighed, but I ignored that, buffering myself in the safe cocoon of this house and my magic.

"Abuelita, hear me," I whispered. "Tita. Come to me. Please hear me. I summon your spirit."

My features in the mirror started to morph, my jaw rounding, the skin around my eyes aging and wrinkling.

It's working. Keep going.

"Tita, can you hear me? Tita. It's me. It's Marta."

The fuzziness of this altered state pulled me under, beckoning me into the same lull of safety as being in her arms. It reminded me of myself as a little girl, wrapping myself around Tita's midsection when I'd had a bad dream and she held me until it went away.

"Mi hija?" came the sound of her voice. It echoed in my head, bouncing off my mental walls like surround sound. "Mi hija, are you safe?"

"Tita," I said on a sob. "We're stuck in the liminal. We need your help."

"Oh, Marta," she said. "We've been so worried."

I couldn't focus on that. I needed to get the point across quickly, just in case things took a turn.

"Tell my sisters," I said. "Tell them we're in the liminal. We're trying to get out on Día de Muertos. Tell the coven to pull us, to summon us."

"You must pray," she said. "The Virgin—"

The connection cracked like static on a bad cellphone call, and I winced as an electric shock buzzed behind my eyes. My magic had started to wane, so I pulled on the earth's energy harder, yanking it into me to feed this tenuous connection. I needed to see her. I needed her wisdom now more than ever.

"Mi hija," came her panicked cry. "Som—ing's com—"

Her voice faded in and out.

"No," I growled, forcing more energy into the spell, grimacing as I struggled to hold it. "Tita, come back."

The vision in the mirror transformed, my abuelita's face dissolving into a thick obsidian cloud of smoke with dark crimson eyes and a big, toothy smile.

"I see you, filthy mortal," it snarled. "I enjoyed the sight of you in the woods with your warriors. Your magic is quite delicious."

I jumped, breaking the connection to my tita's house before grabbing the holy water from the altar and tossing it on the mirror.

"What?" Atlas said, launching to his feet as he ran into the dining room. "What happened?"

"The demon," I said, pointing to the mirror. But the vision had faded and the smoke had cleared, leaving only my reflection behind and droplets of liquid sliding down the glass.

"The demon?" Atlas raised his eyebrows and glanced around, yanking his gun from the holster under his arm. "Where?"

"In the mirror." I explained what happened, trying to stay calm despite all signs pointing to the demon having gotten into my abuelita's house. Was it there in the real world? Had I put her in danger by trying to reach out to her? Or was it here? Was it in the room with us, silently waiting to take us by surprise?

Panic seized my heart, clenching around it so tightly I couldn't breathe. My lungs struggled to pull in air, and I grabbed my hair, my frantic gaze searching around the space as if I would suddenly see her there.

"Hey," Atlas said, grabbing my shoulders so I had to look at him. "Hey, take a deep breath with me, okay?"

"Atlas, what if the demon got her? What if...what if..." I couldn't think straight.

"Listen, your abuelita has been a powerful witch longer than either of us has been alive. If anyone could take that bastard on, it's her."

His words registered, but my emotional mind couldn't latch onto them. All I could focus on was how that evil monster could be ripping her apart at this very moment, and there was nothing I could do to stop it. In fact, I'd *caused* it.

"Look at me," he said. "Marta, Goddamn it, look at me."

With tears making my vision blurry, I glanced at him, focusing on his concerned emerald gaze. "Breathe with me."

He took a deep inhale, and a steady wave of relaxation and calm washed out of him and into me. I sensed his steadiness, the weight of his hands on my shoulders, the feel of the air sliding down the back of my throat and into my lungs.

"Exhale," he said, blowing it out slowly.

Together, we inhaled and exhaled until my blood pressure returned to normal and the terrified side of me retreated into the background, leaving someone much more logical and levelheaded.

Atlas, of course, was correct. Tita was powerful, and her house was warded. After my disappearance, she would have strengthened those protections.

She can handle it. Whatever happens, she can handle it.

"We can't do anything to help her from here," Atlas said. "We have to keep our shit tight so we can get out, okay?"

I nodded and gripped his shirt, fisting the material between my fingers so hard, I dug my nails into the skin on his shoulders. He wiped the tears from my cheeks and nodded. His eyes were so green and comforting, his lips inches from mine. His hot, hard body was suddenly so close and enticing. I remembered how he tasted during the ritual, how it felt with his hands tangled in my hair, how his tongue had wrenched an orgasm out of me.

Atlas was infuriating and irritating, and he lived to argue with me, but I had to admit I didn't *hate* him anymore. In that moment, I thought he was one of the most beautiful men I'd ever seen.

I want him...so bad.

I didn't know my emotions could swing so quickly from one to the other. All I knew was that if I didn't *have* him right then and there, I would die. Simply waste away.

Perhaps he read this in my gaze, or maybe felt it stir in my body, because he looked between my eyes and licked his lips, and that was it.

I pounced on him, wrapping my arms around his neck and slamming my lips against his. He moaned and sank into the contact, grabbing the back of my legs to lift me so I could connect my ankles behind his back. He carried me over to the sofa and sat down so I straddled his thighs, my knees near his hips.

His tongue wrestled into my mouth, and I sucked on it, remembering how decadent this experience had been last night in the woods. It had been a week with nothing more than heated glances and innuendos wrought with sexual tension, but none of that mattered. I *needed* this connection in a way I'd never known before, especially with him.

But fuck it. What happened in the liminal, right?

I went for his belt, ripping it open so I could get to the button and zipper on his jeans. He likewise worked on mine, but when that proved to be too much of a struggle, he grabbed the knife from his holster and flicked it open, slicing down my denim with expert precision. It should have scared me to have a blade so close to my cunt, but the sight of his impatience to get in my pants had me groaning with arousal.

Heat flooded my lower stomach, sinking between my legs, and

once I freed his magnificent cock from his pants, he grabbed my wrists to stop me.

"Wait," he said, clenching his eyes shut as he shook his head.

"What?" My heart clenched. "What for?"

"Marta." His pained voice had me searching for a cut. Had he hurt himself? "Look at me."

I glanced up to meet his gaze with a widened one of my own. He cupped my cheeks and held my head in place, glancing between my eyes.

"How are you feeling right now?" His cock twitched against my bare cunt, indicating the insatiable desire I felt brewing in his sternum. I wanted him. He wanted me.

"Can't you tell?" What kind of stupid question was that? We were blood-bonded. He could sense the inferno inside me.

"I think..." He cleared his throat and closed his eyes again like he was trying to shove away a round of dizziness. "I can't believe I'm saying this, but..."

I whimpered in disappointment, twisting my fingers around his shirt like I meant to pull it over his head.

Under normal circumstances, I would *never* lower myself to beg a man for his attention. But this was one of my warriors...my Atlas... *Mine.*

"Please?" I sounded small and pathetic, even to myself.

He took a deep breath and let it out on a sigh. "Fuck it."

He lined his cock up at my entrance so I could sink all the way down. I didn't need any foreplay. I was wet from the moment he picked me up.

"Fuck." He sighed, wrapping his arms under mine so he could hang onto my shoulders, his fingers digging into the skin near my neck, holding me down. His massive size stung as it stretched inside me, but I welcomed the pain. I loved it, especially when I shifted my hips and he rubbed up against that fantastic spot inside me.

"God, you're so tight," he whispered. "You feel so fucking good. How is it this fucking good?"

"You love when I'm on top of you, don't you?" I said. "You love letting your witch take control."

He laughed and leaned his head back against the couch, exposing his throat to me. "Fucking hell. You can have whatever you want. Take me. Use me."

I rocked my pelvis harder against him, stuffing as much of him inside me as I could get. Euphoria rocketed through my nerves, escalating this untamed desire for him.

"I love draining you, Atlas," I hissed. "Having your cock in my mouth, swallowing you down, it shouldn't be so good, but I can't help it."

"You hate me, witch," he said, digging his hands into my hips so I fucked him harder, faster, more desperately. "I hate you. But fuck, I love this. I love seeing you like this."

A small alarm blared in the back of my mind, reminding me that we were in my Tita's house, fucking on her couch. We were blood-bound to each other *and to Wes,* and maybe we shouldn't be doing this without him. Maybe Atlas was right. Maybe I should stop this. Maybe we needed to slam on the brakes. What if this was the demon's influence? What if I wasn't really the one in control?

But my orgasm crept up on me, heightening the already tight ball of impending ecstasy in my molecules, and I couldn't do anything about it. I dug my boots into the couch, using it as leverage to grind harder, fueled by the little groans and whimpers spewing from his delicious mouth. I pressed my lips to his and captured them, swallowing them down like I was consuming him with it.

All of him.

His blood.

His power.

His soul.

Mine.

Atlas was mine. So was Wes. And I was theirs. I didn't have to like it, and maybe once I got through the endorphin haze of lust, I would realize I didn't. But as he used my momentum against me to drag my cunt along his pelvis, burying him deep inside me, I didn't care about any of it.

There was nothing more important than this moment with him.

"Yes, fuck yes," he cried, his muscles tensing, the veins in his neck standing out. I licked up his throat just as he stilled, his orgasm crashing out of him as his cock twitched deep inside me. It surged into me, and I crested my own pinnacle. The height of my climax yanked me down into a dark abyss of hormones and utopia. Somewhere inside, I sensed a third presence, a third orgasm that had nothing to do with Atlas or me. In the midst of everything, I didn't think much about it; I only used it to further my own pleasure.

Atlas's cock kicked against my inner walls, the warmth of his cum coating my insides, and that should have appalled me, but I only wanted more.

Even as my pleasure subsided, I wanted to keep going. I wanted to drop to my knees and lick him clean until he was hard again. I wanted him inside of me in every way imaginable.

Atlas came to his senses first. He hummed in approval and leaned in to kiss me, sliding his mouth down my jaw to my neck before wrapping his arms around me to lean me in so I rested against his chest.

"I take it you're feeling better now?" he asked with a smile in his tone.

I laughed and nodded, leaning back to look him in the eyes. "I don't know what came over me, but thank you for being here. Thank you for..."

He grinned and rubbed his thumb over my lower lip before glancing down at my shredded jeans between us. "You should grab some clothes before we head back."

As I climbed off him, reality set in. I'd fucked Atlas Colt on my tita's couch. I'd like to think she'd be mortified, but knowing her, she'd probably be thankful I had someone to take care of me when I needed it.

We'd done this...without Wes. We said we wouldn't get jealous. We said what happened in the liminal stayed in the liminal, but did this count? We hadn't talked about it. Where were the lines? Where were the boundaries?

We were bonded. Had he felt it? While I walked into my bedroom at the back, I searched for him and sensed a deep-seated satisfaction, mixed with a small amount of guilt and loneliness, as if he were upset to have been left out.

I'd have to make it up to him. Atlas and I both.

After changing and grabbing a few extra clothes, I found Atlas standing in the living room, re-sheathing his knife and gun. At my entrance, he glanced up and smiled, his eyes sparkling in that after orgasm glow I recognized from the ritual.

"You ready?"

I nodded, grabbed his hand, and we left.

"So, how'd you two make out?" Wes asked when we got back to the estate. He leaned against the doorjamb to the library, his arms crossed, a smug smile on his pouty lips.

I paused and straightened, trying to figure out how to respond. He already knew, so why would I lie?

Atlas barked a laugh and stepped around me, grabbing onto his brother's shoulder to give him a shake. "A little on the nose, brother, but I'll allow it."

Wes raised an eyebrow and smirked.

"I just…" I didn't have the words to describe the way I needed Atlas in that moment. On the ride home, I'd tried to make sense of it, but the truth was, I couldn't.

"What can I say?" Atlas held his hands out to either side. "I'm irresistible."

Wes rolled his eyes and laughed, playfully hitting his brother in the stomach. "Don't gloat. You're hot, but our witch is hotter. If she were desperate enough to fuck you—"

"We saw the demon," I cut in, hoping to avoid the heat snaking into my cheeks and down my neck. I wasn't ashamed of what I'd done. Hell, I'd done way worse before I'd gotten stuck here with them. But the shame of Wes's FOMO snuck into my heart, and I didn't want to make it worse.

"What?" That got his attention.

We walked into the library as I explained what happened, making sure to detail it as specifically as I could remember it. "I think she heard me. I think she understood me, and if she did, she'll get the coven involved. They might be able to pull from their side as we push from this side, and maybe..."

"That's good," Wes said. "We'll keep trying."

"Wes, I'm sorry. I panicked, thinking the demon must have gotten to Tita. Atlas calmed me down, and it just...escalated."

"Hey," Wes said, reaching out to grab my hand and give it a tender, reassuring squeeze. "It's okay. What happens in the liminal, stays in the liminal, right?"

I nodded and pulled him in, rising on my toes to give him a quick kiss. His surprise and delight rattled down to my bones, but before I pulled away, he leaned into my ear.

"Prepare yourself, witch," he said. "It's my turn."

I'd be lying if I said that didn't make my cunt pulse and shiver. I smiled as I stepped back, and he winked.

"How'd you do?" Atlas said from the table where Wes had spread out his research. "Find anything good?"

"Yeah, actually," Wes said, walking over to his brother. "I think I found Constance's death record."

"What?" I hadn't been expecting that. "Where?"

"It's in the coven cemetery back in Scotland," he said. "But I can't be sure. Constance was a popular name at the time, and there are at least five others it could be. But look." He held out a notebook containing a list of names and dates next to them. "Constance Clearwater, date of death 31st of July, 1592. Jonathan Woods, date of death 31st of July, 1592. Xavier Woods, date of death 31st of July 1592. It's the only entry with a witch and two warriors passing on the same date."

"Woods," Atlas said. "They were brothers."

"Possibly," Wes added.

"This is twenty years after her last entry in the journal," I said, skimming my fingers over the letters like touching them would tell me something more.

"Exactly," Wes said. "If it *is* her, and those are her two warriors, then they made it. They completed the soul ritual and lived another twenty years before they died together."

"Cause of death..." I squinted to try to read the words, but they were faded and nearly illegible. "I can't make it out."

"I can't either," Wes said. "But it doesn't really matter, does it? They survived the rituals."

"I don't know," Atlas cut in, rubbing the back of his head. "This doesn't prove they fixed the bond, only that they died at the same time. What if it was the plague or being burned at the stake or some other wild medieval shit?"

"It could be," Wes said. "But we've been researching for weeks. We could spend years digging through this library and still find nothing. I think this means something. I think we should keep going."

Atlas pursed his lips and took a deep breath. "Whatever you say, brother."

We debated and researched until dinnertime, and then I made abuelita's tamales for the guys at Atlas's request. He nearly moaned when he took his first bite, and the sound rattled loose that deliciously perverted side of me that lived to draw that noise out of him.

I was wiped after the visit today, so I wanted to head to bed. But Atlas convinced me to have a drink with Wes and him in the parlor, saying it would soothe my nerves and I deserved it. My bones were heavy, but when Wes pouted and gave me the puppy-dog eyes, how could I say no?

"What are you drinking, witch?" Atlas asked.

"Whiskey," I said. "Three fingers, neat. And I'm only having one. Then it's time to go to sleep."

"Sure," he said with a wink. "You just want to get me flat on my back again, huh?"

I raised an eyebrow and tilted my head as he flashed that adorable grin. Reminding myself I was still supposed to hate him, even if I didn't, I accepted my drink and went to sit next to Wes on the couch, who was currently sipping on a twenty-year scotch. He'd been hesitant to open it at first, but like Atlas said, what was real in the liminal? Did our decisions here affect the other side?

So I said fuck it and welcomed him to it.

"Cheers to blood bonds and dead witches from the 1500s," Atlas said, slumping down on the other couch across from us.

I snorted and held my glass up before taking a sip, relishing the burn that slid down my throat.

"So I have a question," Atlas said, "now that we're lubing up our inhibitions."

A spark of his devilish playfulness twisted in my sternum, and I took another drink in anticipation of where this was going.

"When we hooked up earlier...did you feel it?" he asked, glancing at Wes.

Wes choked on his scotch next to me and wiped his mouth before licking his lips. I focused on that beautiful tongue, recalling how it felt between my legs. Atlas glanced at me with a smirk as if he knew exactly what I was thinking. Maybe he remembered it, too.

"Uh...yeah." Wes rubbed his index finger over his eyebrow. That, too, brought back the sensation of him sliding it inside me. He had beautiful hands, so strong and callused and talented. Truthfully, both of them did. Their fingers had been honed through years of combat training and precise knife work.

"What did you feel?" I asked more to distract myself than to get an answer.

"It was this sensation in my gut, at first," Wes explained. "And then I got hard, just out of nowhere. I was confused. I didn't know where it was coming from. I mean, I was looking through death records. Not exactly the sexiest thing in the world."

He paused to clear his throat and shift his hips, looking between the two of us.

"And then?" Atlas asked, goading him on.

"And then, I couldn't help myself. I had my dick out in the library and I was stroking it before I knew what I was doing." Wes smiled and looked at me. "I sensed you first. I could feel something inside me...kind of how it was at the ritual when I...when we..."

A faint blush graced his cheeks. For being as forward as he was last night and earlier today, the sight of his bashfulness was almost endearing.

"Go on," I said, nudging him with my shoulder. The whiskey hit me harder than I thought it would, but I was a lightweight, so I shouldn't have been that surprised.

"I realized the two of you must have been up to something because by the time I was three pumps in, I was ready to explode. It was compulsive, like I didn't have any control over it. I *had* to do it."

That was how I felt in the moment. That must have been why Atlas tried to yank the emergency brake but couldn't.

"I thought it was the demon's influence," Atlas said, confirming my suspicion. "That feeling of not being in control."

"The demon in the mirror said it could see me, that it saw us in the woods last night. It tasted my magic and said it was delicious." I looked between them as Atlas swirled his whiskey and Wes sipped his scotch. "It was stupid to leave the estate."

"No, it wasn't," Wes said. "You got in touch with Tita. We know what we have to do, now."

A small part of me worried that might have been the demon, too. But no, I'd sensed the connection in my blood. I *knew* it was her.

I hadn't forgotten her other advice. *You need to pray.*

Even as angry at God as I was, I couldn't deny that I would

need all the help I could get. Could I put that aside for the sake of getting out of here?

Anger into faith, faith into action.

"Did you happen to find anything else in the library about how to get out of the liminal?" I redirected the conversation, hoping to distract myself.

Wes shook his head. "I think rewiring the warrior bond is still our best bet."

"If we could share magic...if we could pull from the earth together..."

"I don't know of any other witches that can *give* their magic to their warriors," Atlas said. "Then again, I don't know of anyone who's seen the other side of a liminal and lived to tell the tale."

"True enough," Wes said. "But that doesn't mean we won't be first."

I appreciated his optimism, now more than ever.

Despite saying I would only have *one* drink, I was obviously full of shit because after my glass was empty, Atlas refilled it. The conversation continued, somehow veering into a memory of the night they'd snuck out while their dad was on a hunt and nearly got chewed up by the same demon their dad had been looking for.

"So then this idiot tosses a salt grenade at the son of a bitch, and it fucking catches it!" Wes was laughing so hard at the story, he almost couldn't get the words out. "Boom! It explodes in the demon's face. We run like hell out of there, only to smack face-first into Dad."

"God, he was pissed," Atlas said, shaking his head as he drank his scotch. "I got my ass handed to me that night."

Xavier Colt sounded like a hard man, difficult to live with, let alone have as a parent. I counted my blessings that I had Tita.

"Yeah, we both did," Wes said. "But you always got it worse."

Atlas snorted, his gaze growing distant as if lost in a memory, a faint sense of shame and nostalgia twisting down the connection between us.

"You bet your sweet ass I never did that again," Atlas added with a sense of finality, firmly closing the bridge on that trip down memory lane.

"After that, you were Dad's good little soldier," Wes teased, laughing as Atlas scoffed.

"I had to be," he said. "One of us had to get shit done. We all couldn't run off to college and ignore our responsibilities."

"Hey!" Wes said, shoving his shoulder. "I wasn't ignoring anything. I just...ya know...dreamed about it every so often. And then after Dad died—"

He cut himself off and cleared his throat, the once jovial atmosphere coalescing into reality. I'd almost forgotten I was supposed to hate them. I'd almost forgotten the reason why I never spoke to them, never thought of them, before being matched as witch and warriors. They were there the night my parents died. They could have saved them. They could have done something, anything, and yet...

"I'm sorry," Wes murmured.

I glanced at the half-empty glass of whiskey in my tumbler. "Stop. There isn't enough liquor in the liminal to have that conversation."

"I mean it," Wes continued. "I don't know if we ever...I don't think we've ever discussed what happened."

"And we don't need to now." I finished my drink, set the glass down, and stood. "I'm going to bed. It's been a long day."

"Marta," Wes tried again.

"I mean it," I said. "I just started liking you two. Don't make me regret it. Not now. We have too much left to do."

"He's trying to apologize," Atlas snapped, pushing himself to his feet. "You know, we lost our dad that night, too. It isn't just *you* who's hurt. It isn't just *you* who lost someone."

"I know," I growled, turning to face him, my hands clenching into fists. "And if you had just done something—"

"What were we supposed to do, huh?" Atlas snarled. "Dad

told us to leave. Told us to save ourselves. We didn't have a choice. I mean, Christ, what would you have done?"

The sting of his righteous fury burrowed in my chest, amplifying my own, making it hum and vibrate with potential. I could tear this place down if I let it go unchecked. In that moment, I thought maybe I would.

"You didn't have to listen to him," I said. "You could have... You could have..."

Tears blurred my vision, and my cheeks burned as the weight of their combined remorse pressed on my chest, suffocating me.

What would I have done?

I would have run. If my parents told me to go, I would have gone, especially then. Atlas was twenty, Wes was eighteen. It was their first mission, one they probably shouldn't have been on in the first place. Xavier was a terrible parent, and it was his fault I'd been robbed of mine.

Perhaps Tita had a point about that, too. Maybe I *had* only been looking for someone to be angry at, and they were the easiest targets.

But what did *any* of that matter now? I was bonded to them, as much as I might have hated it. And now, we were stuck in a fucking liminal and we might never get out. A stupid lust demon was banging down every door I tried to open to my coven. Hell, we were lucky the fucker hadn't gotten into the estate yet. We were lucky it hadn't figured out a way to claw us to pieces like our parents.

"Sweet girl," Wes said softly, coming to stand next to me. He pressed his index finger under my chin and lifted my face to meet his, his touch so kind and tender. "We're going to get out of here. We'll do the last two rituals, and we'll claw our way out on Día de Muertos. It's going to work."

I swallowed and nodded, wiping the wetness from my cheeks. "I know."

"We don't have to talk about it again," Atlas said, stepping to my other side. He ran a hand over my shoulder, reinforcing the affectionate sentiment coasting through my tether to him.

"Good," I said before taking a deep breath to steady myself. "Now, about the ritual. We begin at sundown." I went over everything they'd need to do to prepare themselves. Ritual bath and cleansing, of course, as well as added protective ointments and charms. "Since we'll be inside, I'm not worried about anything walking in on us, but just in case."

"Are you sure you're ready for this?" Atlas raised his eyebrows, glancing from me to his brother and back again.

"Are you?" I threw the question back at him. It wouldn't be *just me* who had to bind flesh. It would be Wes and him, too. Constance's warriors had been just as involved with each other as they were with her. The Colts had kissed and whispered filthy words to each other at the last ritual, but that was relatively tame compared to what we'd have to do tomorrow. "Sex magic is incredibly potent, more than blood magic. It's ecstatic. Remember to just...open yourself up to it."

Atlas nodded and glanced at Wes, who swallowed and shifted his gaze to the ground. The awkwardness of what we were about to do hung between us, but I didn't let myself focus on it. I gave them both a kiss and headed upstairs, leaving my door open for them to follow.

"How are you feeling about this?" Wes asked after Marta left. We sat on opposite couches, facing each other, the weight of unspoken misdeeds hanging between us.

"Scared shitless doesn't begin to cover it," I admitted. Maybe I should have been more concerned about...uh...*binding flesh* with my brother tomorrow, but that seemed like the least of my concerns. What the demon said to Marta hung heavy on my shoulders. The library's lack of information on liminals and Asmodeus made my hackles rise. It was almost like someone or something had prepped this space for us, removing anything that might be remotely helpful.

"You've fucked guys before," Wes said. "What happens in the liminal—"

"That's not what I meant," I added, clearing my throat and shifting my weight as he raised his eyebrows and looked at me. I took a deep breath and sipped my scotch to tell my inhibitions to fuck right off. "You know I love you, right?"

He opened his mouth, and his features dropped like he hadn't expected me to say that.

"I'd do anything for you," I continued. "Anything. But man... I'm telling you. Something is off about this place." I clenched my free hand into a fist, almost as if I could *feel* the evil in my blood. "Maybe this ritual helps us, or maybe it makes things worse."

He scoffed. "Worse how?"

"I don't know...just worse." In my thirty-two years on this earth, my instincts had never steered me wrong. My gut usually reacted faster than my brain, and right now, it was telling me to put a stop to all of this. The rituals, the research, our attempts to reach the other side. We were fucking with something we didn't understand, and as much as it felt great, it made me suspicious. What weren't we seeing? What was hidden behind our blinders?

"Atlas," Wes said, drawing my attention back to him. "I've always looked up to you. You're more than a brother to me. You've always been...well...everything. I love you more than my own life, and if I have to step in front of every demon in this fucking world to make sure you and Marta get out of here, I will."

That was his problem. Always so self-sacrificing. Always believing he didn't deserve the life he had, that he was lower than everyone else. It was something our father had put in his head that he'd never shaken.

The moonlight trickled in through the windows, mixing with the soft illumination of the lamp next to him and making his features even more defined. His strong jaw gave way to the curve of his cheekbones and the delicate beauty of his dark eyes. It was fucked up to want him the way I did, and I wondered how long that urge had been there.

"Stop that bullshit," I said. "I'm not going anywhere without you. If you're stuck here, I'm stuck here."

He laughed and shook his head. "It will be fine. Just...be gentle with me, huh? I've never...you know."

"Oh, I know," I teased with a wink. "Don't worry. I have a feeling the magic will make it enjoyable for everyone."

Wes smiled, pulling more to the left than the right, revealing a dimple in his cheek that I'd always loved. Then, he stood, set his glass down on the end table, and nodded toward the door. "I think I'll head up, too."

I nodded, deciding to stay for a few moments alone, just to get my head straight. His footsteps echoed up the stairs and across the ceiling to Marta's room. I focused on the swirling amber in my glass, wondering when my life had taken such a turn for the weird and complicated. It had always been like this, I supposed. Like Wes said earlier, I was a good soldier. I did everything Dad told me to without question. I watched out for Wes, and I protected our secrets, and I volunteered to be matched with a witch when the time came. I pushed hard; I worked my ass off; I did what I was supposed to do.

And what was it all for? Now, I was stuck in a literal version of hell with nothing left to do except fuck my way out.

Life is fucking weird.

When I couldn't sit still any longer, I stood and walked to the window, peering past my reflection to the darkness outside. Stars sparkled overhead, and the trees swayed in the breeze, and it almost seemed normal.

I glanced down at my tumbler again, but when I looked back up, my reflection had changed. It no longer followed my movements, and the version of me in the glass stretched its lips into a wicked grin, one that looked inhuman and sinister. Its eyes clouded over with pitch smoke as its mouth started to move in silent syllables.

Startled, I blinked and shook my head, convinced I'd drunk too much and started to hallucinate. But when I glanced back at the window, the not-me kept talking, forming syllables I could barely understand.

"What?" I whispered, my heart pounding. "What the fuck are you saying?"

"*Atlas,*" came a dark hush from behind me. I jumped, reached for my gun, and turned, ready to fire bullets into whatever it was.

But nothing was there. And when I turned back to the window, it wasn't *my* reflection at all anymore. I stared straight into the dark eyes of my father.

"Holy fuck!" I stumbled back, having to restrain myself from shooting at the glass. "What the hell?"

"*Listen to me,*" it said. "*Don't let him go.*"

"Dad?" I couldn't believe my eyes. Was this really happening? Was this a dream? Had I fallen asleep on the couch?

"*Don't let him go,*" he said.

"Him? Who? Wes?" What the actual fuck?

"*Don't let him go,*" he said again, his voice fading.

"What the hell are you talking about?" I stepped closer, reaching out to touch the window. But he just kept repeating it over and over again.

"*Don't let him go. Don't let him go. Don't let him go.*"

As soon as my fingers touched the cool glass, it shattered, splintering into a thousand tiny shards that exploded around me. I covered my face and ducked to avoid it, but when I glanced back up again, the window was still there. Nothing had happened. I'd imagined the whole thing.

Well, fuck this.

I raced upstairs and into Marta's room, damn near skidding to a halt at the sight of my witch wrapped in my brother's arms. He'd spooned her close to his body, her back up against his chest, his heavy arm over her hip. The sight was so damned endearing, I almost didn't wake them up. But this was too important.

Either I was losing my fucking mind, or my father had managed to contact us from beyond the grave.

"Marta," I hissed, giving her shoulder a shake. "Wes. Wake up."

Marta blinked open her eyes and peered up at me. "What?"

"Something fucked up just happened."

Both the witch and my brother got out of bed, dressed, and came downstairs with me as I explained what I'd seen. But just like before, the window wasn't damaged, and the only person peering out of the reflection was me.

"What do you think it means?" Wes asked. "Don't let him go?"

Marta hugged herself and shrugged. "Are you sure it was your father?"

"Who else could it have been?" I asked, exasperated by the whole thing. This place was killing me, the experience warping my mind until I couldn't tell reality from fiction.

"Alright," Wes added, grabbing my shoulder. "It's been a long couple of weeks. Let's go back to bed, and we can figure it out in the morning."

I shoved him off. "You believe me, right?"

"Of course I believe you," he said. "But there's nothing there now. I don't know what else we can do."

"We believe you." Marta rubbed her tired eyes. "Atlas, after the ritual, we can try to reach him. Maybe ask him what he meant."

I didn't like it, but like Wes said, what the fuck was I going to do about it? I still wasn't sure if I'd made the whole thing up, and I grew even more suspicious about what the hell was going on in this world.

Wes grabbed my shoulders and forced me toward the stairs, leading me up to Marta's room, where he got back in on his side with our witch in the middle. I kicked off my shoes and yanked off my shirt before shoving my jeans down to my ankles so I could step out of them, the vision of my father's pale face dancing behind my eyes.

"Don't let him go. Don't let him go. Don't let him go."

I couldn't shake the dread and unease his words had dug into my heart, and when I slipped underneath the covers, Marta grabbed my hand to intertwine her fingers with mine.

"We'll figure it out, Atlas," she murmured.

"The demon's fucking with us," I said. "We're playing right into its game."

"Then we'll deal with that, too," Wes answered. "We'll fight that fucker off just like we always have."

I tried to find relief in his reassurance, but the twisted concern on my father's face haunted me well into the night. My dreams took me to memories I'd long tried to forget: the sound of his voice screaming at me to take my brother and run, the look in his eyes just before he'd reprimanded me for doing something stupid, the disappointment in his features when my aim was off or I didn't train hard enough.

"I'm sorry, Dad," I told him, panting and heaving air from having sparred with him only to be laid out on my ass.

"Don't be sorry," he snapped. "Be better. Now do it again."

I'd put up my fists and prepare for his attack only to be pummeled by some maneuver I didn't see coming. Dad was merciless with me, but I'd come to realize that it made me stronger.

"Be better," he growled. "Do it again." He punched me. "Again." He kicked me. "Again!" Eyes swollen shut and nose bloody, I put up my fists to defend myself, but now, his eyes had gone dark, and smoke poured from his nostrils and his mouth, his skin sunken in around his skull.

"Dad?" I tried to reach out to him, but he shoved me back, pushing me to the ground before climbing on top of me, his massive weight bearing down on my chest.

"Useless fucking idiot," he screamed, the dark mist pouring out of him, sinking into my lungs, suffocating me. I tried to haul him off, but he wouldn't move. He outweighed me by at least a hundred pounds. "When will you learn, huh? When will you be the fucking son I raised?"

He grabbed my shirt and hauled my upper body off the ground, bringing me close enough to his face so the fog could seep down my throat, choking me. It tasted like ash and brimstone, and fuck, I couldn't breathe. I couldn't move. I couldn't—

"Atlas," said a soft, quiet voice. "Atlas, wake up."

I shot upright, gasping and clutching at my chest. But I wasn't in the training center with Dad. I was in a bedroom. Marta's bedroom. Wes and Marta were next to me, twin looks of concern on their faces.

It was a nightmare. Only a nightmare.

I dug my palms into my eyes and collapsed back on the bed, breathing down the adrenaline of where my mind had been only moments ago.

And then I registered what I'd seen.

Wes was on top of Marta, her legs spread, his torso covering hers, the sheet down around his thighs, revealing his ass and her thighs and...

I glanced back at them and took in the obscene display. Wes held himself up on his forearms by Marta's head, and her ankles were hooked around the small of his back while his hips slowly pistoned into her.

They're fucking.

Right here.

In bed next to me.

"What are you two doing?" I grumbled, my voice raspy and hoarse with sleep.

Marta covered her face while Wes ducked his into the space between her shoulder and neck, preparing to roll off her.

Maybe I should have let him. Maybe I should have been horrified to wake up next to the only other two people in this world, only to find them fucking *without me.*

But...that wasn't my first impulse.

"Don't stop on my account," I said, fire racing down my spine and into my balls.

Wes snapped his head up to look at me, and Marta raised her eyebrows, pursing her lips with intrigue.

My cock gave an involuntary jerk, the strange sensation of being both encased by her warmth and fulfilled by his thick length twisting in my gut.

I should have been pissed or jealous or something. I wasn't.

Instead, I reached down to grab my cock and stroked it while my brother started fucking her again. The way he moved over her and within her filled me with a deliciously sick affection, and her little moans amplified the arousal now coursing through my veins. She sank her nails into his shoulders, leaving little imprints, and he hissed into the torture of it, leaning down to trail kisses along her neck.

Fuck me, but I liked watching them. When I caught him going down on her in the supply closet, I stood transfixed by the strength in his arms as he held her down, by the beauty in her body as she moved against him. I felt that same fascination now. They were perfect together, and watching him take her, hold her, *love* her, made my heart pound against my ribcage, my nightmare long forgotten.

He pushed himself inside with long, slow thrusts, drawing it out so she squirmed under him. And she matched his pace, rocking her hips up to meet him as he bottomed out again.

"Harder," I said, my cock now painfully erect and desperate for attention.

Both sets of eyes glanced at me, Wes's with shock and surprise, Marta's with glee and mischief.

"You heard the man," Marta said, reaching down to grab his ass. "Harder."

"Yes, sir," Wes said, and *fuuucckkk*, that did something to me. He shoved against her, rocking her on the mattress, making her arch up to meet him, exposing her perfect breasts, just begging to be bitten and sucked.

I focused on both of them, memorizing the way they melted together as I stroked myself in time to match his thrusts. Wes looked up at me, meeting my gaze with heat dancing behind his. He licked his lips, and for a moment, only a fraction of a second, I imagined he was drilling into me instead. I fucked my fist, envisioning the way he'd feel behind me, the way his hands would hold my hips, the way he'd sink his teeth into my shoulder.

My pace picked up.

I broke his focus to look at Marta, who also stared at me. She watched my hand under the covers, and when she noticed I was watching, she shoved the sheet away so she could look.

I let her.

I pumped my cock as they fucked right in the bed next to me. Marta reached her climax first, her euphoria exploding out of her in a powerful wave that cascaded into me. My nerves ignited, every muscle in my body responding to the tension in hers. Wes emptied himself inside her, evidently set off by Marta, and I watched the veins in his neck protrude, the broad expanse of his abs coiling as he finished.

The weight of their combined release had me spilling endless streams of cum onto my stomach and thighs, their pleasure becoming mine, mine becoming theirs. On and on it went. I combusted into nothingness and sank back in on myself like a dying star, sucking in air, trying to stay grounded in that room with them.

When I came to, Wes had rolled off Marta and now lay on her other side. She'd scooted closer to me, pushing up on one arm to lean over my torso and drag her tongue along the mess I'd made, cleaning me up.

"Fucking hell," I said, brushing hair out of her eyes. "What a sight."

Once she'd gathered as much as she could, she grinned up at me, and I grabbed the back of her neck to bring her closer, connecting our mouths. She tasted like me and her and *Wes*, and the combination nearly had my cock getting hard again.

Patience. We've got all night.

"Not a bad way to wake up," I stammered, the sound of my racing pulse beating between my ears.

"What happens in the liminal, right?" Marta said, rolling onto her back so she could kiss Wes, too.

He hummed his approval and devoured her mouth, sticking

his tongue in between her lips like he was trying to lick my taste off her skin. And just before she pulled away, he opened his eyes to meet mine, something dangerous and wanton flickering behind them.

Almost like he knew what I'd been imagining. Almost like he'd been thinking it, too. And I didn't know if that thrilled me or terrified me...or both.

I watched Marta draw the pentagram on the library floor in white chalk while Atlas prepared the altar with candles and herbs. We'd already cleansed ourselves and dressed in ceremonial clothes, our bodies ready for the next step.

I still didn't know what the hell I was doing. Yeah, I agreed with Marta. This seemed like the only way to recreate something like the bond we had before, and once we did, we could use our combined strength to open the veil to the other side. But the longer we stayed here, the more uncontrollable my urges became.

This morning, I couldn't stop myself. I'd woken up next to her, registered the heat in my gut, and rolled on top of her before I understood the implications. Was I jealous that Atlas had gotten to fuck her before I could?

No, jealousy didn't even begin to cover it. I ached for her. I yearned for him. And meeting his gaze while I took her called to a primal part of me that I didn't fully understand.

Perhaps I never would.

Now, we'd add another layer to this already fucked-up thing between us. My body trembled with anticipation and something else…something darker and more twisted. That part screamed louder.

"Step inside the circle," Marta said.

Atlas and I did, standing side by side, our bare shoulders nearly touching. She walked the perimeter of the pentagram, pouring a thick layer of salt around us. Nine candles burned around us in a pattern of red, black, and white—three of each for us to represent blood, death, and spirit, respectively. They illuminated the dark space, making it seem more otherworldly and ethereal.

"Fire, we call you." She walked to the next point and set down a bowl of dirt she'd gathered from the coven's cemetery. "Earth, we call you." She placed a long black feather at the next angle. "Air, we call you." Finally, she put a jar of holy water on the fourth point. "Water, we call you."

At the end of the pentagram, the point at the top of the star, she added three items: a length of red ribbon, Atlas's leather pentagram bracelet, and the pentagram I always wore around my neck.

"Spirit, we call you." Then she grabbed the grimoire and turned to face us, setting it down in the center before holding out her left hand. "Remember to let it flow. Don't resist. If this is going to work, we need to be open to receiving the magic…and each other."

"Got it," Atlas said, placing his forearm over hers. I grabbed onto their combined embrace, cradling Marta's elbow in my palm. The minute that the three of us connected, the nascent tie between us burned through my nerves. I took a deep breath, steadying myself, before Marta wrapped a long length of red ribbon around us, circling it over and under until we were sealed together. Then, she did the same with a black ribbon, intertwining it with the red to make a web of deep imprints in our skin.

"Blood for breath. Flesh for flame," she started, urging both Atlas and me to join. We did, saying the rest of the spell together. "I give my body. I speak my name. Pain for promise. Skin for skin. Let no one unmake what we begin."

We continued the chant while the air coalesced around us, growing heavy and thick with energy, vibrating through our skin. Our voices echoed off the ancient tomes and watchful spirits surrounding us, as if they saw our plight and wanted to assist. We could have done this ritual anywhere, but we chose the library for this reason. It was safe, warded, and full of powerful magic she could pull from if needed.

Atlas handed Marta the knife, and I held the chalice under our tied arms, preparing myself for what would happen next. The pain didn't scare me. No, it was what came after, when the sacrifice would pull us into an altered state of consciousness, one that released any restraint we might still be carrying. Like that, I'd let them do anything to me. Like that, I'd do anything to them. And this would be even more potent because of what we'd already done.

Marta sliced down near our wrists, and I held back my wince as the tiny sting reverberated through my body. "One of flesh."

Next, she cut into the middle of our forearms. "One of shadow."

Finally, she cut near my elbow. "One of fate."

Blood welled and came together in the middle, dripping down into the goblet while Marta carved deeper to strip away a tiny bit of flesh from each of us, no bigger than a sliver, but enough to make a sacrifice. Nothing could be given without a gift. Peeling that away, she bent to place it in a bowl, where it burned atop pieces of charcoal, rue, and copal. It sizzled and sparked, but I focused on collecting our blood as the weight of the spell started to take over.

She lifted the burning incense and held it between us, first placing it under her nose to inhale the smoke. She closed her eyes and let out a small moan, like the scent had intoxicated her. When she shifted the bowl to Atlas, he did the same, his features relaxing, his muscles loosening. I understood why when it was my turn. It hit my nose with an earthy potency, and once I inhaled, a wave of euphoria went through my molecules, almost like everything inside me had woken up and fallen into a stupor at the same time.

I was drunk on it, high on the power in the combined essence of the three of us. This was worse than the first ritual. This felt weightless, like I was coasting through the heavens and plummeting into hell in a free fall.

She set the bowl down and took the goblet, where our blood had pooled nearly to the brim. Atlas's heat burned into me from the right, meeting the soft grounded energy of Marta on my left. And when she lifted the cup to her lips to take a drink, my knees nearly buckled. I felt her heartbeat in my chest. I sensed her body like an extension of my own. She handed the cup to me, and I sipped from the brim, gulping down their essence along with my own. It invigorated me, and magic pulsed through my chest and into my stomach like speed, like cocaine, like an enormous burst of adrenaline I'd ever had. I gave the cup to Atlas, who drank the rest of it. Once the blood sharing was complete, the rightness of this moment settled in my veins.

My blood sizzled like the remnants of our flesh in that cauldron. My brain short-circuited and came back online a million times faster. My libido, my yearning for them, amplified exponentially.

I stared at Marta, recognizing the same wanton stare in her eyes as reflected in Atlas's. Now it was time for the final chant. Together, we recited the words.

"Flesh to flesh. Blood to blood. Three hearts bound in shadow's flood. By water and fire, by smoke and pain. What bonds we make tonight will forever remain."

Marta raised a candle to the ribbon around our arms and settled the flame to the edge. I startled, expecting my skin to burn, but only the ribbon ignited. Fire twisted around our embrace like a fiery serpent, disintegrating into dust and magic.

Once it was over, I itched with an aching need deep in my

marrow. Dropping my arm, I glanced at Marta, then at Atlas, the silence between us deafening. I didn't know what I wanted, or... which one of them I wanted first. Marta settled that for us. She grabbed the back of my neck and pulled my face to hers, devouring my mouth with her tongue. I moaned into the contact, desperate for more, wanting to consume her, everything about her. Her lips were so soft and inviting, and she tasted like ambrosia. When she pulled away, I bit back a whine that threatened to tumble over my tongue.

But she went to Atlas next, kissing him with as much fervor and adoration as she had with me. It was beautiful to see. Their fire matched each other, their bodies built to complement his hard edges with her womanly curves. I could have sat there and watched them forever.

She pulled away and stepped back, and I knew the moment had come. This wasn't the careful dance-around-each-other we'd done at the last ritual. I'd licked and kissed his skin, sure. But somehow, that didn't feel nearly as intimate as this.

I grasped for reasons to stop. I struggled against the expectations I'd been raised to believe. He was my brother. He was my adopted father's son. He was everything I'd always wished I could be and failed miserably at becoming. I shouldn't want him like this... I shouldn't...I shouldn't...and yet, I did. At that moment, nothing else mattered. He was simply *mine.*

And I was his. The same way Marta was *ours* and we were *hers.*

I grabbed the back of his neck and pulled his mouth to mine, and we met in the middle like two suns that had finally wilted to the pull of each other's gravity. He sank into the contact, and I shoved my tongue between his lips, wrapping my arms around his neck to get him closer. His chest panted against mine, and the depth of his affection for me, *for this,* barreled through our bond, now more vigorous after the spell.

He fisted the hair on the back of my head and tugged, and I

dropped my hands to his hips, dragging them against mine, nudging my cock up against his. God, he was beautiful. Powerful. Strong. Masculine in all the ways that drew me to him.

This wouldn't be hard, not at all, and I pitied my past self, who had been nervous about doing this. I would delight in pleasing him because it pleased our witch, and it pleased me. We were tied together on a metaphysical level, our blood and flesh now one.

He broke away to bite and kiss down my jaw and over my throat, pausing at my pulse to suck, and I leaned my head back to grant him more access. My toes curled when he hit just the right spot, and a deep guttural groan poured out of my mouth as small, dainty hands went for my linen pants and shucked them to the ground.

Marta stood to my left, completely naked. She'd shed her ceremonial dress and was now working to free Atlas from his. I stepped out of my clothing and helped her with Atlas's, and once we were free from that suffocating constraint, we descended on each other.

Atlas grabbed my dick and stroked it with one hand while he laced his fingers into my hair with the other.

"Did you like fucking our witch while I watched?" he asked, pressing his forehead to mine.

I gulped and nodded. "You're both beautiful when you come."

"Good," he said, shoving me down in front of our witch. "Get her ready for me. I want an encore, and brother, you're the star."

I went willingly, dropping to my knees to stare up at Marta with big eyes, her pupils so dilated, they were nearly entirely black. She looked even better like that from my supplicant position, beautiful and given over to her lust.

"Go on, witch," Atlas said as he stepped behind me to hold me there by my shoulders.

Marta stepped closer and raised a leg, and Atlas grabbed her calf, draping it over my torso so her foot hung down to my mid-back. I spread her open and leaned in, licking a long path up her skin to her clit where I sucked her into my mouth. God, she was so fucking delicious. So drenched. So decadent. The wicked wet sin echoed in my throat, amplified by Atlas's arousal and Marta's eagerness. She sank her fingers into my hair, holding me where she wanted me, and the gentle scrape of her nails ricocheted down my neck and into my spine. Having Atlas watch added gas to the inferno boiling inside me, and the new fury we'd created made it more intense.

"*Yes, just like that,*" she said...but her lips didn't move. "*More. More.*"

"*Fuck, this is intense. I love watching them together. He's so beautiful. She's so amazing,*" Atlas's voice came next, clear as day despite his mouth being otherwise occupied. "*Fuck her harder.*"

I did. I lapped and sucked and raised a hand to push one...then two fingers inside her. The logical part of my mind wanted to take a moment to process this surprising development. We were hearing each other's thoughts, but I was too lost in Marta to focus. I wanted more. I wanted to dissolve into the present and never leave.

"*I'm almost there. Yes, yes, yes,*" Marta chanted, rocking her pelvis faster against my face, and I handled it, keeping pace with her. Her ecstasy rose in me, and Atlas's footsteps echoed as he walked to stand next to her, taking a perfect nipple into his fingers with a hard pinch. She gasped, and it pushed her over the edge. Her climax shoved out of her, into me, into Atlas, and my cock wept from want of attention. My stomach muscles clenched, and I almost spilled on the ground under me, the rage of intensity too much to handle.

When I pulled back, my chin soaked with her cum, Atlas stared down at me with a dark gaze. He leaned down to grab my throat, haul me up, and lick it off my skin, his sick delight at the combination of me and her rattling through him, straight into my chest. It was better than the oldest scotch, sweeter than honey, and he wanted more.

I glanced between him and our witch and back again as unspoken desire bled from my soul.

"Do you want something, brother?" he asked mentally, raising an eyebrow.

"Fuck me," I whimpered. *"Please."*

He chuckled softly and looked at Marta.

"What do you think, witch? Has he been good enough to be fucked?"

She grinned and tilted her head to the side, seeming to assess me. *"I suppose you should have mercy on him."*

"Mercy." Atlas tsked through his teeth and shook his head, tugging me in closer with his hand still around my throat. *"Shall I be merciful, brother?"*

I shivered, my entire body shaking under the weight of his dominance. It gave me such a rush, seeing him like this, knowing I was putty in his capable hands. I almost couldn't stand it.

"Look at you," he teased. *"Such a big, strong warrior turned into a quivering mess by the mere thought of my cock in your ass."*

I quaked harder, and my cock jerked in response. He noticed and reached out to take me, and I nearly lost it all when his warm palm wrapped around the base, sliding up to the head. Fuck, he felt good, and the warmth of his satisfaction pounded behind my chest.

"Witch," he snarled, *"on the ground. Ass up. Head down."*

She didn't normally take orders from Atlas, nor did she usually allow us to talk to her like this. But something in the air was different now. A darkness had overpowered him, overpowered all of us, snatching away any sense of decorum and propriety. This was *his* scene. We were *his* partners. His witch. His warrior. His playthings to do with as he pleased. And I was all too happy to be that for him.

This new side of him should have terrified me. It didn't. It escalated my high. It made me feel more at peace, like all I had to do was what he told me, and everything would be right in the world. It awoke something ancient and dangerous in my own mind, something that rattled against a cage with relentless, unwavering force. I slowly...delicately...unlocked the bars holding it back.

Marta dropped to the ground and lowered her upper body to the floor, reaching her arms overhead. She arched her back and spread her legs, her cunt wet with excitement, shimmering in the candelight, a blatant invitation. One Atlas seized.

"What a sight." He rubbed a hand over her ass, clenching at the fleshy muscle, and I focused on the way his fingers left indents in her delicate skin. Atlas couldn't resist. He kneeled between her legs and leaned down to sink his teeth in. She let out a squeal that turned into a moan when he rubbed her clit, adding the right amount of pleasure to the pain. When he let go, he grazed his fingers over his teeth marks, wondering if there was some kind of magic that would make them permanent.

"Brother," Atlas said as he lined his leaking cock up with her achingly blissful pussy. *"Put your cock in her mouth. If you come before I tell you, I'll make it hurt."*

I froze for a moment, this new monster growling in the back of my mind. I wanted to fuck her, yes, but I wanted him to fuck me, too. I wanted both of them, but not like this. I wanted him in my ass and my cock in her cunt. I wanted to be between them, adored by them, while I lavished affection on both of them.

He didn't have the patience for it. He grabbed Marta's hips and raised an eyebrow in my direction, demanding I listen or suffer the consequences. Somewhere inside, the old Wes scrambled for purchase, but this new version of me wanted to listen. Wanted to obey. Wanted to be good and perfect and *worthy*. And this Atlas, the one that wanted to *take*, he didn't care. I would listen, or he would *make* me listen.

"Is there a problem?"

I gulped and shook my head.

"No, no problem," I said out loud.

"Good." He nodded to the spot in front of our witch. "Do as you're told."

I did. I knelt in front of Marta while she lifted herself onto all fours and opened her lips to take me inside. Fuck, her mouth always felt like heaven. I hissed, and the shock of her warmth hit me twice as he sank deep inside her, all the way down, so her ass met his pelvis.

Fuck, she was perfect. *They* were perfect. I grabbed her hair and held her in place while I took what I wanted from her perfect lips, what I needed, sparing her no pleasantries. I thrust hard before pulling out and shoving myself inside again, just as Atlas did the same to her cunt. The intertwining pleasure, hers, his, mine, it spun around inside me, feeding the monster growing between us, fueling it until it nearly combusted. And just when she was about to hit her apex, Atlas slowed down, retreating just far enough to have her panting around my cock before surging back in again.

I didn't want it to end. I didn't want it to ever stop. And if I played my cards right, it never would. On and on, it went. Atlas brought all three of us right to the edge, her euphoria compounding on mine, mine corrupting Atlas's, his rebounding into her, an infinite cycle that blurred the lines between us. If I stopped to think about it, if I let the useless old me dwell on it, I would have noticed the danger in allowing it to burn out of control. But there was no time for that.

There was only this. Only us. Forever.

I met my brother's gaze over Marta and marveled at the beauty in his breakdown. Sweat beaded and fell down his cheeks; his eyes had gone completely dark, blacking out the white areas around his pupils, and his features twisted in agony. I wanted to come, I *needed* to come, but I was a good boy.

I would wait until I was told, even if it hurt.

"Brother, please," I whined, furrowing my eyebrows as I sank my fingers into Marta's hair. *"Please."*

"Do you think you've earned my mercy?" He was teasing me now, playing with me for the simple joy of watching me falter.

"I don't deserve your ruthlessness."

"Hmm." Atlas leaned over our witch and bit her earlobe, causing her to tremble. *"What do you think? Should I give him grace for going down on you in the closet? Should I let him have his way when he's the reason we're stuck here in the first place?"*

Somewhere in the haze of the magic and the monster, he'd let the vicious side of him turn cruel. I didn't think Atlas really blamed me for our circumstances. But now, he wanted to see me shatter. He wanted to hold me in his palm and smash me to pieces.

"Play nice, Atlas," Marta said. *"He's such a delicate thing."*

I sobbed, my chest heaving with restraint.

"Fine," Atlas said, scooting back from our witch. "Come here."

I nearly tripped over myself to comply, racing across the space between us to lower myself to the ground. I went for Marta first, but he shook his head.

"Oh, no," he said, grabbing either side of my jaw to force my face back toward him. "Lick her off me. Clean me up."

Oh, what a little slut, I was. I grabbed his cock and sucked him deep into my mouth, lapping at the underside with my tongue so forcefully, I yanked his hips forward. He laughed and sank his fingers into my hair, gripping me as he fucked my mouth.

The power in his hold turned me on. The soft velvet of his cock between my lips made my own jump with excitement. And when he hit the back of my throat to make me gag, my lower stomach clenched as tears rolled down my cheeks.

Marta rolled over onto her back and speared her fingers between her legs, soothing the ache he'd left behind. Her eyes had turned the same color as Atlas's, obsidian spiraling in their depths, hinting at the madness we'd unearthed. Atlas urged it on. He tunneled himself deep into me, but that felt amazing. It stroked my own cock as much as it massaged my tongue.

"We've wasted so much time, brother," he said. *"We could have been doing this for years."*

I moaned around him, rubbing my hands up his thighs to his stomach, scratching my nails down his torso and leaving angry welts in their wake. He loved that, too. He worked me into a frenzy, and I felt Marta play with herself, the sensation of her fingers dipping inside her cunt and rolling over her clit amping up my exhilaration as it reverberated through all three of us.

If I didn't stop...if I didn't slow down...

Atlas yanked me away with a growl and nodded to Marta.

"Our witch is lonely," he said. "Keep her company."

Desperate and decimated, I crawled over to her and stroked my cock before placing it at her entrance. In a moment too tender for what we'd been doing, I leaned over her and kissed her, lowering down to my elbows by her shoulders.

"You're so beautiful," I told her. *"Too good for me. Too good for us."*

Sliding inside her forced a sharp exhale from my lungs. She was magnificent, and I loved the contrast of my hard body against her much smaller, delicate one. Of course, that was only appearances. Marta was in fantastic shape, and she'd proven she could take either of us down with a well-timed kick and a sharp blade.

Finish this, the monster said, forcing me to fuck her faster for Atlas's enjoyment.

I heard, rather than saw, him grab the sacred oil we'd used to sanctify ourselves before the ritual, and he poured some on his hands, the scent of rosemary and coconut burrowing in my nose, nearly bringing me out of my trance. I blinked against the flicker of consciousness, the old Wes railing against his cage, telling me to slow down, to realize what was really going on, to shake Atlas out of whatever spell had taken him.

But my brother had waited long enough. He lathered the oil

over his cock and kneeled behind me, rubbing my ass while I rutted into our witch. He teased my opening with his thumbs while I moaned and slowed my thrusts, hanging my head on Marta's shoulder.

The foreign feeling should have scared me, but it didn't. I suddenly wasn't afraid at all. I wanted more. I wanted *this*

"You have no idea how it thrills me to be the first one to fuck you, brother," he said, swirling the pad of his finger around my ass until I whimpered.

"Stop stalling. Do it."

Atlas chuckled and slipped his digit inside, coaxing me open, rubbing against that uniquely euphoric spot that made me arch my back and moan. I'd never done this before, and fuck, he'd been right. I'd wasted so much time.

"There it is," he said with an audible laugh. *"Such a good boy."*

I wilted, my entire body trembling as one finger became two... and two became three. He played with me like we had all the time in the world, and I fucked Marta at the same glacial pace. She moaned and writhed under me, pushing her hips up to meet mine, one hand between us so she could furiously rub at her clit.

When he couldn't stand the separation any longer, he lined his cock up and inched inside.

The sensation was unbearable. So strange. So much pressure. So fucking right. And once the three of us were connected...fully connected by flesh...I couldn't stand it. My brother's bliss poured out of him, ricocheting into me and our witch, and hers reflected back like a mirror. We were starlight and nuclear heat and the entire cosmos condensed into one blinding moment.

Atlas leaned over me and put his hands on either side of Marta's hips, his sweaty chest sticking to my back, his hips fully pressed against my ass. It was too much, and I almost cried out...in pain or pleasure or both, I didn't know. And just when I thought I couldn't take it, Atlas moved and hit that spot inside me again, and I sobbed a groan.

"Yeah, you like, don't you, little brother?" Atlas's arrogant voice heightened my trepidation, and my deviant blood boiled. Because I did. I did like it. And I never thought I would.

Together, we fucked Marta into that library floor. He rolled his pelvis against me, shoving me farther inside Marta, and we retreated in time with each other. I pushed deeper, and he went harder, and we pulled out together.

I looked up at Marta, her features tightened with lust, her eyes long gone to her own monster, the one that lived inside us all.

"Fuck yes," Atlas growled. *"Fuck us both, little witch. He feels amazing inside you, doesn't he? It's even better inside him."*

"Fucking hell, brother," I said, leaning my head to the side so I could lick up Marta's throat, latching on to her neck with teeth and ravishing sucks.

Ever the opportunist, Atlas took advantage. He bit into my shoulder until the skin broke and the rush of his blood filled his mouth, but I didn't care. My utter delight shot out of me and into him. I wanted him to do it again. He scratched down my ribs, his nails tearing a path to my hips, and when he got there, he sat up so he could really fuck me the way he wanted, drilling his hips into me, taking me like he owned me.

And in many ways, he did. He owned me. I owned him. And our witch owned us both.

Hours, days, centuries could have passed in that sweltering room. I'd long ago lost track of time. It didn't matter. Nothing mattered. The magic we'd created had combined with the ancient energy of the books left there, and we descended into it like savages, not cognizant enough to come up for air.

I came a million times over. Atlas spilled into me until neither of us could breathe. Until we couldn't think. I fucked Marta until she lay boneless and sated under me, filling her until my cum seeped out around my cock. Then, I cleaned her up, sucking my own spend out of her body until she couldn't stand it and shoved my head away.

Then we lay in the center of the pentagram on the cold, hard floor, staring up at the ceiling with nothing left inside us. Someone let out a maniacal laugh, a sick, demented sound, and it was only when Marta and Atlas joined in that I realized it had come from me.

Oh yes, the monster was truly awake now, and he wanted more.

I sat at the breakfast table, nursing my coffee and my hangover, wondering where I'd gone wrong. The guys hadn't woken up yet, but I was thankful for the time alone to think. Memories from the night before drifted to the forefront. Atlas's voice, deep, demonic, commanding. Wes's eyes, dark and endless. The untenable rapture coursing my body, insatiable and reckless and terrifying.

I'd known flesh binding was going to be intense. I'd read stories about it before. But not like that. It should have drained me, the way the first ritual did. Instead, I was invigorated, like my skin was on fire and my blood was full of adrenaline and my nerves were firing faster than the rest of me could keep up. I could run a marathon if I needed to. I could scale entire buildings with one leap.

More than that, a flickering alarm kept blaring in the back of my mind, reminding me to pay more attention. I registered Atlas and Wes outside of me, their combined potency nearly over-whelming. The ritual had completed its intended effect, and if we kept going, it would work. I'd bet we were close enough now that I could draw on one of them if needed. But I sensed something else, too. A shadow in the bond. A lingering coldness that shouldn't be there. It flickered like a lone candle at the end of a long tunnel, barely there, almost invisible, but undoubtedly present.

What is that? Where is it coming from?

This wasn't right, and the more I ruminated on it, the more I feared Atlas might have had a point. Maybe we should have taken it slower. Perhaps I should have been more cautious. Something had been unleashed in us last night, something I should have seen coming. I thought we were prepared. I'd made sure we had every protection possible.

What am I missing?

I dug my palms into my eyes and bit back the sting of pain. I had no idea what I was doing anymore. Maybe we should stop this. Perhaps we should just accept that our lives were here now. Stuck together for eternity.

Words echoed in my mind, advice that seemed like it had been given to me centuries ago.

"The time has come when you must fight. You must forsake your rage at what isn't, and focus on what is. You must channel your anger into faith, and faith into action."

Rage into faith, and faith into action. Was it God? Was I supposed to fall to my knees and pray for help? How could I do that when I was still so angry at Him? He'd taken my parents from me and put me here, in some impossible situation.

"You will want to give up. You must not do this. You were given many gifts, mi hija. Do not let them go to waste."

What gifts? After last night, I didn't feel very gifted at all. No, I felt like a naive little girl playing with magic for the first time with no clue as to the consequences of my actions.

I thought about Tita's advice again.

"You must pray."

Would that really help? God and I hadn't had a relationship in years, but what could it hurt? I crossed my hands in front of me and bowed my head, reciting old words that hadn't fallen from my lips in over a decade.

"Our father, who art in heaven, hallowed be thy name..." I finished the prayer and waited for some kind of response, some energetic exchange to tell me it was working. But nothing came, and I shook my head as that familiar resentment settled in my stomach like cement.

Día de Muertos would start at midnight. There was no turning back now. We needed to stick to the plan: finish the soul-binding ritual, open the veil, and push while my sisters pulled. I hoped they pulled. I was banking on Tita giving them my message. And if not, if we were truly on our own, we'd go down swinging. Would it be enough? I wasn't sure. I wasn't sure of anything anymore.

"Hey," came a grumbled voice from behind me. Wes ran his hand back through his hair and limped to the cabinet with the glasses before going to the fridge to pour himself water.

"Hey." I quickly wiped away my tears. *"How are you feeling?"*

He straightened and shifted his shoulders. *"Suspiciously great. Despite the muscle aches. How about you?"*

"Okay," I said out loud. "It seems like the flesh binding is still holding up."

"Uh-huh," he agreed as he took a seat next to me, bouncing his knee under the table. "I'm not sure how I feel about you and my brother being in my head all the time."

I laughed and shook my head. "Same here."

"So...uh...about last night." Wes cleared his throat and sipped his water, shifting uncomfortably like he couldn't stay still.

"It was intense," I said. "But nothing we can't handle."

"Right," he said. "Do you feel any different?"

Like I could run from here to the moon and back? Like unsure about what to do next, combined with debilitating insecurity different?

"Exactly," he said. I froze for a moment before I remembered Wes was inside my head. I was inside his. He'd heard my thoughts.

Wes licked his lips, and my focus dropped to the movement. I remembered that tongue doing wicked things to my skin, making me ache and plead and beg for more. "What do you mean you're unsure about what to do next?"

"I don't think we did it right," I said. "I mean, we're hearing each other's thoughts and the energy in my veins... It's intoxicating. I think I could maybe draw from one of you now, and that must mean we're getting closer to the warrior bond. But...I sense something else. Something sinister. Something we shouldn't have messed with."

Wes swallowed and glanced down, avoiding my gaze. "Something sinister. Do you know what it is?"

"No. I just...I think Atlas might have been right," I said. "I'm not sure we should—"

"Right about what?" Atlas said, suddenly walking into the kitchen to take his spot across from me. He stretched his arms over his head and yawned before grabbing the carafe of coffee between us to pour himself a mug.

"How are you feeling about last night?" I asked, pretending not to notice the apparent tension between them. Wes wouldn't look at him, and Atlas had barely glanced at his brother.

"Fine," Atlas said. "Great. Spectacular."

"No lingering side effects?" I raised my eyebrows, surprised that he hadn't had the same terrifying release as Wes and me.

Atlas straightened and finally looked at his brother. "What? What am I missing?"

"Something's wrong," I added. "There's something we missed. It's like..." I struggled to put it into words. It twisted in my gut like food poisoning, like I might heave and wretch and still not purge it.

Wes tilted his head to one side, cracking his neck before doing the same on the other.

"What happens in the liminal stays in the liminal, right?" Atlas raised his eyebrows. "We said we wouldn't make more of it than it needed to be, and honestly, you both were fucking hot. I've never come so hard in my life."

Heat rushed into my cheeks, and I tried to hide my smile. I could say the same thing, but that wasn't what I was talking about. Atlas was almost unhinged last night, drunk with dominance and magic. And Wes had begged his brother to fuck him like his literal life depended on it.

"Then what did you mean?" Atlas asked.

"I don't know," I said. "There's something else there. Another presence, maybe."

It wanted, it clawed, and it wriggled around in my soul like a maggot in a vat of rotten meat.

"Another presence? That sounds ominous," he said. "Are you saying you fucked up the spell you didn't know anything about in the first place?"

"Oh, fuck off, Atlas." I groaned. "I'm tired, and fighting about it isn't going to get us anywhere."

He scoffed and rolled his eyes, but dropped the issue.

"I've never felt like that before in a ritual," I said. "You might have been right about holding off for a bit. Maybe we should—"

"I'm sorry, what?" Atlas barked, shifting his glare to his brother. "We get this far, we swap blood and flesh and cum, and *now* you want to hold off?"

Deafening silence fell between us. I didn't have a response to his outburst. I didn't know what to say.

"We're running out of time. You said so yourself. Día de Muertos starts tonight," Atlas snarled. "It's too late to turn back."

"Atlas," Wes cut in.

"I want to get out of here," Atlas snapped. "I don't care what the fuck we awakened in that damned library. You convinced me this was what we had to do, so we're doing it."

He was panting by the time he was done, and his frustration echoed straight down the bond into my soul. But there was more to it, a fury he might not have even been aware of. Whatever strange presence I felt, it was in him, too. It was in all of us.

"What's next?" Atlas rubbed a hand over his face and back into his hair.

I sighed. "The soul binding. Tonight. I'm still not sure how we'll react to it." I glanced at the table between us. "But we're out of time. If we plan to do this when the veil is thinnest, that's at midnight."

"Are we ready?" Wes bounced his knee under the table harder, twitching and blinking, biting his fingernails. Had he always done that? I was about to ask him what was wrong, but I never got it out.

A loud blast burst my eardrums, and the windows shattered, shooting glass fragments across the room. I ducked and curled my hands over my head to protect myself, and when I glanced up again, dark obsidian swirls spiraled in thick, angry clouds outside. They beat against the side of the estate, thundering for entry, wailing on the wards.

"Fuck, we have to move." Atlas stood and rushed around the table, grabbing Wes's hand before latching onto mine to drag us into the hallway. We raced past the library into the parlor, coming to an abrupt stop when we realized the magic surrounding us had faltered.

Wisps of smoke poured in from the broken windows as the energy that was supposed to protect the house splintered. It cracked as the cloud invaded it, sizzling and electrifying, sending terror through my bloodstream.

I could fight it. I was amped up on adrenaline from our bond, but my tools were upstairs in my room. I hadn't been as diligent about keeping them on me since we'd been stuck here. We hadn't had any reason to.

"Wes, go get my tools. My satchel and the holy water."

He turned and raced upstairs without argument, leaving Atlas and me to fight off the monster. I didn't know how much good that would do, seeing as it was bigger than any demon I'd ever had to fight. And if it had gotten through the wards at the estate, it was more powerful, too. Fighting back the urge to run, I stood firm and held up my hand, pulling on the remaining energy from the grounds, sucking it up through my feet and into my chest.

"I expel you, demon," I said. "By the ancestors and the great will of my coven, be gone from my sight. You are not welcome here."

Deep, horrifying laughter echoed from all around us, seeming to come from everywhere and nowhere.

"You cannot exorcise me here, witch," it said. "This is *my* realm. You made it for me."

I took a step back and grabbed Atlas's hand as his vitality coursed through my veins. It was weak, nowhere near as strong as it was before we lost our bond, but it *was* undeniably there.

"*Take it,*" Atlas said. "*Use it.*"

I yanked on the tiny sliver of thread tying us together and drew as much of him into me as I could, reciprocating that energy with my own. Then, I chanted in Latin. I said the right words and I channeled the right energy, but the demon only seemed to grow in size. It towered over us, pitch-black mist swirling around us, its beady red eyes glaring down at me.

My spell did nothing. The demon laughed harder.

"I have enjoyed your attempts to defeat fate," it snarled. "Your magic is exhilarating."

I ignored its goading and kept going, kept focusing on my connection to Atlas, on the small trickle of magic I could pull from him, sending it out of my hand in a bright white light. But I was waning fast, and without my tools, I couldn't hold it off much longer.

"*Wes!*" I reached out to him mentally, sensing his approaching presence. He was coming back, descending the stairs, storming toward us. He shoved the leather satchel in my hands, and I reached inside to get my holy water, but the distraction cost us.

The demon pulled on the ancient magic in the earth, tugging it from me as quickly as I could gather it. It fed its maelstrom, which grew to cover the entire lower level as it broke apart the walls and swirled furniture over our heads.

Wes handed Atlas his gun, and the two of them fired salt-loaded bullets into the fray. But it did nothing except piss the demon off more.

I realized three things in a matter of seconds. One: Holy water wasn't going to cut it. Nothing I could do would defeat this magnitude of chaos. Two: The estate was finished. If it had consumed the wards and the ancestral magic, it would have pulled this place down with us in it. And three: We couldn't stay here. We had to flee. We had to get to safety. But in the liminal, I didn't know where that could be.

"Marta!" Atlas screamed in my mind, backing up so he stood at my left while he fired into the tornado of evil. *"Do something."*

"We need to leave," I said.

They didn't wait to argue. The ceiling ripped apart, wood and cement crumbling around us as we took off through the front door. My heart pounded as my feet raced toward Leander's truck. I hopped in the passenger seat while Atlas climbed in the driver's and Wes took the back. He brought the vehicle to life just as the roof collapsed on the century-old building and, as we sped down the driveway, I watched my second home, my sanctuary, crumble into dust and ashes.

CHAPTER 22

Atlas

The spiraling mass of demon smoke followed us down the road, decimating trees and buildings and anything else it came into contact with. I tried to keep the truck steady, but the constant bombardment and loud explosions had me swerving to avoid massive pieces of debris. Marta grabbed my gun and stuck half her body out of the window to try firing at it, but that only agitated it more.

"Where are we going?" I shouted. "Is there any place safe?"

"I don't know," she said, sinking back into the truck. She rubbed a hand over her face and furrowed her brow as her mind raced. *Maybe a church? Maybe Tita's house? But if it got through the wards at the estate, it could get through anything. Where? Where? Where?*

"Wes?" I asked, glancing in the rearview mirror, but Wes only shook his head and bit his lip, bouncing his leg nervously on the ground. His decision paralysis shimmied down the bond, and I slammed my hand on the steering wheel.

"Fuck!" I shouted, but then reminded myself to stay calm. Getting pissed off while we were running away from a monster wouldn't help anyone.

"Saint Michael's Catholic Church is five miles away," Marta said. "I have no idea if it will work, but Michael is the great protector. We might be able to lose the son of a bitch and get some rest."

I didn't have any better ideas, so I turned right onto the road leading to the church and slammed my foot on the brake when we got there, skidding into park right at the entrance. We jumped out and raced toward the front door with the demon hot on our heels, wrecking the trees and buildings on either side of us. Marta and Wes were in front of me, taking the steps two at a time while I shot salt at the monster. Just as I was about to step into the sanctuary of hallowed ground, something ripped the ground out from under me.

Dark smoke wrapped around my ankles, slamming me down on my back. All the air rushed out of my lungs, and I banged my head on the cement steps as the demon lifted me into the air. The world faded out, and for a heartbreaking moment, I thought this was it.

This is how I die.

Funny, I'd always thought it would be some bloodsucking monster or rabid shifter that would take me out. But no. My soul would be an appetizer for Hell's most fucked-up reject. All the shit I'd done. All the cruel ways fate had screwed with me. And this was it. What a way to go.

My dad's mysterious words came back to me.

Don't let him go.

Could this be what he meant? Was it the demon I wasn't supposed to let go of? If my dying meant they were saved, I wouldn't fight it. As long as they were safe.

"Atlas!" Marta screamed inside my head.

"Go! Get to safety!" I tried to tell her, but my consciousness was giving out on me, and the thick swell of red liquid burned my eyes. Blood. I must have banged myself up pretty good if the shit was getting all over the place.

I fought as much as I could, struggling against the beast's hold, but the more I moved, the tighter its vise grew around me. I tried to aim my pistol in its direction, but I couldn't move my body around to the right angle. The evil energy radiated from the demon into my skin, permeating my blood, soaking down to my marrow. My body boiled from the inside out, like every atom, every microparticle, had been set on fire. I was an inferno, ready to implode.

Heart pounding and blood rushing to my head, I almost gave up. Marta and Wes were safe in the church and—

Loud gunshots rang out, the zing of bullets buzzing by my ears. Marta stood on my left, her hands in the air, bright white light emanating from her palms. Wes was on the other side, raining lead and salt down on the demon until it was forced to retreat. The grip on my ankles loosened, and I dropped six feet, landing hard on my back.

I couldn't breathe. I couldn't think. I couldn't move. But Wes put his arms under my shoulders and lifted me, practically dragging me into the church. Once we were inside, I collapsed on the floor, gasping for oxygen and holding my insides together.

"Atlas." Marta scrambled to kneel next to me. "Are you okay? Let me see."

"Is it working?" I wheezed, rolling onto my side to look around at the rows of pews, culminating in the enormous crucifix at the head of the altar. "Are we safe?"

"I don't know," Marta said, wrapping her arm under my back to help me sit up. "I think so."

"It's keeping him out." Wes glanced up at the stained glass above the organ pipes, where the smoke hit the wall and cascaded up the building and over the roof. It covered the rest of the windows and spread out until it blocked the sun, effectively trapping us inside.

"But we're stuck," Marta added. She prodded at the wound on the back of my head, but that felt like a paper cut compared to the burn in my veins. I wanted to tear my clothes off. I wanted to flay my skin from my muscles. I could barely stand her touch.

"What happened to you?" Wes squatted down so he could get on my level, but I still couldn't focus. Their bodies danced in front of me, morphing into two and then three of them before combining into one again.

"It's inside me," I sputtered. The words tasted like venom, and my throat ached to say them.

"What?" Marta hissed.

"It's...inside me. I'm burning. I'm...I'm dying." I scratched at my neck, tearing my shirt away to get at my skin.

"Stop it," Marta said as Wes grabbed my arms to hold me still. "Stop. It's not inside you. It's outside. You're safe."

Trembling and sobbing, I tried to catch my breath, but every movement hurt. I thought I'd never feel good again.

"Hey, hey, hey," Marta said, bringing her brown eyes level with mine, cupping my jaw the same way I'd done to her at Tita's house. "Breathe with me."

I focused on her inhales, sucking air in even though it sliced open my lungs, and I pushed it out when he did, shaking with the force of the exertion.

"Good," she said. "Again."

Together, we breathed down the adrenaline and the lasting demonic effects ringing in my blood. And once the pain started to fade, I relaxed against Marta's body.

"Fuck," I said and lifted my arms to rub over my face. I was covered in scrapes, bruises, and blood. My ankles were the worst of it. Deep searing welts wrapped around my legs just above my socks, blistered and furious. I wasn't even sure I could walk.

"You'll be okay," Marta said. "I've got some herbs and my magic and..." Her voice cracked as she tried, and failed, to hold it together. "You're gonna be okay."

"Don't fret over me, little witch," I managed to string together even though my teeth were chattering. "You still hate me, remember?"

She laughed and pressed a kiss to my temple. "Yeah. That's right."

"Good," I said, patting her arm. "Good. All's right in the world."

Wes walked around the sanctuary, his footsteps echoing off the tall ceilings like war hammers. "How long do you think it can hold out?"

Marta brushed the tears off her cheeks and kissed me one last time before standing. "Certainly longer than we can. We'll have to raid the kitchens and pray something was left here the day we created the liminal."

"And the ritual?" Wes asked. "Día de Muertos?"

Marta took a deep breath and sighed. "I don't know, Wes. We don't have the book or my tools or—"

"We have to keep going," I muttered, trying to push myself up to a seated position. "We didn't come this far only to get this far."

"I don't have the ritual memorized," she said. "Without it, I could—"

"Witches have been coming up with rituals on their own for centuries." My head twinged and my muscles protested the movement, but I still got myself upright enough to lean against the side of the closest pew. "You'll think of something."

She snorted. "You put too much faith in me."

"Well, better late than never," I said, trying to wink. Unfortunately, I was sure I did it with both eyes, not just one.

"We'll stay here," Wes said with a firm nod. "Maybe we can wait him out. If not, we'll do the ritual tomorrow at midnight."

Marta's features dropped, and her quiet unease slithered into my chest. She didn't think she could do it. She didn't think she had the magical capability to come up with it on her own. Truth be said, Constance wasn't much to put faith in to begin with. Why should we care what some ancient old bitch from the 1500s had to say? We had five hundred years of knowledge and experience over her, and Marta was the most powerful witch I'd ever met. If someone was going to get us out of this, if someone could figure it out, it was her.

Either that, or we'd die here. We'd get eaten by that fucking demon or worse, and at this point, I just wanted it to be over. One way or the other.

"Hopefully, we can cross over without him following us. If he does…" Marta trailed off and ran her hands back through her hair.

"If he does, we'll have the full coven on the other side," I added, clutching at my ribs. I was pretty sure one of them was broken. That fucker had dropped me hard.

"I'll go check for food," Wes said with a nod toward me. "Will you do your thing?"

"Right," Marta said, tapping my boot with her shoe. "Let me see that."

She kneeled by my side and tugged my hand away, probing the area with her pointy fingers. It felt like she'd stuck a lance straight through me. I arched off the ground, and she gasped, clearly sensing the sensation in her own body.

"Fuck!" I shouted.

"Don't be such a baby," she said. "It's not that bad. Let me just…" She held her hand up and chanted under her breath, that glowing light pooling in her palms before radiating over me. I sighed as it dissolved into my skin, replacing the tenderness with warmth and comfort and…*snap!* The bone bounced back into place, and I grit my teeth at the sharp agony that ricocheted down my spine and the back of my legs.

"Aww, shit." It was still tender, but when she pulled her hand away, I could finally take a deep breath.

"Now the one on your head." She grabbed my crown and pulled my head down to assess the damage. "Yikes."

"Is it bad?" It felt like my skull had been split in two.

"Look at that! You're as hard-headed as I thought," she said with a snicker.

"Hah-hah." I rolled my eyes. "Very funny."

"You'll survive," she said before placing her hand over the wound and chanting in that same hypnotic rhythm. That, too, stitched itself back together, and suddenly, the roaring pain dulled to a minor throb. "There. Let me see the ones on your ankles."

"No," I said, grabbing her hands to stop her. "You've done enough. Don't exert any more magic. You'll need it to get us out of here."

She glanced at me with her shimmering eyes, so intelligent and mesmerizing. It was difficult to remember a time when I didn't like her, couldn't stand to be around her. Ages had passed since then, even if it was only technically two months. It felt like centuries. We had lived entire lifetimes here in the liminal together.

"Sit with me," I said. "Talk to me."

The glass windows tinkled as the demon pressed in on them, trying to get through, trying to break through the impenetrable force of this holy ground. I ignored it because if I focused too much on it, I'd remember the way it felt with that demon's tentacles wrapped around my legs, and I'd start panicking again.

"About what?" She sat next to me and spread her legs out parallel to mine.

"Anything." I leaned my head on her shoulder, relishing the scent of her cherry soap and her sweat and the soft way her hair brushed against mine. "Everything. What are you going to do when we get out of here?"

She took a deep breath. "Eat a nice juicy steak without it being covered in barbecue sauce."

I scoffed. "You love my cooking."

Marta's torso vibrated as she laughed. "I don't know. Probably never deal with another demon again."

"Oh, come on now," I said, trying to be light-hearted. "This is a once in a million years event. How many demons have the Harlots sent to liminals? They've all gone fine before."

"I think two months stuck in one is enough to make me never want anything else to do with it."

I snorted, but then the silence fell on us, and the soft noises from the demon outside started to grate on my nerves like knives scraping on porcelain plates.

"Thank you," I said, lifting my head so I could meet her eyes.

She furrowed her brows, her confusion seeping into my bones. "For what?"

"For healing me. For putting up with me. For...all of this. We're stronger now because of what you've done." I took her hand and interlaced our fingers, bringing it to my lips so I could kiss her knuckles. I didn't know if it was the blood loss, the concussion, or the brush with death that turned me into a big giant sap, but I felt like if I didn't tell her now, I never would. "I think I'm in love with you, Marta. These two months have been...fucking hell. And I'm sure there's probably about a million other people you would have rather been stuck here with, but I wouldn't have changed anything."

She stared at me with wide eyes, her mouth open, the sharp slice of her shock combining with the warmth of affection and adoration in our tether.

"Don't talk like that," she said, squeezing my hand. "We're getting out of here."

"No, I know," I said. "I just wanted you to know. I thought my brother was the only person in the world I'd ever care about. And now...Now, I can't imagine life without you in it."

"Atlas—"

"I'm serious," I said. "When we get home, when this is all over, I don't want to forget what I felt while I was here. We said what happens in the liminal stays in the liminal, but I don't know if I can commit to that."

She blinked, and tears streamed down her cheeks. I reached up with my free hand to wipe them away, and for the first time since we were stuck here, I leaned in to kiss her without the weight of magic or ritual or demonic influence bearing down on us. It was real, and it was me and her, and *God,* her lips were so soft. It was more than just attraction between us, and maybe it was the impending resolution wearing me down, but I meant everything I said.

Marta was endlessly selfless and brilliant and gorgeous. She was powerful; she'd put me on my ass more than once. When it came to her, I realized there was nothing I wouldn't do to keep her safe, to keep both of them safe.

"Atlas," she whispered when we broke apart. "I don't know how I would have gotten through this without you...without you both."

The sudden silence between us deafened me, and I realized it was quiet, truly quiet, for the first time since we got stuck here. I glanced up at the windows, at the bright sunshine shimmering in through the stained glass, painting the walls in rainbows of vibrant blues and reds.

She followed my line of sight, sickening alarm blasting through both of us.

"Where's the demon?" she whispered.

"Where's Wes?"

Marta shot to her feet. "Wes!"

I loved them both.

I knew that deep in my bones.

And the monster had been clawing at my insides since last night, since I'd unlatched his cage and let him have free roam of my body. He'd seen Marta and Atlas, he'd tasted their blood and flesh, and he wanted more.

"Come to me," he chanted, tearing at my mental barriers with his inky claws. All night and all morning, it had called to me. *"Come to me, and I won't kill them. Deny me, and I'll paint the entire world with their blood."*

At first, I thought I'd been imagining it. We'd been here two months, and I was only now starting to hear voices. But after it attacked the estate, I realized I was the problem. Whatever I'd done during the ritual, whatever I'd allowed to be done *to me*, it had given the demon free rein to invade our wards. It used my energy against us, used my blood against us, and it would keep coming after us until I gave in.

I was the weak link. Maybe I always was. I'd been the one to cause all of this. I was the one who got hurt, who'd been dreaming about the demon pouring out of my mouth and nose.

"I'm already inside you," it said. *"You have no choice. This is your only choice. Come to me, and I'll leave them alone. Let me have you, only you, and I'll let them leave this place."*

I had learned early in life that demons lie. They twist the truth and torment the soul until the human feels like they have no choice but to comply. This happened in Biltmore Forest. This happened all over the world all the time. But I was just so tired of being here, and we were so close to home.

"Come to me, or I'll tear this liminal apart with you in it."

I made sure Marta and Atlas were safe. I got them in the church where the demon couldn't go, and as soon as I could, I got away to get some clarity.

We were reading each other's thoughts now. The flesh-binding ritual had made that permanent, so I didn't understand how they couldn't hear the monster in my mind. But I suspected Marta felt it. That shadow. That darkness she'd sensed this morning. It was me.

I told myself this was the only way to keep them safe. I told myself that I would just let it have me, that they could complete the soul binding, use each other's magic to contact the other side, and slip through the veil at midnight. I told myself they wouldn't miss me, that once they realized what was happening, it would be too late, and they wouldn't be able to stop it.

But as I held my hand on the latch to open the door, I paused, listening to the sounds of Atlas's deep timber.

"I just wanted you to know. I thought my brother was the only person in the world I'd ever care about. And now...Now, I can't imagine life without you in it."

I sensed his deep, abiding affection for her, his love and adoration pouring out of him. And as much as it surprised her, she returned it. Somewhere along the line, her heart had started to beat for him.

I should have been jealous. But like everything in the liminal, that seemed too pedantic to put into words. I ached for Marta, and I yearned for Atlas, and I always would.

"Atlas, I don't know how I would have gotten through this without you...without you both."

She almost stopped me. She almost made me turn back. But the demon wouldn't stop coming for us unless I did this.

This is the best way I can protect them.

I turned the latch as quietly as I could and stepped outside, right into the dark spiraling cloud of evil.

"Alright," I said, closing my eyes. "Take me."

I thought it would hurt more. I thought I would burn and bristle and set me on fire from the inside out, the way it had to Atlas when he'd merely been touched. But no.

A cool gasp of air flowed down my throat and into my lungs, and then I was back in the woods from my nightmare, standing in the salt circle with candles licking flames all around me. The cricket and frogs sang their nighttime chorus, just as they had the night we'd come here, just as they had in every nightmare since.

"Wesson Colt," came the soft, feminine voice. "At long last."

"You wanted me, you've got me," I said, glancing around to see who, or what, I was talking to.

A tall woman wearing a white dress stepped around a tree, her bare feet blackened with soot and undergrowth. Her long blond hair fell in messy waves down to her waist, but her silver eyes cut through me, almost glittering with intensity.

"You've answered my summons," she said, slowly walking around the circle, glancing from my face to my boots and back up again. "Are you willing to pay the price?"

"I want a deal," I said. "That's what your kind does, isn't it? Making deals and condemning souls?"

She laughed, and the sound reminded me of shattering glass, high-pitched, nearly manic.

"What did you have in mind?" She raised an eyebrow and circled the perimeter.

"You want me, you can have me. But you let Atlas and Marta go. You let them leave the liminal. You let them get on with their lives. You and me, we stay here."

At that, she tilted her head to assess me, staying quiet for far too long as she considered. The silence made me itch, made me want to keep talking if only to fill the desolate void.

"You'll give me your body?" She licked her lips, almost too hungry at the prospect.

"If that's what you want. You want to possess me? You want to live inside this skin?"

"Perhaps. It has been a *long* time since I've been invited inside mortal flesh." She hummed. "And what will we do, you and I? We're stuck in this cage. If I possess you, what then? What *fun* can be had when we're one body, one soul, one mind, but we're all alone here?"

I took a deep breath as repulsive images flooded my mind, ones where she chained me down and stripped the skin from my bones, or practiced pulling my insides out until I screamed. Then she'd heal me only to do it all over again. And again. And again. On and on for eternity.

"If you let Marta and Atlas go, if you stop attacking them, if you let them leave, I'll do it." It was the sacrifice I had to make for them. It was the only way to make sure the demon left them alone. I'd do far worse for that.

"So noble," she said. "So heroic. Who knew you had it in you?"

I didn't answer, but it didn't seem like she wanted one from me anyway.

"And why should I take you instead of the witch or your brother? Hmm?" She clasped her hands in front of her. "Either would be a better pick. The witch is strong, and your brother..." She shook her head. "Well, we've been having so much fun with his father where I'm from. Adding him to my collection would be quite extraordinary."

I winced at the thought of my father...*Atlas's* father...in hell or wherever she was talking about. Was he being tortured for all of eternity? Was I bound to end up like him, no matter what?

"I've already got a demon inside me, right?" I said. "The monster. The one who carved up my chest like a Christmas ham the night we got stuck in the liminal. It's *in* me, isn't it? We woke it up when we did the flesh-binding ritual."

She smiled, but it wasn't happy or jovial. It was creepy, like a villain in a horror movie, like other monsters I'd killed when they thought they had the upper hand.

"Yes, it's in you," she said, and it seemed like there was more to the story, more she wouldn't tell me. "No tricks? You don't happen to have an anti-possession charm on you or some protective enchantment that will cast me out as soon as I take root?"

"I wouldn't be here if I did," I said.

"Good." She held out her hand. "I accept your deal."

I swallowed and stared at the outstretched palm, wondering again if I was making the right call. If I didn't do this, we would die in that church. The demon wouldn't leave us alone until it had us, and after last night, I feared another binding ritual would make this monster indestructible.

This is the only way. This is it.

I took her hand and gave it a firm shake before brushing some of the salt away from the circle so she could step inside.

"Tsk, tsk, tsk," she said. "Wesson Colt, I am disappointed in you."

My heart sank before I could regain my courage.

"Didn't your father ever teach you to figure out who you're dealing with before you agree to terms?" She flashed that evil grin again and shook her head.

"I know who you are," I said. "You're an Asmodeian. You're the one who terrorized Asheville and made all those people consume each other."

At that, she laughed and yanked me closer so she could fist a handful of hair behind my head. "No, my darling. I *am* Asmodeus. And together, we're going to raise hell."

I didn't find him in the kitchen or the rectory. He wasn't in the basement or community rooms. My heart pounded with anxious dread, the connection to him now rattling with a sickening urgency. Something was wrong, very wrong. Echoes from the shadow we'd awakened last night reverberated through me, and I was too cynical to believe it wasn't nefarious.

No, I had my suspicions about what it was and what it wanted, and when I rounded the corner toward the priest's rooms, the side door was open wide. This did not make me feel any better.

"Wes?" I held my gun up higher, expecting the demon to jump out of the bushes and attack me.

Instead, the tall, muscular form of my warrior stepped out from behind a giant oak tree, his eyes completely black, his precious lips twisted into an evil sneer, his usually tanned complexion ashen. Despite this, he oozed power and dominance, more than I'd ever seen from him.

"Wes." I took a step toward him. "What happened? What are you—"

"Wes isn't home, *sweet girl*," he snarled. The words came out deep and baritone, almost mechanical in their intensity. "He gave me this little meat suit in exchange for your life. Yours and that imbecile inside."

I choked on a sob, barely able to believe it. Why would he do that? Why wouldn't he come to us? We were so close, we were nearly there. He believed in me. He believed in this. What did he do?

I nearly let myself sink into the recklessness of it, the utter despair of having lost him, but just before those stupid emotions gripped my heart, I yanked myself back to reality.

No.

I wouldn't accept this. I wouldn't allow this. He was coming home with me, with *us,* no matter what fucking deal he made with a demon.

As smoke, they were omnipotent. They could be everywhere and nowhere. They could invade the tiniest cracks in a ward, just as this bastard had done at the estate. But once they took a mortal, once they became corporeal, they were easier to trap. More powerful, of course. They could siphon the energy from the mortal, drain that person's soul dry, which was why so many of them longed to possess a person. As Wes, the demon could eat and fuck and experience the utter joy of killing, instead of simply influencing. But as Wes, I could contain him.

I aimed my gun at the demon's head, but he shook his head and tsked his teeth. "Don't do that, little witch. Could you really watch Wesson's brains paint the woods? There's no undoing that damage, not even after I'm done playing with him."

"Just like a demon," I said. "Making a deal you had no intention of keeping. Is he even still in there?"

"Oh, I very much intend on keeping my side of the bargain," he said. "After all, it's *your* God that demands blind faith with no promise of rewards. My side always does what it says it's going to do."

Demons lie, I reminded myself. *He's lying. Don't listen to him.*

"However, just because I said I would let you go doesn't mean I won't have a little fun first."

He'd barely gotten the words out before he flicked his hand at me, and I flew sideways, smashing into the side of the church. The impact made me lose my gun and knocked the air out of my body, crushing my lungs, collapsing my stomach. I grunted and forced myself upright, reaching for my satchel. But the demon used its magic to hold my hands out to either side, pinning them in place so I couldn't grab my tools.

"Demon of hell," I chanted in Latin. *"I condemn you. By the magic in my veins, by the power in my blood—"*

He tilted his head, and my mouth sealed shut, my lips glued together. Fury raged in my gut, the anger of two months of isolation and generations of pissed-off witches exploding from my torso in a blinding white light. It knocked Wes backward, but I got off the wall, and my mouth finally opened. I held my hands up to project energy toward him, keeping it as steady as I could.

Wes easily got to his feet and mirrored my movement, holding his hands up as that dark smoke erupted from his palms, colliding with my force. They smacked together like a lightning strike, deafening, shattering the surrounding trees. I quickly realized that I wouldn't be able to hold him off for very long. Wes still had his connection to Atlas and me, and he pulled on it, draining me, tugging on my magic and the vibrance coming from my other warrior.

I tried my chant again.

"Demon of hell, I condemn you. By the magic in my veins, by the power in my blood, I demand you vacate the mortal called Wesson Colt." I wrenched the words from my lips, sputtering the syllables with every ounce of power I had left.

He twitched his head and cracked his neck, but only retaliated harder. The metallic taste of copper trickled over my lips, and I didn't know if that was because my nose was bleeding from the exertion or if I'd cut my head when it launched me at the church.

"Give up, witch," he roared. "It's done. It's over. I have you now."

"No!" I screamed, yanking on Atlas's energy, sensing him closer. And just when I thought I didn't have anything else to give, just when I was scraping at the bottom of the barrel for strength, a flash of silver somersaulted through the air, smashing into the demon.

Wes's head flipped back. The black smoke dissipated. And then his body lay limp on the ground.

I glanced at the church, where Atlas slumped up against the doorway, panting in deep breaths. I limped over to Wes and knelt by his body, where a giant silver crucifix lay next to his prone form. Obsidian blood oozed from the wound on his forehead, but he'd been effectively knocked out.

"Fucking hell," I said, pushing to my feet. "Incredible aim."

Atlas nodded and lumbered down to the grass. "Is he out?"

"Yeah, but we don't have much time," I said. "He's possessed. He made a deal with the demon, our safe exit in exchange for him."

"Stupid martyr son of...Help me get his legs."

I grabbed one ankle, and Atlas did his best with the other. Together, we hauled 220 pounds of Wes into the church. We dragged him up to the head of the sanctuary and laid him at the bottom of the giant representation of Jesus on the cross.

"We need to draw a demon trap," I said. "Quickly."

Atlas glanced around for something to use, and I ran into the back room, ransacking the father's office until I found a thick black marker. When I came out, Atlas was digging through the pews.

"Here." I ripped off the cap with my teeth and handed it to him. "You draw it out. I'll get the salt and the candles."

He dropped to his knees and started etching the ancient symbol on the crimson rug, and I winced when I thought about desecrating the church's furniture, but nothing was real in the liminal, right? The real church in the real world was carrying on with its real life, and nothing we did really mattered.

Then I raced around the building to gather the things I'd need. Holy water and blessed wine were easy to find, as were a plethora of incense made explicitly for this purpose. I grabbed rope and a knife and anything else I thought we could use. I returned less than ten minutes later, where Atlas had finished the sigil and was now trying to drag Wes into the center of it. His ribs were still bruised, and his ankles looked like minced meat, but he managed well on his own. I grabbed one of Wes's legs and tugged.

Once he was inside, I doused the rope in holy water and handed it to Atlas so he could tie Wes's hands together. We did the same with his feet.

It must have burned the demon inside him because he groaned and blinked his eyes, turning his head from one side to the other as he came back to consciousness.

"Shit." Hands shaking and legs wobbling, I sprinkled holy water around the circle and chanted protective spells.

"Atlas?" Wes asked, glancing around. "Marta?"

I paused and looked down at him. His eyes were back to normal, and the color had returned to his face. I wanted to believe it was him. I wanted to stop all of this nonsense, and just when I took a step toward him, Atlas grabbed my arm to stop me.

"Don't," he whispered inside my mind.

"What are you doing?" Wes asked, shaking his hands, trying to get free. "Let me out."

"Shut up," Atlas snapped, setting up the candles in equal inter-vals around the circle. "You're a fucking idiot, you know that?"

"What?" Wes glanced at me. "Marta, what is this? I'm okay. I'm me now."

My heart clenched with how much I wanted that to be true, but I knew better.

Demons lie.

This was a trick. There was no way a measly battle and a

crucifix to the head had punched the demon from Wes's body. It would take nearly an act of God, and we didn't have time to wait around for a miracle.

My fingers shook as I tried to strike the match to light the first candle, and I nearly dropped it.

"Fuck," I whispered, trying again. This time, it fired up, and I held it to the wick. But the damned thing refused to light. I tried to ignore the magical implications of that and held it until the flame nearly burned down to my fingers.

"Marta, don't be ridiculous," Wes said, struggling harder with the ropes. "You don't need to do this. Let me out, and we'll do the soul-binding ritual so we can get out of here."

"Listen to me, demon," Atlas said, green eyes blazing as he turned to Wes. "When I get you out of my brother, I'm going to find a way to kill you. Permanently. No going back to hell. Do not pass go. Do not collect two hundred dollars. No more liminals. No more pocket realities. I'm going to stab you in the fucking face and watch you burst into flames."

Wes paused for a moment, his jaw opening as the weight of Atlas's promise landed between them.

"You hear me?" Atlas prodded as he took a step forward and raised an eyebrow. "I promise you this, and I'm a man of my fucking word."

At that, Wes's eyes bled to black again, and he threw his head back to laugh. It wasn't his normal jovial burst of happiness. No, this was chilling and insidious, making my stomach churn with panic.

"Is that what you think, you puny, insignificant warrior? And how do you plan to do that?" His voice dropped four octaves, reminding me of a monster out of a horror movie. Hell, we were in one, weren't we? "Now that I'm riding your brother, you can't kill me without killing him."

I met Atlas's gaze, where he remained as resolute as I'd ever seen him. I tried to swallow my anxiety and ignore the vitriol spewing from the beast. It didn't matter what it said. We didn't come this far only to get this far. We had a plan. We had until midnight to figure it out.

"Demons have been exorcised before," Atlas told me. *"It doesn't matter what deal Wes made. We can undo it."*

I nodded, but I didn't know how to do that without having completed the bond. I could technically pull from Atlas, but would it be enough? Would anything be enough? My faith was at an all-time low. I didn't even have confidence in myself anymore. I was the one who insisted on using the book, on following Constance's demented rituals. Atlas had been right all along. I should have waited. I shouldn't have rushed head first—

"Hey!" he snapped, tracing his tender hands over my shoulders. "None of that. We'll get out of this. We will. You know what to do."

Trying to fill myself with his reassurances, I grabbed the container of salt and walked around the circle, pouring a generous, steady stream to keep us safe.

"You think that will work?" Wes laughed harder. "Idiot humans. Always relying on your sigils and your pathetic beliefs. Where do you think this power came from in the first place? Do you suppose your God gave it to you?"

I pushed those thoughts away, shoving aside any resistance to my faith.

The time has come to fight. You must turn your anger into faith, and your faith into action.

I chanted her words over and over in my head, repeating them as I spread my hands over the incense and chanted empowerment spells.

"No," Wes went on. "We took it. When we rebelled, we clawed at what remained of our power and gifted it to humans in exchange for dominion. You all would still be fish trying to crawl out of water if it weren't for us."

"I give you the strength of protection," I muttered. *"I give you protection. I give you—"*

"Protection?" Wes cackled and yanked at his restraints. "Herbs won't protect you from what's coming, filthy mortal."

I put my hands over my ears to block him out. I'd spent two months falling in love with the way Wes spoke, how he could reach inside me and drag out my insecurities with stone-cold logic. This hurt more deeply than I ever expected.

"Marta," Atlas hummed, kneeling in front of me to pull my hands down. *"Don't listen to him. Demons lie, remember? It'll say whatever it can to get us to do what it wants. Focus."*

"What if he's right?" I whispered, the voice in my head so soft and featherlight.

"He's not. Deep breaths. Inhale. And exhale. Inhale. And exhale."

I matched his breathing until my pulse slowed and the fog in my head cleared.

"What's next?" Atlas asked. "How do we get him out of my brother?"

I shook my head. "I...uh...I don't know. We could exorcise and banish him, but I don't know how to do that. The Harlots forbid it."

It affected the witch who cast it, marking the soul, corrupting it. The witches who were the best at it eventually lost their humanity, almost like they had to sacrifice a piece of themselves for it to work. Lilith had said they went mad, that they were closer to demon than human afterward.

"It steals a piece of the witch's soul," I said. "Nothing is free." I told him the theory about the old stories, and the more I talked, the more crestfallen his features became. "A gift given for a gift received."

"But you wouldn't be doing it over and over again." He grabbed my hands and squeezed them. "Just this once."

"I don't even know if I can banish him from a liminal," I said. "I don't know the steps. I don't know the ritual."

Wes laughed again, this time drawing our attention back to him. "You can't, but I'll enjoy watching you try."

"Oh yeah?" Atlas snapped. "And why is that?"

Wes only shrugged. "Let me out of here and maybe I'll tell you."

"Fuck off," Atlas said. "And shut up before I tape your mouth closed."

"Kinky," Wes said. "Now, I knew you'd like it rough, especially when the witch held you down with a knife to your throat and used your body to get herself off."

I froze, realization dousing me in icy water. It had been watching us the entire time we'd been here. *How?* It didn't give us any signs. It didn't make itself known. If a demon were lurking around every corner, we certainly would have seen it or felt it or...

"But your brother?" Wes shook his head and chuckled. "I'll admit. I've seen some wild things in my extraordinarily long existence, but the last brothers that had such a sordid affair ended tragically with one beating the other's head in with a rock. I suppose it won't be much different this time. Perhaps that's why brothers shouldn't fuck each other—"

"This whole time," I cut in. "You've been watching us this whole time."

"Ding, ding, ding," the demon said. "In a whole wide world of nothing, you were my only entertainment. And hell, were you boring. Bitching and moaning about each other and how to get out. But once you decided to try Constance's little rituals, that's when things got so much more interesting."

My stomach clenched, and I curled my fingers into fists. I knew where this was going, even as the shock and surprise boiled through my blood.

Wes gasped in feigned shock. "What? You didn't know? I had to give you a little nudge, didn't I?"

"You…" All the tumblers finally locked into place. "You gave me the book."

"Right again." Wes heaved a deep sigh. "Getting you to use it took some work. But all I had to do was weave in some influence. A little push here, a little nudge there. Make it unbearable to stay here without touching each other. Make it so even your dreams were infected with me."

"The nightmares," Atlas said. "That was you, too."

"Oh, dear simple warrior," Wes continued. "I've been everywhere the whole time."

"For what?" Atlas rubbed his hand over his face. "What's your endgame? If you wanted us trapped here, why give us the key to get out?"

"Who says it's a key?" Wes raised an indignant eyebrow. "It made you powerful, didn't it? Maybe I wanted to help you. Ever think of that?"

"Oh, right. An altruistic demon with nothing but benevolence in its heart," Atlas growled. "Forgive me for not realizing it earlier."

"That explains nothing," I said. The only reason the demon would give us these rituals was if it benefited it in some way. But how? I didn't see the point. What did it want? Would it really guide us here only for its own amusement? No, I didn't think so.

At that, Wes made a grand show of pursing his lips and shrugging again, suggesting that was all he would say on the subject.

I closed my eyes against the burning ache that threatened to pull me under. I was exhausted and magically drained, and this was the tipping point. The whole time, we'd been feeding the will of the demon. We'd been playing its game like pawns on a chessboard, and now I didn't know what to do next. We couldn't get out of here without Wes, and we couldn't get Wes without yanking the demon out of him, and I couldn't do that without sacrificing a piece of myself with it. I didn't even know if I had the magical juice to do it, period, even with Atlas's help.

"Marta," Atlas said, coming to stand next to me. But I pushed him away.

I needed time to think. I needed space to breathe. I couldn't be here anymore. I couldn't—

"Give me a minute," I said, backing away from him. I didn't know where I was going, only that I couldn't stand to be in that room with the consequences of my conviction anymore. I'd been so sure the rituals would work. I'd been so confident in Constance's instructions, and now my carefully laid plans had crumbled through my fingers.

I found myself in the chapel, staring up at the stained glass portrait of St. Michael with his sword raised above his head. Below his feet, a giant serpent wrapped around the trunk of a tree, its head nearly separated from its body. Objectively, the tableau was beautiful, if a little grim. I watched the fading light pour in through the tiny colored pieces, casting the room in vibrant indigos and emeralds.

I'd never been one to put my faith in a God that would so callously snatch my parents away from me. I'd been angry with Him for so long, I didn't even know where my fury ended and my faith began. But if there ever were a time...if there ever were a place...

I lit a candle and dipped my fingers into the basin of holy water before touching my shoulders, my forehead, and my heart. Then, I fell to my knees right there on the hardwood floor, pressed my hands together at my chest, and closed my eyes.

The words came to me from the depths of my subconscious.

"Padre Nuestro, que estás en el cielo, santificado sea tu nombre; venga a nosotros tu reino; hágase tu voluntad, en la tierra como en el cielo. Danos hoy nuestro pan de cada día; perdona nuestras ofensas, como también nosotros perdonamos a los que nos ofenden; no nos dejes caer en la tentación, y líbranos del mal. Amén."

Our Father, who art in heaven, hallowed be thy Name, thy

kingdom come, thy will be done, on earth as it is in heaven. Give us this day our daily bread, and forgive us our trespasses, as we forgive those who trespass against us. And lead us not into temptation, but deliver us from evil. Amen.

I said the prayer over and over again in my ancestral Spanish, remembering my abuelita reciting the words to me when I was just a girl. We'd kneel at the side of my bed, hold our hands together, and wish for God to watch over us, to guard us through the night. After the third time saying the prayer, I switched to Hail Mary, figuring that since I was making recompense, I might as well run the whole gamut.

"Dios te salve, María, llena eres de gracia, el Señor es contigo. Bendita tú eres entre todas las mujeres, y bendito es el fruto de tu vientre, Jesús. Santa María, Madre de Dios, ruega por nosotros, pecadores, ahora y en la hora de nuestra muerte. Amén."

Hail Mary, full of Grace, the Lord is with thee. Blessed art thou amongst women, and blessed is the fruit of thy womb, Jesus Christ. Holy Mary, Mother of God, pray for us sinners now, and at the hour of our death. Amen.

I imagined the Virgin Mother smiling down at me with open arms, welcoming me back into her embrace after so long apart. Her heavenly warmth enveloped me, soothed away my fears, and gave me strength. I apologized for being so angry, for staying away for so long, and she wiped away my tears with kindness in her eyes.

"I can't do it," I told her. *"It's too hard."*

As she so often did when I was a child, she didn't respond. She simply held me while I cried and lamented my rotten position. I needed to be strong. I needed to find the will to keep going, and I figured since I was standing on hallowed ground dedicated to him, I might as well make amends. I started praying again.

"San Miguel Arcángel, defiéndenos en la lucha. Se nuestro amparo contra la perversidad y acechanzas del demonio. Que Dios manifieste sobre él su poder es nuestra humilde súplica. Y tú, oh Príncipe de la Milicia Celestial, con el poder que Dios te ha conferido, arroja al infierno a Príncipe, y a los demás espíritus malignos que vagan por el mundo para la perdición de las almas. Amén."

St. Michael the Archangel, defend us in battle. Be our defense against the wickedness and snares of the Devil. May God rebuke him, we humbly pray, and do thou, O prince of the heavenly hosts, by the power of God, cast into hell Satan, and all the evil spirits who prowl the world, seeking the ruin of souls. Amen.

When I was younger and full of religious zeal, Tita and I prayed to St. Michael to watch over my parents, to keep me safe, to ensure no harm came to our family and friends. I called to him now for the same reason. I said the prayer three times and visualized my safe space, the one I went to when I needed to ground.

At first, I was alone. Only me and the trees.

Then I turned and there he was. Just as I remembered him. Just as I'd always envisioned him as a child. He wielded his sword of light and stood taller than anyone I'd ever seen, made even more massive by my kneeling position. When I lifted my chin to face him, he smiled down on me like a long-lost friend.

"You've grown," he said.

"You've stayed the same," I replied, to which he let out a loud belly laugh and flipped his sword onto his shoulder.

When he finally sighed and settled down, he looked at me and raised an eyebrow. "I heard your prayers."

Perhaps this was all my imagination, or maybe the liminal had finally taken my last piece of sanity, but that seemed insignificant. I'd called to him for courage. What did it matter where I got it from? I'd always believed in signs and messages from divinity, even when I'd spurned them in my resentment. We witches were closer to the ancestors, to the spirits, because of our magical abilities. If Michael the Archangel deigned to talk to me, I'd be smart to listen.

"Forgive me for my lack of faith," I said. "I've been angry. I've been vengeful."

He tsked through his teeth. "You've been petulant."

I swallowed down the hot rise of shame that crept up the back of my throat.

"I don't know what to do," I said.

"Now, you've lied," he continued. "You know what to do. You're scared to do it."

"Yes," I agreed. "I can't lose him. I can't lose either of them. We need to get home and the demon—"

"Ah, yes. The demon. Asmodeus." Michael rolled his eyes and shook his head. "Annoying little thing, isn't he?"

"How do I get rid of it? How do I save Wes?"

He didn't answer, and when I dared to focus on him, I flinched at his furrowed brows and pursed lips. Disappointment. Was I so arrogant as to question an archangel?

"You were given guidance, witch," he said. "What you do with it is up to you."

Exasperated, I forced back a sob, unwilling to show my weakness in front of one who loomed so large in comparison.

"Turn my anger into faith, and my faith into action," I said, repeating the words from the woman in my safe space.

"Nothing comes free, I'm afraid." He pointed his sword at me, touching the blade under my chin so I lifted my face to him again. "Sacrifice is always painful. I know this better than most. But you must make your choice, and make it quickly. Be prepared to live with it, no matter the cost."

I took a deep breath and opened my mouth to ask another question, but he faded away, leaving me alone with my rumination. When I opened my eyes again, the candles had burned low and their flames danced along the wick, perhaps reflecting my own indecision back at me.

Anger into faith. Faith into action.

Sacrifice is always painful.

My heart clenched at the reality of his words, at what I knew I had to do, but I didn't see another way. I wiped the tears from my cheeks, forced myself to my feet, and turned to head back into the sanctuary.

Don't let him go.
Don't let him go.

Had this been what he'd meant? Was Dad trying to warn me about the demon in my brother? And if so, how did he expect me to protect Wes from this? God, I'd fucked up. I *had* to get it out of him.

My brother stared at me with those demon eyes, and my heart broke in two. How had I let this happen? I was supposed to take care of him. I was supposed to protect him. And here he was, perverted by a fucking monster.

"Aww, don't be too hard on yourself, Atlas Colt," the demon said. "He wanted this. He *begged* me for it."

"Shut up," I hissed and clenched my eyes shut.

"He did this to protect you," it said. "And trust me, he's paying for it now."

I tried to block it out, to ignore the demon's words, but the thought of Wes in there, being tortured by whatever hellscape the demon made for him, made me want to punch holes in the stone walls. My ribs ached and my ankles burned, but none of it compared to the chasm in my chest at the mere idea of losing my brother forever.

"I can tell you how to get out of here," the demon goaded. "I can get you back to the human realm."

"Oh, yeah? And what will that cost me? Want to possess both of us at the same time?" Was such a thing even possible? I didn't know, and I certainly didn't want to find out.

"Wesson has already paid for the information," it said. "All you have to do is follow my instructions to the door and step through it."

"Just like Constance's rituals?" I blew out a disbelieving breath. "That worked out so well for us."

"It got you here, didn't it?" The demon raised an eyebrow on my brother's face, and I wanted to smack it off. "You even liked it, didn't you? The feel of sliding into your brother's body."

"Stop it." I wouldn't have this monster spewing lies about what was or wasn't between Wes and me.

"You wanted it even after the ritual was over. You've wanted it for a long time." The demon laughed. "He liked it, too. In case you were wondering. He wants you to fuck him again."

With facing through my veins, I grabbed my pistol and pointed it at the demon's face...my brother's face. My hand shook as I hovered my finger over the trigger, willing myself not to pull it. I wanted this fucker out of my brother, but I desperately wanted my brother back more.

Footsteps broke my focus, and I glanced up as Marta walked down the aisle between the pews. She'd been crying, her eyes puffy and wet, and I lowered the gun at the resolution on her face.

"Did you figure it out?" I asked when she climbed onto the dais next to me.

She nodded. "Yes. We're going to banish him."

That made the demon cackle harder, raising the hairs on the back of my neck.

"Banish me?" The demon rolled his eyes. "Pretty little idiot, you can't do that."

"Shut the fuck up," I roared and shifted my focus back to Marta. "How? I thought banishing it would hurt you, would make you lose a piece of yourself."

Marta took a deep breath and steeled herself. "Sacrifices are always painful. But we need him back, and I'm willing to do it."

I didn't like the sound of it. I didn't want her to lose anything else to this wretched place. It had already taken so much from her...from all of us.

"Marta," I said, reaching out to cup her cheek so she had to look at me. "We can find another way."

"The veil opens at midnight. That gives us four hours. We don't have time." She leaned into my touch and stepped closer so she could press her forehead to mine. "I'm not leaving here without him."

"Me neither," I said. "That's not an option."

"So we do the banishment," she said. "We get the demon out of him, banish it to wherever it came from, complete the soul binding with Wes, and step through the veil. Easy peasy."

Don't let him go.

Fine. Fucking fine.

"That doesn't sound easy," I retorted. "But I'll go with it. Where do we start?"

"I don't know the spell," she said. "But witches have done more with less, so we'll have to wing it."

"Wing it. Right. Feeling so much better about this." I forced away my frustration and exhaustion to turn to Wes, who had a shit-eating grin on his face that made his obsidian eyes even more sinister.

Marta grabbed the chalice from the altar and set it down at the top of the circle, right near Wes's head. "First, we'll need to cleanse ourselves."

"I didn't see a bath anywhere." So much for ritual oils and protection enchantments.

"Washing our hands will do." She walked to the holy water basin and dipped her hands in, scrubbing them a few times before wiping them on her jeans. I did the same. After that, Marta grabbed some herbs from her satchel and dumped them in the incense burner before lighting a match to set them on fire. She walked around the circle three times, muttering to herself in a whisper too low to hear.

But her thoughts were clear. She was praying, asking God, the Virgin, and Saint Michael for help. She called to Saint Marta, the dragon slayer, for strength. She called to the ancestors to guide our work. She called to her parents for wisdom and love. She called to my father, to my ancestors, to Wes's, for their power and protection.

"I invite you to use me as a channel," she said, closing her eyes and holding her hands above her head. "Let your power run through me. Guide me. Hail and welcome. Hail and welcome. Hail and welcome."

I took a deep breath and stood next to her. When she lowered her palms, she grabbed mine with one hand and interlaced our fingers.

"If you've ever had faith in God, I need you to bring that with you into this," she said.

God and I had never had a heart-to-heart. Monsters, demons, and vampires lived among us, and I didn't trust an omnipotent being that would allow such evil to exist. But... After everything I'd seen, after all I'd been through, how could I admit that such a thing wasn't possible? If we needed God on our side for this, could I set aside my skepticism? Could I pray to someone...something...I'd long since questioned?

Wes writhed on the floor in the middle of the circle, testing the restraints, yanking and pulling his wrists and ankles.

Yes. I could do this for him.

I would do anything for him.

Gods were just another form of magic, another power source. They were real, and they had influence, and if Marta had placed her trust in her God, I trusted her to know it was the right thing to do.

"Okay," I said.

"Do you know the Lord's Prayer?"

I nodded, the words coming to me from the depths of a little boy's memory. Dad had taken us to church only a handful of times, but I'd picked up on enough over the years to know that one piece.

"Good," she said. "Repeat it over and over again. Don't stop, no matter what happens."

My mouth had run dry, and my heart sprinted against my ribs, but I opened my mouth to say the words. "Our Father who art in heaven, hallowed be Thy name..."

I carried on with the chant while Marta gathered more candles, red and black, and interspersed them with the white ones already glowing. She lit them with one match, then returned to the incense bowl and gathered dried flowers from her satchel. Marigolds, from the look of it, but I couldn't be sure.

Then, she placed them in the incense. Next, she pulled something else out of her bag of magic tricks, whispering, "Copal ash for purity and guidance. Light the way. Clear the path."

I finished the prayer and started over again, just as she instructed. But when she held up her palm and grabbed her knife, I froze.

More blood. More sacrifice. Hadn't we given enough?

Apparently not. She sliced open a finger and dripped crimson into the incense burner, where it hissed and cracked on the charred remains of her spell. She stood and walked to me, holding out her palm to request mine. I gave it.

"Stop," the demon hissed. "Stop, you don't know what you're doing."

That was true; we didn't. But we also didn't stop. Marta sliced open the pad of my finger and drizzled my blood on top of hers.

"A gift given in sacrifice. Your blood. My blood." She turned to Wes, her focus narrowing on his shaking form. I restarted the prayer.

Getting his blood took some work. The demon didn't want to give it, and she'd created a protective circle around him, one she had to invade and escape before the demon could do anything to her. Watching her in her element always amazed me. She exuded an elegant strength, even in the face of everything stacked against us.

"You can't banish me from the liminal," Wes shouted. "You'll kill us all."

We didn't listen. We'd had enough of the demon's ramblings, and demons lied. They couldn't be trusted, especially not when one was possessing my brother.

"Finally, a little something extra," she said, retrieving a tiny bottle full of a clear liquid. When she opened it, the heady scent of tequila hit my nose. "Mezcal. Earth to fire. Fire to spirit. An offering given so one may be received." She dumped it into the chalice and took a deep pull before spitting it into the incense, where it reacted to the burning herbs with a sharp flame and a crackling hiss. Marta walked to me, holding out the goblet so I could drink.

I did, only taking a sip before I repeated her motion, spewing the liquor into the cauldron.

"If you put that in my mouth, I'm going to drink it," the demon snarled. "Don't try—"

"No matter," Marta said, dripping more into the incense.

The demon let out another loud laugh before its voice dropped to a low, devilish tenor. "You stupid witch. You can't banish me from a liminal. I *am* the liminal. This world was created for me. I'm the anchor. You get rid of me, and it all falls down."

I stopped my prayer. That sounded a little too close to the truth. The coven had to summon the demon and figure out who it was before the liminal could be made. When I glanced at Marta, she seemed to come to the same conclusion, her indecision and sudden discouragement racing down the tie between us.

"That hits a little too close to home," I admitted. *"What if—"*

"We need to do this," she said. *"Sacrifice is always painful."*

I didn't like it, but she was right. I didn't have any other ideas, and we were running out of time.

In many ways, I'd always existed in liminal spaces. Half witch, half biker. Both Catholic and pagan. Attracted to both men and women. A proverbial pie chart of ancestry that included Mexican, Scottish, and Indigenous roots. Now in love with two warriors. Not that any of these were mutually exclusive. I used to think of it as a detriment, not wholly one or the other, never existing anywhere.

Now, I recognized its strength. I pulled from both Mexican-American brujeria and Appalachian folk magic to conjure my spell for the banishment. I recalled old incantations from the coven and blended them with things my tita did when I was little.

Mezcal for cleansing, coral ash for purity and protection, rue for strength. But through it all, blood. My blood. Atlas's blood. Wes's blood.

Our blood.

Energy surged in my veins as Atlas chanted the Lord's Prayer, and I closed my eyes to visualize St. Michael again, holding his sword under my chin to encourage me. I thought of the woman from months ago. *Anger into faith. Faith into action.*

My fury rolled around my stomach, clenching and unfurling, and I redirected it into power, pulling on the tie thread connecting me to Atlas, increasing my strength.

As the clock neared midnight, I sensed the atmosphere thinning, a shimmer in the air around us. The realms were close now, and as soon as the right time hit, we'd be in the in-between. I needed to work quickly.

"Ancestors, holy spirits, ancient magic, I call to you. Give me your strength." The wind howled outside, hissing through the cracks in the windows and cement walls. My muscles shook with the force building inside me, nearly too much for me to contain. I became full of the potent power of light, of God's almighty wrath, of the same righteous anger my namesake had once used to slay a dragon terrorizing her village. It was like whatever was possessing Wes, its equal and opposite force had taken hold of me.

I let it.

"Asmodeus, demon of hell, I banish you. Leave this man, leave this realm, I command it."

The demon snarled and writhed on the floor, pulling at its restraints while its features twisted into a pained grimace. It mashed its teeth together and roared in the same language it'd used the first time I'd seen it. Ancient Aramaic. Except now, I could understand it.

"You cannot banish me, witch," it spat. *"I am the liminal. I am the force holding this realm together. You'll kill us. You'll kill us all."*

Again, I didn't listen. Alarms blared in the back of my mind, and I ignored those, too. I was so full of certainty and arrogance that I barreled my way through any hesitation.

"I give of myself to see you gone," I said. "Flesh to flesh, and bone to bone. I give of myself to see you gone. By smoke and shadow, by blood and breath. We summon darkness. We summon death. The demon amongst us, what bears our name, I banish you from here to whence you came."

The world blurred, the howling air racing around us, spiraling into a hurricane that picked up books and unlit candles and pew cushions. My hair lifted from my face, my clothes beat against my skin, but still I pushed forward, determined to see this through.

I wouldn't leave here without Wes, no matter the cost.

"Take our flesh, our fire, our breath. Let our souls be bound in death. What feeds on lust, we cast you to hell. Bound to the dark where demons dwell."

"*No!*" the demon snapped as black smoke rose out of Wes's nose and mouth. It fought the banishment, trying to reel itself back in as I repeated the enchantment. The words came from somewhere else, something divine and full of ancient rage. I let it flow. I watched Wes struggle on the ground as the atmosphere charged with electricity. It zapped against my skin like sticking my tongue on the end of a battery, but I relished it.

The power was intoxicating, and I understood then why the Harlots had forbidden this type of magic. I could do this forever. I could channel this ethereal energy and command every monster to do as I wanted. I'd never know another day of hardship. This was what witches were made to do, and I lamented the twenty-four years I'd spent on this planet not having tasted it.

"*Wes, if you're in there, chant with us. Help us.*" I sent the message along the weak telepathic bond between us, praying he might hear it. When I glanced up at Atlas, his intense stare focused on the demon clawing its way out of his brother, his jaw square, his lips twisting the syllables of the spell.

A loud crack sounded overhead, and the roof of the church lifted off the building, floating into the maelstrom. The walls chipped away, dissolving into little bits of dust like an enormous tornado had whooshed it to Oz. I remained undeterred. We were almost there, we nearly had it...

But time had never been on our side. In the frenzy of the ritual, the clock had struck midnight. The veil was opening. We had precious few minutes to step through it, and I didn't know if I had the strength to hold it all together.

Liquid dripped down my lips and over my chin. I ignored it. The same heated tingle flowed down the side of my neck and jaw. I ignored that, too, so single-mindedly focused on the task, I didn't realize what was happening.

Atlas took my hand and interlaced our fingers together.

Together. Together. Together.

We are three souls together.

Three souls combined.

Never torn apart.

Three souls.

The world started to blacken, the bounds of reality fading in and out. Something snapped inside of me, a thick, heavy weight giving way as the rest of the black smoke poured out of Wes's body. His chest arched off the ground, and a gut-wrenching scream tore out of his chest.

We're hurting him.

No...we're killing him.

I tried to stop it. I tried to calm the storming chaos, but we'd come too far. I'd invoked too much. I couldn't see the end. My veins burned as every molecule in my body incinerated, blasting into nothingness. Still, the world fell apart. Trees folded into the gale-force wind. Houses. Cars. Entire buildings. Until finally, there was nothing except three of us inside the protection of the circle with the swirling world beyond.

My knees gave out, and I sank to the ground, Atlas collapsing next to me. I grabbed Wes's bound palms with my free hand and clung to him, pushing whatever energy I had left into his prone form.

His pain became our pain, the sickening decay of evil spreading from him to me and from me to Atlas. Like our pleasure had once, this wretched, overwhelming agony rebounded, circling through our connection until it drove needles into every inch of my skin. We were flayed alive. We were gutted with our insides spilling out.

We were pulled to every corner of the universe, our atoms splitting and multiplying and splitting again.

In that moment, I wished for death. I wished the liminal would take us, that it would stop the pain and the misery and let it be over. I wished for anything to make it end.

"Ancestors, please. Help us. Hear us. Please."

All of the preternatural radiance whirling around us collapsed, coalescing into the center of my chest like a dagger to the heart. I arched into it, howling and screaming for release, my eyes blown open but seeing nothing, my head turned toward God but receiving no grace.

And then the world faded to black.

I stood in a dark space with nothing around me. Atlas was on my left, his hand still clasped in mine, and Wes was on my right, no longer bound and wailing. We looked the same as we had in the liminal, our clothes torn and dirty, our hair in disarray, but there were no other indications that we had survived.

"Where are we?" Atlas asked, glancing around.

"No clue," Wes said.

"Did it work?" Atlas looked past me to his brother on my other side. "Did we banish the demon?"

No one answered because we weren't sure. Something had happened. That was certain. But I didn't feel right. I didn't feel *whole.*

I wanted to punch Wes for what he'd done. I wanted to kiss him now that he was back. But there would be time for that—eternities upon eternities. We weren't in the clear yet. This place wasn't home, and until we got there, I couldn't give up the good fight.

Up ahead, about a hundred yards, a small flame flared to life and flickered in the darkness, the only light in the space.

"What do you suppose that is?" Atlas asked.

I narrowed my eyes, and when I couldn't make out anything else, I took a step toward it.

"Whoa, wait a second," Wes said, tugging me back. "We don't know what that is."

A soft humming echoed on the horizon, something soothing and familiar, but I couldn't quite place it. Whatever it was, I wasn't afraid of it, and I figured that was a good place to start.

"We should go toward it," I said as I moved forward again, bringing both of them with me. Atlas groaned, and Wes reluctantly agreed, but they both stepped ahead. We held hands and walked for miles, decades, the songs lulling us in. Joy rang through my chest, some long-forgotten happiness that I hadn't felt in ages. It reminded me of home.

I picked up my speed at the sensation, and more flames joined the solitary one, becoming a field of dancing fire, beckoning us. The singing grew louder, providing a chorus of voices that yanked at my spirit.

"It's the veil," I said. "It has to be."

We sprinted now, our hands still joined, our steps in time with each other. Marigolds suddenly appeared under our feet, acres of them in bright tangerines and vibrant lemons. Laughter spilled out of my chest as we reached the candles, the faces of my warriors illuminated by the fiery call of our family.

Finally, a chestnut door appeared, seemingly connected to nothing except the jamb. But I knew what we would find on the other side. The voices of the living rang out, willing us to come to them.

"We just need to—" I dropped their hands and reached out to touch the doorknob, but Wes grabbed my wrist to stop me.

"We don't know what's on the other side," he said.

"This is the veil," Atlas confirmed. "But the veil to what? It could be the living or the dead over there."

"I sense them," I said. "My sisters. This is it. They're calling us home."

Wes looked from me to Atlas and back again.

"Together, then," Wes said, putting his hand over mine.

"Together," Atlas agreed, and placed his palm on top of Wes's.

Then, as one, we opened the door.

I opened my eyes and sucked in a gasp, focusing on the stars overhead. They twinkled off in the distance, casting a backdrop to the full moon radiating through the treetops.

The full moon.

It wasn't waning. It wasn't—

"There she is," came a familiar voice from above my head.

"Bridge?" I croaked. My voice sounded hoarse like I'd been in the desert for two months instead of the liminal and, when I lifted my hands to rub my face, my muscles twinged in protest.

"You bet your sweet ass, Marts." She leaned over me with a smile, and the sight of her bright blue eyes nearly brought me to tears.

I tried to sit up, but I got woozy and fell back again.

"Whoa, take it easy," she said. "You've been through a lot."

"Wes? Atlas?" The thought of them sent a sudden panic through my chest. Had they made it back, too?

"Over here," Atlas said from my left. He was propped up against a tree, grinning as Leander prodded at his ankles and Val took his pulse. Wes sat on the other side, garnering the same attention from Circe and Gullevig. The rush of their presence coursed through my veins, settling in my chest like warm soup in a blizzard. We were back. We were together.

I wanted to be happy, to be overjoyed that we'd done it. We'd gotten out of the liminal. But even in that moment of blessed reunion, I sensed the *wrongness* in all three of us, almost like I'd left my entire life somewhere else with no way to go back to get it.

"Is she with us?" Crunching leaves preceded the tall, statuesque form of Lilith, the Harlots' president and high priestess of our coven.

"She's here," Bridge said. "We've got them."

"Good." Lilith squatted down so she was eye level with me and grabbed my chin between her index finger and thumb. She stared into my eyes with her umber gaze, unnerving me with its intensity. As the leader, she had more power than any of us could ever know, and when she looked at me like that, I was terrified of what she might see.

Could she tell what we'd been through in the liminal? Could she see what I had to do to get free?

Lilith raised an eyebrow and pursed her lips before pushing to her feet.

"I want them all in quarantine until we can figure out what happened," she said before turning to walk away.

My heart sank, and I tried again to stand, to go after her and tell her off for thinking I would go into isolation. I'd just spent two months there, for fuck's sake. But maybe she had a point. Something was still off, and when I lurched to my feet, I got dizzy again. Bridge grabbed onto my arm to keep me up.

"*It's okay,*" Wes said, reaching into my mind. "*They can't take us away from each other. We're home now, and that's all that matters.*"

I nodded and let Bridge guide me through the woods, the same forest where we'd fallen into the liminal at the beginning. I glanced over my shoulder at Atlas and Wes just behind me, being helped by my other sisters and warriors. But when we got to the cars, they tried to put Atlas and Wes in separate vehicles.

The thought of being parted from them, even for the drive back to Asheville, ripped my heart apart. I wouldn't tolerate it. I couldn't stand it. The jolting force of panic squeezed my lungs until I couldn't breathe.

"No," I protested, digging in my feet. "We go together."

"Marts?" Bridge furrowed her brow at me. "You okay?"

"Bridge, I go with my warriors," I said. "Don't force us apart."

"It's only an hour drive," she said. "Are you sure you're okay?"

"Please," I said, gripping her hands, sinking my nails into her skin. "Please, we need to stay together."

Atlas and Wes made a similar fuss a few feet behind me as they attempted to explain that they would be getting in the truck with me, or the Harlots would have to knock us out again.

Two months ago, the mere mention of having to spend an hour in a car with them would have had me growling and rolling my eyes. Now, I feared what would happen when we were apart. Blood binding, flesh binding, and...whatever had happened at the end, it tied us together in ways that were likely unhealthy. And when the rest of the coven found out the extent of it, I feared they would do everything they could to break it apart.

Witches weren't meant to bond to their warriors like this. It wasn't supposed to be sexual, and it definitely wasn't supposed to entail shared thoughts and physical sensations. Witches were meant to pull energy from warriors, and warriors were meant to protect their witches. And that was it.

This... This would shock the coven.

"Fine," Circe said, holding her hands up to take them off Wes. "They go together."

She gave Bridge a wide-eyed look that said, "What the fuck?" and nodded both of my warriors toward the truck in front of me. Atlas slid into the left side, and Wes climbed into the right side, and once I was in between them, only then did I feel any small measure of peace.

It didn't last. On the ride home, Leander drove while Bridge explained what had happened from their perspective after we'd disappeared. Being in the back of this pickup was strange. We'd spent the last two months driving it around like we owned it. Of course, like Atlas had once flippantly said, nothing was real in the liminal. We *hadn't* been driving this truck. We *hadn't* really been living at the estate. Had the magic been real? I still felt it in my veins. I still radiated with the aftereffects of banishing the demon. It would take me a lifetime to figure out where the lines were between reality and what had happened to us.

"We knew you were in the liminal," she said. "But we just didn't know how to get you out. We couldn't summon you from the liminal without summoning the demon with you, and we couldn't destroy the liminal with you in it. Banishing the demon was out of the question, so we just kept researching, kept trying to figure out a way to contact you."

I grabbed both of my warriors' hands and gripped them tight, refusing to lose myself in the memories of what had happened right before we'd gotten out: the swirling vortex, Wes's screams, the blinding pain. I couldn't process that and Bridge's story at the same time.

"It's okay," Wes reminded us. *"We're okay."*

Were we? Was Wes still Wes? Not even an hour ago, he had a demon squirreling around inside his body, Atlas had been enraged by his brother's violation, and I'd been overcome by enough divine magic to rip the liminal apart.

"How'd you end up doing it?" Atlas asked, seeming to take the question right out of my head.

"It was when you talked to Tita through the mirror," Bridge answered. "She said you mentioned Día de Muertos. I'm ashamed to admit I didn't think of it myself. Of course that would be the perfect time. The veil is thin." Bridge looked over her shoulder at me, casting a raised eyebrow at our joined hands. "I'm sorry I couldn't get to you sooner, Marts. I really tried."

Tita had saved me in the end. With the coven pulling from this side and me pushing from that side, I'd had enough power to complete the spell. I should have been thrilled at the thought of seeing her. Instead, I just felt...numb.

"What happened at the ritual?" I asked, ignoring her apology. "After we fell in, did we just...disappear?"

"Yes," Leander answered. "Your bodies, along with the demon. You fell into the vortex, and it closed around you, and we were all left standing there with our thumbs up our asses, not sure what to do about it."

"Lilith was pissed," Bridge said. "I'd never seen her so angry. It took all of us to get you out tonight, a full coven. The magic was... overwhelming."

Yeah, I can imagine.

Atlas snorted, evidently having heard that, and Wes sighed, glancing out of the window.

"So what happened on your end?" Bridge asked. "How'd you end up getting out? Is the demon still in the liminal?"

I didn't answer because I didn't know, and I was too exhausted to explain. I gripped Wes's hand tighter and leaned my head on Atlas's shoulder to let my eyes close.

"We'll talk about it later," Bridge said. "Get some rest."

I did.

I woke up in a dark room, staring at a ceiling I'd seen a million times before. For a moment, only a heartbeat, I thought it hadn't worked. I thought I was back in the liminal, that this never-ending nightmare had played the cruelest joke on me by letting me believe we'd broken free, only to swallow us back up the moment we weren't looking.

But then a throat cleared from the corner of the room, and I came face-to-face with the vice president of the Royal Harlots, Circe. Her dark hair was braided back away from her face, revealing her intense black stare and pointed pursed lips. She had one ankle propped up on the other knee, her leather boot glistening in the low light, and judging by the way she pulled on her cigarette, this wasn't going to be a happy conversation.

"So," she said, tapping ash into the tray on the table next to her. "How's it going?"

I grimaced and tried to push myself into a seated position, only for my tired muscles to give out on me. I flopped back onto the pillows. Then, I realized we were alone. Atlas and Wes weren't here with me.

"Where are they?" I asked, my tone sounding more demanding than I'd intended. I searched my body for them, sensing our tender thread pulling me down the hallway. Wes was about a hundred yards to the right, Atlas farther on beyond him. The first was still asleep, dreaming about blood rituals and my eyes when I stared up at him from between his legs. I decided not to question how I knew his dreams and focused on Atlas, who was facing his own inquisition from Valkyrie. His annoyance and frustration pooled in my chest, amplifying my own.

"They're fine," Circe said. "As I'm sure you know."

"What's that supposed to mean?" I hadn't told them anything about the liminal or what we'd done there. I hadn't given them very much at all, so unless Atlas was spilling his guts, which I doubted, I didn't understand how she could have access to that information.

"You know what it means," Circe said, taking another long draw on her cigarette before pointing it at me. "You've been a very naughty witch, haven't you?"

I took a deep breath and tried to steady it on its way out, every nerve in my body aching for me to find my warriors. We couldn't be apart. It physically hurt to not be near them, and that, of course, raised a whole host of other concerns. What had we done to get out of there? What had we sacrificed?

"I didn't—"

"Don't lie to me," Circe said. "You're blood sworn to the coven and to the MC. Your colors come first. Remember that."

"We were stuck in the liminal," I explained. "Our bond was gone."

Circe raised an eyebrow in a simple gesture for me to go on.

"I didn't know how to get out," I said, wondering how much I should say. Between the three of us, we hadn't come up with a cover story, but I also didn't see the point in lying. Lilith had looked me in the eye, and whatever she'd seen prompted her to demand we be kept in quarantine...and separated from each other. I put a hand over my heart as it clenched. I needed to be with them. I needed to be surrounded by their energy.

In the end, I told her as much as I could. I explained how we'd found Constance's book and the rituals inside. We'd researched for weeks before we tried the first one, but when all of our roads turned to dead ends, we didn't think we had another choice.

"We had to get the bond back," I explained. "We had to figure out how to get out of there."

I divulged all of it, down to the flesh-binding ritual and the demolition of the estate. The demon had been watching us the whole time, nudging us in ways we didn't anticipate. When I got to St. Michaels and what had happened to Wes, I paused. If she knew he'd been possessed, if she knew what I'd done to get us home, I wasn't sure how she'd react. I trusted my sisters, but like she said, the coven always came first. Would she expel me? Would she banish all three of us?

Atlas and Wes would be fine. They'd lived their whole lives on the fringes of the Harlots. But me...this was my world. My family. My sisters.

"Go on," Circe said. "How did you finally get rid of the demon?"

"We banished it," I stated. "But that destroyed the liminal."

"You banished it?" Circe raised her eyebrows. "You used a forbidden ritual to toss a demon back into hell."

"Yes," I said, squaring my jaw, tilting my head up higher to meet her stare. "I'm not ashamed of it. Not even guilty. I knew the price, and I paid it willingly. I did what I had to do to get us home." I paused to swallow down the heat rising in my cheeks. "I'd do it again if it got us the same result."

"Why?" Circe pursed her lips and shook her head. "Why banish it? Why not go through with the soul-binding and use all that residual magic to open the veil?"

"That was the plan," I explained. "Until..."

I was terrified of what it meant. The memories of what happened after were hazy. I remembered the pain. I remembered bleeding from my ears and nose. I remembered clawing my way to Wes and clinging to Atlas and then...something shifted inside me. If I had to guess, I'd say it was my soul being cleaved into pieces. It was the sacrifice demanded of a witch that dabbled in banishment.

Nothing comes without a price.

Sacrifice is always painful.

To send a soul to hell, the practitioner must give a piece of herself to go with it.

Except...

I'd expected hollowness. I'd expected emptiness and apathy. Instead, something else squirmed around inside me like a parasite, like a cancer. I could sense its presence but didn't know exactly what it meant or what it would do.

"Until?" Circe said, bringing me back from my thoughts.

"What will Lilith do with us?" I asked instead of answering. "I botched the liminal ritual. I used old magic to create something unknowable between me and my warriors. I banished a demon to hell, knowing it was forbidden. Will she kick me out? Strip my patch from my cut and forbid me from the estate?"

Circe took a deep breath and grabbed her pack of cigarettes, pinching one between her teeth before using magic to light it with her hand.

"Don't know," she replied. "It depends on how honest you are."

"Do you think I'm lying?" I hadn't been, not about the things I actually told her.

Circe's assessing gaze narrowed, and I sensed Wes start to wake up. He was looking for me, looking for Atlas, panic squeezing his chest when he realized he was alone.

"No," she finally said. "But I think there's something you're not saying, something you want to keep hidden."

"I spent two months in the liminal," I said. "There are a lot of things I want to keep hidden. Lots of things I wish I could forget."

"Hmm," Circe hummed a gentle agreement.

"I had to do what I needed to save him," I said. "You have to understand. I wouldn't come back without him."

Understanding dawned in her widening eyes. "Which one?"

"Does it matter?" I asked. "The demon possessed him, and I love him, and I would do it again to save him."

"One of them was possessed?" She ran her hand over her face. "Jesus, Marta. Are you sure it's gone?"

I didn't answer because I wasn't.

"Fucking hell." Circe blew out a breath. "If it were up to me, I'd be giving you a fucking medal. Two months alone with your warriors and a demon?" She laughed. "I don't know many witches who could go through that and live to tell the tale."

I tried for a smile, but it felt fake even as I pushed the corners of my lips up.

"But it's not up to me," she said. "It's the coven. We all have to agree, and honestly, the way you three looked coming out of there did not spark optimism."

"What do you mean?"

"Your eyes were black," she said. "You were covered in soot and brimstone. You reeked of magic, like it was clinging to you, refusing to let you go." Circe blew out a thick cloud of smoke and shook her head. "It was the stuff you only hear about in old wives' tales."

"I had to invoke certain...energies," I said, glancing down to my lap, refusing to meet her scrutinizing gaze. "I couldn't do it alone."

"I don't doubt that," she said. "But if you're a threat to the coven, a threat to the Harlots, we can't let you stay. You know that, right?"

I nodded. "My tita?"

"She's here," Circe said, nodding toward the door. "She's been waiting for you to wake up."

"Can I see her?" My heart tugged at the notion that she might say no. "Even though I'm in quarantine?"

Circe thought for a moment before nodding. "I'll go get her. Don't tell Lilith."

She rose and walked out of the door while I tried again to push myself upright, now having enough strength to do it. I took a deep breath, closed my eyes, and checked in on my warriors. Atlas had finally been left alone, now ruminating over what they would do with me.

"Not going to leave her," he thought. *"They can go fuck themselves, and if they try to keep her from me, from us, I'll—"*

"It's okay," I told him. *"Don't let them see you sweat."*

"Little witch." He sighed. *"Did you tell them the truth?"*

"Most of it," I said. *"I left out some bits at the end."*

"Good," he replied. *"I miss you. I'm coming to see you."*

"No, stay there for now. Let's see how this plays out."

Silence and then a reluctant grunt. *"Fine. But don't think you're—"*

The sound of Tita opening the door cut him off, and my weariness warred with utter joy at the familiar sight.

"Mi hija," she cooed as she came closer to sit on the bed. I wrapped myself in her arms, holding her tight as she whispered prayers of thanks to the Virgin and God and all the fucking saints that I'd made it home. We held each other for a long time, probably longer than was necessary, and I berated myself for not feeling...more.

I wanted to cry. I wanted to break myself into pieces and flay myself open. But there was just...nothing. That wrongness infected me. It swallowed up all the emotions I should have had and sucked them down into a bottomless void. My abuelita had been the one stable person in my life. More mother and father than grandmother, she'd raised me as her own. She loved and cared for me when no one else would, and yet...I couldn't bring myself to show any emotions about being back in her arms.

That concerned me, too.

"Let me look at you," she said, pulling away to cup my jaw with her firm hands. Her careful gaze ran down the length of my face as she pushed a piece of my hair behind my ear. "Oh, you've been through it, huh?"

I nodded. "It was..."

"You're different," she said. "You're stronger."

"Perhaps," I admitted. "I don't know if that's a good thing."

She smiled and leaned in to kiss my forehead, the touch comforting in its familiarity. How many times had she done this in my life? Thousands? Millions? And this time, it seemed to startle me. Like whatever was in me would sink its teeth into her, corrupting her as thoroughly as it had me.

"Tita, I—" I cleared my throat and shook my head. "I think something's wrong with me." The words came out in a hushed whisper. I didn't want anyone else to overhear, which was stupid because there were ears *everywhere* in the estate.

"Shhh," she said with the same kind smile that she always used when I came home with a skinned knee or a bruised ego. "It's over. Whatever happened is gone. Whatever it is, we'll figure it out."

"They might take my patch," I said. "They might…"

"If that's the case, then we will figure that out, too." She pulled me back into her arms. "My sweet Elizabeta. My Marta. You have survived so much for someone so young. And you know what? You will survive this, too."

My heart squeezed as I wrapped my hands around her back and clung to her, suddenly feeling like that little girl again, the one who had found out she'd been made an orphan.

I didn't know what would happen now, where I would go or what I would do.

But I remembered what St. Michael had said to me.

Sacrifice is always painful.

I made my choice, and now I had to be prepared to live with it, no matter the cost.

I stood in front of Lilith with the rest of the coven circled me. Bridge hovered off to my left, her brows furrowed as she tried to give me a reassuring grin. She'd been part of the conversations around what to do with me, but despite being my cousin and my best friend, she couldn't tell me what they'd decided.

It had been three days since we'd been back, and I hadn't been permitted to see Atlas or Wes. A Harlot was with me every minute of the day, standing guard or escorting me through the estate. My warriors were still close, but their absence needled under my skin like a tattoo, slowly piercing me into delirium. I needed to be near them, skin to skin, bone to bone.

But that, too, was part of the reason I probably should maintain my distance. I didn't know or understand what I'd unleashed in us, and I didn't trust what would happen when we were finally reunited.

"Marta," Lilith said from her spot at the head of the table. Circe sat on her right, smoking a cigarette, and Rhiannon, the Harlots' enforcer, sat on her left with her hand crossed in front of her. "It's good to see you up and walking around."

"Thank you," I said and straightened my shoulders. "It's good to be home."

Lilith nodded, her focus unnerving me, making me want to explode or rage just because of how much I knew she could see. I might as well be naked in front of her, all my scars on show, all my faults bared for her judgment.

"You were trapped in the liminal for two months with your warriors," she said. "Circe has told me your side of the story, just as Valkyrie and Gullveig have collected versions from the Colts."

I swallowed, knowing our stories had more or less lined up. Both Wes and Atlas were reluctant to admit what had driven us to use a banishment spell, knowing it would create even more hesitation from the Harlots to welcome us with open arms. But I couldn't keep it from them, as much as I initially wanted to. It was up to me to protect them, all of them. If I were a threat, let them do with me as they will.

"I must admit," Lilith continued. "I'm impressed. That you managed a blood binding, a flesh binding, and a banishment all by yourself speaks to an...unknowable power."

Unknowable.

I licked my lips and glanced at the ground, perhaps sensing where this was going. Lilith didn't like unknowns. The safety of the Harlots depended on the rules of magic, the discipline of order, and a strict hierarchy of strength. I'd upended that in a variety of ways.

"I'm told you invoked St. Michael, that you called divinity into yourself."

"I did," I said, the ghost of that incredible energy flickering through my veins. It combined with that mysterious darkness, that emptiness, and sparked a small fire in my gut. I feared I'd never be rid of it, not truly.

"You're aware that banishment is forbidden," she said. "It always comes with a cost. It's the reason we created liminals in the first place."

"Nothing is free," I said. "To banish a soul, you must give a piece of your own."

"Indeed," she said. "And still, you did this anyway."

"I didn't see any other way to get out of there," I said. "I couldn't reach the coven. The only contact I made was with my abuelita, and even that was cut short by the demon. I would do anything to protect my warriors. Anything."

Lilith nodded. "I believe you."

I sighed as a weight lifted off my shoulders, but the clenching in my gut didn't release. There was more coming, and I prepared myself for the fallout.

"Even still, when I look at you, I see something else in your eyes...something missing."

I cleared my throat. "The binding rituals I did with my warriors tethered us in ways I don't truly comprehend. Being apart from them—"

"That's not what I mean," she cut in, balancing her elbows on the arms of the chair so she could bring her fingers together in front of her mouth. "You know as well as I do that there is no such thing as light and dark magic. There is only order. Only chaos. As wielders of magic, it is our duty to balance these two forces, to maintain what is just and limit energetic disruptions."

I nodded and bit my bottom lip, now seeing where this was headed.

"More importantly, it is my honor and my obligation to keep the coven safe."

"I understand."

They would kick me out. They would strip my patch, my cut, and my magic. They would—

"It is not your fault," Lilith said. "What happened was divine intervention. You were meant to go to the liminal. You were meant to bond with your warriors."

That had me snapping my head up, furrowing my eyebrows. "What?"

"We will rework our ritual to ensure it does not happen again," Lilith said. "I'm sorry we failed you. I'm sorry we didn't get you out of there sooner."

Shock trickled down my chest and settled into my gut like lead.

"I fear the damage to your magic may be too far gone, but as long as you are a Harlot, we will work to set things right." Lilith glanced around at our sisters, all of them nodding in blatant agreement. "In the meantime, you will remain at the estate with your warriors. Six months of probation so we can be sure there are no lasting effects."

"Probation?" I blinked. "You're not taking my patch? You're not shunning me?"

"Shunning you?" Lilith snorted and shook her head. "If the ancestors have set you on this path, I am in no position to argue with them."

I should have been relieved. I should have fallen to my knees and thanked Lilith for her mercy and the ancestors for guiding me to this precipice. But the everlasting numbness only spread. They were making a mistake. The hollowness in my soul would tear this place apart. The lingering shimmer of whatever overtook me in St. Michaels would one day explode, and I wouldn't be able to control it.

"I believe whatever divinity there is...God, the ancestors, the deities...they give the hardest battles to the strongest warriors. You faced an impossible situation, and you walked through hell to survive. I am not fool enough to spurn a gift like that."

"We will help you, sister," Circe said. "So will it be."

"So will it be," the rest of the Harlots echoed.

"And my warriors?" I asked. "What becomes of them?"

"I understand you are more deeply bonded to them than what is expected," Lilith said. "Even now, I can see their auras intertwined with yours. Be careful."

I took a deep breath, understanding this for what it was: cautionary advice.

"I will admit, it did cross my mind to try to separate you," she said. "Warrior bonds are not meant to be so codependent. Warriors are meant to protect their witches, to put themselves in front of danger, to sacrifice their bodies should the need arise. I fear what such a loss would do to you."

She spoke from experience, having lost her own warrior years ago. She'd never taken another. If that loss cut her so deeply, I couldn't imagine what would happen to me if I lost Atlas or Wes. Or God forbid, both of them. The thought of it nearly made me panic.

"Be that as it may," Lilith went on, "we are stronger together. If you have the likes of Michael the Archangel on your side, if you can channel such power, I will not be the one to stand in its way."

I couldn't believe this. I'd been preparing myself for a downfall, for exile. Not a slap on the wrist and a warm welcome home.

"Is there anything else?" Lilith asked, looking around. When she was greeted by silence from my sisters, she nodded. "Very well. Marta, I caution you to use this gift wisely. I have faith that you will seek help should you need it. In the upcoming weeks, you will meet with Gullveig and Hella to recount the precise rituals you used, so that we may better understand how it might have impacted you."

"Thank you, Lilith." I nodded.

"Moving on," she said with one final glance in my direction. "What do we know about the Bloody Femmes? Have they been seen riding through our territory again?"

Gullveig gave an update while Aradia pulled up some files on her computer, detailing their last known location. I tried to stay present, to keep my attention on church, but my thoughts went to Atlas and Wes. They were standing their own trial with the other warriors, and when I closed my eyes, I yanked on the bond.

"It's over," I said. *"Probation and a watchful eye. They're not kicking me out."*

"That's great," Atlas said.

"The other warriors are skeptical," Wes added. *"But happy we're back. They want to watch us, make sure we're not a threat."*

"They don't realize our little witch is the real threat," Atlas said.

I internally snorted and shook my head. *"I miss you."*

"We'll be together soon," Atlas said, sending a light caress of affection down the bond between us.

The meeting went on around me, and when Circe called it over, I turned to head back toward my room. The separation from Atlas and Wes ached like a lance to the chest, but I tried to take comfort in the fact my coven wouldn't take them from me. But... that hollow void inside twisted around my heart, and I knew we weren't out of the thick of it, yet.

This may have worked out in our favor, but something still wasn't right. Something loomed just over the horizon, just out of reach, and it was barreling toward us with breakneck speed.

I fucked up. I knew making a deal with the demon would cost me, but I didn't realize exactly how much. I'd been so ready to sacrifice myself to save them, I didn't count on them doing the same to save me. Atlas, sure. He'd run through hell if it meant finding me on the other side. But Marta? I expected her to be the voice of reason. I expected her to read the cards on the table, take her chips, and yank my brother out of there.

I didn't think they'd burn it all down to make sure I left with them.

I was thankful, infinitely so, but now the shame ate away at me like a sculptor chiseling away at marble. Something wasn't right in me, in *us*, and it was my fault.

The Harlots kept us isolated for three days afterward, someone always on guard in my room to make sure we didn't see each other. But on the fourth day, we were brought before the rest of the warriors to stand judgment.

Technically, the warriors were an extension of the Harlots. Lilith and her council reigned supreme, and their choices shaped how the warriors operated. But that didn't mean we weren't an entity in our own right. In the end, the warriors had decided to let the chips fall where they may. Leander reiterated that we would be watched, that we would need to play by the rules or face the consequences.

We agreed, of course, but it didn't change how I felt on the inside.

My broken soul had followed me out of the liminal, and if I stuck around, I would bring everyone down with me. I'd given up more than my free will when I let that demon possess me. Atlas and Marta thought they'd banished it, but something still wasn't right. That monster, that darkness inside me, slithered around my chest like a hookworm, battering against the farthest recesses of my mind, wrapping its clawed fingers around the bars of its cage and shaking the confines of my control.

Eventually, it would overpower me, and I didn't know what would happen when it did.

I have to get out of here.

I'd never felt that impulse as strongly as I did while walking back to the estate. We went through the motions. We ate dinner with the rest of the warriors and the Harlots, celebrating our safe retrieval and a return to normalcy.

It will never be normal again.

Marta emerged from the crowd and rushed toward us, wrapping her arms around Atlas first before doing the same to me. The connection between us sizzled at the proximity, reminiscent of how it felt after the rituals, but now... more. Different. Intense.

After the party ended and most of the others dispersed, I disappeared into my room alone and quietly shut the door, knowing tonight would have to be the night. Sitting on the edge of my bed with my head in my hands, I realized I couldn't stay here any longer. I could put them in more danger by waiting around to see what would happen.

The separation would hurt, but we'd survived worse. *They'd* survived worse, and they deserved better.

I sensed my brother coming closer before the door to my room opened, and he stepped through.

"Atlas," I said, my heart twisting at the sight of him in sweat pants and a black T-shirt. After everything that happened, I only found him more beautiful. Now that we were on the other side, the *human* side, perhaps I should have felt ashamed of my attraction to him. What happened in the liminal had *definitely not* stayed in the liminal.

"What are you doing here?" I asked. "Where's—"

"We haven't had a chance to catch up since we got out," he said, crossing his arms as he came to stand in front of me. His biceps bulged under his shirt, and I ignored the twist of heat in my gut at the sight. We may have told the others how deeply we were connected, but we hadn't shared everything with the rest of the class. They didn't know what transpired between Atlas and me. It wasn't their business. "I should beat your ass for leaving Marta and me that night in the church."

I sighed, perhaps knowing this was coming, and forced my tired muscles to stand.

Whatever we'd done to get out of there had amplified the bond, and now, I didn't know where I ended and Atlas began. In many ways, our lives had always been like this, more extensions of each other than separate beings. The magic had only made it physical instead of metaphorical.

It was the first time we'd been alone together since we got out, and the sudden pang of what I'd done echoed in my chest like the world's loudest tuning fork.

"Atlas, I'm sorry. I shouldn't have—"

"I could fucking clock you right now, you know that?" He scoffed and shook his head. "But I love you too damned much, and I'm just so fucking happy to see you."

I couldn't stand the separation anymore. I rushed to him and threw my arms around his neck, yanking him closer. He returned my hug, squeezing our chests together, tucking his face into my neck. The warmth of his body soothed some of the ache in my heart, and when I sensed our witch getting closer, I glanced up at the door just as it opened.

Marta stepped through, her gaze shifting between the two of us before she launched at our embrace. I wrapped an arm around her as hers came to my hips, and together, the three of us took our first collective deep breath since coming home.

"You're such a fucking idiot," she said when she stepped back. Her dainty hands balled into fists, and she shoved my chest, knocking me back a step. "I could kill you."

"I know." I hung my head. "I thought I was saving you. I thought you'd both get out if it weren't for the demon."

"We had a plan," she snarled, trying to keep her voice low. "We were going to get out anyway."

"You didn't know that," I admitted. "It was going to tear the place apart with us inside it."

"I had it under control," she said, but even as the words infiltrated the space between us, I tasted the lie in them. None of us had control. We were puppets, toys, entertainment for a nasty soul that had ripped its way out of hell and refused to go back.

"What happens next?" Atlas asked. "We're under the microscope, but if I have to be apart from you two again, I'll fucking lose it."

"Me, too," Marta said. "I think whatever I did in the church has made the bond—"

"Unbearable," I finished for her. What I didn't say, what I couldn't say, was that I still felt *it* inside me. When the demon took hold, when I finally gave myself over, it settled in my soul like a permanent brand, fiery and cold, stinging and scalding. I would never be able to get rid of it entirely, and I worried about what that would mean for them. How much did the rituals truly connect us? Were they in danger because of what I did, what I'd become?

"We made our choice, and now we live with it," Marta said. "It will be a while before we fully understand the consequences."

"What happens in the liminal stays in the liminal," Atlas said.

"Let's hope it's that easy." Marta rubbed her hands over her face and back through her hair. "All I know is I've been itching since we've been home. Being with you, being here, this is the first time I've been able to breathe."

"Same here," Atlas said. He wrapped his arms around her shoulders and pulled her into his body for another long hug, pressing his lips against her forehead and inhaling her deeply. And suddenly, I felt like an intruder on their intimate moment. My mind conjured images of me in Marta's bed, Atlas standing at the edge with his hands on his hips, unsure if he should join us.

I didn't remember anything about what happened after the demon took hold of me. One second, I was standing outside, making the deal, and the next, I was on the ground, writhing and burning as the world spun around us. I'd awoken to the worst pain I'd ever experienced while Atlas screamed and Marta exploded with bright white magic. Then, we were in the veil.

Marta and Atlas explained the highlights to me. The demon had tried to battle Marta, and Atlas knocked it out. They dragged me into a demon trap and banished it, but doing so had cost her.

She had to give up a piece of her soul to do it.

But that didn't seem like the end of the story. Something was missing in me, too.

"Come on," Marta said, nodding to the bed. She grabbed my hand with her free one and tugged both of us over to the mattress. She slid into the middle while Atlas circled to the other side, and I climbed in behind her.

We lay like that for a few moments, listening to the sounds of each other's breathing, and I debated with myself about whether I should tell them the truth. But in the end, how could I keep it from them? They deserved to know.

"There's something wrong with me," I admitted. Both Atlas and Marta turned to face me. *"I think...I think the demon's still inside me."*

"No," Marta said. *"I banished it."*

"I feel rotten," I continued. *"It still burns."*

"It's the liminal," Atlas explained. *"I feel it, too. Whatever we did in that church fucked us up."*

"I'm empty," Marta said, glancing down as she interlaced her hands with mine. *"I know I banished Asmodeus because a piece of me is missing. Wes, we all feel it."*

Not like this, I wanted to say. I'd been corrupted. Couldn't they see that? Couldn't they sense it?

"I think we all need a distraction tonight. We can figure it out tomorrow." Marta grabbed my hand and brought it to her mouth. She sucked my index finger in between her lips and rolled her tongue along the pad, sending a sharp strike of pleasure straight down to my balls. Atlas watched with rapt attention, his emerald eyes glittering in the moonlight.

This was the first time the three of us had been together. Alone. Without the haze of ritual and magic clouding our minds.

"Please?" Marta asked both of us. Our thoughts had bled together over the last few days that now it was nearly second nature to receive her desperate pleas. I glanced over her shoulder and raised an eyebrow at Atlas, pushing all thoughts of what would happen after far from my mind.

"Our little witch is needy tonight," I teased.

"So needy," he replied.

"Should we indulge her?" I clicked my tongue against my teeth and withdrew my hand from her mouth, lowering it to wrap around her throat, holding her head in place.

"It would be cruel not to," Atlas said, curling his lips into a devious grin. He leaned in and pressed his mouth to hers, and I moaned at the sensation on my own lips. His. Hers. The blend of them together was so wickedly damning, I couldn't help the shift of my hips against her ass. My cock brushed along the thin clothing between us, and I dropped my forehead to her crown, sliding my hand along her ribs to her hips.

She bucked against me, rolling her pelvis to increase the contact, and that almost broke me. Fuck, I wanted this. I wanted this so damned bad, but I also didn't want to corrupt them any more than I already had. That demon had shredded my soul, warped it and twisted it, and I couldn't be sure I wouldn't hurt them with it.

One night. Have one night. Then that's it.

A sharp clench tugged at my chest, and Marta glanced over her shoulder at me with furrowed brows. Perhaps she had felt the yank inside me, or maybe heard my thoughts. If she did, she didn't mention it, only rolled so she could cup the back of my neck and bring my mouth to hers. I lapped at her, tasting both my witch and my brother, and the combination made my cock rock fucking solid.

She pulled back from me and glanced between Atlas and me, seeming to question whether what we'd found in the liminal would follow us outside of it. Two months ago, this was a line neither of us would consider crossing, but now...to hell with it. I crashed against him, all teeth and tongue, and he groaned into the contact, the rush of his arousal coursing under my skin.

I wanted him. He wanted me. And we both wanted her.

A thick masculine hand grabbed me between the legs as a softer feminine one grappled with the hem of my shirt, yanking it up so she could claw at my stomach and chest. Her nails sank into my skin, and I moaned as I rolled onto my back.

They descended on me like ravenous beasts, and I couldn't help myself. I relished the feel of being under them. Marta stripped off her tank top and shoved her shorts down to her ankles and off her feet. Atlas worked on my sweatpants, shucking them down my legs before he settled himself between my thighs.

"Can I sit on your face?" Marta asked.

"Fuck, I might die if you don't," I answered, and I had barely thought the words before she straddled my head and lowered her delicious cunt to be devoured. Tasting her that first time had been

heaven, but this was absolute euphoria. We both moaned at the first swipe of my tongue over her clit, and then a warm, wet mouth wrapped around the tip of my cock, and I bucked off the mattress.

"Oh, such an eager slut for my mouth." Atlas hummed, kissing along the underside before flicking his tongue over the head. I gasped, but all I breathed in was Marta's pussy, and she tunneled her fingers into my hair, gripping and holding me the way she wanted. I sucked in time with Atlas's ministrations, each swipe of his vicious tongue sending shock waves through both of us. Through all of us. So connected were we that we became one body, one bundle of nerves, beckoning to explode.

Marta's muscles tightened around my head, her nails sinking into my scalp as she threw her head back on her shoulders, riding my face as the crest of her orgasm rose inside her. I felt it. I sensed it coming. And with the way Atlas stroked my dick, fucking me back into his throat, I didn't think I could hold out through it.

She let it take her, shouting, *"Yes, yes, right there, I love your mouth,"* through the bond. It cascaded into me, surging into Atlas, whose throat groaned around its hold on my cock. She gushed on top of me, and I couldn't help my dirty thoughts.

"So fucking wet. Fucking drenched. Delicious." I sucked her hard. *"Use me. Fuck me. Give me your cum, sweet girl."*

I panted and gripped her thighs, sure I might blow any second. Just before I did, Atlas pulled back and slowed his pumping, laughing as he bit and kissed the inside of my thigh.

"Slow down, little witch," Atlas said. *"You've got us both wound tight."*

"I want you," she said as she climbed off my body and settled near my ribs. *"Inside me. Both of you."*

I was ashamed of how much I wanted that, too. What remained of the monster rattled its cage inside my mind, reaching through the bars to sink its claws into my brain. I'd thought I'd left it in the liminal. I thought it was the demon all along. But whatever had seized me that night came with me out of it, and now I didn't know what to do.

Atlas licked his lips and grinned, pushing up so he could stretch out on top of me and press a salty, wet kiss to my mouth. I wrestled with his tongue, letting him have control, letting him use me as he rubbed his cock against mine.

Fuck, it turned me on. It brought me closer to busting again, and I didn't want to embarrass myself.

"Come on, little brother," Atlas said. *"Our witch wants us inside her. We've got to work her up to it."*

I shuddered at the thought of our cocks inside her at the same time, rubbing up against each other, spilling inside her tight cunt. His cum. My cum. Together.

I took a deep breath and nodded, forcing away my trepidation. Like this, everything could have happened to someone else. When I was with them, I felt complete and whole in a way that scared me. And I would ruin it to keep them safe.

I licked Marta's nipples while Atlas worked one, then two fingers inside her, using his other thumb to rub over her clit and coax her legs farther apart. She rocked her hips into him, desperate for more, and I bit her tender flesh to tug, making her squirm and moan. Her soft skin yielded to the depraved way I handled it, and I moved to the other side, gently kissing the triangle scar over her heart before giving her left nipple the same attention.

"Think you can handle three fingers, baby?" Atlas cooed.

I grinned when she whimpered and moaned an audible, "Yes."

Unable to stand the separation, I trailed down her body until my fingers joined my brother at her cunt, where I dipped my index finger inside her. Together, we worked her tight hole open, massaging her pleasure centers, reveling in the way we felt it inside us, too.

I could have spent eons fucking her, sliding my fingers against Atlas's while she writhed and sobbed under us. But I wanted what she wanted. I wanted something more depraved, more delectably wanton, than anything I'd ever experienced. Now that she'd dangled it in front of us, I couldn't wait to sink into it, to let it consume me.

"Are you ready for us, little witch?" Atlas asked, kissing the inside of her knee.

"Yes, please. Yes, more." She rolled to face Atlas as he moved to her side, and I pushed up behind her, lifting her leg so it balanced over his hip.

"Relax," I told her as she shivered. I ran a hand along her rib cage and down to her hip, and she preened into the touch, tilting her head back to kiss me. I devoured her mouth, coaxing it open so I could lick her tongue. Atlas palmed his cock and stroked before brushing the head along her entrance, gently slipping in with a few timid thrusts.

"Oh," Marta cried, arching into me. I squeezed her breasts, her hips, her thighs, anywhere I could get my hands to ground her.

"Fuck, you feel so good," Atlas said. He leaned in and kissed her neck, lapping up the column of her throat to her jaw and mouth. The heady scent of pinewood and cherry assaulted me, and the combination of them sent me into a frenzy. I needed and I yearned and I fucking couldn't stand it. How would I ever live like this? How could we expect to keep this from the rest of the coven, the rest of the warriors?

"Get in here, brother. You need to feel her. I have to feel you," Atlas pleaded, and I rushed to comply. I grabbed my cock and lined myself up, the velvet heat of him sending a pulse up my spine and down the back of my legs. She was soaking wet, but that didn't make it any easier to shove my way inside. Atlas was steel, and she was soft silk, and I could only hang my head on her shoulder and gasp.

It took a couple of thrusts to get myself halfway in, but Marta clamped down on us, one hand coming to Atlas's shoulder, the other reaching behind me to grip at my neck.

"It's so much," she said, and fuck, I knew. I felt it like a sledge-

hammer between my legs, both the tight squeeze of Atlas and me inside her and the pure delirium of my cock rubbing up against his. Our balls brushed together, and that nearly undid me. I gripped her hip for leverage to slightly pull out, only to surge back in deeper. Harder. All the way.

Once I was fully seated, Marta moaned and arched into it, pulling in deep inhales and letting out shuddering exhales.

"Fuck, it's good," Atlas murmured, kissing her neck. I rocked against them, finding a rhythm with Atlas's thrusts so that we were fucking her together, fucking each other, and my grip on reality started to break. Fire licked through my abdomen, tingling down to my feet and up the back of my spine. I lavished attention on her shoulder, her neck, that soft spot behind her ear, and then my lips found my brother's. I consumed them, too. We licked each other and her and melted into this magnificent, overwhelming bliss.

It went on and on, me fucking them, them fucking me. Hands and fingers spread everywhere. Atlas's grip on my hair, my delicate attention to Marta's clit, her grasp on my wrist and the other hand around his neck. I caught the green glint in Atlas's eyes and the sweat trickling down his neck. I wanted to lick it away. The flush on Marta's skin reeled me in, rosy and pink and altogether beauti-ful. *We* were beautiful like this.

We were magic.

We worked each other into a frenzy, pleasure circling between us like a soundtrack on repeat.

"You like your warriors inside you?" Atlas said when he started to reach his peak. *"You like the way we take you at the same time? You want to drain us both, huh? Such a greedy little thing."*

Marta laughed and fucked us harder. *"Not as greedy as you. To want both your brother and me? Such gluttony."*

That sent me over the edge. Yes, I did want her and my brother. Yes, we wanted too much and not enough. And I shouldn't. This snarling, vile thing inside me reared its head, and I restrained myself from letting it go, letting it have free rein. It was easier to keep it contained when I was with them, but even then, it was a dangerous, reckless beast.

I fucked them harder, focusing on how Marta's cunt tightened around us, her internal muscles quivering with impending release. And when it hit, it ricocheted into both Atlas and me, setting us off. Heat scalded my nerves. Energy bloomed in my gut, something powerful and strangely unique.

"I love you," she cooed. *"I love you both. So fucking much, it hurts."*

"Fuck, I love you, too," Atlas replied.

I should have said it back, but a blinding light exploded out of us, shaking the furniture in the room and rattling the windows in the frame. Lightning lit up the sky, rolling thunder echoing the booming in my chest.

"Fuck, fuck, fuck," Atlas roared, and I rocked my hips harder, milking the last bit of cum out of both of us. I wanted them to have it all. My brother coated my cock, each hot spray like a balm to my agitated, blistering soul.

We lay connected for a while afterward while I kissed every inch of Marta's skin and whispered things like, "Such a sweet girl," and "So perfect for us, perfect for me." She trailed her hands over Atlas's chest and twisted them in my hair, hugging both of us closer. We softened inside of her until we eventually slipped out, and when it was over, truly over, I petted them both until their breathing evened out, both of my beloveds succumbing to deep sleep.

I knew what I had to do, but the knowing did not make it any easier. Marta wouldn't forgive me for this. Atlas wouldn't rest until he tracked me down. But deep in my heart, it was the right thing to do.

I'd infected them. I was filthy, dirty, rotten to the soul. I was the one who'd been tainted, and if I stayed with them, I'd drag them down with me. Better to find a place to decay in solitary peace.

After I climbed out of bed and gathered a few necessities, I wrote a quick note telling them not to follow me. I placed it on the bedside table and stood at the doorway to memorize one last image of them, one last thing to carry with me. Their hands twisted together. Their legs intertwined under the covers. Their rising chests as they breathed in tandem.

My heart broke, but I'd never wanted this life. And now that I was stuck with it in ways I'd never imagined, I had to do what was necessary, even if it hurt.

I made my choice, now I live with the consequences.

I blinked back tears, and I left.

Time had a habit of simply...carrying on.

Waking up in bed with only Atlas fractured me more deeply than anything else ever could. I should have seen it coming. Something wasn't right, and in retrospect, I understood it had been Wes's shame and hesitation. He left us a note, three stupid sentences that left a chasm in their wake.

I'm sorry. I love you. Don't look for me.

-Wes

Atlas wanted to tear out of the estate, track him down, and kick his ass. Perhaps some small part of me wanted the same. But I was broken and numb.

The emptiness inside me made going through the motions of everyday life strenuous enough. Going after him when he didn't want to be found sounded like trying to move a mountain with a shovel—a journey of a thousand miles, indeed, but ultimately pointless.

Days passed. I got up. I ate. I visited with my abuelita, whose intelligent eyes saw far more than I'd ever want her to see.

"Come help me in the garden," she'd say, pulling me outside as she insisted fresh air would do me good. "Tell the plants your troubles."

"They don't care about my troubles, Tita," I'd reply.

"Nonsense. The plants love to gossip." It was her way of trying to cheer me up, but it did little good.

At night, I'd crawl into bed with Atlas and try to find some small measure of relief in the feel of his skin on mine, but it was never enough. Not for either of us. Without Wes, without one third of my blood and flesh, we were a dead ship, floating in the ocean with no way of finding land.

"Wes, come home," we'd call, reaching out through the infinite expanse of our bond to locate him. But the more distance he put between us, the harder it was to sense him. That had more consequences than we'd ever thought.

After a week apart, I sat in the library while Gullveig and Hella analyzed the ritual I'd recreated from Constance's book. We couldn't find the damned thing in the human realm, and I'd started to wonder if it hadn't been *created* for us by the demon itself.

"You performed the blood bond with this?" Gullveig asked, raising an eyebrow. "Spells like this haven't been practiced since the height of the witch craze."

"I know," I said. "We were wary of using it in the first place, but..." *We didn't have a choice.* I stopped before I said the words because I'd been repeating them incessantly for days. Gullveig and Hella looked at each other, some silent communication passing between them that suggested they had concerns about my mental well-being.

Honestly, same.

"Okay, walk us through it again," Hella said.

I did, and when I was through, they still weren't convinced that it would have been strong enough to have the effect it did.

"We were in the liminal," I told them. "The magic had different properties there."

I didn't mention that the demon had been watching and guiding the entire time. How much of what happened was because of me, and how much was because of the demon's influence? I may never know.

When they grew tired of my sullen attitude and dismissed me, I went to the training center to let off some steam. But my workouts were mindless, just me drifting through the motions, never really committing to any one thing or the other.

I went to the woods to center and ground myself, hoping I might see the woman again, the one with the powerful advice. When I only found myself in my sanctuary alone, I drew as much strength as I could from the earth, but even that paled in comparison to what I'd once been able to do.

Wes's departure had left a gaping hole inside my soul, and no matter what I did, it wouldn't heal. His abrupt absence ached like fire under my skin, like acid in my veins. The physical pain was one thing, and it was agonizing. But the emotional turmoil of not having him near made the numbness even more profound, the hollowness from the liminal amplified. Atlas said Wes had probably left because he thought he was protecting us, that he thought he was dangerous and didn't want to hurt us. If he really felt the demon was still inside him, I understood. But we were all suffering, and being apart wasn't the answer.

By week three, I'd stopped sleeping through the night. And by week four, I could barely eat.

At least Atlas seemed to be in the same boat. We fed on each other's irritation, and any reconciliation we may have found by surviving the liminal together slowly peeled away. We were always meant to be a three, and without Wes, our triangle would never be complete.

"I've had the guys running facial recognition," Atlas said from across the table, sliding his roasted vegetables around on his plate. He had deep purple marks under his eyes, and his cheeks had sunken in on his face. Quite the pair we made. "We think we got a hit out in Albuquerque."

I swallowed against my dry throat and shifted my lifeless gaze to his. "Yeah?"

"Yeah," he said. "It makes sense. He'd find a populated spot to blend in. He'd work somewhere dealing in cash, so he didn't leave a paper trail. Fuck, I bet he even changed his name to something normal like John Smith."

"Atlas." I sighed, running a hand over my face. "It's been a month. Just let it go."

He narrowed his eyes at me, squaring his jaw to prepare for a fight. The angry rush of fire reverberated down my sternum, expanding from him into me, replacing the aching chasm with something tempestuous and volatile.

"Who the fuck are you?" he spat.

I tried not to flinch. "What?"

"Who is this fucking shell sitting in front of me?" He threw his fork down and leaned back in his chair, crossing his arms over his chest. "The witch from the liminal would have chased his ass across the world and dragged him back by the scruff of his neck."

That hurt more than anything else he could have said because it was true. The person I was before the banishment spell would have sprinted to the edges of hell to find someone she cared about, someone she loved.

"Is that who you're hanging around to find?" I raised a brow. "The witch from the liminal? She's gone."

"Right." He scoffed and rolled his eyes, escalating my ire.

"I'm serious," I snarled. "If you're still here for her, you're wasting your time. I don't know where she is, but just like Wes, she's not coming back."

"You know, I thought after everything we've been through, everything that's happened, you and I would finally be on the same page." He shoved back his chair and pushed to his feet.

"Same page about what, huh? How fucked up it is that we did

this to ourselves? How screwed up we are inside? We kicked a demonic bees' nest and now we're dying from the sting." My voice rose as I matched his stance, pushing to my feet, letting the rage of Wes's abandonment add fuel to the inferno inside. "When will you get it through your thick fucking skull? He's not coming back. He doesn't want us."

The "He doesn't want *you*" went unsaid, but Atlas startled like I'd said it anyway. Perhaps he heard it in my thoughts. Perhaps he already suspected it, just as I did.

"You're giving up, and it's repulsive," he growled, slamming his hands on the table.

I leaned forward, baring my teeth as I let my wrath consume me. "If that's how you feel, then get out."

His features tightened and his muscles tensed, our anger bouncing back and forth between us.

"Go on," I snapped. "Go!"

Atlas straightened, grabbed his stuff, and walked away. The sound of the slamming door behind him reverberated through the house, and his retreating presence picked at the scab in my chest.

Wes was gone. Now, Atlas was gone. And I was alone.

I thought he might come back once he cooled off, but he didn't. I went to bed by myself that night, purposely trying to ignore the hole inside my body where they once resided. We hadn't sealed the soul bond, and this fractured thing between us only cracked further with each second that we weren't together. If I closed my eyes, I could see the fissures spreading like a broken window, each delicate slice spreading further as I breathed.

I thought about reaching out to him telepathically. Who really knew where I ended and they began? Our thoughts and feelings had become unified so quickly, I didn't have time to learn how to control it.

In the end, I went on with my life. I did the assignments Lilith gave me. I met with Gullveig and Hella and tried to recount the steps I'd taken as best as I could. But they didn't have any solutions, either.

"The other warriors will go after them," Hella said, putting a hand on my shoulder in a reassuring pat. But that only made it hurt worse, the foreign touch so blindingly *not them*.

"They won't let Atlas and Wesson abandon you like this," Gullveig added. "Though, when they return, I might light them on fire myself."

I tried to smile, but it didn't feel real.

Nothing felt real.

I walked through life with the vague sense that I'd left the realest part of me in the liminal, and I would never get it back. I survived the days like a ghost, haunting the estate, hardly able to look my abuelita in the eyes without the perpetual shame of being a husk swallowing me whole.

"You're not eating," Bridge said from across the breakfast island. We sat in Tita's kitchen for family dinner. My cousin had already finished her empanadas and housed an entire plate of rice. I pushed my food around with my fork, hardly able to stomach the smell, let alone the taste.

"Not hungry," I replied.

"We're worried about you." She reached out to grab my hand. "Atlas and Wes will—"

"I don't care what Atlas and Wes do," I snarled.

Bridge raised an eyebrow. "You're full of shit. And if you keep this up, I will help Tita tie you to a chair and shovel food down your gullet."

She was joking, but I didn't laugh. This endless nothing inside of me was more than Atlas and Wes leaving. Their absence stung, sure, but the numbness had been there as soon as we got home. It could have been why they had to leave in the first place. Tita served us pie, and I put on a good show of saying the right things and trying to look happy, but I knew she wasn't convinced.

The next day, I hit rock bottom. When I tried to ground in

the woods, my one piece of solace in this infinite droll of existence, the magic wouldn't come. I called to the ancestors, I beckoned the trees and the earth for help, but I got no response. I opened my eyes and stared at my hands, flexing my fingers as if that would somehow make them work. But when I focused my energy and tried to shoot magic from my palms, nothing happened.

"No." I tried again. Same result. I fell to my knees as a sob poured out of my throat, the first real emotion I'd felt in four weeks. This wasn't exhaustion or depletion. This was my own idiocy. I'd fucked with fate. I'd fucked with a spell that was banned because of what it cost, and here were the consequences. My warriors, gone. My magic, gone. My soul in pieces.

And it was all my fault.

I banged my hands into the ground until my knuckles bled. I screamed at the heavens and God and Michael and anyone listening. I decried the ancestors and the fates. How fucked up was it that they'd put me in this situation, forced me to act, and then punished me for what I'd done?

Anger into faith. Faith into action.

Tita would tell me to pray about it. She would tell me to light candles and appeal to the Virgin. And hadn't that been precisely what I'd done in my darkest hour? Hadn't that been my last resort when I didn't know how to get the demon out of Wes, and I didn't think I was strong enough to carry on?

Would it work now?

I clasped my hands together and said my prayers, three times for each of them, calling out to The Virgin and God and St. Michael. I wanted to feel that rush of divinity again. I waited for their wisdom and ethereal grace. But it never came. Nothing came.

Royally pissed, I slammed my fists down, smashing them into a snarled, decaying log, and suddenly, an enormous blast shot out of me. A tremendous wave of obsidian decimated the wood, sending bits of earth into the air, propelling me onto my back. It was like a valve had been loosened, and whatever was inside steamed out in a boiling wave of fury.

Blinking, I stared at the wreckage, unsure of what I'd done.

Black. Darkness. The demon.

I was truly screwed. Even if Atlas and Wes never came back, I couldn't stay here. I couldn't draw from the earth. I couldn't harness my birthright. Whatever I had now was uncontrollable and rotten, now perverted by my own arrogance and recklessness. What happened in St. Michaels had created a void inside me that nothing could fill, and the only people who brought me peace, who understood, were gone.

I thought about keeping it to myself and disappearing in the night like Wes. But that didn't sit right with me for a multitude of reasons. I'd taken an oath of loyalty to my coven and the MC. I'd sworn my fealty in blood and magic. If I had nothing else, at least I had my word.

"It shot out of me like the first time a witch discovers her magic," I told Gullveig and Hella the next day. "Except it was black. Not white."

They blinked at each other, mouths open and eyebrows halfway up their foreheads.

"Has that ever happened before?" Hella asked.

"No," I replied, digging my nails into my palms to keep from exploding. Even sitting there, I sensed it well inside of me, drawing from the absence of my warriors, feeding on the desolation and weakness.

"I think we're outside of our element here," Gullveig said as she rubbed a hand over her face.

I agreed.

Week five brought a visit from our friends in the national chapter of the Royal Bastards MC. Hellsing was the resident demon whisperer in Louisiana. He and Lilith were friends, having learned the craft together in their childhoods. He'd been tasked with a run-through of our territory and wanted to stop in to visit.

Hellsing was tall with long dark hair and a piercing gaze that unsettled me, but as soon as it connected with mine, I sensed the power inside him. He had exorcised even the worst hell spawn and managed to keep his soul intact. After dinner, he approached me before I had a chance to hide.

"Let's take a walk," he said, nodding toward the back door.

I didn't see how I had any other choice, so I went with him, hugging myself against the chilling autumn air. Winter would descend soon, and even though it didn't get bitterly cold in North Carolina, I sensed the world dying in my molecules. Perhaps I sympathized.

He was quiet for the first few minutes as we wandered into the woods, the sounds of crunching leaves under our boots providing a backdrop to my pounding heart. Finally, once we were out of earshot from the estate, he pushed his hands into his pockets and turned to face me.

"Gullveig tells me you're having trouble with your magic," he said.

I swallowed down my indignation. Trouble was putting it mildly. "I can't ground. I can't pull from the earth."

He nodded but stayed silent, waiting for me to continue.

"I'm shooting darkness out of my hands. It's like...like I'm infected."

His eyes narrowed, and he tilted his head to the side. "There's more."

I was hesitant to tell him. After all, he wasn't a member of the coven, but something told me to be honest, that if there was one person who could help me, it was this biker who had been through hell and back. He had no reason to judge me, nothing to gain or lose from telling the others.

I bared it all. I explained the rituals and the demon and what happened at St. Michael's. Maybe I was just tired of trying to figure it out. Maybe I wanted him to stab me in the chest and banish me with the others. When I was finished, something hot and sticky slid down my cheek, and when I wiped it away, my fingers were tinged pink.

Blood.

More blood.

He took a deep breath and let it out on a sigh.

"You know, there's all different kinds of supernatural in this world," he said, glancing out toward the tree line. "Shifters, vampires, demons. Witches that pull from the earth and warrior bonds that don't act the way they're supposed to. My magic isn't like yours. I'm a different breed, but we all must work with what we've got."

"You should exorcise me while you've got the chance," I said, shaking my head. "Tell the others I attacked you or something."

He snorted a laugh. "No, I don't think that's the problem."

I glanced up at him and loosened my hold on my midsection. "No?"

Hellsing hummed. "Seems to me you started something and never finished it. Whatever was in Wesson spread to you and Atlas, maybe more so you because of your magic."

"You're saying there's a demon in me." I searched my soul for the truth in this, but all I found was the chasm of loneliness and pain the Colts had left in their wake.

"If you had to give up a piece of yourself to banish the demon and you were connected to the others at the time, they must have given up a piece of themselves, too." He pursed his lips and shrugged. "Evil clings to emptiness like that. You give an inch, it's going to take a mile."

"How do I get rid of it? How do I get myself back?"

"Can't say for certain," he admitted. "But if I were you, I'd finish it. Spread it out between the three of you."

"I can't—I can't do this to them." I couldn't ruin them more than I already had.

"It's already done," he said. "The three of you can already hear each other's thoughts, feel each other's pain and emotions. They agreed to share your magic, right?" He turned and started walking again. "Seems like the most logical thing to do next."

"They're gone," I said. "They left me, left this."

"Hmm." He glanced toward the sky and took a deep inhale. "Beautiful day, isn't it?"

His sudden change in topic momentarily threw me, but I glanced upward and noticed three crows circling above us, cawing and dancing with each other.

I always believed in signs from the earth. Whatever I needed, She provided. And now, with that image in mind, I breathed a little deeper.

CHAPTER 31

Atlas

I sat in my car outside the bar, watching through the windows like some fucked-up stalker. I sensed him close by, which meant he must have sensed me, too. He'd be a fucking idiot not to. Of course, of all the stupid things he'd ever done, this would be the stupidest. Not to mention the most hurtful. I could wring his pretty little neck. And when I got my hands on him, I would have to convince myself not to take it too far.

He left us. He fucking left us. *Again.*

And this was about getting him back, about convincing him that it was reckless and stupid to run off.

He'd always been self-deprecating, convinced he wasn't strong enough for this life, that he'd be better suited to something easier, more normal. Well, tough.

We didn't get to choose. We were warriors, and we were fated to be with Marta. After everything, after the liminal and the rituals and that one night of pure, agonizing bliss, nothing could convince me that wasn't where we were meant to be.

The thing that pissed me off the most, the thing that really twisted my insides, was that he'd left *me*. All these years we'd spent together, attached at the hip, and he leaves without so much as a goodbye? No. I wouldn't accept it.

That shit at St. Michael's had punched a hole inside all of us, and where Marta had filled hers with depression and Wes had filled his with avoidance, mine simmered with rage. I was angry. All the time. And the only time it abated was when we were together for that one blissful night. That had to mean something.

He rounded the corner at the other end of the bar to set drinks down in front of three people, and the sensation of being near him again sizzled up my spine like I'd been struck by an electrical wire. His regret and shame coiled deep inside me, mixing with my fury, creating something tumultuous and turbulent. He must have felt it, too. His back straightened, and he glanced over his shoulder to scan the place. I sank farther into the darkness.

"Atlas?" came the voice inside my head, the one I'd longed to hear for five weeks. He looked like shit. Dark circles hung under his eyes, accentuating the puffy bags, and his cheekbones were even more pronounced. Judging by the way his clothes hung off his body, I'd say he'd lost at least fifteen pounds.

Not eating. Just like Marta. Christ, these two were going to give me a damned stroke.

I purposely blocked him, trying to cut off the tether so he didn't bolt. I knew my brother well enough. Once he realized I was here, he would run. And Gods above, I hoped he did.

After confirming he was, in fact, here, I went to the shitty pay-by-night motel where he was staying and parked around back. The sign flickered on the dark street, making it seem more like a scene from a horror movie. And I figured that fit the vibe well enough. There'd be no sappy rom-com reunion here. If things didn't end in blood and violence, it wouldn't be on brand for him and me.

I easily picked the lock and went inside, closing the door behind me and glancing around the empty space in the dark. A few of his clothes were folded on the extra bed at the far end, and his backpack lay in the far corner, the light of his laptop echoing through the space. Figuring I was in for the night, I sat in the cuck chair and waited. His shift was finished in an hour, so it wouldn't be too long before he showed up.

While I sat, I let my anger fester. I let it turn into a boiling, rotten thing deep inside me, one that consumed my soul so much it hurt to breathe. I hoped he put up a fight. I hoped he ran. I would need some way to get out this excess energy before I dragged him back to Asheville, forced him to his knees, and made him beg for Marta's forgiveness.

Then, we'd both make him understand that running wasn't an option, not anymore. He wanted to do these fucking rituals. He was the one who convinced me there was no other way. Now, we had to live with the consequences. He didn't get to hide his head in the sand and pretend like it never happened.

My thoughts drifted back to that night in the parlor after they'd gone to bed. The vision of my father in the window still haunted me, but his words were part of the reason I came.

Don't let him go.

Was this what he meant? Had Dad become a messenger of divination in the afterlife? After all these weeks, I still didn't understand it. But I'd made my peace with it. I was the one who was supposed to look out for Wes, and I might spend the rest of my life proving I could. But that was where Dad's bullshit ended. Being better, stronger, faster had gotten me here, sitting in a shitty motel in the dark with half my fucking heart in Asheville and the other half trying to hide from me. There was no such thing as perfect, and I was fucking exhausted from trying.

Dad could get fucked.

A few minutes after midnight, his sulking presence inched up my spine again, and the key twisted in the lock. I braced myself as the door swung open and he flicked on the light.

"Hello, brother," I said.

He startled and turned to face me, his features falling into a flat expression. He must have known I was here. He must have felt me the same way I felt him. Up close, I saw how the stress of being apart had affected him. He looked even more gaunt and forlorn, and the emptiness behind his eyes sparked the overprotective drive that had always lived inside me. I wanted to lash him for leaving me. I wanted to launch myself into his arms and never let him go again.

"Atlas," he murmured.

I raised an eyebrow. "I'd say it's good to see you, but you look like hell."

He gulped, visibly swallowing down his shock and rancid anticipation.

"What are you doing here?" He stayed frozen to the spot, the door still open, the flashing red light from the motel sign adding to the scared aura he threw off.

I gave a sad laugh and tilted my head to the side. "What do you *think* I'm doing here?"

He glanced at his feet and curled his fingers into fists at his side. "How did you find me?"

"I've known you almost your entire life," I said. "I'd find you anywhere."

His heart tugged at that, and he bit it back, shoved it away, telling himself he didn't deserve it. And wasn't that a fucking sad song stuck on repeat? Wes never thought he deserved me. He didn't think he deserved Marta. How wrong he was. For there were no three greater fucked-up individuals in this world, and that alone meant we would be best off with each other.

"You're lucky I found you before the rest of the warriors," I said. "They wouldn't have let you finish your shift."

"Are you here to tell me I made a mistake? That I should come home?" He looked up at me, his eyes rimmed red like tears were threatening to spill over. "If so, you're wasting your time. I'm not going back."

"We'll see about that," I said.

"You can't force me back, Atlas," he said. "I'm doing you both a favor by staying—"

"A favor?" I barked an incredulous sound. "Look at you!" I waved a hand at his general appearance. "How do you think Marta's been doing, huh? Better yet, how do you think *I've* been doing?"

"I can't care about that," he said. "I have to protect you."

"By running away." I rolled my eyes. "Typical."

He squared his jaw, his gaze turning fiery and defiant as the insult landed somewhere around his ego.

Finally. The reaction I wanted.

"This isn't college all over again," he said. "We're not kids anymore, Atlas."

"You're Goddamned right." I stood and stalked closer to him. "We're adults. So it's time you start acting like it."

"A warrior protects his witch," he said. "This is me protecting her...protecting *you*...from what's inside me."

I leaned in close, bringing my face inches from his. "And what makes you think it's not already in both of us, too?"

That surprised him. He blinked, and his mouth fell open as he reeled back from me. "What?"

"That's right, brother," I said. "Blood bound. Flesh bound. And whatever the fuck that was in that Goddamned church. Marta's a mess, has been for weeks. And me?" I blew out a sarcastic breath. "It's taking everything in me not to drag you out to the car by the scruff of your neck."

Wes winced and looked to the ground again. "I'm sorry."

"I don't care about your apologies," I snarled. "I don't want to hear them."

"Then what do you want?" His voice came out small and timid, reminding me of all the times Dad had reprimanded him as a child, and he'd have to eat crow to get back in the bastard's good graces.

But despite it all, despite the rage and the uncontrollable wrath scalding my veins, I still wanted him. He was still the most beautiful man I'd ever seen, and I'd probably go to my grave yearning for the taste of his lips on mine.

"So many things," I whispered.

"Atlas, I..." He was suddenly so unsure of himself. Perhaps I hated that the most. That I'd made him like this. That we'd done it to each other.

"Here's what we'll do," I said, putting my hands on his shoulders. The touch coasted through my body like a live wire, and when I slid them up his collarbones to his neck, the feel of his skin made me want to forgo my plans altogether. But no. I had to stay strong. I had to earn this, to prove to him I wanted him, that he was better off with us than he was out here, wasting away in some shit-hole town in the middle of nowhere. "We're going to fight for it."

He furrowed his brows and pulled his lips between his teeth.

"If I win, and I'm going to, I get to do whatever I want with you. Up to and including dragging your sorry ass back to Asheville. If you win, I'll leave you to your misery."

He sighed, the weight of this confrontation melting from his bones. He wanted to give in, I could feel it. But he also didn't want to come back and face the music. He couldn't accept that we'd love him despite whatever this was, that he deserved us and we thought he was worthy of that. My brother was always his own worst enemy.

"Just like old times, huh? Wrestling over the last cookie in the pack?" He smirked and shook his head, trying to look away again.

I held his jaw firm, forcing him to meet my stare, keeping him in place so he could see how serious I was. "I'd say our witch is a far better prize than a fucking cookie."

At the mention of *our witch*, something switched in his gaze, something softening and heating at the same time. He darted his tongue out to wet his lips, but my focus dropped to that movement, my mind going to the last time that perfect mouth was wrapped around my cock. Long gone were the shame and guilt of feeling this way about him. Society's rules didn't matter in the liminal, and now that we were back, it seemed that they didn't matter in the real world, either.

A heartbeat passed between us, one where I silently asked if he was ready, and he silently accepted the challenge. Then he shoved me back as hard as he could and took off into the night.

I righted myself and raced after him. He was taller, but I was faster, and I always had been. But where would be the fun in catching him right away? He headed for the tree line, launching over a fallen log before disappearing into the forest cover. Heart pumping, legs scrambling, I vaulted over the same obstacle and scrambled through the undergrowth. Leaves crunched under me as my panting drowned out the chorus of the night.

He hit the gas pedal as he dodged between trees, and I sprinted to keep up with him, finally catching him around the hips and tackling him to the ground. But he was quick on the defense, elbowing me in the ribs as we fell. I grunted and curled to the side, but it was enough for him to bolt to his feet and take off again.

Motherfucker.

I bit back the torment of the hit and pushed upright. It had cost me, and he was further ahead this time. But my time in the gym had done me good, and I made up the lost ground. He pivoted to the left, and I anticipated the move, catching him around the waist this time, so we fell to the side.

"Oh, little brother," I teased. "So predictable."

He bucked his hips and shifted his weight so he had the advantage, moving himself on top of me. But I countered with a headlock and used his momentum against him. We rolled so he was face down on the ground with me spread out on top, my chest to his back. Wes wasn't one to give up easily, so he threw his head back and nearly clocked me in the nose. I reared up in time to miss it, but my grip on his neck faltered, and he pushed me off him.

I didn't think he'd be one for cheap shots, but he kneed me in the gut and swung at my face, jabbing me in the jaw hard enough to hurt but not enough to ring my bell. When he tried to run again, I grabbed his ankle and sent him flying forward. He rolled to his back just as I climbed on top of him, my knees on either side of his hips, and I smacked him on the cheek. Hard. Harder than he'd hit me.

My brother's face whipped to the side, but he recovered and came back with a vengeance, arms flailing, hips arching, legs kicking. I nearly lost my seat as he swung at me again, fist flying toward my face. I caught his wrist and pinned it above his head, bringing my face millimeters from his.

Then I felt the cold kiss of steel at my neck and froze. The fucker had pulled a knife on me. My fault for not specifying no weapons.

"What now, big brother?" It was dark, and the waxing moon didn't provide enough light through the shadows of the trees to fully make out his features, but I nearly laughed as one of his eyebrows crept up his forehead and he twisted his lips into a wry grin.

I sucked in a breath as gently as I could, fully aware that this version of Wes might slit my throat and leave me for dead. Still...it turned me on, and that said more about how fucked-up I was than any blood-flesh-demon binding ritual ever could.

"You think I'm scared of your little pig-sticker?" I tutted and leaned into it, bringing my lips closer to his. "Go on."

He heaved deep inhales, either in recovery from our chase or the precarious circumstances in which we found ourselves, and my focus dropped to his beautiful mouth. Wes looked at mine, too, and I used that one moment of distraction to twist his weapon hand away from him, grab the knife, and toss it to the side.

Wes tried again to toss me off him, shifting his torso to use my weight against me, but I expected that, and I leaned to the other side to offset it, grabbing his free hand to pin it above his head next to the other one.

"Fuck." He groaned, now entirely held down. He tried kicking his legs behind me, but I wouldn't budge. Not even when he arched his back and twisted side to side. I only tightened my grip on his arms.

"Give." I stared down at him, fury mixing with the pure elation of having won, and my cock twitched, now fully hard behind my jeans.

He squared his jaw and glared, but I was delighted by that, too. At least his angry defeat wasn't the empty, guilt-ridden zombie I'd met at the motel.

"Give!" I shook him to get his attention, maybe snap him out of his determination to win, to stay away from us.

"Fine," he snapped. "Give."

I smiled, and my wrath melted away. "There's a good boy."

"Fuck off." He arched his hips in a feeble attempt to move me, but I held firm, and when his thick, heavy cock came into contact with mine, my grin widened.

"Well, well, well," I teased, leaning forward to brush my nose against his. "I think he likes it."

"Get off me." He tried to lift his arms, but the combined weight of me and gravity held him down.

"No." I trailed down the side of his cheek to his jaw, ghosting my lips along his face in a whisper kiss that made him shiver. He wanted to relent, I sensed it clear as day, but he also didn't want to give up the fight. He thought he was still protecting us. He thought he didn't deserve us.

Stupid little brother.

"When are you going to get it?" I murmured, pressing my lips to his ear. "I love you. *We* love you. And there's not a place in this fucking world where you can hide from that. I won't let you."

He choked back a sob as I pinched his earlobe between my teeth and pulled. That gasping sound quickly turned into a moan, and I knew I had him.

Fuck yeah.

"You shouldn't," he whimpered.

"Too bad." I leaned down to kiss his neck, just above his pulse, reveling in the shiver that raced down his spine. "I do. I always have."

When I lifted back up to face him, his features softened, and something like adoration met me in his eyes. It was sweeter and more endearing than any expression he'd ever shown me, and when his eyes dropped to my mouth again, I decided to indulge us both.

I closed the distance, placing a tender peck there first to check the waters. But fuck, the sensation of his soft, perfect mouth rattled down my body, and I couldn't help rocking my pelvis into his, sliding our cocks against each other.

When I pulled away, he chased after me, connecting our mouths again in a thundering release of tension and years of devotion. I groaned into the contact and opened my mouth to wrestle my tongue in between his lips. Even this, the bastard fought me on. He nudged against me with his own, desperate to get inside me, biting and licking and sparring.

But I wouldn't let him. *I'd* won this round, and we both knew what that meant. I pulled away from him and released my grip on him, sliding my palms down his arms, the triangle scars on my hands rubbing against flesh and soft cotton. When I got to his shirt, I balled it into a fist and yanked him up.

"I'm going to fuck you now," I said. "It's going to be rough, and when you come, just know *that's* what you deserve."

I'd always admired Atlas, especially when he got like this. All surly and mean, taking what he wanted and screw anyone who got in his way. Except now that I was on the receiving end of that, I couldn't help the tiny bit of fear that swirled with my excitement. Maybe he read this in my eyes or felt it across the bond because he flashed me that lady-killer grin and winked.

"I told you if I caught you, I would do whatever I wanted with you." He sat back on my hips, pressing his full weight on my throbbing dick, and pulled the leather out of his belt buckle. "Time to pay up, little brother."

The jingling metal echoed off the trees, and somehow, that sound made this more real.

I love you. We love you.

It repeated in my head as he shoved his pants down, took out his cock, and scooted up my body so his shins pressed my biceps into the ground. He sat back on my chest and stroked his shaft inches from my face, little drips of precum leaking out of the head.

My mouth watered, and as much as I had fought him, fought *this*, I had secretly hoped it would end up here. My muscles trembled and I stared up his long torso, the heat in his eyes propelling me forward. I lifted my head, trying to lick him, but he pushed my forehead back down.

"Patience," he said with a chuckle. "So greedy. You must have missed my cock almost as much as me, huh?"

It brought up memories of being in the liminal with him, when I'd shaken as he'd taken me as hard as he wanted. Of course, that hadn't really been me...or rather, it hadn't been completely me. In the weeks since I left them, I'd come to realize the demon had me then. It had probably had me the entire time we'd been there, since it sliced open my chest and infiltrated my dreams. But I pushed thoughts like that away. They didn't have any place here with my brother and me. No, the only things allowed here were the woods and the moonlight and the mischief in Atlas's eyes as he worked himself inches from my face.

"Now, are you going to be a good boy and let me fuck your throat?" He raised a condescending eyebrow, and every self-respecting cell in my body told me to fight him.

But now? Fuck, I sank into submission with all the grace of a newborn donkey. My knees shook and my heart raced, and if he didn't do something soon, I might lose my nerve.

"Yes," I finally croaked, nodding quickly.

He hummed a laugh and threaded his fingers through my hair, gripping the crown tight.

"Open your mouth," he said.

I did, and he leaned over me to spit on my tongue. It should have repulsed me, should have made me feel degraded and humiliated. I deserved it, he said. I deserved worse, I thought. But it had the opposite effect. I moaned and let him slap his cock against my tongue, playfully batting the tip against my skin.

"Lick me," he commanded, and I rushed to obey, lapping at the underside, the head, the slit, anything I could reach. Like this, he was utterly in his element, so powerful and controlling, and my conscience stopped riding me. I didn't have to think about Marta or my absence or the shame ruining everything that was once good about me. I only had to do this one thing. I only had to stick out my tongue and do whatever my brother told me to do.

The monster at the back of my mind, the one constantly beating against metal bars and begging to be let out of its cage, was notably gone. Quiet. Wordless. Blessedly absent.

The silence was intoxicating, and when he finally stuffed himself inside my mouth, I relaxed into the eternal peace of *him*. Just him. I sucked and softened my jaw, letting him press in and out. He tasted like salt and sweat and *Atlas,* and the combination added to my blissed-out state. Warmth rushed around my own cock as the tie between us blazed to life. I didn't think I'd ever get over that, the strange symbiotic limerence of our blood bond. Being this far away from Marta made it feel incomplete, and her absence from this whole experience plucked at the strain on my heart.

He said he loved me. He said Marta was a mess without me. And it hit me then, while I was sucking my brother's cock. All the times they'd shown me. When they wouldn't leave me in the liminal. When Marta smiled up at me first thing in the morning. When we took care of each other for two months while fighting over laundry and dishes in the sink.

Maybe he was right...Maybe I let this burning shame inside of me get the better of my senses. Maybe I was flawed and imperfect and fucked-up, but maybe that was enough. Just like they were beautiful wrecked and broken, and that was enough for me.

I'd been such a fucking idiot. I shouldn't have left him. I shouldn't have let my guilt eat me alive. I should have listened to my brother from the start. We were in this now, the three of us, and now that the train had run off the tracks, I had to keep my hands and feet inside the vehicle until it imploded.

"There ya go. That's right, let me have your throat," Atlas cooed, pulling out only to thrust in deeper. He hit the back of my mouth, and I focused on breathing in through my nose to keep from gagging, but fuck, even that turned me on. My eyes watered, and drool dripped out of the corners of my lips, but pinned down as I was, there was nothing I could do but endure it. Of course, someone like Atlas fucking my mouth was *hardly* something to endure. No, I cherished it. I let him use my mouth however he wanted because he was my brother, and I loved him, and we were intertwined in ways that could never be undone.

Hadn't I insisted on this? Hadn't I been the one saying what happened in the liminal stayed in the liminal? And now with his full weight on my chest and his cock in my throat, I found myself infinitely thrilled that he hadn't listened to that.

It was fucked up, certainly, but we'd been fucked-up our whole lives, and why stop now?

He stilled his movements and pulled out, giving me a chance to suck in a deep gasp of air.

"Aww, look at how adorable you are." He swiped his thumb under my eyes to brush away my tears and wiped the corners of my lips. "Such a pretty little cocksucker."

I panted while he undid my belt, zipped down my jeans, and flipped me over. I barely had time to brace myself before his tongue was in my ass, licking and swiping and forcing my face down to the ground from the sheer exhilaration racing through my blood.

"*Yes,*" I cried, unwillingly sending the telepathic moan straight to him. He laughed and tongue-fucked me harder, and my cock leaked onto the undergrowth, an obscene display of just how much I loved it. I scrambled for purchase on the ground, but my muscles trembled so hard, I couldn't hold myself up. And when he pressed a finger inside me, I nearly collapsed.

"Look at this tight little hole," he taunted, coaxing his finger in deeper. "I'm going to wreck you, brother, more than I did in the liminal. And I think you like that most of all, huh?"

"Fucking hell, Atlas," I managed to grumble.

"Aww, such niceties now that I'm finger-fucking you," he said. "I ought to pound you into the leaves for the way you coldclocked me."

"You deserved it," I said, pushing back on him to urge him on. My cock throbbed, and when one finger became two, he pressed on a spot inside that surged a wicked, filthy ecstasy straight up my spine and down into my balls. I tucked my face into the crook of my elbow and sighed, the pleasure too great, the agony far greater.

I whined when he pulled his fingers out of me, surprising myself with how much I desperately wanted him to fill me again. But the sound of a bottle cap had me looking over my shoulder at him as he squirted lube onto his palm and rubbed it over his cock.

Fucking hell. He brought lube?

"You're Goddamned right," he said. "I told you I was going to win, and I meant it."

"You couldn't have known that," I said as he lined the tip of his erection up at my entrance and nudged it in. The first prodding pressure had me arching off the ground, wincing against the stretch.

"Oh, I knew that, little brother," he said, grabbing my hips. "You wanted me to win. You wanted me to track you down and find you and make you pay for it."

The idea of being seen, of being known, so completely brought tears to my eyes, and I blinked them back as he pulled out only a fraction before pushing in again. This time farther. This time harder.

"You wanted me to punish you," he hissed, his tone light and breathy. This was affecting him as much as me. How long had we danced around this thing between us? How long had it been there, unearthed, biding its time, waiting to burst to life with so much ferocity, neither of us could hold it back? "Tell me, do you feel punished?"

At the words, he shoved in as far as he could go, bringing our pelvises flush, his balls slamming against mine. He hit that spot again, the one that made my cock leak, and I melted into the ground with a silent plea and a very audible grunt.

"Wes," he said, leaning over me so his mouth was by my ear. "Answer me."

"Yes," I said. "I've been punished."

"Good," he said. "I forgive you for taking off. Our witch will forgive you, too. Now you must forgive yourself."

It broke me. With his cock balls-deep inside me and the weight of his affection rushing through my blood, I collapsed in on myself. I almost sobbed.

"Can you do that for me?" he asked, pressing a delicate kiss to my ear. "While I fuck you, I want you to focus on letting go of all that bullshit. You don't need it anymore." He inched out slowly, so fucking slowly, and then pushed back in, and I saw stars. The euphoria was nearly unbearable, and I wanted more. I wanted it harder, rougher.

"Say it," came his voice again, followed by a hard bite near my shoulder. "Tell me I love you."

"You love me," I repeated.

"Good." He fucked me again, his fingers digging into my hips, the squishy sounds of our bodies rubbing together nearly perverse. "Say you love me."

"I love you," I answered immediately.

"And how do you feel about our witch?" he asked, peppering kisses up the back of my neck and to the other side.

"I love her, too." The words rang true as they left my lips.

"Do you think she loves you?" He rolled into me, pressing against my insides in the way only someone so profoundly connected to me could ever know.

"Yes," I cried. "Yes, she loves me."

"That's a good boy." He pulled off me, and a sharp thudding pain hit my ass cheek, forcing me to suck in a rough gasp.

He spanked me. That fucker actually spanked me.

"Don't you fucking forget it," he snarled before he smacked the other side, too.

Then he fucked me in earnest. He rutted into me, holding me

down by the lower back while he painted my ass red. And fuck, I loved that, too. I muttered obscenities, things like, "Harder," and "Please," and "Deeper, please deeper." Atlas obliged me.

I came much earlier than I wanted, the explosion rocketing through my body like a meteor crashing into Earth's atmosphere. My toes curled, my teeth clenched together, and my fingers turned to claws in the dirt, but my God, it was terrific. I blasted into orbit and floated to the stars, my vision damn near blacking out. I spilled onto the ground under me without Atlas ever having to touch my cock, and he just laughed and laughed and fucked me harder.

"How embarrassing for you," he said. "Can't even stand a cock in your ass for more than five minutes."

"Fuck you," I sputtered, trying to regain my focus through the haze and the sudden dizziness.

"That's the whole point," he said.

It went on for an eternity, the two of us in those woods. He made me repeat the words until they numbed my tongue. *I love you. You love me. I love Marta. Marta loves me.* And I felt them in my bones.

Just when he was on the precipice of his own climax, just when I sensed the imminent implosion, he leaned over me, twisted my face around so he could bring his lips to mine, and he whispered, "Now, tell me you deserve it."

I was afraid to utter the words, fearing how they might settle into my bones and never leave.

"Tell me you don't have to protect us," he said. "Tell me we protect each other. Together. And don't you dare fucking lie to me."

Despite it all, I managed a quiet, "We protect each other together."

He kissed me, his climax finally ripping through him, tearing into me through the bond. It set me off again, and I rutted into the dirt like a teenager on prom night, desperate to find any friction to ease my agitation. His orgasm rebounded, surging out of me and into him and into me again.

It was torture. It was bliss. It was heaven and hell and everything in the universe combined.

When he rolled off me, he collapsed at my side and closed his eyes, panting and sweaty and fucking beautiful in all his powerful glory. I lay boneless on my stomach, my arms tucked under my head, my face tilted toward him so I could focus on all the tiny details that made him so...*him*.

The shape of his cheeks as they curled into his jaw. The brush of light brown hair near his ears. The tiny jump of his heartbeat at the pulse in his neck. The way his strong hands sloped into his fingers, such violent weapons that had been coated in blood more times than I could count. And yet, he used them to bring us here, to bring me back from the brink, to remind me who I was and, more importantly, who I belonged to.

"Thank you, Atlas," I said.

He pulled his lips into a slow, lazy grin and rolled toward me, leaning in to give me a soft kiss.

"Come home to us," he said. "You need us. We need you."

I nodded and gave him another quick peck before wrapping an arm over his ribs to pull him in close, nuzzling my head under his chin and inhaling him deeply. He smelled like sweat and pine and him. He smelled like home.

We lay under the stars for a while and listened to each other breathe before Atlas rolled on top of me and took me again. That time was slower, languid, a necessary reconnection. And when he'd had his fill of me, he yanked me to my feet, took me back to the motel, and forced us both in the shower. Then, we started the long journey home.

I sensed them coming before I saw them. The void in my heart filled with their presence, the rough grit of Atlas's whirlwind personality and the stoic shame of Wes's guilt. I was in the library at a table in the far back, researching soul bonds. After my talk with Hellsing, I thought about asking the coven to perform a separating spell. If my tie to my warriors was causing me to lose control of my magic, maybe it would be better to sever it cleanly.

But the more I read, the more I realized that wouldn't be possible. What we'd done was permanent, and severing it would have detrimental effects on my psyche. Besides, I would need them to do it anyway, and I wasn't sure when or if they'd ever come back.

When I heard heavy footsteps on the wood floor, I swallowed down the tiny flicker of anticipation. They might have returned only to tell me they were done with the life altogether. And if that was the case, why not just stay away? I'd gotten the message, loud and clear.

Their beacon burned brighter inside me until it grew into an inferno, and when I glanced up, my warriors stood at the end of the row. Atlas had on jeans, boots, and his brown leather jacket, sporting a black eye and a smug grin. Wes wore a dark hoodie and a matching shiner that spoke of how their reunion had gone.

I raised an eyebrow and closed my book. Everything in me wanted to run to them, to pull them both into a hug before dragging them back to my room and taking out the six weeks of anxiety on them with sweat, cum, and blood. I forced myself to stay still.

"Welcome home," I said as I glanced between them.

Wes took a deep breath, steeling himself for what he wanted to say. "Marta, I..." He shook his head. *"I'm sorry."*

"Out loud," I said, trying to push his presence away from my mental solace. "You don't get to be in my head. Not yet."

"I'm sorry," he said. "I shouldn't have left. I thought I was protecting you, but I just made things worse."

"Worse? For me?" I scoffed and rolled my eyes. "I'm fine. Look at me." I gestured to myself and the library and the piles of books stacked around me. "Doing great."

"Don't be like that," Atlas said, taking a step forward. "You're wasting away. We all are."

"Atlas Colt, the great reconciliator." I let out a sardonic chuckle. "Don't make me gag."

"I fucked up," Wes continued, moving to stand next to me. "This thing, this void, it's still inside me. I can feel it, and I didn't want it to spread. I didn't want it to hurt you. I thought leaving would help...somehow."

"Did you think that before or after Atlas fucked—"

"Hey," Atlas snapped. "Cut the shit. You're allowed to be mad. Just don't be cruel."

"Why?" I barked. "That's your job?"

Atlas tilted his head and raised an eyebrow, but his brother was undeterred.

"I was dealing with my own shit. It's not an excuse, but I understand now," Wes said, his voice quiet. He dropped to his knees at my feet and rested his hands tentatively on my calves, his eyes pleading, the agony of his distress seeping through the bond despite how much I didn't want to feel it. I didn't want to feel anything. But I did. And I couldn't stop it. "I think Atlas is right. We need to be together. We need to stay together. We can't survive alone. I love you, and if you can find it in your soul to forgive me, I'll spend the rest of our lives making it up to you."

I love you.

My resolve crumbled, and the weight of his confession anchored me to the present, one where I had my warriors back and they wanted to stay, and I was being a bitch just to save my pride. Their absence had hurt, yes, but forcing them away would only do more harm than good. I needed them. We needed each other.

I leaned forward and cupped his jaw, the touch sizzling down my hands, into my arms, and straight to my heart. The emptiness plaguing me for the last six weeks suddenly overflowed with the magnetic adoration between us. We had survived hell, and nothing could shake that bond.

"Don't you ever leave me again," I murmured, pressing my forehead to his.

He gripped my wrists, the weight of his fingers pressing into my pulse like he was hanging on to life itself. "I won't. I swear it."

I lowered my head to press my lips to his in a tender kiss full of release and forgiveness. When I pulled back, I took a deep breath and looked at Atlas, who beamed like he'd just witnessed pure beauty in its rarest form.

"And you," I said, pushing to my feet. I stalked around the table, dragging my fingers against the cool wood until I stood in front of him. I should be furious with him. Our last conversation ended with him storming out and me sinking into chaos. But he'd brought Wes back to us. He'd come home. He hadn't given up, even when I was at my lowest. He'd earned my gratitude. "Thank you."

"Yeah, don't mention it," he said with that smug expression that made me want to punch him just to wipe it off his face. "I don't suppose I get a kiss, too, huh?"

I pressed my body against his and wrapped my arms around his neck, pulling him down to connect our lips. He hummed into the touch, and when we broke apart, a sense of rightness settled in my gut. I felt complete in a way I never had before.

"You know, I may have forgiven you both, but Bridge and Tita are another story."

Atlas winced, and Wes had the decency to look terrified.

"What are you researching?" Wes asked, glancing down at the books on the table.

"Right." I nodded and ran my hands back through my hair. "I think I know what happened to us, and what we have to do about it."

I explained what I'd learned and watched as Atlas's features dropped into frustrated reluctance. At least Wes seemed curious enough to pick up a book and flick through its pages.

"No," Atlas protested. "No more rituals. No more spells."

"If it fixes things," I said, "it could be worth it."

"We're back together now," he continued. "That's enough."

"No." I flexed my fingers, remembering the black mist pouring from my palms. "We need to see it through. My magic mutated because we didn't finish it. Besides, whatever void is inside us, whatever this is, spreading it out will even the playing field. It'll help."

Atlas crossed his arms over his chest and pursed his lips, petulant but willing to concede my point. Wes hummed and shrugged.

"Worth a shot," he said, which earned a groan from his brother.

"Yeah, I've heard that before." Atlas pinched the bridge of his nose and grabbed a book, settling in next to us to see what he could find.

Just like old times.

Later that night, after we'd discussed it until our eyelids grew heavy, they followed me back to my room, where I closed the door and quietly turned the lock into place. I didn't know what the others thought about both Atlas and Wes sharing my bed, nor did I care. I was sure they gossiped in dark corners and spread rumors about the brothers that fucked the same girl (and maybe each other?) but I let them talk. No one else could know what it was between us. No one else had been there, had lived through the things we had together.

We took our time undressing each other, kissing and worshipping our favorite parts as the soft rustling sounds of clothing hit the floor. Atlas laughed when Wes bit a ticklish part of his ribs, and Wes sighed when I licked a long line up his throat.

Our thoughts blended together, a mix of *"More"* and *"Please"* and *"I love you, I love you, I love you."* The combined sensations could bring me to climax on their own, and when we fell into bed, a tangle of limbs and mouths and tongues, we explored each other's bodies like it was the first time. We loved and we caressed and we reconnected in the only way we'd ever known. And when it was over, we fell asleep wrapped around each other like daylight may never come.

Life went on.

True to form, both Bridge and Tita reprimanded my warriors with sternly pointed fingers and a litany of expletives that promised the unholy wrath of hell should they ever think of taking off again. Then Tita served them lemon cakes and hot tea and told them she expected them to come by this weekend to help her rebuild part of her greenhouse that had fallen in during a recent storm.

The other warriors were less forgiving. Leander and Caspian put the Colts through the ringer. Despite explaining what had happened and why they'd left, the warriors didn't abandon post when things got tough. It was one of their guiding principles. In the end, Atlas and Wes escaped with a severe reduction in responsibilities for up to a year. No missions. No weapons. Supervised reconnaissance only. They'd broken their trust, and it would take a long time to get it back.

Two weeks after they returned, I had Lilith's blessing to

complete the soul-binding ritual on the sacred grounds out in the woods. It made sense. This was where it all began for us, all those months ago when the ancestors plucked their name out of an ancient chalice and tied them to me forever. We'd bathed each other and rubbed protective oils on our skin, pausing at the scars on our chests and palms. We prepared the altar with rue, roses, lavender, and candles. We'd dressed in white ceremonial robes, the same ones we'd used in the liminal, and when the full moon rose in the sky, I sent the guys ahead of me, knowing I needed to make one more recompense.

I went to the small altar I'd set up in my room, the one where I'd placed a small crucifix, a seven-day candle dedicated to the Virgin, a miniature sword, and a tiny plastic dragon. Then, I fell to my knees, clasped my hands together, and prayed.

I'd been so angry at God for so long, but after everything I'd been through, I didn't see the point. I'd wasted so much energy being hateful, sure that God had fucked up somehow, that His plan for me was bullshit. Now, I understood. *Anger into faith. Faith into action.*

If nothing else, I had faith in myself. In my warriors. And without God, without the solace I found in this daily meditative prayer, I wouldn't have been able to do what I needed to do to survive. I'd never been sure if the visions I'd seen at that church in the liminal had been real, but what did it matter? It got me through. It gave me the strength I needed, and for that, I'd be eternally grateful.

So I said my thanks. I told the Virgin my worries. I asked St. Michael for bravery. And as always, I requested that St. Marta guide me. Warmth enveloped me, like They had heard my prayers and given me Their blessing.

Then I went to join my warriors in the woods. I walked barefoot on the dirt pathway that led into the trees, remembering how I'd made this same journey the night they became mine. I'd been terrified, and the same sense of anticipation filled my chest now.

That emptiness had gone away with them back, but the parasite remained. The chaos in my hands still shot black, and if this didn't solve it, I didn't know what to do next.

Faith, Tita had told me. *Have faith.*

I clung to those words as I broke through the tree line, but standing around the periphery were other members of my coven. Lilith stood at the head, her hands clasped in front of her. Bridge and Val were off to the right, Circe and Hella to the left. Aradia, Hekate, Isobel, all of them. They'd all come.

"What are you—" I couldn't even finish my sentence, the shock and surprise rattling my nerves.

"Marta of the Royal Harlots MC," Lilith said, taking a step forward. "You wish to complete a soul bond with your warriors."

"Yes," I said, furrowing my brows. "But I didn't think..."

"We're your sisters," Lilith said, placing her hands on my shoulders. "If this will help you, we'll help you. It's a powerful ritual, and you don't need to stand alone. Never again."

Tears burned my eyes, and I blinked them back, swallowing down the overwhelm of being a part of a family like this. Even though I knew I'd do it for any of them, their showing up for me like this ached in the best way.

"Thank you," I said, nodding.

"Chin up," she said, tucking a finger under my jaw to lift my eyes. "You'll be okay. We're here for you."

She stepped aside, and I walked to the altar, where Atlas and Wes stood, waiting for me. I took a deep breath and began by calling the elements and welcoming the ancestors, asking for their help with this work. Then I cast the circle around us, invoking protection and love and divinity. Once the candles were lit and the full moon beamed down on us, I went to the chalice at the center of the altar and poured some of the wine, having already been blessed and cleansed. I focused inward, trying to find the earth and ground in this, our most hallowed space.

Firelight flickered over my warriors' faces, casting their features in soft shadows and delicate tangerines. It was time.

"No going back," I told them.

"I'm ready," Atlas replied.

"Let's do it," Wes said.

I grabbed my knife and pricked the end of my pointer finger, holding it over the chalice when it bubbled with blood.

"By flesh once given, by blood once shed. We summon not, but seal instead. The rift that fed on fear and flame, we close with heart, with soul, with name." A few drops sizzled into the murky red liquid, but the spell had already started to twist down my spine, tingling in my legs, twisting through my chest and over my scalp.

I handed the knife to Atlas, who opened his finger to do the same thing.

"Three divided," Atlas said, "now made one. Darkness shared, its rule undone. Let shadow's reach be spread and small, so none may bear the whole of it all."

His blood made the same crackling noise as mine when it landed in the mixture, and the magic intensified in my bones, scalding and furious.

It's working.

Atlas gave the knife to Wes, and he cut himself over the chalice, his serious gaze meeting mine as he did.

"Soul to soul, we weave this thread," he said, "Not for life, nor love, nor dread. But that which bound us once in pain shall never find that path again."

After he finished, I picked up the chalice and brought it to my lips, gulping down our combined essence. The energy in the atmosphere picked up, the circle flaming to life, the candles burning brighter. Smoke filled the valley, and my sisters began chanting, invoking ancient, powerful magic that intensified the ambiance.

Atlas drank after me, his thoughts churning, his anxiety

warring with elation as it slithered through our tether. When he swallowed, the circle sparked to life like fireworks.

Wes drank next, and that was when it hit. My muscles tensed, and something shoved me in the chest, toppling me over. Atlas grabbed one hand, and Wesson grabbed the other while they joined palms across from me. That emptiness inside me, the darkness, the flagrant void of whatever we'd brought back with us, circled through our connection like a whirlwind, picking up steam.

Memories flashed through my mind like a movie montage. I saw the two of them as boys, huddled together in a motel bed, watching a horror movie and trying to scare each other. Next came me as a girl, cuddling with my father on the couch while my mother read me a bedtime story. Them learning monsters were real, Wes's eyes wide, Atlas's toothy grin big with excitement.

On and on the memories went.

Me on my father's lap while he taught me how to hold a knife.

Atlas kissing a girl for the first time at age twelve and thinking it was grosser than he expected.

Wes getting an A on a paper in middle school and realizing he was smarter than his father had ever given him credit for, that he could actually do something with his life.

Atlas going on his first mission and chopping the head off a vampire, returning home covered in blood and aching for a hug no one would give him.

Wes going to homecoming in the best suit he could find at the thrift store, praying for a normal life, knowing it would never happen.

Me learning my parents had died and crying myself to sleep in Tita's spare bedroom.

Atlas and Wes burying what remained of their father's corpse, each wishing they could hold hands and cry, knowing their father would be appalled if they did.

I watched their lives play out in my mind. They bore witness to every pain I ever had, every struggle I'd ever endured.

Finally, the darkness ebbed, and a vibrant energy took root. I pulled from the earth and spread it out to them, gifting them with this piece of me. It reinvigorated what we already had, making it infinitely more potent and powerful.

When we opened our eyes again in that sacred clearing, we were one soul. One person in three bodies. One consciousness living together.

And I felt my magic roar to life.

CHAPTER 34

Epilogue

MARTA

Two Years Later

I sat in the back seat of Atlas's car and stared at the dark, decrepit building in front of us. The broken windows and decaying brick hinted that the place had been abandoned for eons, which made it a perfect spot for vampires to nest. Wes loaded his gun with iron bullets in the passenger seat while Atlas drummed his fingers on the steering wheel and glanced around.

"You sure this is the right place?" Atlas asked.

"Absolutely," I replied, double checking my knives on my holster. Firm and steady, just like I wanted.

"Looks creepy," he replied with a sigh.

"How many you think are in there?" Wes pursed his lips and ducked his head to better take in the eerie view.

"Isobel said ten, but you know how vampires are," I replied.

Of course they did. They'd been hunting vampires since before I graduated high school. And besides, in the two years since the soul binding, they'd come to know everything I knew. There were no barriers between us anymore, no secrets, no hidden trysts in dark closets. I thought it would be strange to have such a profound connection to two other people, but it had only made us stronger.

We were deadly on missions, working as a unit, anticipating each other's moves and countering with hive-mind precision. Witches weren't supposed to be this close to their warriors. We were meant to do the dirty work while they protected us and watched our backs. But I wouldn't have it any other way. Atlas, Wes, and I completed each other in truly miraculous ways.

Atlas matched my competitive nature with quickness and skill, and Wes met my intelligence with competence and inquiry. When I reached a blind spot or did something impulsive, they brought me back to earth. When Wes questioned himself or sank into a shame-ridden spiral, we reminded him why we loved him and how cherished he was. And when Atlas needed to vent excess energy, we let him take it out on us again and again and again.

When I was first bound to them, I never thought there would be a time when I would say I was thankful for it. I imagined being pissed at the ancestors for the rest of my life. But now, I understood why it had to happen this way. For me, there were no others.

"I don't see any signs of vampires," Atlas said. *"No rotting corpses. No amputated body parts."*

"Doesn't mean they're not there," Wes countered. He pulled back the chamber on his pistol and glanced at me. *"Should we do this?"*

Atlas heaved a deep sigh and opened the car door to step out. I said a quiet prayer to my divine cheerleaders and followed him, cracking my neck and swinging my arms to warm up. My magic pooled in my stomach, coasting out of me and into them, amplifying our strength and reinforcing the protection I'd already placed around them. We silently walked to the front of the building, where Atlas pulled his gun and held it up. Wes walked around him, barrel already aimed, and I went in second, brilliant white light licking off my fingertips.

A loud hiss echoed from our right as a vampire jumped out

from the shadows. Gleaming teeth reflected in the moonlight, but Atlas was quicker. He shot the thing in the head, and it fell to the floor, limp and boneless.

"They know we're here now," I said as footsteps sounded overhead and fierce, terrifying snarls reverberated around us.

We attacked as a team. Wes fired at one rotting bloodsucker while I fried another with my magic. Atlas nailed a female between the eyes seconds before it tore into Wes's neck. I scorched a hulking male and flung a knife into another, smiling as the handle stuck out of the bastard's chest. Wretched blood splattered my face when Wes shot one just as it descended from the second floor to jump on me.

The three of us cleared that building like trained mercenaries, dropping vampires left and right. When we finished the second floor, we thought we were done. We thought we'd gotten them all. But a tiny body shoved out of a corner and tackled me to the ground, managing to get its hands around my neck before I could stop it. For being so small, it was stronger than me, and even when I brought my elbows up to break its hold, it didn't let go. I tried to blast it with my magic, but I couldn't breathe, and I struggled to focus.

"Filthy fucking witch," it roared, its eyes gone red with lust and hunger. "I bet you taste like sugar."

Wes barreled into the room and shot it three times in the back, but it didn't move. More disgusting crimson leaked onto my clothes, coating me in the foul-smelling decay. I felt it before it happened. Wes drew on my magic, sucking it deep into himself, and I gave it freely. He held up his hand, and glorious white light poured from his palm, incinerating the vampire on top of me, reducing it to ash and brimstone. It crumpled in my grasp.

I sucked in air as Wes held his hand out to me, yanking me to my feet.

"Thanks," I croaked.

"Anything for you, sweet girl." He leaned down to kiss me as Atlas came into the room.

"Fuck," he said. "We missed one, huh? You okay?"

I nodded, and Atlas wrapped his hand around my neck, tugging me close so he could kiss my temple.

"Let's torch this place and get out of here," Wes said, nodding toward the stairs leading to the first floor.

As I followed him, I thought again about where I'd started and how far I'd come. This life wasn't perfect, but I'd like to think my parents would be proud of me, that they were somewhere in the afterlife, cheering me on.

ATLAS

I'd always hated witches, even while knowing I'd likely be bonded to one. But never in a million years did I think it would be her. We fit together like two pieces of a puzzle. Add in Wes, and the whole picture made sense. She was beautiful and fiery and smart as a whip, and the first time she put a knife to my throat, I thought I'd come in my pants like some prepubescent boy. It was still one of my favorite memories.

As for my brother, I'd always loved him. That love had morphed and changed over the years, but we'd grown to be extensions of each other. There was no me without him. There was no him without me. It probably wasn't healthy, and anyone with half a brain would say it was fucked up, but screw 'em. Now that we were soul-bound to each other, no one else could ever understand what it was between us.

The other warriors had never said anything to us, and I figured that was because they realized it wasn't their business. Or maybe they had always suspected we were fucking anyway and didn't need any confirmation. I didn't fucking care.

After we set the abandoned building on fire with the dead vampires in it, we drove back to the motel, blasting AC/DC and Led Zeppelin the entire time. Marta sang at the top of her lungs, her carefree smile easing the anxiety in my chest. I'd nearly lost her when Wes left, but that seemed like so long ago, it hardly registered anymore. I was thankful to have her back, have them both back. My brother joined her during the chorus and pumped his hands in the air, adrenaline from a good fight coursing through his veins, making him giddy.

Fuck, I loved seeing them like this. I loved watching them be happy, almost as much as I loved making them happy myself.

I'd once lived to be my father's perfect soldier. I'd once given everything to this life out of a sense of duty and honor, hardly a care for my own wants and needs. But now, I had the two most precious people in the world next to me, and I understood that nothing was more important.

When we got back to the motel, reeking like a decaying corpse and covered in blood, we stripped off our dirty clothes and huddled together in the tiny shower. There was barely enough room for Marta, let alone the addition of two huge dudes like Wes and myself. But we made it work. I scrubbed the guts out of Wes's hair while he washed the flaking dried crimson from Marta's skin, and then the two of them took turns tormenting me with soft kisses and gentle caresses over the areas they knew drove me wild.

Then, we fell into bed. I fucked them both that night before I fucked myself on Wes's cock. For appearing like such a calm gentleman, the man took his aggression out on us when we were alone. He was all bites and scratches and hard, piercing thrusts. He nutted before I'd even got going.

"Aww," I teased. *"Such a quick trigger. Must be so hard for you. Do you like it when I let you fuck me? Do you like it when I take what I want and leave you panting?"*

"Fuck off," he managed to whimper.

Marta laughed and positioned herself under me with her cunt in my face, which I took advantage of by stuffing my nose between her legs and sucking her clit in my mouth. She reciprocated by coaxing my cock to the back of her throat, milking me from the outside while Wes did the same from the inside.

It was pure fucking bliss. We brought each other to climax again, the shared pleasure circling through us with no signs of slowing down. And when we finally called it a night, I watched them fall asleep tangled in each other. Legs over waists. Hands intertwined. Her exhales becoming his inhales.

I'd never felt so safe and warm, so protected and adored. Maybe it was the lingering high from the vampire hunt or my pathetic bleeding heart, but I lay awake and stared at the ceiling, watching the shadows from the trees drift over the popcorn plaster. I thought about how we'd been raised, how my life had brought me here.

My dad raised me to be stronger, better, faster. Always fighting. Always winning. Softness was weakness. But he was wrong. Softness was a strength. All my anger ever got me was cruelty and rage. I'd been swinging at pieces of myself, my guilt, my grief, my doubt, like they had to be destroyed. But they weren't flaws. They were what made me human. I could still be strong and let others see the more vulnerable sides of me. I could move slower, breathe deeper, be softer. The worst sides of myself, the parts I never let anyone else see, they didn't make me weak. They made me alive.

Wes and Marta made me alive.

"Atlas," Marta whispered, rolling over to face me. *"Are you okay?"*

"Just fine, little witch. Go back to sleep."

She snuggled closer and wrapped an arm over my chest, tucking herself against my side and nuzzling her nose into my neck. *"Tell me."*

I shook my head and sighed. *"You ever think about the liminal?"*

"All the time." She hummed and pushed up on her elbow so she looked down at me, her dark eyes sparkling in the moonlight. *"What about it?"*

"I'm just...I'm just thankful for you. That's all."

"I'm thankful for you, too, Atlas." She leaned down to kiss me.

I hugged her close and kissed the top of her head, finally letting myself close my eyes and drift into sleep.

WESSON

I woke up before Marta and Atlas the next morning and stood at the end of the bed to stare at my brother and our witch. They were cuddled close together, all of their skin touching, and the sight almost made me jealous. No matter how we fell asleep, they always gravitated toward each other in the middle of the night like two ends of a magnet finally finding each other. But being so tied to them helped me realize there was nothing to envy. They had their own thing, just as I had mine with each of them.

And besides, they were so damned adorable together, I almost woke them up with my filthy mouth on their skin and dirty words whispered into their minds. Instead, I went for a run to stretch my legs. The sun rose over the horizon, and the crisp spring air soothed the ache in my muscles from a hard-won fight the night before.

I used to think I wasn't cut out for this life, that *any* other existence would be better than the course I'd be put on. My fear of not being worthy, of not being *warrior* enough, ate away at me until it was all I could see. Everyone I'd ever known had died because of what we did, and I thought if I ran far enough away, nothing could ever hurt me again. That I could never hurt anyone else.

I'd only hurt myself in the process.

Two years later, I saw things more clearly. I deserved love from the people who loved me, despite my flaws. I deserved to have everything I ever wanted. I wasn't bad or evil. In this life, there was no such thing. Only chaos. Only order. Only shades of gray.

Perhaps I should have been more ashamed of myself for the relationship between Atlas and me. Our father would be rolling in his grave if he knew, and if anything I'd believed about the ancestors was true, I imagined he was groaning in the afterlife and demanding to be brought back to the living realm if only to kick our asses for it.

Fuck him. Fuck all of them.

Atlas and I were meant to be as we were, and in some twisted way, we'd always been like this. Marta had only made things better. She fit between us like fate and destiny had created us at the same time, only to separate us so they could watch us scramble to find each other again.

For the first time, I could say I loved my life. And I had no regrets.

Maybe we'd think about having kids of our own one day. Maybe we'd raise them differently. Maybe we'd tell them they could be whatever they wanted, and if they showed signs of magic, we'd encourage them to explore it however made them feel good.

I snorted and shook my head. We'd probably just fuck them up in different ways, but that's the nature of life, wasn't it? I tried my hardest, and I'd survived *in spite* of it.

After three miles, I got back to the motel just as Marta was waking up. Atlas had already showered and now stood in front of his backpack wearing nothing but a towel wrapped around his waist. Water dripped down his muscles in tempting rivulets, damn near making me drool. He could always bring me to my knees.

Marta flicked her gaze to me, having plucked the thoughts out of my head, and flashed me that wicked grin. She'd been thinking the same thing.

"Hey!" Atlas pointed at both of us. "None of that. We're on a schedule here. We've got to get back to the estate before they send someone to track us down."

"Look at you," Marta piped up. "Being so professional and punctual."

"Hmm, quite out of character, isn't it?" I raised my eyebrows and stripped my sweaty shirt over my head, making Atlas's gaze catch on my naked chest. And that was the main difference between us. I liked him freshly showered and waiting to be soiled. He liked me already wrecked, so he could see how much dirtier he could make me.

"We've got ten minutes," Marta said, pushing up on her hands and knees to slink across the mattress, stopping just at the edge so she could nudge her nose along the growing bulge behind the towel.

"Ten minutes?" Atlas scoffed but arched his hips into her touch, threading his fingers through her hair. "You two deviants will have me strung out in that bed for at least an hour."

I walked closer and stepped behind him, wrapping my arms around his waist so I could dance my fingertips across his lower stomach at the edge of the towel. He shivered, and I laughed. "Methinks he doth protest too much."

Marta parted the barrier separating him from her and leaned in to give his cock the faintest lick. He groaned as his head fell back on my shoulder, and we knew we had him.

Yes, this life was tough. It kicked my ass most days, and I had more scars than I could count, both physical and mental. But in moments like this, when I had my brother demanding more and my witch teasing every inch of our skin, I knew it was all worth it. I'd do it all again if I had to, and I'd fight like hell to keep it.

The End

Want More?

Thank you for reading! If you enjoyed this book, please consider leaving a review. They help other readers find my work and enable me to keep writing. (Seriously, I am a sucker for validation and have a praise kink. Plz love me.)

You can stay up to date by joining my newsletter. ANNNDDD you get free smut just for signing up.

https://jenadoyle.com/join/

(No spam, only smut. I promise.)

I'm also @thejenadoyle on all the socials. Be sure to follow me for book recs, pictures of my cute dog, and all the news about upcoming releases.

Acknowledgments

Dear Reader,

This book was truly a labor of love. It took me longer to write than I intended, mostly due to life and work and *gestures around broadly*. Its original release date was supposed to be October 23, so let's just pretend we're still in the spooky Halloween / Día de Muertos mindset, okay? When I only had 75% of it written by the beginning of October, I knew I had to push it back. Thank you for being patient with me.

Regarding the magical elements herein: I am a practicing witch and have been for many years, so I drew on my own practice and unverified personal gnosis for many of them.

However, I am not of Mexican heritage, nor do I practice American Brujeria. For that, I relied on "American Brujeria" by J. Allen Cross and "Mexican Sorcery" by Laura Davila. Both were fantastic and incredible works, and even if Marta wasn't from this background, I would have picked them up just to learn more about this type of magic. For more specific Appalachian guidance, I read "Backwoods Witchcraft" by Jake Richards and "Roost, Branches, and Spirits" by H. Byron Ballard. All of these resources are available on Amazon if you'd like more context.

Marta's interaction with Michael the Archangel was inspired by my own relationship with the Norse Goddess, Freya. When I was at my lowest point in life, when I literally could not go on another day, I found the craft. I threw myself into my own under-standing of spirituality, determined to find a reason to keep going. And so I soldiered on, even if it hurt, even if I hated every second. One day, a few weeks later, She came to me during a meditation and told me "not to fuck it up." (Her words, exactly.) It took me a few hours to understand what She meant. But then I realized, by taking it day by day, by immersing myself in a spiritual and magical practice, I'd saved my own life. And now, I had a second chance.

Now, whether deities really exist or not is wayyyyy above my pay grade. Did I imagine her ethereal presence? Was it only a figment of my own subconscious? Was it my "Capital S Self" telling my other parts to get their shit together? *Emphatic Shrug* I might argue there's no difference. But I can tell you this...I try every day to follow her advice. I'm still trying not to fuck it up. Some days, I succeed. Some days, I tell myself to try again tomorrow.

So, where do we go next? Well, I need a break. I originally intended to do a second RHMC novel next year, but at this point, I don't think that's going to happen. This world has been so much fun to create and build, but I don't know when I'll be back. You let me know if you want another. Right now, my muse is running on cigarettes, caffeine, and twenty minutes of sleep. Every time I open my laptop to write, she groans and rubs her temples and lets out an annoyed huff. We must appease the muse, my friends. Make sure you follow me on the socials for updates.

I have so many people to thank for this one. First, to Alex LaBruyère for her incredible encouragement and sympathetic ear. She allowed me to vent, cry, and scream when life got to lifeing, then she told me to pull up my big girl panties and get back to it.

To the incredibly talented and overwhelmingly generous Crimson Syn, thank you for listening to me ramble about this fic. Thank you for helping me navigate the sometimes tricky waters of writing and publishing. And thank you for doing all that you do for so many authors.

To my beta reader, Leslie Grace — You are a rockstar! Thank you so much for walking down this windy road with me and for the happy hours where you helped me fix my plot holes and figure out what I'm doing with my life, in general.

To my editor, Misha, thank you so much for being on my team. Your reassurance means the world to me, and at this point, I don't know if I can write a book without your expert eyes going over it and telling me I'm doing a good job!

To my sensitivity reader, Maria. Thank you, thank you, thank you. I bow to your kindness and willingness to trust this new-to-you author when I reached out to you and asked for help with the Mexican cultural elements.

And finally, to you, dear reader. If this is your first Jena rodeo or if you've been here from the start, thank you for giving Marta, Atlas, and Wes a shot. I hope I did their story justice. And at the very least, I hope you had a bloody, smutty good time.

Cheers!

-Jena

Jena Doyle writes dark motorcycle club romance, queer fairytale adaptations, and paranormal smut for all the good girls who love a tattooed hand necklace. When she's not dreaming up dirty words, she enjoys traveling, binge-watching trash TV, and dabbling in all things witchy-woo-woo. She holds a Bachelor's degree in English / Creative Writing and has been known to ramble at great length about Shakespeare's gay agenda. Jena currently lives in West Virginia with her partner and their snuggly pup.

instagram.com/thejenadoyle
facebook.com/thejenadoyle
tiktok.com/@thejenadoyle

Also by Jena Doyle

MIDSUMMER

We Wild Things (Prequel Novella)

Midsummer

Samhain

Solstice

Beltane

STEEL ROSES MC

They Called Him Saint (Prequel Novella)

Crimson Chaos

Savage Saint

Oleander Oaths

Mischief Mayhem

Ruthless Reign

ROYAL BASTARDS MC: HELENA, MT

Blood and Whiskey

Blood and Magic

Heats and Holidays (Novella)

Blood and Trouble

ROYAL HARLOTS MC: ASHEVILLE, NC

Filthy Little Witch